Royal Journals

Abroad In NYC

by

Summer Reads

Royal Journals

Copyrights © 2025 Summer Reads

All rights reserved.

No part of this book may be reproduced, stored in a retrieval system, or transmitted in any form or by any means—electronic, mechanical, photocopying, recording, or otherwise—without the prior written permission of the author, except in the case of brief quotations embodied in critical articles or reviews.

Ebook ISBN # 978-1-969775-09-3

LCCN: 2025920825

Contents

Introduction

Hello Reader,

Thank you for taking the time to read my story.

I started my career as a public servant with the local fire department. That led to my lifelong career in the medical field, ending in Radiology. After being hit in a car accident, I could no longer safely take care of my patients and retired from the medical field as COVID shut down the world.

I started creating fictional stories when I was a young child. Three or four pages would round out my short stories. As I became older and life was more demanding, I wrote less and less, but became a devoted reader—mostly in the summer, when I had more time. Detailed dreams have always been a part of my life. I never did anything about them; they were just there—my own personal movie theater. The vivid ones would hang around in my mind for a few days. Then, it got to a point where I would have the same dreams over and over again. Sometimes exactly the same as before, sometimes from a different perspective.

Two years ago, I started jotting down some of my dreams. I gave my characters names and created their backstories. Before I knew it, I was having new dreams, and they were using my characters' names. What? After organizing all my dreams and writing out a long timeline, I realized that I had a book.

I then began writing Royal Journals. After several months of constant writing, I felt like I had come to a stopping point—but I was nowhere near the end. When I did research on how large I should make a novel, I came to realize that I had multiple Royal Journals. The current book I was writing was actually #2 of the series. It was shaping up to be five or six books long.

I got into writing book #1 when all my dreams changed. I was no longer re-dreaming of my known characters. I'd quickly take notes and get some details or twists written, then I'd get back to my task. Before I knew it, I was off on a tangent with a different series, Our Angel.

Now I have about twenty or more different types of stories started, a few complete books, with several more that are close to being done. They range from Mafia, Romance, Drama, Erotica, Thriller, Werewolf, and a sprinkle of Humor—sometimes several in the same book.

I hope you enjoy what my crazy mind has come up with.

Summer Reads

TikTok - books by summer reads

Instagram - books_by_summer_reads

To my wonderful husband, Bill. Thank you for all your support—even when times were scary, you encouraged me to continue.

To my best friend, Jamie. Kicking ass and taking names while spreading sunshine. Love you, Girly.

Thank you both for giving me the confidence to publish even when I didn't think I was ready.

Royal Journals
Through Life, Music, and Love
Abroad in NYC

Written by Summer Reads

This collection of journals, notes, and various letters is meant to be listened to with music. If a song's title and artist are announced, listening to the song while reading will help you understand the mood and feelings of the characters.

All song information was found on Wikipedia, and the credits are listed at the end of the book.

This book includes adult situations that a young adult could face in today's crazy world—the emotional, the erotic, and physical scary trauma.

Lilly Reads Journals

Lilly woke up after a good night's rest. While lying in bed, she started thinking back on what she had already learned about her mother, and she could hardly believe what had happened so far. To think that she was finally reading about her mom's life, which she had always been so curious about.

At this point in the journals, her mom was only in her early 20s and had so many crazy experiences. Lilly's heart was racing just thinking about it. She felt like she needed to talk to Uncle Jasper, but how do you approach someone about something so private and sensitive?

"Excuse me, Uncle Jasper, were you really my mother's first fuck?" Like that would go over well. And how would his husband take it if he was in the room? Lilly laughed to herself. She got up and went downstairs to scrounge some breakfast and load up with snacks for today's reading.

She got downstairs and noticed that no one else was up. "Hmmm," she wondered where Chris and Philippe were. She decided on just fruit and yogurt for breakfast, so she gathered her supplies and decided to go past her brothers' rooms. When she got to Philippe's room, he was still sound asleep. She then went next door to check on Chris, but his room was empty.

"Hmmm," she wondered if he was already off to town. She pushed into his room and noticed his bed was already made. Did he not sleep here last night? What had he gone off to do? She would have to ask next time she saw him. She turned and went to her room to continue down the path of her mother's memories.

She opened the trunk and pulled out the next book and pages strapped together. A loose page fell, and she picked it up. She looked on both sides, and there was no number on it, so she started to read it to try and figure out where or when it went in the collection.

Jessie

Jessie walked down the hall from holding, towards the courtroom. His chains rattled rhythmically on the floor with each step he took. The song *"Show Me the Meaning of Being Lonely"* by the Backstreet Boys popped into his head, and he started singing to himself.

Show me the meaning of being lonely.

Is this the feeling I need to walk with?

Tell me why I can't be there where you are?

There is something missing in my heart.

He had lots of time to think these last few days while locked up and waiting for the preliminary hearing. Replaying every decision in his mind that led to today, he would have changed only two things. First, he would have told Eve sooner that he loved her and fought harder to keep her. Second, he should have killed Adam years ago.

He entered the courtroom and saw his father and lawyer already seated at the desk. Behind them was most of his family. He nodded to his father when he looked up at him. Opposite were the plaintiff lawyers for the state of New York. Behind them were various reporters and a courtroom sketch artist.

The guard escorted him to sit behind the desk, removed his cuffs, and he sat down between his father and lawyer. His nerves were in high gear while he listened to all the chatter around the room. His father softly rested his hand on his shoulder. Jessie turned and looked at him. "Breathe, son. We will get through this." Jessie nodded as he pressed his lips together.

"All rise," the court officer called out. Jessie stood up along with everyone else. "The Honorable Margaret Martin is now presiding." Jessie was suddenly glad to see Judge Martin. A wave of relief washed over him. He has had several cases with her in the past, and she knew his character as a lawyer for women's rights and protection. He looked at his father and smiled. However, his father kept his poker face on, but nodded his response to Jessie.

"Please sit," Judge Martin said, and everyone sat back down in their seats. "Plaintiff, your opening statement."

A lawyer Jessie didn't recognize stood up. "Your Honor. The state of New York seeks two counts of vehicular homicide against Mr. Jessie Cooper on the grounds of premeditation." Jessie heard the gasps of his family behind him as his father held Jessie's nervous leg from bouncing uncontrollably.

Lilly

Lilly's hands were shaking, and she was crying so hard that she had to stop reading. She set the next large group of paperwork on the bed and went running to her aunt's room with the loose page. When she got to her room, she started banging on her door. "Auntie," she kept on banging. "Auntie, I need to talk. Right now!" She kept on banging until the door flew open.

"What's wrong, my Darling Girl?" Lilly started bawling her eyes out and gasped for air as she held up the page. Her aunt took the page and started to read it, then stopped. "I told you not to read pages out of order. Now this will always put a shadow in your mind." She pulled Lilly to her as she shook her head.

"It was loose and fell when I picked up the next section," Lilly blubbered out and gasped for air. "I didn't know…" Lilly shook her head and gasped again. "Where it belonged," she finished.

Sophia held onto her tightly as they slowly walked back to Lilly's room. She started to whistle and then broke into an older song— *Patience* by Guns & Roses.

They entered Lilly's room, and Sophia walked over to the trunk, whereas Lilly continued to her bed.

"I'm sorry you read a part out of order," Sophia said as she started flipping through the bottom sections. "Ah, this is where it goes," she said as she re-filed it into the stack. "Next time, if you find a loose page, don't read it. Just bring it to me. I'll make sure it gets to where it needs to be."

Sophia walked over and sat on the corner of the bed. "Try not to let that little section plagues your mind. Go forth with an open heart and an open mind, and just let the story unfold as your mother voyaged through it."

Lilly took a deep breath and picked up the next section. "August 2022? Is there one missing? There's a two-year gap from the last one."

Sophia shook her head. "Unless a book magically shows up, there is a gap. Remember, the first book was as she recalled it. It's logical to have some gaps. I believe from here on, she wrote as she experienced life."

Sophia got up and gave Lilly a kiss on the head. "Come see me before you go to bed for the night to check in on your progress."

Lilly looked back up at her and nodded. "Okay. I already grabbed a small breakfast and some snacks. I'll see you for lunch or dinner?"

Sophia smiled as she got up. "I guess it depends on how deep you are into the reading—if you can peel yourself from it enough to be social with us." She winked and then waved goodbye before closing her bedroom door.

August 2022 Abroad in New York

Entry 1: At the bar is a good place to start.

Jessie set his head down on the desk and closed his eyes. On difficult days like today, he wished he could talk with his mother. Thinking of her made him a bit sad, flashing back to when he was ten years old and she was diagnosed with breast cancer. He didn't understand then what it would mean, but she battled with it for another eight years before she passed away. She always supported his dreams of the performing arts and was the only one to attend his plays in school. Most importantly, she was the buffer between him and his father. That all changed after she was gone.

After class, Jessie walked out, upset with today's testing. It's not the direction he wanted to go in his life. Hell, he really had no clue what he wanted to do except party, have fun, and fuck every girl he could. He did know that he wanted to be rich. When he was a kid, he always figured he'd take over the family plastic and rubber company. But his father never took him under his wing to show him the way. At this pace, that is nowhere in sight. However, he was so tired of his father running his life and telling him what to do or how to live his life. If it were not for the monthly allowance from his father, he'd up and take off.

His school week was over, and he was ready to party for the long weekend. He called his number one friend with benefits to see if she was free to help him blow off some steam. Conveniently, she was and was hanging out with friends near the bar. As he got close, he saw her hot ass, wearing stilettos and a miniskirt that hardly covered her cheeks. "Hey Babe, you're looking hot tonight," he said as he approached her.

"Oh, yeah? You need a date for a party tonight?" she replied, turning to face him. He slowly smiled and shifted his weight to the hip.

"I'm looking for something a bit quicker. You got time for a BJ?" he asked.

"I sure do, honey," she smirked. He nodded his head yes, and she walked him to a quiet part of the alley. He leaned back against the wall and let her take over from there. She unzipped his pants and fished his semi-hard cock from his briefs. He leaned forward slightly to watch her, just as she took him in her mouth. The visual and the sensation of her wet suction made his cock fully hard.

He leaned back again with his hands behind his head and closed his eyes as he listened to her wet sounds while she moved up and down on his shaft. She placed both her hands on his ass and squeezed occasionally as she took him deep in her throat. A moan escaped him as she did different movements with her tongue and changed the suction intensity.

Slowly her speed increased, and before too long, she was at full speed on his shaft. Shortly after, he felt the pressure of his orgasm build, and he placed a hand on her head to keep her all the way down on his shaft as he erupted in her throat. She swallowed each of his salty flows and slowly licked his shaft, then moved up and down a few more times until he started to soften.

He helped her to stand up, then tucked himself back in and zipped up as she wiped the excess fluid off her face. As they walked back down the alley, he smacked her ass and said, "Thanks, Babe." Then they parted ways at the end of the road. She went back to the corner with her friends, and he walked on to the bar to meet up with his roommate, Adam.

Adam

Adam was glad to be done for the day. He was tired and mentally drained after today's class. He was not looking forward to Friday's test but was excited to return home for a quiet weekend. He could then express his displeasure to his father about taking law classes. He understood and agreed with the reason—to be able to understand business law and write contracts for the construction sites—but all the other mumbo jumbo had driven him nuts. His love of buildings had nothing to do with divorce law. Working on a double major for the last three years had him exhausted. He just wanted to concentrate on architectural design. Fortunately, the end was in sight for both this spring.

He pushed his way through the door of the bar a little too hard to blow off some steam. He noticed Jessie was not there. Figured he was running behind or had an errand to run first. Jake was not at the counter, so he headed to his usual spot. Jake was probably in the back doing chores. "Be right out," he heard Jake call.

He unloaded his heavy bag off his shoulder and took off his coat. He thought it was going to rain today. Otherwise, he would have left it at home. Now he was sweating in the August heat. He stopped in his tracks as he could smell something soft in the air. He took a deep breath in. Not something Jake would be cooking; it had an erotic flair to it. He could feel a deep desire growing inside his pants but squashed it down before it got out of control.

Jake appeared with a stack of napkins and silverware that he would soon wrap together for the dinner rush. He set them on the counter and walked over to him. "Evening, Son. What can I get for you?" Jake asked with a smile.

Adam had been a regular for the last three years. He started coming here when he and Jessie became roommates. It is far enough from school so if they get too sloshed, no one from school should notice, and close enough to the condo if they need to walk, due to the lack of any taxis. "Just the usual, please. It'll be an early night. I have a big test tomorrow," Adam replied.

"Sounds good," Jake responded, turned, and headed to the bar, and Adam set up the table for a round.

He cracked the cue ball to spread the balls around. After sinking a solid ball into the side pocket, Jake returned with his 7 and 7 drink and a small bowl of peanuts. He placed all of it on the small side table. "Thank you," Adam said and handed Jake a 20-dollar bill. "Keep the change."

Jake nodded his head in acceptance. "Thanks. Have a good evening." They smiled at each other, and Jake returned to the counter. Adam wondered if after graduation he would come back to this place to just hang out and relax. He watched as Jake wiped down the bar and then took a glass of water to the far side booth.

That is when he saw the woman with the luscious, flowing locks of red hair. How did he not notice her when he first arrived? With her hair pulled back, he could see every detail of her beautiful face. Her clothes were loose, but he could see her frame and her curves. He smiled as he found the source of the erotic scent. His body responded instantly.

Unfortunately, his boxers offered no support to hide his full arousal, and he was forced to sit down until he could gain control of his erection. She had to be about 5'5"—about a foot shorter than him. Just right. He sipped on his drink as he watched for thirty minutes. Jake went over paperwork, and she held up one item at a time for him to look at.

Jessie and four others breezed in the door at the same time. He caught Adam's attention and waved as he walked his way to join him at the table. "You got started without me," Jessie said while he looked at the pool table.

"Sorry, I was gonna try and have a round finished before you got here. I only sank a solid in the side pocket. Do you want to start over or just play stripes?"

Jessie examined the table from three sides and replied, "I'll play stripes." He grabbed a cue stick and started hitting balls around the table.

After a couple of turns, Adam's hard-on was well under control again, and they finished out the game. Jessie had set up the next round and broke the balls. Adam was good until she practically walked right up to him. She was an arm's length away from where he stood. Her scent put his body into overdrive. His heart pounded and every hair on his body stood on end. He just needed one more stimulation and he would burst in his pants.

He had to sit down again to hide his now swollen member, who had a different plan. He wanted to talk to her. He needed to know who she was and figure out why his body reacted this way to her. Jessie turned to Adam, "Your turn," and held out the stick.

Adam whispered, "Dude, seriously! I can't right now." Adam looked down and then back up at him. Jessie noticed the bulge Adam tried to hide and started to laugh. Jessie looked around and noticed the girl at the counter with the owner.

Jessie sat down next to him and whispered, "Why don't you go and introduce yourself?"

Adam looked at him in disgust and whispered, "Which part should I introduce first? My dick will get there before I do." Adam's eyes went big, then they both laughed.

"Then I'll go talk to her," Jessie said and started to get up. Adam pulled him down with a hard thud on the seat. "Ouch, bastard. That hurt!" Jessie exclaimed. "Just for that, I'm finishing your drink." And with a quick movement, he chugged down Adam's whiskey. A sour expression appeared on his face.

"Ha! That's what you get for drinking someone else's beverage." They both laughed. The door chimed and Adam watched her as she left. That's when his heart sank.

"Your last chance. Don't just sit there. Go after her," Jessie pointed. Adam just stayed in the seat. At least he overheard a part of the conversation that she would be back tomorrow.

"You need to take the Saran Wrap off your dick and use it more often. There are a ton of hot girls around who would love your cock," Jessie emphasized.

Adam shook his head and sighed. "There's more to life than just fucking the next girl in line. Besides, I'm around girls all the time and none of them affected me like she just did. There's something special about her."

Jessie laughed. "Bullshit. They're all sluts. One way or another, all they want is your money or your dick. The sooner you figure that out, the better," Jessie snickered. Adam sighed. He knew that was not true.

Eve

Eve sat in the corner booth at Jake's Bar and Grill. She had her current project spread out for the owner to pick the 'like vs. dislike' items. She was busily working on her tablet, entering images and dimensions into the design program. The model of the bar was starting to look good. Looking around, there were only a few people there—a couple of guys sitting at the bar celebrating something special to them and two more in another booth eating an early dinner.

Suddenly she got a sinking feeling in her stomach. "Bordel!" she slightly cursed aloud. What if this is a gay bar? Then these last few weeks of research and stalking would have been for nothing. She paused her thoughts for a moment. Well, not nothing. At least she will have accomplished a site design for class.

She was glad that her interior design school was not that far away, considering how big the island of Manhattan was. Two years of interior design and foundation study at the Architectural Association at home in France was plenty for her requirements. However, she wanted to experience a different, more modern culture before tackling some of her future problems back at home. Her area was growing fast after the COVID shutdown. Space was limited since the town is registered with the historical society. Not many changes could be made without prior approval. So, growth outward and remodeling of non-traditional buildings were required.

The door chimed, and it pulled her from her thoughts. It announced the arrival or departure of a patron. She casually looked over and saw the addition of the tall, dark-haired man. He walked straight to the pool table and unloaded his bag and coat. She instantly recognized him as one of Jessie's friends from his many posts. Her heart started to race. Then she thought, if this was a gay bar, then that may not be a friend, but a partner.

She glanced over again and studied the man as Jake was talking to him. He's a good-looking man with a distinctive lower velvet voice. Easily could be 6'3" or more. She could tell that he took care of himself and wondered if it was from work or working out. She pondered a little more on the partner aspect and would have to watch a little more to see how they interact. She went back to work on her tablet.

Hopefully, Jessie would arrive soon. Several times on his Instagram page, he would post pictures from this location. After all her research, it comes down to today and tomorrow. She knew that he would most likely be here tomorrow. It was the only regular post he made. By setting up the schedule to deliver her presentation tomorrow, she would increase her possibility to 'bump' into Jessie.

The owner, Jake, came over with a glass of water and sat down across from her. He is a nice and kind older gentleman. She could tell that he had been here for a long time. He knew nothing about her original intention, but only that she was a student that worked on projects. So perhaps other students have gone through the same process with him before. They chatted for a bit, picking out what he liked and colors that went well together for his taste. She got so wrapped up in what they were doing that she did not notice people arriving—

Including Jessie.

Jake had to get going to serve customers, so she thanked him for his time as he slid out of the booth. Just then, her phone chirped with an alert. She looked at the message and saw the Instagram picture of Jessie and his tall friend at the pool table. She smiled and giggled at the funny faces they were making.

After she composed herself, she put the phone down and glanced over at them playing pool when she heard the distinct sound of a new round being started. She finished making the changes that Jake had mentioned. She could easily make her final presentation right now, but she wanted to freshen up and put on something nicer to catch Jessie's full attention.

She made her tabletop jukebox selection, and since not that many people were present, her selection of *"Every Breath You Take,"* by The Police played right away. She hummed along with the thought of spying on Jessie as she packed up all her drawings, color samples, and textiles. She peeked over at the guys, and Jessie was sitting down while his friend was lining up a shot. She continued to sing softly to herself as she waited a few minutes while she finished her snack.

When Jake came out of the back room with a load of clean glasses, she made her way to the end of the bar closest to the pool table where Jake was putting the glassware away. She spoke loud enough over the music, and for the guys to hear, "Can I make the presentation tomorrow at this time? It will only be a few minutes of your time."

She smiled because she could hear the guys talking to the left of her. Jake agreed, and they shook hands. She turned her back to the guys, picked up her bag, and went out the door. She doubted that at this time she would attract his attention since she was wearing her favorite comfy clothes that hid her body and a baseball cap to help block her face.

But tomorrow will be a different story.

Entry 2: Jake's Presentation

Adam had fussed over what to wear for a few hours last night instead of studying like he should have. He understood this chapter, so he was not worried about the outcome. He finally settled on an outfit that would accentuate his muscles without visibly showing them. However, he was unable to find any briefs that would hold back his outward physical attraction. He would just have to make do and try to control himself.

He thought about how Jessie was the opposite of him. He would purposely unbutton his shirt to show off his little chest hairs and flirt like the player that he is. Showing off his package to attract a girl for the night was part of his normal routine. It truly bugged him how he used girls for sex and then moved on to the next one without a thought. He shook his head.

During class, his mind raced through his test. The answers poured from his mind and out of his hand. It even surprised him how quickly he turned in his test. Ultimately, he would find out how he did when he returned on Monday.

Adam made it to the bar as quickly as possible after class. He bounded through the door like a jack-in-the-box toy and stopped at the threshold. After looking all around, he found that no one was in the bar. His heart was racing, and his breath was heavy from rushing so much at the anticipation of seeing her again. He slowly walked in and took a seat at the bar to calm his breathing.

"Hey there. Little early today. How was your test?" Jake asked as he came around the corner with a smile. Adam instantly relaxed and breathed a calming exhale.

"Well, to be honest, I was in a hurry to get here today." Jake looked at him with a confused face.

"Can I get you something to drink?" he replied.

Adam thought about it. "Thanks, but no, I need a clear head today. Just a 7-Up, please."

Jake reached for a glass and filled it up and slid it over to him.

"So…" Jake paused. Adam looked up at him, waiting for him to finish his sentence that never came.

"So, what?" Adam asked. Jake looked at him with a side glance.

"You said you were in a hurry to get here today. Normally your friend doesn't get here for another hour or more. So, what's the hurry?"

Adam leaned back in the seat, closed his eyes, and took a deep breath as he remembered the image of the girl from yesterday. "Do you believe in love at first sight? Because I saw my future wife yesterday." He opened his eyes and looked back up at Jake. His face changed to an intrigued look.

"She was here working in the corner booth and you were talking to her for a bit." He looked over in the direction where she was sitting. "Then she came up to the bar before leaving."

He looked back at Jake and was trying to read his face before he replied. "The redhead?" Jake smiled. Adam's heart started racing again. He put his arms on the counter and rested his head on his hands, taking deep breaths to calm down.

"She's going to be here tonight," Jake responded.

Adam slowly sat up. "I know. I overheard the conversation yesterday. That's why I raced here today." Jake's smile grew, seeing the time-old desire on Adam's face.

"My problem is that when she's close to me, I can't control myself." Adam hung his face in shame. "I want to talk to her, but I don't want to give off the wrong impression that I'm only interested in her for sex." He looked at Jake with a raised eyebrow.

"Oh, because you get TOO excited," Jake responded in emphasis.

Adam looked at him with worry. "Exactly," Adam practically whispered. "It would be nice if I could talk to her without my friend around. I just know he will make it that much more difficult for me, if not make moves on her himself, ruining any chance I would have with her because I'm the friend of the idiot who used and dumped her." He took a deep breath and then refocused on Jake's face. "I know I can't ask you for her personal information, but anything you could share with me would be appreciated."

Jake took a step back and smirked his lips. Adam could see he was pondering what to do. After what felt like an eternity, Jake came around the bar and sat next to Adam on the barstool. "Son, you have been coming here for years now. You have always been wonderful to me and even helped with the occasional problem that has arisen in the past, without question. As far as I can tell, you are one of the good guys and wouldn't use any information I give you for harm." Adam sucked a deep breath in anticipation and waited for him to finish.

Jake pulled a pen and business card out of his pocket. "Her name is Eve, and she's here from France," he said as he wrote her name on the card and slid it toward him. He giggled lightly. "I was just thinking that you guys would be Adam and Eve." He let go of the card in front of him and tapped on it. "This is the school and program she is in. You could contact them. Let them know that I sent you."

Adam leaned over and full-arms hugged him. "Thank you so much," Adam said softly before letting go. Adam had taken French in high school, but over the course of the last few years, he had forgotten most of it. He smirked his lips as he thought about picking it up again. Yet another thing to add to his already busy schedule.

Then he had a wonderful thought that might just work. He pulled out his phone and looked at his schedule. He was jam-packed for the next couple of weeks. He looked at the number on the card and called the school. After a couple of rings, the answering service picked up. Dang, he thought to himself. It won't be until Monday that someone hears this.

At the tone, he left a message. "Hello, my name is Christian Stratford. I'm the CEO of Community Construction. My friend Jake owns a bar on 57th and 7th by Carnegie Hall. He had one of your students, Miss Eve, doing a presentation. Jake was sharing her concepts with me, and I was impressed with her design work. I was wondering if she could also work on a project for modernizing our offices. Would love to get started in a week or two."

He left the office number and hours and ended the call. He then sent a text to the office manager that he would be expecting a call from either the school or a student. He gave a list of a few days and times in his schedule that he would be available. He trusted her to follow the instructions without too many questions. But he knew at some point he would need to explain the situation. He let out a heavy sigh as his stress level decreased.

After he was done, Jake questioned, "I thought your name was Adam?" He looked at him puzzled.

Adam smiled. "It's my middle name. That's what my friends and family call me since I'm a junior. That way there is no confusion on who is being talked to at gatherings." He held up the card. "Can I keep this?"

Jake nodded his head yes. "I hope everything works out. You're a good kid."

The door chimed and a group of people came in for some libations.

Jake got up and walked around the bar to greet his guests. Adam picked up his pop and bag and went to the pool table to start playing a round while waiting for Eve. As he set his things down at the side table, he decided to pick a song to play for when she arrived. He started going through the available selections.

Eve

Eve was antsy all day at school. Her foot would not stop tapping as her anticipation grew. Time could not go by any faster, and yet she had to remind herself to slow down and breathe. If she got there too early, she would miss the opportunity she originally set. Just like her mother, traveling to Scotland to find her father, she was also set on finding a good man who could complement her and her duties. This was the boldest she had ever been, and she hoped it would not all blow up in her face.

She is currently 22 but will be 24 when her student visa expires in a year and a half. If this attempt failed, it would shorten her time to look. And if subsequent attempts failed, then she would have to return to France and start over, shortening her peak fertile age to start a family and provide an heir to her rapidly shrinking family tree. She would then have to think logically and think less of love for her goal as time passed. Thinking about going back home and dealing with the limited aristocratic selection churned her stomach. Having already tried and failed a couple of times, it took a toll on her soul.

One of her girlfriends from the design class asked if she was okay. Eve reassured her that it was just nerves for her upcoming presentation. That was the farthest from the truth. She loved the design she had prepared and could talk about it for hours, without stopping. Already knowing ahead of time that Jake was not going to change anything, and it was just for her program, took the stress off. She was just going to share images and her 3D concept, and then thank him for his time.

Last night she tried on most of her dresses and narrowed them down to two. She figured that when she was ready, the correct dress to wear would talk to her. That would save her precious time. She also lined everything out in order of how she was going to need them to help speed up the process. She only packed one pair of heels with her, so all her dresses looked great with them. She hoped he was taller. Sometimes it is hard to tell in pictures how tall someone is. The few short moments that she had to glance at him yesterday, he was either sitting down or bent over the pool table. Here's to hoping, and she silently wished herself luck.

Before long, class was over, and she rushed home to get ready. The day was hot, so she needed to rinse the sweat off and look fresh for the evening. A cool shower was just what she needed. Right after, she put her hair in hot rollers. She started with simple makeup because she did not want to look overdone or give off a high-maintenance vibe. She has always been a simple or often no-makeup kind of girl. Even though she was raised to be prim and proper, she enjoyed being rugged and carefree. He would need to know this side of her sooner rather than later.

She walked over to the dresses she chose last night and decided that they were way too formal for such a hot day, and she would be uncomfortable. She put both back and decided her slim burgundy sundress would be better. She is not going on an official date yet, so she could save those for next time. She slipped it on, smoothed it out, then checked her look in the mirror. The color of the dress made her hair look like a bright fire. She smiled, thinking of her father's hair color and hoped that her colors would pass on to her children.

She checked the clock and was ahead of schedule. She could stop off and get a cool drink before going in to help with her nerves. She quickly brushed her teeth, so her smile would be as bright as her hair. She grabbed her tablet and purse, then she was out the door. She managed to catch a ride quickly, and traffic was lighter than normal, so she had even more time to kill. She decided to wait in the coffee shop that was kitty-corner to the bar. From there she would be able to see the traffic going through the doors. She placed her order and picked a window seat.

She tried to go over the possible conversations they could have. Should she walk up to him or see if he comes to her? Should she be flirty or play coy? As time went by, she started to worry that he was not coming today. What if there was a crazy reason for him to change his routine? Checking the time, she only had a few minutes left before the time she told Jake that she would be there. Would she need to draw it out even though she told him it would be a short presentation? She could just sit at the bar and have a drink. Eating would be out of the question. She snickered. Wouldn't want any food stuck in her teeth when trying to make a good first impression. All the planning does not matter now. Time was up, and she needed to leave.

She grabbed her belongings but left the drink she did not finish with a tip on the table and started to the bar. Breathe, girl, just breathe, she kept reminding herself as if she had forgotten. The heat of the day instantly made her glisten, and she hoped that it would not be too bad by the time she got in the door. Just as she crossed the street, Jessie came around the far corner. 'Merde!' He is right there. Do I say hi or pretend I don't see him? She debated as the distance closed between them. Cars started honking as the frustrated drivers voiced their opinions, and she looked in their direction, losing her concentration on him for a moment.

She reached the door at the same time as he did. "Hello, sexy!" he said as he put his hand on the door to open it for her but had not opened it yet, effectively blocking the doorway. She looked at him and started to smile. His blue eyes caught her attention, and she blushed. "Let me buy you a drink since we are going the same direction?" he asked. She opened her mouth, but the words would not come out. She looked down in frustration. Blowing it. Come on, girl. Talk to him.

She looked back up and mustered all her courage. "Thank you, I'm heading in to have a meeting with the owner." Her face blushed darker. Just breathe, girl, come on.

"Hmmm, well, maybe after, when you're done?" He moved slightly closer. She couldn't help but smile bigger.

"That would be nice. Thank you." He held out his hand, and reactively, she accepted. Her hand had tiny pin needles at the contact. Then they walked through the door together.

'I did it. I actually did it.' Her brain screamed. She created and executed a meet-cute, and it went perfectly so far. She wanted to jump up and down, then scream from the top of her lungs, but she swallowed that feeling down as fast as she could. He walked her to the counter and then parted ways. He walked to the corner where his friend waited by the pool table. She watched him join the existing game, glancing at her from time to time.

An erotic wave started to roll through her, but she fought that feeling. "*Adore You*" by Harry Styles started playing. She loved this song and started singing along with it. It is a good song for how she was currently feeling. She turned back to the counter and concentrated. Now for a quick presentation, and then she could go and visit with Jessie and get to know him.

Jake came around the corner. "Hello, Eve. You're right on time. I like a girl who is punctual." She smiled at his kind words.

"Is now an okay time? Do you have a couple of free minutes?" she asked with sincerity.

"Now is a great time," he responded. She brought out her tablet and started the program with her drawings while he was mixing drinks behind the bar. She slid the tablet over so he could see from his side.

"You can use your finger to move around the room, zoom, or double-tap to walk," she said as she demonstrated. Eyeing the jukebox selector, she slid it closer and made a choice. "*Dreams,*" by the Cranberries played right away.

"This looks great, darling. The colors are perfect to what we discussed. You really nailed it," he expressed with joy. He then looked over her shoulder and back to her. "Would you be a dear and take these two drinks to the guys at the table while I look over the images?"

She smiled, knowing it was the direction of the pool table he was referring to. "Sure, it would be my honor." She grabbed the drinks and turned. She saw Jessie sitting with his friend, and he waved her over. A few short paces and she was standing in front of both of them. The erotic wave hit again, and her heart started pounding faster. She could feel her cheeks start to heat up.

"I'm sorry, I have no idea what drinks these are, just helping Jake for a moment." She held both of the glasses out for them to take. Jessie's friend grabbed the clear one with bubbles. Probably a pop. She wondered if he was going to be driving. Looks like he is unhappy. Hope he does not feel like she is trying to cut in. Jessie stood up and took his drink while also softly touching the back of her hand in the exchange. She felt tingles go up her arm and started to blush again.

"Ah look, she blushes easily," he said to his friend. "Are you joining us?" Jessie asked.

"I'm sorry. Just here to deliver your order. Enjoy!" She smiled at them both and then returned to Jake, who was intently looking at her drawings. She sat down on the barstool and tried to calm herself.

"Some of these changes I could do without hitting the budget too hard." Jake pointed to a few of the items. She clicked on another tab and a list of materials displayed the potential cost. She then sent the presentation and materials list as an attachment to his email.

"I sent everything to your email. All items here can be found at local stores. The list shows where it can be found and its cost. That way you can pick and choose," she explained.

He leaned in and whispered, "I have a friend that could use your help. Can I give him your number?" She leaned back in a bit of shock. She had not thought about trying to network today. It would help to build her portfolio.

"I do not mind giving my number to you, but I do not give my number to people I have not met in person. You have my card from the school. They can contact me there first. It helps me, so I can do a little research before I show up."

She smiled, reached into her purse, and pulled out a couple more cards. "Just in case you need more." She wrote her cell number on one of the cards and slid them to him and smiled. "The school will be in touch for a quick review of the process. Please be honest. It's a way we can learn and grow. Thank you so much for your time." She extended her hand for a shake. Surprisingly, he cupped her hand. She was not used to this level of familiarity with a stranger. It made her blush slightly, but the way he did it felt sincere.

He looked over her shoulder and then back to her, pulling her in slightly. "He wants to talk to you, but he's a bit shy." She thought that was odd since he seemed so forward earlier.

She looked over her shoulder just far enough to see the two guys and then refocused on Jake. "We just met. He asked if he could buy me a drink." She blushed a little more.

"Really? What can I get you?" he asked. She thought for a minute. She did not want alcohol to interrupt her thoughts or reactions.

"Do you have root beer?" she asked. "It's typically not stocked in France." He grabbed a glass and filled it with the foamy beverage. "Thank you so much," she said as he handed it to her.

"Don't do anything I wouldn't do." He winked and went back to work. She sat at the bar and took a sip of the beverage and licked her lips in an attempt to remove the foam. 'Deep breath, girl. You need to calm your racing heart,' she told herself. She sat there gathering her items together and was taking another sip when she felt a hand on her shoulder. She turned to see who it was, hoping that it was Jessie, and it was.

He laughed and wiped the foam from her upper lip. His finger left a warm trail where it had touched her. She blushed again. "Thank you for the beer," she said and held up her glass. He clinked cheers with his own.

"Hey babe, you wanna join me for a round of pool?" She looked over at the table and then back to him. She smiled as she felt her devil horns grow.

"I do not know how to play. Will you show me?" she asked sheepishly. That was a big fat lie. She grew up playing in the family game room. She was quite skilled at Snooker, English billiards, Three-cushion billiards, Four-ball, and Eight-ball. However, she thought it would be fun to pretend to have him teach her. He held out his hand. After already touching him at the door, she was not ready for him to be handsy. No matter how much she had been planning this very moment. There was a feeling that she could not place.

"My name is Jessie. I'll teach you. It's really easy." He pointed to his friend. "My roommate's name is Adam."

She uncontrollably giggled. "C'est dingue. My name is Eve." She inwardly cheered. They are roommates and not partners. That's a good sign.

She handed her drink to him to hold and then picked up her items to follow him to the small table they were seated at. She set down her items while facing them both. "Hello. My name is Eve." She put her hand out to shake the roommate's hand. His grumpy face faded, and a smile grew in its place as his hazel eyes sparkled with energy.

He shook her hand. "Bonjour, beautiful Eve. Je m'appelle Adam." And then he softly kissed the back of her hand. She felt her face burn as her face turned deep red. He spoke to her like her father did with her mother. Eve's heart started racing again, and her eyes lit up.

"Parlez-vous français?" Other than at the French embassy, she had not met anyone else who knew her native language.

His eyes went wide. "I'm sorry, that was the only French I know."

Eve smiled. "You said it with a very nice pronunciation. I bet you could learn it quickly if you tried." Her hand was growing intensely warm in his and her heart was not slowing down.

Jessie grabbed her other wrist. "Come on, babe, I'll show you how to play." He pulled her from Adam's hand. She saw his face get angry again. Oh, no. She is causing turmoil in their friendship. "Eve, this is a pool table." She turned her attention to Jessie. "The white ball is the cue ball. That's the one you will always hit. The goal is to knock the other balls in the pockets before sinking the black eight ball. One player will be solid color, and the other player will be stripes."

She looked at the table and already saw several plays she could make. "Okay, how do I hold your stick?" He moved behind and slightly to the side of her, then grabbed her hand and placed it on his upper thigh before he whispered in her ear.

"You can hold my stick later tonight if you want?" She pulled her hand quickly, turned to face him, and took a step back in shock at how forward he was. "But this is how you hold a cue stick," he kept on talking like he did nothing wrong.

Suddenly, there was a loud bang on the table behind them. They both turned to look at the noise and saw that Adam had slammed his hand on the table. "Dude, you okay?" Jessie asked. Adam just sat there, giving Jessie a glare. "Anyways…" Jessie continued and turned back to the table. "You hold it like this." He stood at the table and demonstrated. Then he handed it to Eve. "Aim the stick to hit the white ball to hit the red ball so it goes in the side pocket."

Eve held the stick and then leaned over the table. She purposefully aimed to scratch, moved her arm back and forth, then took the shot, barely clipping the cue ball. She made a sad face. "I missed." Jessie laughed, and Eve smacked him playfully on the shoulder. He then spooned in behind her and guided both her hands. Eve's body lit up at the closeness, and her heart started to pound again. Adam groaned behind them, but she ignored him. He can be a grumpy gus all he wants. She was going to concentrate on Jessie.

"Let me try again," she demanded, and she moved him out of the way with her hip. This time she took aim, lined it up, and sunk it.

"Wow, that was great," Jessie exclaimed as Eve handed the cue stick back to him. Jessie put his hands up and said, "No babe, it's still your turn. When you make your shot, you keep going until you miss," he explained. She made sure that he won by a landslide. She wanted to string him along for a bit and didn't want to put a chink in his ego.

After two rounds, she noticed the time. "Oh my gosh, it's getting late. I need to find a new building and design a couple of rooms for class on Monday." She backed away and turned to the small table to collect her belongings when she saw Adam's sad face. "It was nice to meet you. Maybe next time you could join in." She smiled. Just then, Jessie grabbed her around the waist, surprising her and blocked her in between them.

"Could I convince you to take this party back to my place?" She got goosebumps up her arms, and the hairs stood up on her neck. She wasn't sure if it was a New York thing or just him, but he was a bit too forward for her liking.

She mentally kicked herself. Look who's stalking someone, hypocrite.

"I'm sorry, I do not go home with strangers, especially late at night. But I'll make you a bet." She turned to see him.

"I'm intrigued," Jessie responded and pulled her closer.

"Let's play one rounder. The loser buys the winner dinner next Friday, wherever they want." She watched and waited for his response.

"Deal." He let her go and started to set up the table again. She set her items back down, leaned in, and placed a hand on Adam's shoulder. He felt warm, almost febrile. Perhaps he's not feeling good, and that's why he's been so cranky.

She whispered, "Adam." He looked up, and they were face to face. His eyes widened. "Place a wager against Jessie for me to win. I'm gonna clean the table." She winked and turned back to the pool table. Jessie had gone over to the jukebox and selected a song to play. *Put Yer Money Where Yer Mouth Is*," by Oasis started playing. "I think I've got this game down now. Can I break this time?" She looked back at Adam and raised an eyebrow.

"Sure, babe. Just make sure you hit it hard," Jessie added. Eve turned and faced the table.

"Jessie," Adam spoke up as he pulled out his wallet. "I'll place a 20 wager that she wins."

Jessie laughed, pulled out a 20-dollar bill, and walked over to him. "I'll take that bet. Easy money for me."

"Are you boys done?" She took the pool stick from his hand and let her fingers trace across the back of his hand. She smiled because, after she studied Jessie's playing style, she knew she had this in the bag. Plus, a date for next Friday with Jessie, and she helped his friend earn some money.

This turned out to be a wonderful day.

Entry 3: Honest Talk Between Men

Walking down the street from the bar, Adam was fuming mad. He had kept his anger under control in the bar, but now it was boiling over and he wanted to smash Jessie's face in. Suddenly, he stopped.

"I can't fucking believe you!" Adam screamed at Jessie. Jessie stopped and turned to face him. "Over the last few years, you have brought girl after girl to your room, just to boot her to the curb," he yelled again.

Jessie shrugged his shoulders. "So what? I like having sex, and I like variety," He replied nonchalantly. Adam smashed a fist on the top of a garbage can he was standing next to.

"Then, when I expressed interest in a girl for the first time, you couldn't just keep your hands off her," Adam yelled again and started walking away.

Jessie started to follow. "Fuck off, dude. It's not like you were going to make a move. You just sat in the corner like a little shy schoolboy. I'm the one who invited her over. I'm the one who engaged in a conversation. I'm the one who got a date with her. Not you. You sat there and did nothing but be a little bitch all evening," Jessie responded angrily.

Adam stopped in his tracks. He was right. He had done nothing but sit there, being angry. That was her first impression of him, and he hated himself for it. He wanted to get to know her. What was it about her that got his heart racing?

"Well, you knew I was nervous and overly excited. You could have invited her to sit with us. But instead, you groped her all evening. You even forced her hand onto your junk and she pulled away. Why she stayed, I have no idea," Adam fought back. "Plus, she hustled you into a date. She told me to make the bet because she was going to win." Adam snickered.

"Bullshit. It's like I told you. They are either into your money or your dick. She pulled back. That means she's looking for money." He waved his finger in Adams face. "And her hustling me into a date just proves she's looking for a sugar daddy." Jessie paused and an evil smile grew on his face. "Either way, I'm still gonna fuck her," he said spitefully.

Something snapped in Adam and he instantly boiled over. He wrapped a hand around Jessie's throat, squeezed it, and forcefully took Jessie to the closest wall. "If you hurt her or her feelings, you're gonna be mopping your blood up off the floor!" he yelled while pointing a finger in his face, then he let go and walked home without him.

Adam made it to the condo two hours before Jessie returned home. By that time, he had cooled down. Jessie slowly opened the door and looked around, and Adam was sitting on the couch.

"Come in, Jessie, we need to talk, without the anger." Jessie slowly closed the door behind him and went to sit on the opposite couch. Adam could smell the alcohol on him. He must have gone back to the bar for several more rounds.

Adam leaned forward and looked Jessie in the eyes. "I want to apologize for my behavior. That is not the type of man I am or want to be. I'm sorry if I hurt you." Jessie didn't say anything. He just leaned back a bit more on the couch. Adam took a deep breath and continued.

"You and I treat people differently. Especially women. Sometimes it really drives me nuts. When a friend tells you that they have feelings for someone, that is when you help your friend. Seeing you flirt with her—it ripped me apart, and your comment pushed me over the edge." He leaned back and waited for Jessie to reply. Adam could see he was thinking.

"So, what do you want me to do? I have a date with her. Want me to blow her off?" Jessie asked quietly. Adam was trying to think of possible outcomes, but his mind was just crazy.

"You already screwed me over. If the date goes well and you get along, or if it doesn't and you split, I will always be the 'roommate.'" Adam used air quotes to make a point.

"So, you want me to go on the date?" Jessie asked in surprise. Adam hung his head and breathed deeply.

"Yes, go on the date, but please don't be your usual horned-dog self." Jessie leaned back and put a foot on the table.

"And what if she initiates another date or sex?" Adam's heart started to pound and his hands twisted into fists.

Adam leaned forward and stared Jessie in the eyes again. "I stand by what I said earlier. If you hurt her, I will hurt you." Adam got up and walked to his room and shut the door behind him. He walked over and flopped down on his bed. A song popped into his head, so he put in his earbuds and made his selection to listen to *"Jessie's Girl,"* by Rick Springfield.

Entry 4: Returning Home Dad's Help

Friday after class, Adam was driving slower than normal. He should have called for the car service, but it was too late now, since he was almost home. Being preoccupied with Eve and Jessie, he just couldn't seem to keep his mind focused on the road. He was hoping that their date next week would tank or she would see through his player ways. "Fuck!" he cursed to himself. He could be so smooth when he wanted to be. He wished he could just get rid of Jessie altogether.

"No, no, no. I'm not going down that rabbit hole," he told himself. That would be bad, and with his luck, he'd get caught in a heartbeat. He'd just have to get him out of the equation some other way. Adam pulled up to the house and took a deep breath to calm his nerves. He parked out front since he would be leaving tomorrow night to return to the condo. He would have to deal with Jessie all week prior to his date. He shook his head and wondered how many other girls he would parade through the condo before then.

"Adam!" his mom said in surprise as he walked into the house and set his keys down. "We were not expecting you until dinnertime. Why are you home so early?" she asked.

"Hello, Mom," he replied as he gave her a kiss on the cheek. "I have some business to discuss with Dad. Am I interrupting anything?" he asked with a puzzled look in her eyes.

"Nope. He's done with physical therapy for the day. He's just relaxing right now. You can go see him," she responded with a smile.

"Thank you, Mom." He gave her a hug before heading upstairs.

Just as Adam was about to knock on his parents' bedroom door, his dad called out, "Come in, boy. I saw you coming a mile away."

Adam laughed. "You know, one of these days you'll get an eyeful, and you're going to end up removing all the interior cameras," he said as he came into the room.

"Oh, yeah? You plan on bringing someone home and having your way with them all over the house?" His dad wiggled his eyebrows. Adam laughed and then shut the door.

"You never know. Maybe sooner than later." His dad looked curiously at the door. "Really, we need privacy for business? Anything going on in the office can be said in front of your mother." His dad looked worried.

"It's not about work, Dad." He pulled up a chair and sat next to his bed. "It's about Mom." Now his dad really looked worried. "Easy, Dad." Adam waved his hand and then leaned back in the chair as he tried to gather his thoughts. He closed his eyes and just let the frustration go. "Back when you met Mom, she was dating someone else." Adam sat up again and faced his dad.

"Oh, that kind of talk. Well, a little bit beyond the birds and bees chat," he laughed, but Adam didn't. "Oh, that serious? Why don't you just start from the beginning?" his father smirked. Adam leaned forward and grabbed his dad's hand with his and rested his forehead on the back of his dad's warm hand. "Just breathe and let it out, Son. No judgments here."

Adam stayed there for a while and started thinking about the progression of his dad's MS. His body had slowly become less mobile over the years. Having the security systems in the house gave him a way to be connected. The door opened. "Hello, Beautiful. We are having a guy's talk. Please give us a few."

Adam knew without lifting his head that his mother was in the room, but he waited until the door closed to continue. "Thursday, I walked into the bar to play some pool before going home. My body felt her before I even knew she was there." Adam lifted his head and looked at his dad.

"What do you mean your body felt her?" his dad asked with big eyes. Adam looked down at his groin and then back to his dad. "Oh, it's a blessing and a curse. Just like two sides of a sword. Anyway, sounds like you had a chemistry reaction," his dad added with a smile.

"I had to remain seated or else I'd be sticking out. That's not how I wanted to make a first impression. Anyway, Jessie was there, and he knew I was interested in her. She had an appointment with the owner the next day, so I got there early so I could meet her. I don't know if Jessie was waiting outside, but when she arrived, Jessie had already introduced himself and invited her to play pool with him. By that time,

I was pissed off, hard as hell, and not much of a conversationalist. Now, she has a date with him, and I'm left to watch from the sideline."

Adam took another deep breath and let go of all the stress. "I don't know what to do from here. I want him out of the picture so I can get to know her, and well..." He paused and sang, "I want Jessie's girl." His father laughed at his singing.

"You're wondering how I won your mom's heart while she was dating someone else." Adam raised his head and slowly placed his dad's hand back to a flat position. "I will tell you what my father said to me. Take notes." Adam took out his phone and started a new memo page.

"First and foremost, you will always be a gentleman. Open car doors, hold your hand out to help her in and out—which conveniently gives you an opportunity to kiss her hand. Open regular doors; also gives you the opportunity to put your hand on her lower back. Always pay. It does not matter what. Don't let her split the check."

Adam's fingers were flying on the little keyboard, then he giggled. "I kissed her hand when we met. Think it's from all the years of watching you and Mom."

"Second. Always tell her she's beautiful. Even if she's crying and her face is a mess. Lifting her confidence will boost her confidence in you." 'Check,' Adam thought to himself.

"Third. Always be her protector. Whenever there may be danger, her honor, or feelings, prove that you'll be there for her. It builds trust." Keep her close, watch for danger, other men. Adam kept typing.

"Fourth. Always show affection. Hugs, kisses, sit next to her with your arm around her. When she's comfortable, she will return the affection. Gently touch her hand, arm, or leg when she shares a part of her life or insight into her past."

Adam loved all of this and was mentally seeing it already.

"Fifth. Dance when you get the chance. Even if it's just the radio in the living room. It's the closeness and moving together that forms a bond. Especially if it's a love song. You may want to create a playlist." Adam smiled as he continued to type.

"Sixth. At some point, you're going to need full courage and tell her how you feel. She's not psychic. Make it clear. No wishy-washy terms." Adam took a deep breath and slowly let it out. "I know you get nervous and shy. But sixty seconds of courage can change the course of your life." Adam stared at his dad for a moment before returning to his notes.

"Seventh. You'll know when, because you'll feel it, but be the first to say, 'I love you.'" Adam smiled because he already wanted to say those words.

"Eighth. Don't wait too long, propose and get your ring on her finger. Find something beautiful that has a significant meaning to you both. Like birthstones." Adam nodded as thoughts went through his mind.

"Ninth. Never forget her birthday, Valentine's, Christmas, or anniversary. Put them in your phone. Write them out on the desk calendar. Now, let me be clear. I'm not saying shower her with lavish, expensive gifts. But a gift that has meaning goes a long way." Adam nodded again, firmly agreeing with him.

"Tenth. Never drink more than one alcoholic beverage. Just in case you must drive or take her home. No girl who is thinking about the future wants to see a guy she's interested in get drunk and sloppy. It will leave a negative view and an untrustworthy image in her mind."

"All common sense so far," Adam said as he finished his typing and looked back to his dad.

"Good. Now, how to get rid of the other guy without hurting him permanently. Unless you want that?" his dad asked as he raised an eyebrow and he waited for Adam's response.

"No, not permanent. I just want him out of the way so I can have more one-on-one time with her," Adam responded with a smirk.

"Good. Didn't know if I had to call in a favor." His dad started laughing. "Let's start with being sneaky. I know it's not normal for you, but you are now in a war for a woman's love. You want to make sure that what you do will only affect the intended target. No accidents. If you accidentally dose her or someone else, it could cause serious problems." Adam nodded his head in understanding.

"1. When staying up late, put him to sleep. Slip him a dose of a sleeping aid. Make it look like he had passed out from drinking or just tired from a long day." Adam typed the info in as he thought about how he could slip something in his drink or food.

"2. When sleep is not an option, keep him in the bathroom. Ipecac will induce vomiting or laxatives to loosen his bowels. He may choose to stay after the episode, but you can encourage him to leave to prevent the spread of an illness."

Adam started to laugh. "That's smart, now that everyone is so up on precautions since COVID," Adam added as he shook his head.

"3. When there may be sex, reduce his ability to get an erection." Adam's eyes went big. "I'll get you in contact with my friend, who is a pharmacist. He will assist you. It comes in a liquid or a powder. He needs to consume a certain amount each day to cause impotence."

Adam tapped his finger on his lip as he had a thought. "He makes a protein shake every morning. It comes in a jug of powder." Adam smiled at the evil idea.

"4. Where there may be trust, remove his credibility. This may be easier for you since he's already a player. She just needs to see him with another girl. Set up security at the condo and record his next visitor. When she comes over, prevent her from entering and play the video." Adam's wheels were spinning now. This part would be easy.

"Son, you must make sure to offer her support and take her away from the situation. She's gonna go through different stages. Fighting mad is usually the first. So be prepared to receive a swing that was intended for the other guy. There will be sadness, so have tissues and a shoulder to cry on. Then find a way to burn off the energy. Don't have rebound sex. Go for a run together, batting cages, dancing at a club is always good." Adam smiled as his dad talked about all his strong suits.

"If all that doesn't work, just let me know and I'll have him whacked." Adam looked at his dad in shock. "Aw, come on, boy, you should know by now that I'm kidding. I'll put in a PO for some equipment for your new home security. If you head to the office tomorrow morning, you can have most everything set up by Sunday evening. I'll contact my pharmacist friend in just a few minutes. He will let you know when to pick up 'your prescription,'" his dad winked at him during the accents.

"Thank you, Dad. Sounds like I need to go shopping for a few items also. I may leave after dinner to get started."

"No. By the sounds of it, you have already had a long day. Stay the night and be fresh tomorrow." Adam thought about it. A night away from Jessie may be good as he made his plans.

Entry 5: Schedule an Interview

Eve was in a glow all weekend long after coming face to face with Jessie. She would play back the whole encounter from the door until she left, after giving her number to him. But now it's Monday at 4 p.m., and she has not heard from him. How are they going to meet up for a date if they don't talk? She knew she should have gotten his phone number. But after swindling him into a date, she didn't want to seem desperate.

Now she's having a sour taste in her mouth because of being ignored, and mentally kicked herself repeatedly for not getting his number. But she didn't want to be the annoying, clingy girl. Replaying the memory has a different effect now. What did Jake mean when he said, "He wants to talk to you, but he's a bit shy"? Jessie was anything but shy. She pondered on that for a while.

After confiding in a few of her class girlfriends, they decided to have a group date. That way the other girls could check him out. And if he bailed, at least the group of girls would have a fun evening out. Eve really liked that idea.

At the end of class, the teacher called Eve up to her office. "Hello, Mrs. Johnston. You called for me?" Eve asked as she knocked on the door.

"Yes. Please come in and have a seat." Eve sat down, not knowing what to expect, and smiled at her instructor nervously.

"Your work has been very exemplary during your time here. Tell me, how did your presentation go on Friday?" Eve leaned back for a moment to recall.

"I think it went well. For what he said in response to my images and 3D presentation," Eve twiddled her fingers a bit out of nervousness.

"His review was all top numbers. But what had me call you into my office today is that he shared your information." Eve smiled and nodded her head.

"He said that he has a friend that could use some help with updating. He asked for my phone number, but I gave him the school card for a contact." Mrs. Johnston smiled.

"That's good. Keeps you safe that way. Well, during the weekend, we got a call requesting you for your assessment and presentation. The name is Christian Stratford of Community Construction." She slid the memo page across the table and Eve picked it up to study it.

"Looks like I have a phone call to make and some research to do. Architecture plans, any archive images, history of the company. Do you need me for anything else?" Eve asked.

Mrs. Johnston shook her head no. "All good here. Keep up the good work." Eve got up, shook her hand, and was on her way. 'I must go back and give Jake a big hug,' Eve thought to herself.

Eve found a quiet area of the school to make her phone call. Hopefully, they will be open. It's 4 o'clock already, and some businesses close at this time. But, with it being a construction company, perhaps their office hours reflect site hours. She dialed the number, and they picked up on the second ring.

"Hello, thank you for calling Community Construction. How may I direct your call?" The woman's voice on the other line sounded older but very pleasant. Perhaps she's been with the company for a long time.

"Hello, my name is Eve. I'm a student at the New York School for Interior Design. Mr. Christian Stratford called for me. He got my business card from Jake," Eve bit her lower lip as she waited for the woman to respond.

"Yes, hello Ms. Eve, I'm Ophelia, the office manager here. I was expecting your call. Mr. Stratford is currently out of the office, but I have his available days to schedule a meeting. How much time do you need?"

"First meeting usually lasts about an hour. Depends on how much of a change he is looking to make and the overall size of the space," Eve smiled to herself.

"He has a little time this week. Would this Friday 3 p.m. till 4 p.m. work for you?" Eve's heart sank a little.

"I'm sorry, during the week, I'm in class until 4 p.m. From where I am, by taxi and good traffic, the earliest I could make it would be 4:30 p.m. So 5 p.m. to be safe, so I'm not late. If he has any time spots open after then during the week or anytime on the weekends is good for me."

Eve heard her hum while turning pages. "Ah, next Saturday is a planned in-office day. He could meet you then, and I will make sure not to double-book. He's usually very busy with paperwork in the morning. Would 1 p.m., just after he returns from lunch, work for you?"

Eve was looking at her calendar and noticed that the first weekend in September is a normal U.S. holiday. "That's Labor Day weekend. Are you sure he's not busy with a family function?"

"Oh my, you're right. Good catch. Well, he has it marked as coming in. How about we schedule for that day and I will verify. The number you're calling from, is this your number or a school number?"

"This is my cell number. I'm good with a call or text. Thank you so much for your time, Mrs. Ophelia." They said their goodbyes, and she ended the call.

Her heart was beaming again. Now, time for some research. She would have two full weeks to gather as much information as she could.

Adam

Adam was done with school for the day but did not feel like being social with Jessie after class. He decided to head back to the condo instead. Getting some work done would take his mind off his studies for a while at least. After walking in the door, he tossed his bag onto his bed and decided to fix a quick dinner to eat in his room.

He grabbed a plate and served up some leftover takeout stir-fry and re-warmed it in the microwave. A bit of grapes and a cold glass of milk rounded out his meal. He made sure to shut and lock his door so Jessie could not just walk in and bug him.

At this time, Jessie should be arriving at Jake's bar. After finding that Adam is not there, he will probably drink too much and pour himself in the door later. If Adam was lucky, Jessie would bring a girl back, and he'd save the images from the newly installed home security system.

Just then, his pocket buzzed. It was an automated text from the pharmacy. His new prescription was ready. He's scheduled to have it sent by courier tonight, since his days are busy. Soon, Adam can mark another check on dad's list. He hoped this stuff would work. He wondered how long Jessie would have to ingest the substance before it would have an effect. Well, since he's not going to hover, he will never truly know.

His phone rang and he saw Ophelia was calling. It's important when she called, so he answered right away. "Hello, Mrs. Ophelia. How can I help you?" he asked, knowing how busy she can be.

"I had the student from the design school call and schedule." Adam's heart instantly started racing.

"And…" he asked, trying desperately to sound calm.

"During the week she has class until 4 p.m. So, meeting before 5 p.m. is difficult. You marked that you were coming in the following Saturday. We tentatively scheduled for 1 p.m., just after your lunch break. However, I just wanted to verify it, since it's a holiday weekend."

Adam opened his calendar to check. He forgot about Labor Day weekend but did not have any plans other than working Saturday. Perhaps he will have to do a BBQ on Sunday with his parents.

"Thank you for checking. Yes, I plan on being in. But let's change it from 1 p.m. to noon and do a working lunch. Could you find out what she likes and please get that ordered for us to deliver about 12:15?" he asked as his heart calmed down.

"Not a problem. I'll take care of it. Anything else?" she asked.

"It may seem odd, but could you also find out some of her other favorite things?" He paused.

"I'll see what I can do," she replied.

"Thank you, Ophelia. You are a lifesaver," he added before saying goodbye and hanging up.

His heart pounded in his ears. He lay back on his bed to soften the pressure in his head. It would be two weeks before he could see her again without Jessie. That meant he had enough time to start to relearn French. He opened his phone and started to download a language app. He closed his eyes while waiting for the download to complete and couldn't help but dwell on the fact that they had a date this Friday.

He could imagine Jessie's slick hands grabbing at her during their date. "Ughh," he vented. He sat up and quickly ate his food so he could finish work. Then he was going to hit the gym to work off the frustration. He could see himself spending a lot of time there in the next few weeks.

Entry 6: Karaoke with Girls / Date?

Eve feverishly worked all week on her new assignment. Spending time with the county assessor's office to get blueprints took a while. The building plans were from 1890, and completion was in 1893. There had already been a few remodels recorded, and finding all the alteration copies was a challenge. In the archives, she was able to find several owners over the 130 years, Mr. Stratford being its current owner for 38 years.

Diving headfirst at full throttle helped her ignore the fact that Jessie had not called her all week. Here it is Friday, the day of their date, and she has not heard a word. "Merde! Stop thinking about him," she grumbled to herself. Some of the other girls looked at her. She took a deep breath and calmed herself down.

Stephanie got up and walked over to her station. "It's a good thing we have plans for tonight, since he ghosted you. There are so many jerks in this town. Finding a good man is hard. You're typically not going to find a good one at a bar or a dance club. Those are more for fun-time boys. Have fun now, maybe a one-night stand. You have to look harder for the man in the crowd."

Eve was confused. It happened all the time with American English slang. "I'm sorry. What does the word 'ghosted' mean?" Stephanie giggled, pulled up a chair, and sat down.

"It means that he was there and seemed interested and then disappeared, invisible, like a ghost. A real man gives you his number or exchanges numbers because he wants to hear back from you. If he doesn't, he's not really interested in something serious."

Eve shook her head. "Okay, I understand." Just then, her phone rang. She didn't recognize the number. "Hello?" she answered, wondering who it may be. Not many people have this number.

"Hey Babe. How's it going?"

Not recognizing the voice, she paused and looked at the number again before continuing. "Who is this?" she furrowed her eyebrows.

"Babe, it's me, Jessie. The guy you hustled into a date." Shock took over her whole thought process. She quickly tapped the speaker button on so Stephanie could hear.

"Hmmm. That sounds familiar. Are you the guy that I gave my number to a whole week ago? Is that really you?" She looked at Stephanie and winked. "The guy who ghosted me." Stephanie winked back at her.

He laughed. "Sorry, Babe. That wasn't my intention. Wow, it's been a crazy week in school. Where did you wanna go tonight?"

She leaned back in the chair, crossed her arms, and watched Stephanie. "Well, since I thought you ditched me, I made other fun plans." There was dead silence on the line. For a moment, she thought the call had been dropped.

"Oh, okay. I was looking forward to seeing you all week. Umm, can we meet after?" His response sounded genuine. She looked up to Stephanie for advice. Stephanie quickly wrote out on a scrap piece of paper, 'group date.' Eve grew a devilish smile, understanding what she meant.

"I guess you could join in, but it requires your participation. A bunch of my friends and I are meeting at Duet 53 at 7 p.m. It's just a couple blocks south of Jake's bar. Bring four or five of your friends."

She could hear him writing the info down. "Sounds good. Looking forward to seeing you again. Later, Babe," he said before hanging up.

"Well. It looks like tonight may be more interesting than we originally planned," Eve said. Stephanie was nodding her head with a big grin. "It sure does." They both laughed.

After getting a quick bite for dinner, Eve went back home to change her clothing choice. She was going to wear the same sundress from the day she did her presentation, but now she didn't want to wear the same thing twice in a row to meet Jessie. Now sliding hanger after hanger, her eye settled on her green dress with a black lace overlay. Her feet were already tired from today. If she wore her heels, she would be taller, but her feet would be screaming by the end of the evening, so she opted for her black flats.

Jessie

Per Eve's request, after Jessie hung up the phone, he texted a few friends to add numbers for the evening. He then called Adam.

"What do you want?" Jessie cringed, since Adam didn't sound happy as he answered his phone—probably because he knew today was the date.

"Hey man. I kinda screwed up." Jessie could hear weights drop to the floor and knew Adam was at the gym.

"What did you do?" Adam asked, with a bit more anger in his voice.

"I forgot to call Eve earlier in the week." There was a pause for a moment.

"You fucking idiot. Now what?" Adam asked.

"Well, I just got off the phone with her. Since she hadn't heard from me all week, she made other plans with friends. But she wants me and a few friends to join in the fun. She said participation is required. Whatever that means," Jessie smirked his lips as he explained.

"And you're calling me because?" There was silence for a bit.

"Guess I have to spell it out for you. Please come tonight. She knows who you are already. It will be a chance for you to get to know her in a group setting."

Adam

Adam liked that plan. Maybe even make up for his behavior, last time they met. "When and where?" he asked. He recognized the name and location instantly as a karaoke bar. This was right up his alley. However, Jessie will probably hate it. Even better, he grinned at the thought of Jessie embarrassing himself on stage. "Is she coming to our place first or meeting there?" Adam asked.

"She wants to meet there. Do you want to share a cab there?" Jessie asked. Adam thought, Sure, his way of getting out of paying for a lift. But either way, he'd have to get there and back. Besides, Jessie may have passed out, he thought to himself.

"Sounds like a plan. Let's leave at about 6:30 p.m. Bye." He already knew that he was going to order the car service. That way he knew Jessie would get home safely. And, if things went well, he would spend the evening with her instead. Adam was currently at the gym. He had planned on working his frustrations out all evening this way, but now he had to hurry home to shower and change for the night.

Spending a few minutes in the closet, he picked out simple black slacks and a white polo shirt. The whole time, he was racking his brain for a good song to sing. Now lying on his bed, he was thumbing through all the soft love songs he had until he found one. He put his earbuds in to listen so Jessie couldn't hear. It was perfect to make his point. He hoped she would like it also.

Eve

Eve and her four co-workers arrived at 5:30 p.m. for ladies' night so they could get a table close to the stage and still be able to see the door for when the guys arrived. For some of them, knowing guys were coming made the whole situation feel like blind dates—except for her and Jessie. A whole bunch of them had already signed up for time spots. She picked a 7:15 spot for herself and a 7:30 for Jessie. Anyone else he brought would have to pick their own.

The girls were all having such a good time singing, dancing, and drinking. Most everyone forgot that the guys were coming. They had several drinks and food by the time a bunch of guys walked into the building together. Suddenly, her tummy fluttered with excitement. There were four guys that Eve did not recognize, and then she saw Jessie and Adam.

Eve cheered loudly and waved to get their attention, and the whole group migrated to their table. All the guys spread out among the girls and started talking. She stood up to greet Jessie and Adam and gave them both kisses on the cheeks. "Thank you for coming."

"Hey Babe," Jessie responded.

"Hello Beautiful," Adam added.

"Us girls have already started, some are already three sheets," Eve giggled as she pointed to Cathy. "Jessie, I signed you up for the 7:30 spot, but you still need to pick a song to sing." She turned to face Adam. "I'm sorry to you and the other guys." She shrugged. "I didn't know who he was bringing, so you will need to sign up. Hopefully, it's not too late. But I don't have school tomorrow, so I can stay up." She turned and pointed to the stage. The boys walked off together, and then she sat back down.

Eve's giddiness had taken over, and she was glad to visit with Jessie again. After all the guys were done signing up, they came back to the table. Jessie sat on her left, and Adam was on her right. "Well, this is cozy," she blushed slightly. "I'll be up soon. What song did you guys pick?" Eve asked.

"I've picked one of my favorites," Jessie responded. "But I've never done this before, so forgive me if I suck at it." Eve smiled and nudged him with her elbow.

"It's all about having fun and enjoying each other," Eve smiled. He then rested his hand on her leg. Eve suddenly got nervous, but he wasn't moving his hand around, so she'd let it go for now.

"I picked a different song. I have not rehearsed it much either. Hope I do it justice," Eve responded as she turned to face Adam. "What about you?"

Adam rested his arm along the back of her chair, leaned in, and spoke soft and low. "I picked a song to show my low end. I hope you like it." His low reverberations gave her full-body goosebumps.

"Oh yummy, so velvety," she responded, rubbed her arms, and blushed again. "I can't hardly wait." She smiled.

Adam sat up straight. "I'm gonna get some drinks. You guys want anything?"

Jessie leaned over. "You know what I like. Thanks."

Eve smiled. "I've already had a few, so I'm good. Thank you."

Adam leaned his head, "How about a water or a pop?"

Her eyes lit up. "Oh my, yes please. A root beer would be nice." She smiled as he reached for her hand and gave it a soft kiss.

"Your wish is my command." Then he turned and walk to the counter.

They called her name, and another wave of butterflies hit her tummy, so she took a couple of deep breaths. "I'll see you all in a few," Eve said as she got up. Jessie nodded and waved as she walked to the waiting area. She took a couple more deep, soothing breaths while waiting her turn. After the previous song ended, the stage man handed her the microphone and her song displayed: *Only Girl (In the World),"* by Rihanna.

Her girls instantly cheered. The lights were bright, but as she looked out into the crowd, she could see Jessie sitting and Adam standing at the table, clapping. 'Breathe girl,' she reminded herself. The music started and she powered through.

I want you to love me, like I'm a hot ride

She sang and slowly moved her body back and forth with the rhythm. She concentrated on not being pitchy and stuck to the beat. She partially closed her eyes to block the brightness of the lights. They were giving her a slight headache.

Want you to make me feel like I'm the only girl in the world

She continued to relax as the song progressed through the chorus section.

The crowd was cheering so loudly that she couldn't tell who was who. She knew that her accent would hinder some of the words. But it was a challenging song, and she gave it her best.

After her song was over, she made her way down the steps, and all the girls were there to greet her. Now she could enjoy the rest of the evening and relax.

As she walked to the table, Adam surprised her when he came up to her and gave her a big hug. "That was wonderful. When does the tour start? I'll be your first roadie."

Eve laughed, and they turned to sit down. He's more friendly than last time. However, she could see that something was off in Jessie. Nerves were probably getting to him.

"You're up in a few minutes. Don't stress too much. Just take deep breaths and pretend you're the star and own the stage. Or alone in the shower. Whatever works for you. No one cares if you say a word or note wrong. We all have done it. Mostly, just have fun."

She gave him a hug and then sat back to relax. Adam sat back down next to her again and leaned his arm across the back of her chair again. She could feel the heat on her back. It felt nice since she always seemed to be cold.

Shortly, they called Jessie's name to get in line, and he got up from the table without saying anything. Eve reached for his arm and gave him a squeeze. "Have fun." And then she let go of him.

Once Jessie was out of earshot, Adam leaned in and whispered, "He's had a long day—long week, really. I don't see him staying up late tonight. I'll make sure he gets home safe. But my song is later, so I'll be here for a while."

Eve smiled and whispered back, "Thank you for letting me know." Eve then got a quick scent from Adam aftershave and leaned forward. Her body got warm, and her heart started to race as an erotic wave started in her.

He then raised his hand and placed it on her back and pulled her gently closer as his other hand picked up hers. "Now that we are alone for a few, I need to apologize for last week."

She turned to him. "For what?" she asked.

"When you arrived, Jessie and I were in the middle of an argument. Instead of setting my frustration aside, I sat in the corner like a bear. I should have been more of a gentleman. Please forgive me?" He then kissed her hand.

She leaned her head to the side. "I saw you were upset, but since I didn't know you, I figured you would work it out. Everyone has rough days, and that one was yours. How could I hold that against you? I was not upset or offended. So, you are forgiven." She smiled and nudged him with her shoulder.

"Since you brought it up. What was the fight about? Lover's quarrel, perhaps?"

He had a shocked look on his face for a moment.

"Jessie and I are NOT partners. Just roommates. We are both straight," he responded with a serious look in his eyes and face.

"Well, that's good. When I was doing my research for Jake, it seemed like only guys frequented the establishment." She winked at Adam. "In today's times, you never really know unless you ask."

Even thought about it for a moment. From the outside looking in, one could see how that would look. "Adam? You still haven't answered my question."

"Oh, I'm sorry. Jessie was being a selfish jerk when he should have been a friend when his help was needed," he replied with pressed lips.

This made Eve think. Jessie's being a jerk to his friends. What would he do to me?

"When did you learn to play pool? You're obviously a shark by playing coy and then suckering him into a bet that he would lose." She saw the curious look on his face.

Eve smiled. "When I was young, we had a billiards room. My father taught me to play all types of table games." Her smile faded slightly at the memory of her father teaching her how to aim and plan moves.

"We had air hockey in our game room. I got good at all my angles," Adam added.

Eve frowned. "Clearly, by my accent, English is not my first language. So sometimes translations..." she shrugged her shoulders. "They confuse me. I'm sorry to ask. How do you play hockey in the air?"

Adam laughed and slightly squeezed her. "You never have to apologize for asking for clarity. It's a table like pool, but air blows through small holes, keeping the puck floating. You have to guard your goal while trying to hit the puck into theirs."

Eve was thinking. "So, the table is a machine that blows air. This sounds like fun. I'll have to try it someday."

"How long have you been here?" Adam asked with big eyes She was surprised that he was continuing the conversation.

"I have been here for six months of a two-year student visa. I'm working on getting different design knowledge. Are you from here?" she asked, now that he was talkative.

"I grew up in a town called Roslyn Heights, a short distance from here on Long Island. My dad worked in the city, and I would shadow him on the weekends. I've lived here in the city for a few years now. I'm working on my double major in Architecture and Law. Have you done any sightseeing or tours?"

Eve shook her head no. "I've been so busy with classes that I haven't really had the chance."

Adam smirked, knowing that feeling. "I'll have to help you with that. You can't travel all this way and not see the sights."

Eve smiled. "I'd like that. I did see the Statue of Liberty from the airplane before landing. Did you know that there are more than thirty of them in France?"

Adam laughed. "I knew there were a couple in Paris, but not that many." He shook his head.

"There is one in Bordeaux, near where I live in Sarlat. It's a replacement from when the Nazis stole it, but still just as nice," Eve added. "Oh, look." She pointed to the stage. "Here comes Jessie." She refocused her attention. Jessie took the microphone, and she could see his personality filled the stage. The monitor displayed *"Money,"* by Pink Floyd. She recognized the band and song. "This should be an easy song for him to sing."

She sang along in her mind as she focused on his natural ability, letting out a cheer here and there. "He's doing so well," she said loud enough for everyone at the table to hear her.

The whole bar and their group cheered and clapped as Jessie came back to the table, including Eve. She got up and gave him a hug. "That was excellent for your first time. You looked like you had done this before. How do you feel?"

"That was fun. I'm just very tired all of a sudden." Eve gave a pouty face.

Adam chimed in. "It's been a long day. I can have the car take you home and then come back for me." Jessie's face lightened as he smiled.

"Would that be okay?" He let out a slow, long exhale.

"Dude, staying safe is always a priority. That's why I have the car service tonight." Jessie nodded his acceptance, then made his way around the table, said his goodnights to his friends, then came back to Eve.

"I'm sorry that I'm not better company tonight. I'll have to make it up to you. Especially since I bombed on this date and didn't even get to buy you dinner." He slipped a paper in her hand as he kissed her on the cheek goodbye.

"Okay. Sounds good to me," she replied with a slight pouty lip.

"I'll be right back in after he leaves," Adam nodded before they turned around.

She watched as the two guys walked away. When they were out the door, she looked at the paper in her hand. "Here's my number. Something just you and me next time." She tucked the paper in the corner pocket of her clutch just as some of the girls came up to her. "You are so lucky to have two guys fawning over you."

Eve was confused. "What are you talking about? I'm on a date with Jessie tonight."

"Well, just in case you hadn't noticed, when you were singing, Jessie was staring at his phone the whole time. Adam hasn't taken his eyes off you all night." Eve looked back at the door to see if the guys were still outside.

"Thanks," she replied. That made her think about the fight they had when Adam called Jessie a jerk. And the girls warned her that this town is full of jerks. Was she wasting her time with this whole endeavor, and should she just wait until she returned to France to find a suitable husband? Could she find someone who could love her for her? Or would it be a marriage without love? She wanted a love like the love her parents had. Passionate.

Without warning, Adam scooped her up, and he started to swing her around. She couldn't help but cling both her arms around him to stop the feeling of falling as a giggle escaped her.

"You look so beautiful tonight. Standing there, you look like a beacon of light." She blushed instantly. He slowly set her feet down but kept her body close to his. He claimed her left hand with his right, and they transitioned into dancing with the rhythm of the song being sung. He then leaned in and started singing softly in her ear.

"*I can't believe we're finally alone. I can't believe I almost went home. What are the chances? Everyone's dancing, and he's not with you.*" Eve got goosebumps running down her arms. She recognized the song but didn't know the artist. She leaned in closer.

"Who sings that song?" she whispered back.

Adam gave her a spin out then pulled her back into his arms. "Dove Cameron. Its title is *Boyfriend*."

They didn't talk much, but song after song, they kept dancing and spinning. Sometimes he would hold her from behind. She enjoyed the feeling of being held in his arms. From time to time, she could feel him tuck his head into her as if he was going to kiss her. She instinctively leaned her head back for more access, but then he would slowly pull away, leaving her heart racing with anticipation.

Eventually, they called his name. He would be up after the current singer. "Have fun," she waved goodbye.

"Always," he responded. He took her hand and kissed it again before turning for the stage.

She could feel her flush growing. Finally, she had some time to sit for a bit and get something to drink. Her beverage was warm now, but she didn't care. She needed something wet down her throat. After a few gulps, the root beer was all gone. She went to the counter to get some ice water this time. She sat down at the table with two glasses, one for her and Adam.

She couldn't help but notice that all the girls were looking at her as they giggled. "What?" She held her hands up and shrugged her shoulders at them. They all laughed and then turned back to the stage. She shook her head at them. They were probably laughing about her and Adam. Go figure.

It was Adam's turn on stage, and his large frame was hard not to stare at. The blacklight made his shirt glow, accenting his muscular physique. Eve fanned herself as she suddenly felt flush. *"Your Man,"* by Josh Turner came on the screen. Eve did not recognize the song's title or the artist's name, but the crowd lit up. The sound of a slide guitar gave away that it was a nice, slow country melody. Then Adam started singing in his low voice.

The crowd erupted, and Eve cheered. She had goosebumps all over her body from his sultry tones. She was amazed at his low range. But most of all, he kept looking at her like he was singing to her directly. She leaned forward to concentrate.

Eve's heart felt like it was racing out of control. She could actually feel her temperature rising, almost by the second. The song was so seductive, and she felt like she was being pulled under. There was an ache growing in her that she had never felt before. Like a sea siren, his sultry voice called to her. Her whole body pressed in on itself, like a warm, weighted blanket had been placed on her. She was in awe of his energy to command the crowd.

Other than the occasional shout-out of appreciation, the crowd was mesmerized. Even Eve felt like she was glued to her seat. There was no way she could have gotten up if she wanted to.

And all at once, her pounding heart could be heard in her ears, and the room was darkening. That was odd with so many bright lights on the stage, but it was obvious. Everything around her was dark, except the bright lights shining back at her. She could hear the crowd cheering for Adam, but even that was sounding far away, steadily becoming quiet. What's going on?

Her body had become so heavy, she couldn't hold her arms up anymore to clap, and they just dangled by her side. Someone called her name. They sounded so far away. She couldn't move enough to respond. What is happening? Where did everyone go?

Adam

Adam watched Eve during the whole song. He wanted her to know that it was meant for her. He could see her watching him intently. As Adam's song was finishing, he saw Eve sitting still at the table. She was so energetic just a few minutes ago. Now, she looked frozen, and her eyes seemed like they were glazed over. Something didn't sit right with him.

At the end of his song, he tossed the microphone to the stage manager as he ran off the stage. The crowd was cheering, but all he could think about was getting to her. He came around the corner and slid to a stop next to her.

"Eve!" he exclaimed, but she didn't respond. Shit, he thought to himself. Did I accidentally get some of the sleep aid in her drink? He was careful. Even Jessie didn't fall asleep this fast. He softly felt her wrist for a pulse and could feel her heart was racing.

Eve moved in his direction and put her hand on his. Her eyes rolled, but she was clearly not focusing on him. She felt cool to the touch. This isn't a sleep aid. This was something else.

All her friends suddenly came over with scared looks on their faces. "Did you see anything? Somebody did this to her." They all looked at each other. One of the girls finally spoke up. "We spiked her drink shortly after she sat down, but she didn't drink it. She was so uptight about tonight. We just wanted her to relax and have fun." All her friends looked guilty.

"Which she was. We should have gotten rid of it, but we all forgot," another girl spoke up.

"When you went on stage, she chugged the whole thing down," a third girl replied.

Adam was suddenly so mad. He smacked his palm on the table, and all the girls jumped. "What did you give her?" he yelled so loud that it even scared him a bit.

"Just a Valium."

"And how many glasses of alcohol before then?" he demanded.

"I think three, but that was from 5:30 until 7 when you guys arrived," the first girl answered.

"Way too much for her size," he muttered to himself. His adrenaline had kicked in hard. He carefully scooped her up and held her close since she was not holding on. One of the girls set her bag on her lap, and he was off to the car.

His driver, Derek, saw him coming and popped out to open the door. "Where to?"

"I need to make a call. Her friends slipped her a Valium with alcohol mixed. I'd rather she woke up in her place so she won't be scared. I just don't know where she lives."

Derek opened her bag and found a wallet. He removed the identification card and found a key ring. A bouncer ran up to Adam and demanded to know what was going on. Adam then placed her in the car and quickly explained the situation again. Not giving him any room to argue, Adam went around to the other side and shut the door.

"Let's hope this is her address," Derek said as they took off.

Eve was quiet as she lay there. She looked so peaceful as she slept. He reached for her hand and held it. He sighed, then pulled out his phone. He contacted his father's on-call doctor. Adam arranged for the office to send a nurse to meet them at the apartment, check her vitals, and give her fluids if needed. If her condition got worse, the hospital was nearby.

They pulled up to a brick building. "I'll go check first and will call if I made it in," Derek announced. After a few minutes, Adam got a call from him. "There is no elevator, and she's on the third floor. I'll make room for you to carry her into her bedroom."

"Thank you." He hung up and went around to pick her up. When he opened her door, she looked at him for a moment.

"Your swong was wonbebfur. I lobbeded it," she drunk-mumbled before she fell back to sleep.

"Come on, Beautiful. It's time to get you into bed." His adrenaline was still running through him, so he easily picked her up.

This time she clung to him. He made quick work of the stairs, and Derek stood at the front door. "You feeeel so goob ti hooold." He just smiled, knowing that all his workouts were for a moment just like this—to be the man she needed him to be.

Eve

Eve was dancing with Adam as the music softly played. His low voice vibrated in her ears as he sang. She could feel his muscles in his shoulders and down his arms as she held onto him. His hands on her back, holding her tight to him, and she felt so good being pressed to his chest. He gave her a spin, and she ended up with her back to his front.

He slid her hair to the side and started to kiss her neck, slowly moving upward. Moving her jaw toward him, they locked lips and started kissing passionately as his hands began to explore the front of her body. She reached up and anchored her fingers in his hair, pulling him harder into the kiss. One of his hands claimed a breast as his fingers found the nipple.

She gasped, and he slipped his tongue into her mouth, deepening the kiss. She had the need for more as her desire grew. His other hand slid down under her clothing and began to massage her clit. She moaned loudly against his mouth at the intense pleasure, and he rubbed harder and faster.

She could feel the orgasm growing fast from deep inside. Her other hand reached behind her, and she found his penis bulging in his pants. At her climax, she screamed, "Adam…"

Eve suddenly woke up. Her body was buzzing in an after-orgasm glow. She had never experienced that before. She lay still as her breathing mellowed and the sexual waves subsided. That was an intense dream. She looked to her left at the window. She recognized the view as her bedroom. It was sometime in the early morning because it was still dark. Her body felt heavy, like bricks were holding her down. She turned her head and could see someone in white sleeping at her desk.

She tried to speak, but she could not get the words out. Her arm had a bee-sting feeling. When she looked down at her arm, she saw the IV there. Something had happened. She remembered being at the club and watching Adam singing. How did she get home? Why couldn't she remember? She wiggled her toes and then her fingers. She got her ankles to move and then her wrists. She worked her left knee and then her right. She managed to kick a pillow off the bed. Left elbow, but held her right one still for the IV. Stretched her hips left and right, shoulders, neck.

"Good morning." The gal at the desk was now next to her. Eve opened her mouth, but nothing came out. She let out a fast breath and hit a fist on the bed in frustration.

"It's okay. Your boyfriend brought you home. He sure was worried about you." Eve looked out into the living room and reached.

"Oh, he and his driver left after I arrived. There just wasn't enough room for everyone to stay here last night." What driver was she talking about? "My name is Mary. Your boyfriend called my boss, and I was sent here to take care of you. I'll be right back." Eve could hear her in the kitchen banging around and then the sound of the microwave.

A minute later, she came back in with a teacup. She pulled a small chair from the kitchen, placed it next to the bed, and sat down. "I will put a little on the spoon and then in your mouth. Swish it around your mouth and then swallow. We will do this a few times until your voice feels better." Eve nodded her head yes. "After that, I'll sit you up and you can finish the cup on your own."

Eve looked at the clock but could not quite focus on the little numbers. She looked at the nurse and then tapped her watch. Mary looked at her and then read the time. "4:25 a.m."

Wow, she slept more than six hours. But the hangover sucks. Sip after sip helped to lubricate her throat. All her spit glands were dry, but the tea felt great, lubricating each new area with each small sip. Eventually, she was able to squeak out some sounds.

"Well, that's progress." She set the cup down and, as promised, helped her to sit up. Eve scooted back against the headboard and Mary handed the tea from the nightstand to her.

The warmth in her hand felt great as she breathed in the steam. "What happened?" Eve squeaked again.

"Oh, your boyfriend left a letter for you. Do you want me to read it while you drink?" Mary asked as her eyes sparkled in the low light. Eve nodded her head yes and Mary went to the living room and grabbed the letter from the coffee table. She broke the seal as she sat down.

Beautiful Eve,

I had a wonderful time with you tonight. I wish it could have continued. However, your girlfriends wanted you to relax and slipped a Valium in your drink first thing. But during the evening you didn't drink your beverage, and they forgot about it. Until you chugged it all down after we finished our dancing.

Please don't be too mad at them. They all feel awful and are waiting to hear from you so they can each apologize for their actions. I contacted our family doctor, and he said that I could take you home to rest but had the nurse come to monitor you, just in case. So, I had my driver take us to your place.

I would have stayed but felt there was not enough room for all of us. Please call me when you can. The time does not matter. I probably won't be sleeping well until I hear from you anyway.

Jusqu'à la prochaine fois,

Adam

P.S. I put my number into your phone.

The nurse lowered the letter to her lap. "I'm the one who would file a report if you wished to."

Eve looked at the nurse with a tilt of her head before she whispered, "What do you mean, file a report?"

Mary folded her fingers and explained, "I can fill out paperwork about being illegally drugged against your will. The person or persons would get into trouble and probably go to jail."

Eve leaned her head back and breathed deeply for a moment. She remembered the girls all looking at her after she returned to the table. She thought it was about Adam, but it must have been about that instead. She sat up straight.

"No, I would not like to make a claim. My friends made a mistake that they will not make again. I will make sure of that after I'm done talking to them. Besides, I'll be okay once this all wears off. Plus, if I make a report of something like that, my aunt will make me return home right away. I do not want that. I'm mid-semester in my school program." 'And I need to figure out if I want to pursue finding a husband,' Eve thought to herself.

They chatted for a while about some of the side effects, but she was past the worst. Eve moved to get up, but the nurse had her wait. So, she asked the nurse for her bag. When she opened her phone, it was on the contact page, and Adam's number had been programmed.

That sneaky man. She selected to send a text message. No need to call this early and wake him up. 'Thank you for being my hero tonight. But really, I can't say thank you enough. Tonight, could have gone so wrong.' 'Stop, stop, stop,' Eve thought for a moment. 'Let's not go there,' and she reworded the message.

'Thank you for being my hero. I truly appreciate you. I also had a good time. Jusqu'à la prochaine fois, Eve.' She remembered the dream and felt flush. She sent the simple message and set her phone down. She took another big sip of tea and felt the heat and moisture soothe as she swallowed. Then her phone rang. She looked and saw Adam calling.

"Hello?" she answered in her squeaky voice.

"Hello, Beautiful. I'm glad to know you're doing better," he sounded exhausted.

"I hope I did not wake you up," she softly asked.

"No, I've been awake all night. But now I can rest knowing you're doing better." Eve felt her face blush again.

"I can't thank you enough for taking care of me." She bit her lower lip as she finished so she wouldn't go dark.

"It was my honor to take care of a damsel in distress. And as a lawyer, it's kind of my responsibility to do so," he added.

"Oh, I see. Well, either way, thank you again," she pressed her lips, not knowing what to think of that.

"You're welcome." There was an odd pause before he continued. "What are you doing this Wednesday?" he asked.

"I have class until 4 p.m. After that, I'm free," she replied.

"That's great. I'm having a surprise birthday party for Jessie at my place. Would you join us?" he asked.

"That would be nice. You know, I could get him out for a little while so you can set up, and then we could return to the party." She offered.

"Hey, that would be even better than what I had planned." They finalized their plans and then hung up.

She looked at Mary. "I think I'm going to be good. I'm gonna take a shower and start my day. I have a bunch of work to do before my next meeting."

Mary came over and checked her pulse and blood pressure, looked into her eyes, then took her temperature one last time. "Yep, I agree." She removed the IV and applied gauze and a waterproof bandage for the shower.

"Thank you so much." Eve stretched out her hand, and they shook before Mary left her apartment.

Entry 7: Jessie's Date

Saturday evening, Eve went digging and found the small piece of paper in the corner pocket of her clutch. She didn't want to wait until the last minute like he did with her. She programmed the number into her phone and then called. It rang a few times and then went to voicemail. "Ugghhh," she voiced her displeasure to herself. She was hoping to talk directly to him.

"Hello. This is Eve. I was hoping to cash in on your rain check. I'm fairly busy next week except for Wednesday. I'm in school till 4 but I could meet you somewhere around 5 or 5:30, depending on if you need me to get dress up. Let me know if it's going to work or not. Bye."

She hung up the phone, frustrated and hoped that he wouldn't ghost her again. She took a deep breath and slowly let it out. Hopefully, he doesn't wait till the last minute to respond either. All of that would be another red flag jerk alert.

She sat at her desk and started working on concept drawings for the preliminary meeting when her phone rang. The display showed Jessie's name. She quickly accepted the call. "Hello?"

"Hey babe. Sorry for not answering, but I forgot to save your number. I don't pick up on calls I don't know. So, thank you for leaving a voicemail. YES!" he exclaimed. "I would love to go out on Wednesday for dinner. But remember, you need to pick the place. I don't care if we go in shorts and flip-flops or if you wanna get all sexy for me. By the way, it was a bit loud last night, but I wanted to say you looked gorgeous in that black and green dress. It was such a contrast to your bright red hair."

Eve could feel the heat on her face as she started to blush. "Thank you. I will do a little research and try to find something in between us. What area do you live in?" Eve asked as she silently hoped he didn't live on the other side of the island.

"I live at the Solow Residential building on the south side of the park. Not far from the bar where we met," he replied. "The law school I go to is a few more blocks west from there," he added.

"Okay, I'm just a few blocks north, near the Lenox hospital. I will find something and let you know," she felt relief settle in knowing he was closer.

"Sounds good. Later, babe," he responded before hanging up.

She opened the search on her tablet. Daniel on E 65th looks good. They have European-style food, and they open at 5, required RSVP though. She smirked her lips. It may be difficult to find a reservation on such short notice. Then she found out Perrine on E 61st is open most of the day. They have a mixture of foods, but an RSVP is recommended for dinner there also.

"Dang," she sighed. Then she saw PJ Clarke's on 3rd. Best burgers around and not as expensive as the other two. That sounded good. Fill up before hitting the party.

She got up and started going through her dresses. Since it's his birthday, she picked her black with gold flower knee-length cocktail dress. But this time she would wear her heels. Hope he didn't mind that she may be a little taller. She took a picture of the dress and heels and sent a text to Jessie. "Can you dress to keep up with this?"

He responded a couple of minutes later, "I see you want to dress up and get sexy for me. I can keep up for sure. Where are we going?"

She smiled as she read his message. "PJ Clarke's on 3rd at 5 p.m. Just a couple blocks east from you."

"Sounds like a plan. I can't hardly wait to see you again."

"Great. See you in a few days." Eve was so happy that she started to dance and swing her hips to the rhythm in her mind. And then she started solo singing "*Woman,*" by Doja Cat.

Jessie

Jessie walked over to Adam's door and knocked, even though it was already slightly open.

"What's up?" Adam said as he opened the door all the way.

Jessie felt a bit nervous. "Hey. Just wanted to be open and honest." Adam looked at him with a raised eyebrow. "Eve called and we scheduled a follow-up date." Adam lowered his head and softly nodded. "Sorry man, I'm letting her take the lead," Jessie said softly.

Adam raised his head. "Any chance you will be bringing her back here afterward? If yes, I'll head to the gym for a few hours."

Jessie thought about it. Would be nice to get a release for his birthday. "Maybe. She sent me a picture of her sexy outfit for the evening. Want me to show you?" Jessie fumbled with his phone.

"No." Adam held up his hands to block the view. "When?" Adam asked.

"Wednesday evening." Jessie paused and shifted his weight.

"How about you send me a text when you know. That way I can take off before you get back." Adam let out a slow breath.

"Okay." Jessie shrugged his shoulders as he replied and walked back to his room. He stopped and looked back as Adam had shut his door.

Adam

Damn, that girl is good. He has no clue as to what is coming. He picked up the phone and texted Eve. 'He took the bait. He was talking about your dress. What are you wearing?' He sat there eagerly, waiting for her to text back.

'I'm glad to finally have a date with him and to be able to help with the party at the same time.'

He noticed that she didn't say anything about the dress, pressed his lips flat and waited. A couple of minutes later, he finally broke down and responded. 'You didn't answer my question.'

'You will see it when I show up,' Eve quickly responded.

She's being coy and smiled at the thought. 'How will I know what to wear? I don't want to be over or underdressed.' He grinned as he probed.

'I guess you'll have to see what Jessie is wearing when he leaves. Or you can ask to see the picture I sent him.'

He frowned a bit. He didn't want to seem like he was going back on what he said to Jessie. 'Guess I will have to wait.'

He was looking forward to his surprise on Saturday for her. He couldn't hardly wait to see her reaction and get to spend time alone with her. No Jessie, no group, just them and their time together.

He started a group text and advised all their friends about the updated plans for the party. He laid back on his bed, closed his eyes, and went through the mental checklist for the party.

Jessie

Jessie was on top of the world today. Everything just seemed to be falling in line. It started with waking a few minutes before his alarm went off. He got up and was out the door quicker than normal, so he took the earlier bus. That got him to school 45 minutes earlier than normal. He was able to use that time to review before the test and felt great while taking the test.

He made it back to the condo before Adam did. He found a birthday card with a wrapped brownie snack on the counter that he had left for him. He smiled as he read the card, then munched on the treat as he went to his room. He snagged a quick shower and started to get dressed in his new suit he picked out on Sunday.

If she was going to be that fancy, he needed to step up his game. Plus, an outfit like this had many uses: weddings, funerals, formal events, dates. He smiled as he looked at it. His mom would be proud. She was always trying to get him to clean up. He shook his head at the thought.

Mid-dressing, he heard Adam arrive. "You home?" Adam asked loudly.

"Yeah, dude. I'll be out in just a minute. Thank you for the card and treat. It was perfect to help tide me over until dinner." He finished getting his coat on his shoulders, slipped his dress shoes on, and stepped out into the living room. "What do you think?"

Adam turned when he came out and had a shocked look on his face. "I didn't know you owned a tuxedo."

Jessie did a spin to show off the whole outfit. "I got this on Sunday. Armani. You like it?"

Adam stood there, slowly nodding his head yes. "You guys going to the theater?" Adam's eyes were practically popping out of his head.

"Nope, just dinner," Jessie responded and posed like he was on the runway.

Adam smiled and let out a laugh. "Okay, James Bond. Be a gentleman, so I don't have to bust your nose on your birthday and get blood all over your new outfit."

Jessie smirked at Adam's warning, turned, and went to his room to finish getting his hair ready. He wanted to be there before 5 p.m. so he could see her walk in. He only had a few minutes left before he had to get going.

He didn't know why, but he was nervous for the first time in forever. Normally, he didn't care about what was going to happen on the date, but more about what happened after the date. But tonight felt different.

He kept taking small sips of the ice water to cool down and soothe his throat. He was not used to wearing so many layers anymore and had to dab his forehead to keep the perspiration off his face. He decided against drinking alcohol so he wouldn't do or say anything inappropriate because of intoxicated mouth.

He even picked up a bunch of flowers from the street vendor on his way. There were several different flowers with a variety of red, like her hair. It had been since high school when he last bought flowers for a girl. He pressed his lips flat as he thought back to the bad memories before shaking his head clear.

"Concentrate on the now, dumbass." He took a deep breath and slowly let it out as he looked around. The way she hustled him into a date, he figured she would have picked an expensive place. However, PJ's is known for good food without hitting the wallet too hard. They were so overdressed for this restaurant, but at this point, he didn't care.

He just kept on watching the door. And then she breezed in. The picture she sent of the dress didn't do it justice after seeing it on her. It hugged her and accentuated her curves, yet left room for his mind to wander. His heart started to race as her soft perfume wafted his way. It was very erotic, and he felt himself stir in his shorts. He stood up and hid the bouquet of flowers behind his back. She was talking to the waiter, then he pointed in Jessie's direction.

In slow motion, she made eye contact with him, and he watched in delight as her face lit up.

"Fuck," he thought to himself. He could swear his heart stopped.

In that moment, he felt the world change around him.

Eve

Eve was looking forward to tonight's date since she made the call on Saturday. She used the excuse of needing to go get records to get out of class early. That way, she had extra time to get ready. She was calm all evening until she walked in the door of the restaurant. She got a wave of butterflies and took a calming breath, and then she saw Jessie standing there, waiting for her in a quiet corner booth.

He looked handsome in his tux. She bounced a little with happiness and then walked to him. When she got there, she kissed him on both cheeks. "Hey babe." He held out a beautiful bouquet of different red flowers.

"Jessie, they are beautiful. Thank you." She then hugged him.

"Not as beautiful as you. You're killing this dress." He spun her around so he could fully see her and he sucked in a deep breath. "It's going to be damn hard to keep my hands under control tonight. I already want to touch you." He leaned in and slowly moved his fingers along the bare skin of her arm, and goosebumps raised at the sensation.

She caught her breath as her heart raced and her face flushed. He raised his fingers to her face and softly traced her jawline. "The color of your face gives you away." He slowly closed the distance and kissed her lips. She loved that they were soft and warm, and her whole body instantly warmed up.

His kiss only lasted for a moment before he pulled back and reached for her hand as he led her to the table. 'Damn, I could have kept on kissing him,' she thought to herself. 'I'll have to get some more of that softness before we get to the party,' she continued to think. She slid into the booth and was surprised when he slid in next to her instead of across from her. She felt herself blush again.

"Now what are you thinking to cause yourself to blush?" He smiled at her.

"I was not expecting you to sit next to me. I thought we would be across so we could talk."

Jessie smiled, leaned in, and whispered, "Yes, but this way I can whisper in your ear things I don't want others to hear." Her blush deepened. He then slid in a little closer and rested his hand on her leg. Just like Friday, there was no moving around.

'Okay Eve, now is your chance to start. Will this work? Only time can tell,' she thought to herself. "Are you from here?" She already knew he was from Texas, but she wanted to get him talking.

He laughed. "Everyone can always tell where I'm from by my southern accent. But I guess to you, we all have accents." He took a sip of his water. "I'm from Texas. My whole family is Southern all the way back to the beginning." He smiled, and she giggled at his response.

"Except for my father, who is Scottish, my whole family is French. Now that goes way, way back. Like to 1000 A.D. We have huge portraits on the wall and everything." She teased him.

"Damn. Talk about knowing your lineage," he smirked.

Eve shrugged her shoulders. "Well, back then, it was all about lineage and getting to the throne. I'm glad it's not like that anymore. The royal rule is over, but there is still some aristocratic nonsense that got handed down to me."

"I'm glad to be born in today's day and age. I wouldn't want to be born before the discovery of antibiotics or vaccines. Living a longer, healthier life is better than dying by age 30," Jessie laughed.

"I fully agree with that. Plus, I'm glad not to be married off at the age of 12 and expected to start popping out babies. Back then, most died in childbirth. They were kids having kids." She scrunched her face at the thought. He then started moving his hand on her leg, and her face relaxed.

"Unlike today. Now we get to live life and have fun first before deciding to start families. Sex for procreation has changed to sex for pleasure." His hand was making a straight line to her border, and he was leaning into her neck. She quickly stopped his hand, but his mouth made a soft pass along her jaw. She had an "oh" moment, and her heart started to pound with anticipation.

She wanted more, but she hardly knew him. She dipped her head a little and then looked at him. "We can save that part for later if that's okay with you?" She felt her face blush deep red this time. "I'd like to chat for now and get to know more about you," she smiled.

He leaned back a bit and then whispered in her ear, "Okay, we can save that part for when we are in private." Then he squeezed her leg a little. Her phone chirped and she sent a quick text. "You got work going on?" he asked.

She smiled. "No. That was my security team. They were making sure I didn't need help. Plus, they will check in from time to time. I'm doing something different from my normal routine. I need to respond, or they will send in SWAT." She wasn't kidding about that, but he laughed like she was joking.

"It's all good. Girls need to be safe when seeing a new person until they get to know each other better." He sat upright and gave her just a smidge more room, but kept his hand on her leg.

"You previously said that you guys are in law school. How long does that take?" She turned so she could try to face him better.

"It's three years after getting a bachelor's as a prerequisite. So, it feels like forever. I saw you discussing decoration stuff with the bartender. You're in some sort of design program?"

"Yes, interior design. I did a couple of years back home, and now I'm here on a two-year student visa. But I've been here for six months already. The goal is to update older homes to look fresh and modern again. This will be useful back home."

"So, you're only gonna be here for another year and a couple of months?" he asked.

"That is correct." She looked down at her hand and started tapping on her ring finger. "Unless it's made permanent," she softly added and then looked back at him.

His head softly bobbed up and down. "Kinda nice knowing there's a timeline."

"You understand then?" Her eyes went big.

"Yes, I do understand," he smiled.

That's good,' she thought to herself. Otherwise, it would be hard for her to explain in the translation.

Their conversation kept on going during dinner. They both agreed to share a dessert. She saw the time and knew they needed to get going. She turned to Jessie and rested a hand on top of his. She started to slowly move her fingers on his. When he looked at her, she asked, "Would you like to take this date back to your place?" She could not help but smile, knowing what was waiting for him.

He got a big grin on his face. "Time for some privacy?" He smiled a little bigger.

"Or maybe something else." She winked. "I just need to check in first before we go." She sent a quick message to Adam that they would be finished soon. Then she let security know they were moving on to the birthday party at his place.

They slid out of the booth, flowers in her arms, and made their way to a taxi. His place was not that far away, but walking in her heels would have been a challenge, since he seemed to be in a rush now. Perhaps she played that card a little too strong. She's not used to being the aggressor in a relationship.

A short trip later, they were getting out and made their way up the elevator. Jessie had her cornered while his hands started to roam her body. He placed small kisses in random spots, her body was covered in goosebumps. The doors opened and he pulled her with him. As they got to the door, she was bouncing a little in anticipation. She grabbed him and leaned him against the door.

"I just wanted to apologize." She planted a hard kiss on him and started to wrap her arms around him. He broke the kiss by pushing back a little.

"Let's take this inside." She took a step back and smiled as she hid her face in the flowers.

"Okay. If you insist. Let's go in."

Jessie

He swung the door open and turned for her hand, but she just stood there smiling. "Come on in. I'll show you around." He turned on the lights since it was dark.

"Surprise!" Voices were yelling from everywhere. He turned, and his friends were standing all around the condo. There were decorations everywhere. All types of food on the island and cocktails on the counter. For most of the day, he thought almost everyone had forgotten about his birthday.

He turned back to Eve and raised an eyebrow. "You knew about this?"

She blushed. "Guilty." She batted her eyelashes at him. He reached for her, but this time she took his arm and moved with him as they met with his friends.

They eventually ran into Adam. "Thanks for this. It truly has been a good day," Jessie said. They hugged and patted each other on the backs. The music was going, the drinks were flowing, and everyone was having a good time.

The party started to calm down after a few hours. "I have something for you," Eve said as she pulled him aside to his room. He shut the door when they were inside. She sat down on the bed and pulled a small box from her clutch then handed it to him.

"You didn't!" he exclaimed. The overexcitement may have been from the alcohol, but he truly appreciated the thought. Seeing her on his bed added to his all-night erection. He opened the box and saw a gold bracelet with his initials engraved in the center. "This is wonderful." He pulled it from the box, and she helped to fasten it to his wrist. He admired it for a moment.

"Thank you so much. It's been forever and a day since I've been given a meaningful gift from a wonderful girl." He smirked and leaned his head to the side and watched her blush grow from her neck and consume her whole face. "I have something for you also." He reached into the nightstand drawer and pulled out a condom.

She had a shocked look on her face. She couldn't even pretend right now. Her body was screaming out for him to touch her.

"I know that you want some of this." He pushed her over and landed on top with his pelvis firmly between her legs. He quickly unzipped and had the condom on in a flash.

"Jessie, my body is not ready for this." He softly covered her mouth.

"Shhhh, or everyone will hear us." With the other hand, he lifted her skirt and slid her underwear to the side. She mumbled through his fingers and placed her hands on his chest. He positioned the head of his shaft and pushed in.

"Damn, babe, you're so tight." He pushed in again and started a slow rhythm. He felt so good stuffed in her tight pussy.

"I'm not gonna last long. I've been solid since I saw you walk into the restaurant." He wanted to kiss her. No, he needed to kiss her. He removed his hand from her mouth so he could make the connection, and she moaned.

"Oh, Jessie, please." He crashed his mouth onto hers because he had to have all of her at that moment. After trying to deepen the kiss, he traced his tongue along her lips, but she wasn't opening for him. He slowly moved his hand to her breast, slid the top of her dress down, and found her nipple, then gave it a firm pinch. She gasped, as he hoped she would, and he took the opportunity to slide his tongue in.

He let out a soft moan of pleasure as it became very slippery, and he just sped up. Soon enough, he felt his climax peak. He broke the kiss and leaned his head back and enjoyed the feeling of a whole-body orgasm. He went limp and laid on her for a moment while breathing deeply. That was intense and wonderful.

His body had never done that before. There was something about her that was different, wonderful, that beckoned to him. And he could hardly wait to find out.

"That's what I've been really needing. Now my birthday is perfect. Thank you." He whispered softly in her ear and then placed a kiss on her neck, just next to her ear.

Adam

As soon as Jessie left, Adam sent the group a message again. 'All clear.' A few minutes later, people started showing up and helped with decorations, chairs, food, and alcohol. He got music going, and they were all having a good time visiting, when he got a text from Eve. 'Finishing soon.' A few minutes later, he got a message from Jessie.

'Coming home with Eve.' His blood boiled a little, but he knew she had to get him to bring her home.

Everyone found a comfy spot and held still. Adam turned off the lights and went to hide in the corner by his room. The front door cracked open. He heard Jessie invite Eve inside. As soon as the light came on, everyone yelled.

Jessie looked like he was going to have a heart attack. The shock on his face was perfect. Then he turned and held out his hand, and Eve joined him. She was now on his arm with flowers from the evening. Holy shit! A new suit and he bought a girl flowers. Maybe he is turning over a new leaf. Or maybe the threat of violence is keeping him in line.

He kept on watching them as they made their way through the room. The dress she was wearing was gorgeous. The black and gold accented her natural coloring. The heels she was wearing made Jessie look shorter but made her body look leaner. His body fully reacted to the vision. But he kept his distance since it was Jessie's party. Eventually, they came face to face. "Happy Birthday."

"Thanks for this. It truly has been a good day." They hugged. He turned to Eve, smiled, and lifted her hand.

"Hello, Beautiful." He then gave her hand a kiss.

She giggled and gave him a hug and kissed him on both cheeks. "This place is amazing. There are so many people here," she smiled.

"Thank you. I know you guys just ate, but there is food on the island and mixers on the back counter," he added.

"Thanks. Think I'll just get some water. Do you know what Jessie would want?"

"I sure do. I'll get it." He walked over to the counter as she went to the fridge. She grabbed a bottle of water and returned to stand next to Jessie again. When he came back with his special drink, Jessie thanked him. He felt a bit guilty, slipping a sleep aid into his drink on his birthday, but he needed to stick to the plan.

He smiled at Eve. "Hope you have fun." She smiled back and nodded. He returned to floating around the room and visiting with friends, but he always kept Eve just within his sightline. After a couple of hours, people started to leave, and overall, the party was getting quieter. He saw Eve pull Jessie to his room, and then the door shut.

His blood pressure went through the roof and his heart was pounding in his ears. He heard Jessie for a moment with a loud, excited voice. Then it was quiet. At least he couldn't hear anything over the noise of the party. Shortly after, they emerged.

He was leading her by the hand instead of her clinging to his arm. His heart started to calm down, but then he noticed her flushed cheeks were not her normal blushing. She wasn't smiling like she normally does. In fact, she looked mad. Jessie was showing off a new bracelet that Eve had given him. But her body language was not reading happy. Adam needed to know what happened while they were alone.

He walked over to them, and Jessie turned to show Adam the bracelet. He saw the initials and thought it was nice. But he still needed to know. "Everything going, okay?" he kept his eyes on Eve.

"Yeah, man. Having a great time, thanks to you." He noticed that Eve didn't smile. Her lipstick looked smudged. Were they kissing? He looked closer at Jessie, and her color was clearly on his lips.

"It's getting late. I need to get going." She pulled from Jessie's hand and started for the door. Adam quickly caught up to her.

"Do you need me to take you home?" She looked him in the eyes, but her face seemed mad. If he didn't know any better, he would even say she was pissed off.

"I'm good. Thank you. I just need some quiet time to myself. It's been a busy night." Right then, he knew Jessie had crossed the line and made her mad. She was gone quicker than a flash of lightning. He needed to know what had happened, but it would have to wait until everyone left. There were only a few people hanging around, and he knew that, with a few subtle clues, they would leave.

He found the flowers that Jessie had given Eve still sitting in the sink. Something happened for sure. He looked over his shoulder at Jessie, who was happy and chatting with friends. He picked up the flowers and put them in a vase with water. He put away the food and alcohol. Another couple left after saying goodbye to Jessie. He then turned the music off. The last group said their goodbyes.

Jessie flopped down on the couch, leaned back, and set his feet on the table. Adam sat across from him but leaned forward, ready to pounce. He could see Eve's lip color on him, and his blood started to boil. "How did dinner go?" he asked as he wanted to strangle him.

"We talked the whole time. I never knew that just talking to someone would be so nice. It's crazy how far back she can trace her family." Adam breathed fire but fought to calm himself down.

"And how is it that you guys both came back at the same time?" Adam glared at Jessie.

Jessie rubbed his fingers on his temples while he thought for a moment. "We were getting along well. After dessert, she straight up asked me if I wanted to take the date back to my place. I wasn't about to refuse that offer. As agreed, I let you know we were coming." Jessie still held his head while he rested back and his eyes closed.

"And then you guys went to your room," Adam probed.

Jessie softly smiled. "It's always nice to get a gift for your birthday. Best birthday ever, since I was a kid." Adam sat there, fuming for a moment. These are not the answers he needed so he could pummel his face in.

"Anything else?" Adam asked. However, Jessie didn't respond. He leaned forward and wiggled Jessie's foot.

"You still awake?" Adam watched as Jessie's breathing was steady. He should have asked the questions sooner, before the sleep aid kicked in and he fell asleep on the couch.

He pursed his lips as he thought. Perhaps he just surprised her with a kissing moment after she gave him her gift. He took a deep breath. Or she truly was just getting tired. She had class all day, and it was pushing close to midnight. He took another slow and deep breath in and out to calm himself down.

Adam got up and slowly leaned Jessie over, put a pillow under his head, and covered him with a blanket. He laughed. That new tux is going to need a pressing after sleeping in it. Then he turned off the lights.

Eve

"Ma'am. Are you okay?" The taxi driver looked at her through the mirror as her tears were starting to fall down her cheeks.

"I'll be fine. It's just been a long day," she replied. He slid the window open and handed her a couple of tissues. She accepted them and wiped her eyes, then blew her nose.

"Obviously you're upset. Your night not going as planned?" He made a slight frown on his face.

She sighed. "Something like that." Her tears started to fall again, and she breathed heavily.

He pulled the car over and turned to face her. "Do I need to take you somewhere safe to get help? A friend's place, or…?"

She lowered her head. "No. It's just been an emotional day. Too much drinking and not enough food." She looked back up at him. "I promise that I'll be okay. Please proceed." He nodded and continued taking her back to her apartment.

After she got home, she still didn't feel right. Deep down, she felt used, dirty even. She peeled everything off to take a hot shower. She noticed bright blood on her underwear. She knew it wasn't that time of the month, so she grabbed some paper and pressed. Her undercarriage stung. She pulled the tissue away and there was more.

He had torn her with his force when her body was not ready. She got into the shower and started thinking. It's been one hell of a week. First, her friends drugged her. Now the man she was interested in for a possible relationship had forced himself on her. Perhaps she should just call it good and end her studies at the conclusion of this semester.

She started to cry again as everything poured out of her.

September

Entry 1: The Referral Interview

Eve settled her conversations with her friends during the week. She voiced her concerns about being drugged against her will, and they all profusely apologized. She knew that it would take some time to allow renewed trust in them, but she only has so many friends here.

Otherwise, the next few months will be hard and lonely before she leaves at the end of the semester. Eve decided to finish out one year and then return home. She has not informed her aunt yet because that needs to be at the last minute, so she doesn't pull her early.

She was withdrawn the last couple of days. She's gotten even less sleep than normal but still felt like she couldn't share her problem with the girls. Not yet, at least. She was still unsure herself as to the course of action to take. One side wants to beat the shit out of Jessie. The other side understands how she led him on, making him think she wanted sex. How he went about it was not okay.

He needs to know what he did to her. At some point, she will have to make him understand the position he put her in. That weighed heavily on her mind during most everything she did. But, for right now, she needed to set those thoughts aside and concentrate on her interview with Mr. Stratford. If all her research was right, he would be in his 60s.

As with older generations, they don't have much of a digital data trail. But either way, she was going to put on a smile and look the part. In the archives, she found one picture of him, and he looked taller. So, she didn't mind wearing her heels. She picked out her knee-length black pencil skirt and a burgundy silk blouse to accent her hair. She hoped it would be appropriate for what he was used to.

Eve managed to make it to the building with a few extra minutes. She decided to head in early and cool off from the heatwave. She was in awe of the stone and tile work. She just had to touch and feel the texture as she climbed the flight of stairs to the office.

"I can hear your heels clicking on the steps. Are you Ms. Eve from the design school?"

Eve heard the familiar voice from the phone echoing from above. "Hello. Yes, that is I. Are you Mrs. Ophelia?" Eve asked as she picked up her pace. She reached the top step and went around the corner. An older receptionist was sitting at the desk. She probably has been with this company since its creation.

"Yes. Very nice to finally meet you. Mr. Stratford is busy right now with a call, but when he's ready, you can go in. There is a waiting room to the right." She pointed, smiled, and went back to her work.

Eve turned around the corner and saw several large blueprint drawings on the wall. She set her bag on the couch and studied the images. About 10 years in between each of them. The oldest being drawn in 1960. She rested her hand on the frame and studied the lines. She closed her eyes, and she could imagine the foundation, walls, stonework, and roofline being built. In her mind, she could move around the space and place lighting and furniture in the spaces.

Eve heard Ophelia stop her typing. "Hello Adam," she heard her say.

Eve opened her eyes and looked over her shoulder. It was Adam. Her Adam was standing there, smiling at her. A smile instantly filled her face. Eve turned to face him, and she started bouncing with giddy excitement, and her heart started to race. Suddenly, she did not feel so down. She took a couple of steps in his direction to close the gap and fully hugged him.

It felt great to hold him and to have his arms around her, even for just a moment. She pulled back to kiss him on both cheeks but was surprised that he also did the same. He reached for her hand.

"Hello, Beautiful." He then raised her hand and kissed it softly. The heat from his lips instantly transferred to her hand. Still holding her hand, they walked over to the couches.

"I wasn't expecting to see you here," she said as her smile grew.

"I go to school during the week and work most weekends here. My dad started this business." He turned to look at Ophelia. "Our office manager has been with us since the beginning," he continued. Ophelia didn't look up but just bobbed her head up and down.

"That's wonderful," Eve responded. Adam turned to face the pictures.

"These four blueprints are my dad's handiwork. You can tell by the size and irregularity of the lines that they are hand drawn."

Eve turned to him. "I can close my eyes and see the building grow. Imagine walking in the spaces and see where to put furniture." She pointed to a print to the left.

"This is a mid-century modern house. Sloped roofline, big open space, large windows, central fireplace, minimal furniture." She paused and looked at Adam, and his eyes looked like they were glowing in excitement.

He stepped closer. "That is how it was originally drawn. But the customer didn't like some of the features, so they were altered after this original rendering. This one here on the far left is one of mine."

Eve paused, then it finally clicked in her brain, and she started laughing. He looked at her, confused. She reached her hand out and squeezed his arm.

"I'm sorry. Last time we talked about your work at the bar, the music was a bit loud. I thought you said you were an architectural lawyer. At the time, I thought, 'Why would a building need a lawyer?' But it all makes sense now. You are an architect and a lawyer." She laughed again, and he joined in. She stepped closer to him so she could see his drawing better.

"You can tell by the thin, crisp lines that this is drawn on a computer," he added with a chuckle.

"It's also a single floor plan to a high-rise building." She looked at him. "You can tell by the size of the support columns, elevator shaft, and the number of stairwells," she said as she pointed to spots on the image.

"All the buildings in this city are relatively new compared to the ones back home. Perhaps one day you can come tour around. Who knows, maybe even impact the way you design." She smiled and gave him a wink.

"These blueprints are wonderful. But not everyone can imagine the after design. Have you thought about putting in flat panel screens?

You could make them look like pictures with framework. That way you can rotate images. Show the blueprint. Then rotate to images of the groundwork, framing, landscaping, and so on until the finished product is displayed. So instead of five static images on the wall, you could potentially have thousands of images, and your customers who have a hard time seeing past the paper can better understand."

Eve's heart sank when she saw the look on Adam's face. She took an uneasy step back. "Oh, I'm sorry if I overstepped. I just love buildings. They all have stories to tell."

Adam closed the distance and pulled her into a side hug. "Don't be sorry for speaking your mind. This is why you're here. Plus, that's why I became an architect. I love buildings also."

"Excuse me." Adam and Eve both turned to see Ophelia, and she tapped her watch.

"Oh, your appointment," Adam said as he picked up Eve's bag. "Let's get going on the tour so you can see the area."

They walked the one level in just a few minutes. There were offices along the outer wall and open space inside with cubicles. They discussed his ideas for needing a larger conference room and making it feel less like a newsroom.

She would need to come back when it's busy to see the workflow. Maybe even get employee ideas and needs. They returned to the main office where she expected to meet his father, but the room was empty.

"Adam. Where is Mr. Christian Stratford? I thought I was going to meet him today?" She paused to look at the empty desk.

He walked back to her and lifted her hand. He then guided her to a plush seat in front of the desk and set her bag down next to it.

"Mr. Christian Adam Stratford Sr. is my dad. I'm Christian Adam Stratford Jr. My dad goes by Chris and I'm Adam, so there is no confusion in conversations," he said as he sat down behind the desk. However, she was still confused. "What's troubling you, Beautiful?"

She looked up at him. "It's just that… I'm just confused. Why would your father call to have me come, just to have the meeting with you?"

He laughed and pulled a business card from his pocket and slid it to her. She recognized the school business card, but her name was written on it.

"I'm the one who called. I got your card from Jake. I wanted to spend time with you without any distractions. At the time, I didn't know how to reach you."

She pursed her lips, still confused. "So, you don't really need me to help here? It was just a ruse so we could visit?" Anger was filling her now. She grabbed her bag and slung it to her shoulder as she stood up to vent.

"Adam, I spent two weeks doing research in preparation for this meeting. I don't appreciate being lied to, just so you can visit with me." He bolted up from the desk to block her path. "It's been a very difficult week. I don't need to add this to the pile." She vented a heavy breath.

He wrapped his arms around her and tucked his head down into her hair. "No, that's not it at all. That came out wrong. We really do need your help. Yes, I wanted to visit with you, but the project is real. Please don't be mad at me. I wasn't trying to trick you. I swear. I just thought it would be a nice surprise that it was me."

She could feel his warmth as he surrounded her. She leaned her head into him and started to cry. All the pain from the week was coming out again.

"I'm so sorry. My trust in people has been strained this week. Starting with my friends drugging me and the misunderstanding with Jessie. I just haven't been in a good place this week." She reached up and held his back with both her hands. She noticed he felt so good to hold.

Adam squeezed a little harder and then eased his hug. He then grabbed a tissue from the desk. "You are always safe with me. Anytime, for any reason, just let me know, I'll be there for you." He lifted her chin to face him and helped to wipe her face. Suddenly, she wanted to kiss him but knew it would be inappropriate, but she felt her face blushed anyway. "Please say you understand?".

She took a deep breath and relaxed her nerves. "I understand." She then rested her head back on his chest.

They stood there in silence, holding each other until there was a knock on the door. He let go and took a step back. "Are we okay now?"

"Yes, I'm better now." She smiled as she looked him in the eyes, "Thank you for your support."

She blushed again. He put his hand on the back of her neck and bent down. She thought he was going to kiss her cheek, but then he changed direction, and caught her off guard. His lips pressed onto hers. They were soft yet firm at the same time and her heart fluttered out of rhythm as her body began to melt into him.

She grabbed the front of his shirt and held onto him as his other hand firmly pressed on her lower back. The kiss felt like an eternity. A feeling of belonging there took hold of her. He ended the kiss and placed his forehead on hers. After taking a couple of deep breaths, she opened her eyes and smiled at him.

She noticed that there was now a bag of food on the desk. She didn't hear anyone come and go. Now, she really wondered how long they stood there kissing. Ophelia must have seen them kissing and left them alone.

He guided her back to the seat and slid a side table closer. He opened the bag and turned to her. "Your favorite food is Mexican?" His eyes were big again.

"Yes." She smiled. "Well, Spanish."

"It's my favorite also," he said as he pulled out a tray for her and set it on the table.

"You didn't have to do this, but thank you."

He handed her utensils and a napkin. "It's my pleasure." He smiled and they dove into their meal and work.

It was 2:30 by the time they wrapped up their meeting. She got his email so they could send images back and forth. They planned to have a budget meeting in a few days at the condo.

She would have to set things straight with Jessie before she would feel comfortable there.

Adam

Bright and early Saturday morning, Adam decided to walk to work. It's only a few blocks away from the condo, and he could use the stretch before being stuck in the office all day. However, today he was on cloud nine because he gets to visit with Eve. He arrived just as Ophelia was unlocking the door. "Good morning."

She jumped. "Oh my God. Good morning, Adam. You scared me. I wasn't expecting you in for a little bit."

He gave her a little pouty lip. "Sorry for scaring you. I wanted to talk to you about my meeting today."

They walked in together and he sat next to her desk. He poured out every detail from the last couple of weeks. The good, the bad, and all the desires. That way, she would not be surprised by any action that may happen in the near future.

He laid out the plan to have her notify him when Eve arrived so he could come out and show her around. They would then eat lunch in the office and work on the details for about an hour.

He was busy drawing on his current project when Ophelia sent him a text. "Beautiful girl is here to see you."

His heart started to pound in anticipation. He's been looking forward to this. Her smile and giggles filled his dreams, both awake and asleep. Getting to visit and dance last week was wonderful, but it's hard to get to know someone when it's loud around. Then it turned into an emergency.

He looked at the clock and noticed she was early. He smiled. 'Good work ethic. Dad would like that.' He thought to himself as he got to a stopping point and saved his progress. Checked himself in the mirror and then headed out to see her.

He went out to the reception area and Ophelia pointed to the waiting room. He could smell her before he even turned to see her.

There she was, leaning against the wall, studying one of his dad's drawings. She looked absolutely, gorgeous. He couldn't help but smile. Her black skirt hugged her curves and the burgundy shirt accented her hair perfectly.

She turned to him and her face lit up. He wasn't expecting her to hug him as she did, but he completely enjoyed it. Learning from last time, he did the double cheek kiss like she does. He took her hand. "Hello, Beautiful." Then kissed her soft hand. Still holding on to her, he led her over to the couches.

"I wasn't expecting to see you here." She still had a look of happiness and confusion on it.

"I go to school during the week and work weekends here. My dad started this business." He turned to the desk. "Our office manager has been with us since the beginning." He smiled at Ophelia.

"That's wonderful," Eve responded as he turned to face the pictures.

"These four blueprints are my dad's handiwork. You can tell by the size and irregularity of the lines that they are hand-drawn." Eve faced him.

"I can close my eyes and see the building grow. I can imagine walking in the spaces and see where to put the furniture." She pointed to another one of his dad's drawings. "This is a mid-century modern house. Sloped roofline, big open space, large windows, central fireplace, minimal furniture." She paused and looked at him again.

His heart thundered in his chest. She's describing the building exactly how he feels when he does the drawing. He moved to be closer. "That is how it was originally drawn. But the customer didn't like some of the features, so they were altered after this original rendering. This one here on the far left is one of mine." Adam waited for her to look, but instead, she started laughing. What could be so funny about his work? He was trying not to take any offense to her change of mood.

"I'm sorry. Last time we talked, the music was a bit loud. I thought you said you were an architectural lawyer. At the time, I thought, 'Why would a building need a lawyer?' But it all makes sense now. You are an architect and a lawyer." She started laughing again, and he could see the confusion. She stepped closer to him, but now she was looking at his print. He let out a soft breath of relief.

"You can tell by the thin, crisp lines that this is drawn on a computer," he added.

"It's also a single floor plan to a high-rise," she quickly added. He was shocked that she knew that so quickly. "You can tell by the size of the support columns, elevator shaft, and the number of stairwells." She pointed to spots on the image as she talked. Man, she really is paying attention.

"All the buildings in this city are relatively new compared to the ones back home. Perhaps one day you can come tour around. Who knows, maybe even impact the way you design." She smiled and winked at him. He would love to tour around with her. Travel to see different buildings around the world.

"These blueprints are wonderful. But not everyone can imagine. Have you thought of putting in flat-panel screens? You could even make them look like pictures with framework. That way, you can rotate images. Show the blueprint. Then rotate to the groundwork, framing, landscaping, and so on until the finished product is displayed. So instead of five static images on the wall, you could potentially have thousands of images, and your customers who have a hard time seeing past the paper can better understand."

That was something he never thought of. He wondered how much that would cost. "Oh, I'm sorry if I overstepped. I just love buildings. They all have stories to tell," Eve said as she made the cutest pouty face.

He just had to hold her. "Don't be sorry for speaking your mind. This is why you're here. Plus, that's why I became an architect. I love buildings also." He felt his heart swell with affection for her.

"Excuse me." Adam turned to see Ophelia, and she tapped her watch.

"Oh, your appointment." Reality kicked in and he picked up Eve's bag. It was heavier than he expected. What did she keep in here? Bricks?

"Let's get going on the tour so you can see the area." He opened the door, and Eve walked in. He leaned over to whisper to Ophelia. "That's a great idea she had. Look into five screens for the waiting room. Power, wiring, monitors, and so on. Get me a cost." Ophelia nodded.

He took Eve to see where the offices were along the outer wall. He didn't like the way the cubicles looked. They needed a larger conference room. He had a few ideas but needed help. After the tour, he led her to the main office.

"Adam. Where is Mr. Christian Stratford? I thought I was going to meet him today?" He paused because he forgot to explain.

He walked back to her and lifted her hand, then guided her to a seat in front of the desk and set her bag down next to it. Now's as good of a time as any to explain. "Mr. Christian Adam Stratford Sr. is my dad. I'm Christian Adam Stratford Jr. My dad goes by Chris, and I'm Adam so there is no confusion in conversations," he responded and sat down but she still looked confused. "What's troubling you, Beautiful?"

She flashed him a different look than he was used to. "I'm just confused. Why would your father call to have me come, just to have the meeting with you?"

He couldn't help but laugh. He pulled the business card from his pocket and slid it to her. "I'm the one who called. I got your card from Jake. I wanted to spend time with you without distraction. At the time, I didn't know how to reach you."

Her confused look didn't go away, but her tone changed. Her shoulders raised up like she was ready to swing a fist. "So you don't really need me to help here. It was just a ruse so we could visit?"

Oh, shit! Now she's getting angry at me. What happened? We were talking just fine. She suddenly stood up to leave. His heart pounded at the thought of her leaving, mad at him.

"Adam, I spent two weeks doing research in preparation for this meeting. I don't appreciate being lied to, just so you can visit with me."

He ran as fast as he could. He couldn't let her go mad. "It's been a very difficult week. I don't need to add this to the pile." All he could think to do was to hold her.

"No, that's not it at all. That came out wrong. We really do need your help. Yes, I wanted to visit with you, but the project is real. Please don't be mad at me. I wasn't trying to trick you. I swear. I just thought it would be a nice surprise that it was me."

He could feel her shaking. She was cold to the touch. Something is going on. She leaned her head onto his chest and started to cry. Oh, shit! What is going on?

"I'm so sorry. My trust in people has been strained this week. Starting with my friends drugging me and the misunderstanding with Jessie. I just haven't been in a good place this week."

Then it dawned on him. She's traumatized from the night of karaoke. But what misunderstanding did she have with Jessie? The image of them coming out of his room popped into his mind. He felt her hold his back, and he calmed at her touch.

Adam pulled her in a little more and then softened. The tissue on the desk was just within reach. "You are always safe with me. Anytime, for any reason, just let me know. I'll be there for you."

He lifted her chin to see her better, then cleared her beautiful face of her tears. His heart pounded again in his ears. He wanted to kiss her, but she needed the gentleman right now. He could see her face blush. Fuck, his desire is killing him. "Please say you understand?" He could see she was relaxing.

"I understand." She then rested her head back on his chest.

God, she feels so good to hold. She fits right in my arms. Then Ophelia knocked. It was reactive to let go and take a step back. "Are we okay now?" He silently prayed she was feeling better.

"Yes, I'm better now." She smiled as she looked him in the eyes. "Thank you for your support."

Her blushing again was his last trigger. He couldn't take it anymore. She could hate him later. He just had to find out. His hand palmed the back of her neck and leaned down to kiss her.

Her lips were petal soft on his. He could feel his heart pounding along with hers and he felt her pull him in. He reached with his free hand to explore more of her as he could feel himself letting go.

If he didn't end the kiss here, he was going to cross a line, and he didn't have permission yet. He breathed heavily in anticipation, resting his forehead on hers helped his heart slow down. In the back of his mind, he knew Ophelia had come and gone discreetly. This was exactly why he had discussed the meeting ahead of time. The bag of food on the desk smelled good, and it pulled both of their attention.

He guided her back to the seat and moved the table closer, then opened the bag and was in shock. "Your favorite food is Mexican?"

"Yes." She smiled back at him. "Well, Spanish."

"It's my favorite also," he replied. He pulled out a tray for her and set it on the table.

"You didn't have to do this, but thank you." Her smile grew larger.

He handed her utensils and a napkin. "It's my pleasure." He smiled. It truly pleased him to make her happy. He was going to need to be patient with her emotions. She was still recovering. He shouldn't have kissed her.

But it had just felt right.

Entry 2: Chat with Jessie

Eve left the meeting with Adam feeling wonderful. That was the best she had felt all week and hoped there would be more days like that. However, she knew that if they were going to keep meeting at the condo, she would need to have a conversation with Jessie. She sent him a text. 'Are you home? I need to see you.' She caught a cab and started heading in the direction of the condo.

A few minutes later, he responded, 'Ya, babe. All private here for as much of me you want to see.'

Her stomach churned. This was going to be difficult. 'I just needed to talk. I'll be there in a few minutes.'

Eve paced outside the door for a good ten minutes, just trying to think of the right wording. She did not want anything to get lost in translation. Her hands were shaking and she couldn't get them to stop. She almost left when the door opened.

"Hey, babe. I didn't hear you knock. You've been out here long?"

She took a step back and froze. "No." He opened the door all the way.

"Well, come on in," he said as he waved his arm to the side. She walked in slowly and shut the door. He was going in and out of his bedroom, but she knew not to follow him there. "Can I get you something to drink?"

Eve saw a glass of what looked like alcohol on the counter. "No, thanks. Have you been drinking?" She needed to know if he was sober enough to have this conversation.

"I've had a couple. But I'm not driving." He moved toward her and she counter-moved around the island. He stopped. "What's going on? Why are you avoiding me?" He leaned on the island.

"We need to talk about what happened on Wednesday." She pressed her lips flat.

He smiled. "That was a great day." He held up his arm. "Still got it on."

She half-smiled. "It's nice that you appreciate a few things." He looked at her for a moment and then asked again.

"What's going on?" He leaned forward and reached his hand closer.

"You did owe me a date, and it just happened to coincide with your birthday. So, I worked it out with Adam to keep you entertained until they were ready for you to return to the condo."

"I know. After everyone yelled surprise, I asked if you were part of it. You said guilty. So, what's with the recap?" He leaned up.

"Well, after a while, I wanted to give you my gift, but I didn't want to make a fuss in front of everyone so, I asked you to come to your room. You shut the door, but I didn't think anything of it. I gave you my gift and it seemed like you liked it."

He reached his hand out again. "And my other gift was wonderful also," he said as his smile grew.

Eve stepped back and leaned against the counter. "I didn't give that to you. You took it from me. You forced yourself on me and you hurt me." Eve was breathing heavily as her frustration was released.

Jessie leaned up. "I thought you wanted me to. At dinner, we agreed to keep that part for when we were in private."

She took a deep breath as her hands made fists. "We were not in private. The condo was full of people. You pushed me back on the bed. I told you my body wasn't ready. You covered my mouth, telling me to be quiet. That made it difficult to talk, let alone breathe." Her tears started to prickle the back of her eyes and they were threatening to fall. She fanned herself as she tried to breathe normally.

In a louder voice, she continued, "You really hurt me." She took another breath. "You don't treat people like that." Her tears freely fell now.

She turned to get a napkin from the counter and wiped her face. Instantly, he had his arms wrapped around her from behind. Eve went from sad to raging-bull mad in a heartbeat.

She started to squirm and twist as she resisted his hold. Her hands were pulling on his, and she was kicking in every direction. "I'm sorry if I hurt you. That wasn't my intention. I just thought you wanted a quickie."

Eve's heeled foot landed square on his bare foot, causing him to yelp and lean forward. Then she whipped her head back, colliding hard with his forehead. He released her and she instantly spun around to slap him. It was the hardest she's hit anyone and her hand stung from the impact.

She quickly moved to the other side of the island. "You do not have permission to touch me," she yelled at the top of her lungs. She picked up the vase of flowers from their date and threw it at him. She missed by a mile, but broken glass, water, and flowers went everywhere. She flew out the door before he could follow her.

Adam

Adam's phone buzzed. Announcement: Front Door. He saw it and put it down. He was not expecting a package, so it was probably just a neighbor walking by. His phone buzzed again and again. After the fifth buzz, he opened the monitoring system. "Eve!" he said out loud. What was she doing there? He rewound the video to the beginning.

He could see her walking down the hallway from the elevator, but she didn't knock on the door. She paced back and forth. Her hands were moving and she was talking. Was she on a phone call? He sped the video up to where Jessie opened the door. She suddenly looked scared. The door fully opened and she slowly walked in.

Adam switched to the living room camera. She's holding still and it looks like Jessie's getting laundry ready for the pickup. He comes back to her and she moves away from him. He can see that they are talking, but every move he makes, she counters to keep away now. She shifted to keep the island between them. Something is not right here. She's behaving like she does not trust him. Adam mentally kicked himself for not installing the cameras with audio. He got up and ran for the door.

"I'm leaving. Something came up," he said to Ophelia as he ran past. He got out onto the street and traffic was jammed. It would be faster to just run a few blocks. He checked the phone occasionally, as he was dodging around people. They were still talking and she looked madder. When he got to a red, do not cross sign, he was just around the corner and half a block from his building.

He checked the phone and he saw red. Jessie's holding her from behind and she's kicking, trying to get free. He could see the fear in her face. They slammed heads and she got free with an added swing slap. He could see that she was yelling. She threw the vase and left in a hurry. The light turned green and Adam sprinted as fast as he could.

He rounded the corner and he could see Eve getting into a cab down the block. Panting, he wasn't going to catch her before she left, and running to her place was beyond his current stamina. He decided to continue jogging down the block and head upstairs to have a little chat with Jessie.

When Adam got into the condo, Jessie was leaning on the island. He took a couple of paces to close the distance and Jessie stood up straight. Without warning, Adam struck a fist across his face, sending Jessie crashing to the floor. "I told you that if you hurt her, I hurt you." He then took a step back. "I don't know what happened the evening of your birthday, but it clearly changed her. And just now, you couldn't just keep your hands to yourself. Don't touch her ever again."

Adam breathed heavily as he hit his fist on the countertop and then took a deep breath to slowly blow it out. "You're a good friend to guys, but you treat women wrong. Whatever you did wrong, she called you out on it. Learn or get the fuck out of my condo. Think on it as you clean up this mess. Your mess."

Adam turned and slammed the door shut behind him. He stood in the hallway to calm himself down. He was going to Eve's next and didn't want any residual anger showing. He went to the street and caught a cab. He had a few minutes to think before he knocked on her door. His heart slowed and he could finally breathe normally again. He got out of the cab when it pulled up to the address. Her place looked so much different by day, compared to when he carried her in at night.

He gently knocked on her door. There was a little noise, and then he heard footsteps. She opened the door just enough to see who was there. He could see the signs that she had been crying, and his heart sank. He held his arms open for her. She opened the door all the way, instantly started to cry, slammed her body into his, and hugged him. He wrapped his arms around her and squeezed.

They stood there in the hallway until he decided to scoop her up and take her inside. He shut the door with his foot and walked over to the couch. He slowly sat down so he wouldn't crash with her and just held her as she clung to him. Her crying came to a stop after a few minutes, and her breathing was easing. He softly pulled her hair back and wiped her face clear with his thumbs.

"I knew something was wrong the evening of his birthday party. You confirmed it in the office today." He paused to gather his thoughts. "As part of our construction business, we install security systems. I have a couple of cameras at the condo, but I chose video only." He slowly let his fingers move on her arm.

"I saw you arrive at the condo and pace back and forth. Then you went inside. However, I couldn't hear the conversation, but by your body language, I knew you were upset and defensive. Then he grabbed you, and you fought with him to get free." She started to breathe heavily again, and so did he.

"I got there just after you entered the taxi. So, I went upstairs. With one swing, I knocked his ass to the ground and told him to never touch you again."

Eve hugged him tighter.

"Wish I could have seen that," she breathed into his ear. Adam paused. He wondered if he should show her or if it would just add to the trauma she was already dealing with.

"I have it on my phone if you want to see it," he replied.

Eve sat up. "Really?" Her eyes went as large as saucers.

"Are you sure? I don't want to add any more damage to what you're already feeling." He waited patiently for her to respond.

She sighed and was quiet for a moment. "I do. I think it would be nice to see."

Adam shifted his weight to the right so she could sit to the left of him. He then dug his phone out and opened the monitoring system. He rewound the camera to the time he walked in the door and handed it to Eve to watch. It only lasted for a few moments, but Eve's eyes went huge, and she covered her mouth. Then she played it again without the shock. Then again, with a grin on her face.

"Oh, Adam. I'm so sorry. I broke your vase." She looked at him with sorrowful eyes.

He gave her a squeeze. "Don't you worry your beautiful head about it. We need to work on your aim, but the vase went out in a blaze of glory." He smiled as his hand made an arc in the air, then his fingers exploded. "You don't ever have to go back to the condo. I completely understand if you don't want to be there." She eased up her grip on the phone and sat up.

"I don't mind being there, so long as you are there," she smiled. "I just don't want to be there alone with him again," she said as she handed the phone back to him. "One thing I did notice." She looked at him.

"What's that?" He reached for her hand and started to softly rub his thumb. He loved watching her blush.

"I don't know if it was the camera angle or just seeing you flex for the first time. Your back and arm muscles look like the Hulk." She smiled and leaned against his shoulder and wrapped her arm around his. "Thank you for standing up for me. I really appreciate it."

He opened his music app and stood up. He took a step back and slid the coffee table out of the way. "We can order food for delivery later tonight." He held his hand out for her. "But for now, may I have this dance?" She giggled and reached for his hand. They stayed up late, chatting about anything that came to their minds.

Entry 3: Honest Talk Between Guys

Early Sunday morning, when Adam left his room, he saw several books on the coffee table. There were a bunch of papers laid around with a stack of post-it notes. He looked at a few of the books: Dating Playbook for Men, Dating for Dummies, Learning to Read Body Language, and about four others. Adam smirked his lips. Guess he's gonna try and learn. That's good, he thought to himself.

He was on his way home to spend the day with his parents. He sent Eve a text about where he was going to be and was out the door. The quick 45-minute drive got shorter each time. Then again, he had Eve on his mind the whole time while replaying yesterday's events. The office meeting, then his fight in the condo, and spending the evening at Eve's consumed most of his thoughts throughout the whole day. When thoughts were overwhelming, he would send a quick message to Eve to check in and see how she was doing.

He got a few quiet minutes with his dad to catch up on the war against Jessie for love. Adam sat on the bed to face his dad. "Well, I have good and bad news."

His dad's eyebrows raised. "Really? Do tell." Intrigue was written all over his face.

"The good news is that Jessie screwed up big time and he's out of the picture. The bad news is that he hurt her somehow, and she doesn't even want to talk about it or be alone with him." Adam pressed his lips together in thought.

"So, he emotionally hurt her? Or was it physical? Either one is not good." Chris smirked his lips to one side.

"I'm not sure. It was the evening of his birthday. When they arrived, she was happy, smiling, and holding onto his arm. Towards the end of the party, they were in his room for a few minutes. When they came out, he was showing everyone the gift she gave him. But she was different. Not smiling. He was pulling her by the hand. She looked red-hot mad. Like when Mom gets mad." Adam took a deep breath to calm himself.

"At our Saturday meeting, a couple of days later, she confirmed that something had happened but said it was a misunderstanding. From there, she went to see him at the condo. I saw the alerts on the phone and watched in horror as they got into a fight and he grabbed her from behind when she was not looking."

His dad gasped. "I showed up after it was all over and punched his ass to the ground. I told him to grow up, learn to behave better, or get out. I then went over to her place and was her support all evening." His dad let out a big sigh.

"Oh, son. You'll have to slow down and wait for her to heal. That poor girl. Follow the steps and you'll be fine. Pay attention to her body language for clues." They were both quiet for a few.

"Like I'm not busy enough, but I've started learning French again. It's her primary language. When we first met, I greeted her with a little and her eyes lit up. But lessened when she found out that was all I knew. She said that what I said sounded excellent and that learning may be easier than I thought."

His dad bobbed his head up and down. "Plus, it helps to know the language when traveling." Chris raised an eyebrow. "When all of this works out, I'm sure at some point you guys will return to France to meet her family and for follow-up visits," Chris added. "How goes the chemical warfare?"

"I don't know if his libido has been affected yet. I have not heard any complaints, but I don't think he has had any late-night adventures since starting his new shake additive. The sleeping one worked great for the night of karaoke. He went home, and we danced together all evening. I even got to sing to her. That was until she was drugged by her friends."

"Wait. What?" His dad had a shocked look on his face.

"She was nervous prior to the date, so they spiked her pop with Valium to help her calm down. The problem was she didn't slowly drink it as they thought she would. She had alcoholic beverages before we got there and she chugged her pop down after we were done dancing. It knocked her on her ass. I ended up calling the on-call doctor for help. I took her home and a nurse came to stay with her," Adam responded.

"Wow, what a crazy week it's been. Hopefully, things slow down a bit." Chris pressed his lips flat, but a smile tugged at the corner of his mouth.

"Only time will tell. Love you, Dad." Adam leaned over and hugged his dad.

"Love you too, son." Chris leaned his head against Adam's shoulder.

In the evening, after his parents retired to their room for the evening, he decided to press some weights in the gym. He and Eve arranged to have a phone call, so he called her up.

It rang a few times before she picked up. "Hello?"

"Hello, Beautiful," he responded.

"Can we chat later? I'm standing here naked, about to climb into the shower."

Adam's body jolted with the visual and he almost dropped the weights onto his foot. "Damn, Beautiful. You can't tell a man that. I almost killed myself just now. It gets the brain going and I lose concentration."

She laughed. "I'll call you back when I'm done." They said their goodbyes and he hung up the phone. He kept on working his muscle groups.

It was sometime later and he was about done when she called back. "Hello?"

"Bonjour." Her voice always sounds so happy when she spoke French.

"That took you long enough. Clean everything three times?" he asked jokingly.

"Just certain spots." He could hear her softly laugh. "It takes time to wash all this hair. And then dry it so I don't get sick."

"Hmmmm, I see." He envisioned her in the shower again. He blinked to clear his mind so he could concentrate. "Okay. Are we still meeting on Wednesday evening?"

"That's the plan. I get out of school at 4 p.m. I can kill a little time if you need me to. Let me know when you are on your way. And then I'll head in that direction. I have a list of all the ideas we discussed. I have not done any research yet. Need your input on what you like so we can get the budget squared away. Then we can meet the following week with my images," she finished.

"Sounds good." He was counting his reps in his mind.

"You sound distracted. What are you doing?" He dropped the bar of weights on the floor.

"Making my hulk muscles stronger for you." A devilish thought came to mind. "I've been working out… naked, while waiting for your call." There was a crashing sound and then he could hear her laughing in the distance. "What was that noise?"

She stopped laughing enough to answer. "I fell off the bed."

He chuckled. "Payback for teasing me earlier. Anyway, I have to go and take a shower myself. I need to wash all this sweat off." He said goodbye and ended the call. Now he was going to take a hot shower and he still had her on his mind. 'Think I'll release some pressure also, so I'm not blue later,' he thought to himself.

Monday, he drove straight to school. He knew there were going to be a couple of long days with class and study group. After he got home late that evening, that's when he learned that Jessie had called out sick. He was nose-deep in his new studies. Adam decided to offer his help if he was willing to listen. They got to talking about body language and made a game of it: Guess my mood? By the end of the evening, Jessie was getting better.

Tuesday, by the time he got home, Jessie was full tilt learning. Adam's never seen him so dedicated, not even to his schoolwork. He sat down and asked if he wanted to hear his dad's wisdom list, modified and condensed for Jessie to absorb, of course. He seemed eager and willing, so Adam went over the list to compare to the books.

"First and foremost. Manners begin with being a 'man'," Adam emphasized the word. "Days of being a selfish boy are over when you start this path. Do I make myself clear?" Adam asked before proceeding. Jessie leaned forward and nodded his head yes.

"Before sex list," he started as Jessie looked at him intently. "That means, no sex for now. Building an emotional connection takes time. It also makes the physical connection better down the line. Be a gentleman. That means a man who is gentle. Kiss her hand when you first see her for the day. Open the doors for her. Always pay." He watched as he took notes. That should go against one of his primary codes of women's behavior.

"Second. Never drink more than one alcoholic beverage. No girl wants to see a guy get drunk and sloppy. It will leave a negative view and an untrustworthy image to her." That will be a challenge for him, being a big drinker.

"Third. Always compliment her. Lifting her confidence will boost her confidence in you." That should come naturally to his flirty behavior.

"Fourth. Always show affection. Hugs, kisses, sit next to her with your arm around her. When she's comfortable she will return the affection. Gently touch her hand, arm, especially when she is sharing." Adam knew that Jessie didn't like to kiss. Or, the one-night stands in his case. That one's going to take some work.

"Fifth. Dance when you get the chance. Even if it's just the radio in the living room. It's the closeness and moving together that forms a bond." That's gonna be another easy one for him.

"Sixth. Always be her protector. Whenever there may be danger, her honor, or feelings, prove that you'll be there for her. It builds trust. Sound familiar?" Adam waited for Jessie's response on that one, but he remained quiet.

"Seventh. Never forget important dates. Birthday, Valentine's, Christmas, or anniversary. A gift that has meaning is better than an expensive one." That's going to go against the grain. Thinking of a gift, let alone a thoughtful one, will be difficult.

"Eighth. At some point, you're going to need full courage, open yourself up and tell her exactly how you feel. She's not psychic. Make it clear." Adam paused to let Jessie catch up.

"Before or after sex." Adam waited again.

"Ninth. You'll know when, because you'll feel it, but be the first to say 'I love you.'" Adam doubted that he would get to this stage in the next few years.

"Tenth. Don't wait too long, ask her to marry you. Find something beautiful that has a significant meaning to you both." He knew Jessie would probably never get to this point but put it out there anyway.

"Now you can add my dad's list to your 'How to be a good man' file. How likely are you going to follow any of the information?" Adam had a serious doubt about the whole situation. Jessie sat up.

"I'm going to try." He held up a fist to his face. "It took something big for me to realize that I was fucking up."

"So, listen dude, Eve will be coming here tomorrow evening for a work meeting. She does not want to be around you. You will be on your best behavior. This will be your first test. Pay attention, mind your words, and for God's sake, apologize so she hears you." Adam got up and gave him a soft push on the shoulder. "What are you doing about school?" he wondered, since it seemed like Jessie was avoiding it at all costs.

Jessie leaned back, stretched, and then tucked his hands behind his head. "I don't know. Law is my father's path for me. Do I continue and try and find a lane that fits me the best? Or do I stop now and try and figure it out? I really don't know."

Adam was shocked. It seemed like Jessie was stuck between a rock and a hard place. If he walked away from law school, he was sure his father would completely cut him off. What would he then do? Work a minimum wage job while trying to figure it out?

"That's a tough situation. If I was in your shoes, since I already put in the effort, I would finish school, find what fits best, and then find my passion with the income work brings." Adam stretched. "I have a bit of studying to do and then I'm gonna get some sleep. See ya tomorrow." He turned to walk to his room.

"Hey, man." Jessie called out and Adam turned back around. "Thank you for your help. I've been needing guidance that I should have had a long time ago," Jessie said with a smile.

Adam smiled in return. "You're welcome."

Entry 4: Budget Meeting

Adam checked in with her off and on through Sunday to make sure she was doing okay. He was out of town, seeing his parents for the rest of the holiday weekend. It was mostly simple chat, but every time her phone buzzed, she got excited. She decided to test the waters and see what he would do. Late Sunday, when she was expecting him to call, she pretended to sound like she was in a hurry. "Can we chat later? I'm standing here naked and about to climb into the shower."

She heard a bang sound and giggled. "Damn, Beautiful. You can't tell a man that. I almost killed myself just now. It gets the brain going, and I lose concentration."

She laughed. "I'll call you back when I'm done." She was not the greatest at flirting, but she got the reaction she was looking for.

She sketched on the bed for a good hour for their meeting before returning his call. It ran several times before he picked up. "Hello?"

"Bonjour." Ugh. She needed to remember to respond in English.

"That took you long enough. Clean everything three times?" he asked. There was a tone of teasing in his voice. Two can play this game.

"Just certain spots." She laughed as she remembered using the water wand on jet spray against her undercarriage until she climaxed. "It takes time to wash all this hair. And then dry it so I don't get sick."

"Hmmmm, I see." His laughter was soft in her ear. "Okay. Are we still meeting on Wednesday evening?"

She took a deep breath and slowly let it out. "That's the plan. I get out of school at 4 p.m. I can kill a little time if you need me to. Let me know when you are on your way, and then I'll head in that direction. I have a list so far of ideas. I have not done any research yet. Need your input on what you like so we can get the budget squared away first."

"Sounds good." There were a weird rhythmic sound and an awkward silence before she worked up the courage to ask.

"You sound distracted. What are you doing?" There was another bang of something heavy hitting the floor.

"Making my Hulk muscles stronger for you. I've been working out, naked, while waiting for your call." Eve sat up fast and fell off the edge of the bed, sending the phone flying across the floor. She was laughing hysterically as she crawled under the desk to retrieve it.

"What was that?" She could hear his concern through the phone.

She got her laughter under control before answering. "I fell off the bed."

He laughed at her. "Payback for teasing me. Anyway, I have to go and take a shower myself." She blushed as she thought of him taking a shower. They said their goodbyes and ended the call.

She fanned herself to cool off. A playful shower didn't sound half bad right now, she smirked to herself as she eyed the shower wand.

Wednesday came slower than she wanted. But now that it was here, the day seemed to fly past. To make things go even faster, Adam was done early, and she still had a few hours left of class. She still needed to pick up her gift that she ordered while on the way to his place.

Mrs. Johnston called Eve to her office. "Are you doing a follow-up with the referral?"

"I had my initial meeting on Saturday. It went well. There were several ideas discussed for the space and their current needs. We have a budget meeting today after class."

Mrs. Johnston looked surprised. "Would you like to go early and get set up?"

"Really? I could use the extra time," Eve responded.

"You have my blessing." Mrs. Johnston waved goodbye, and Eve didn't hesitate as she flew out of the door.

She was home, changed, and out the door with her preliminary work, drawings, and cost list. More than anything, she was looking forward to seeing Adam again, and yet a bit nervous at the same time. But she knew she would be safe with Adam there. She sent a quick text: 'Done early. On my way. Will be there in about 20 min.' She had to make one stop and then back to business.

She almost knocked on the door when Adam opened it. "Hello, Beautiful. You have to see this for yourself. You are not going to believe this. I think something loosened when you slapped and I punched him." He held out his hand, and she gladly accepted with a smile. They walked into the living room to see Jessie with books everywhere and Post-it notes stuck in them, along with a notebook that he was writing in.

"Eve!" Jessie said excitedly, popped up, and she instantly took two steps back toward the door, pulling on Adam's arm. Adam turned to face her.

"He's learning. I never thought I'd see the day." He turned back around and stepped aside. Jessie slowly walked up to Eve looking sheepish. Eve's body started to shake as her feet were frozen in place. "Easy, Beautiful. I'm right here. He won't do anything stupid, or I'll loosen something on the other side of his head," Adam added, and she took a deep breath.

She knew it was going to be difficult to be here, but she didn't imagine her body would react like this.

"I have been a self-centered screw-up for a long time. No woman has ever said anything before like you did. And then getting my face slapped woke me up." He paused and smiled at Adam. "Then bashed in, made me take a good hard look at myself." He lifted his hand and held it out for her. She looked at Adam with straight terror and then back at Jessie. "I won't hurt you," he said, and then lowered his head.

Eve looked up at Adam again. Adam smiled and nodded his head, yes. She trusted him, so she slowly placed her other hand in Jessie's. He then lifted it and gave it a soft kiss.

"Last time, I was trying to apologize for my actions. But, I didn't read your body language enough to notice how upset you were." He looked up at her. "I am truly sorry. I hope one day you will be able to forgive me." He stood up taller. "Will you please sit on the couch so I can show you what we have been working on?" His other hand swung towards the living room.

Her eyes flashed to the couches and back to him. "I will sit next to Adam," she said quietly, then pulled her hand from his.

"I understand," Jessie responded with a soft nod.

She stepped into Adam as a shield, and he wrapped his arm around her. "What are you seeing now?" Adam stood protectively.

"She's shaking and trembling in fear. Fear that I caused. I am sorry. I now know better and want to do better. It will take some time, but Adam is working with me." Jessie walked back to the couch and sat back down among his work. "As I go along, would it be okay if I ask you a question here or there for a woman's point of view?" Jessie asked with big hopeful eyes.

She looked at Adam. "I think another point of view, especially a woman's, will help him learn," Adam replied with a soft smile.

Eve could hear her heart thumping in her ears. "If it's an appropriate question. If you ask me anything rude, then I'm gone," Eve responded. Jessie nodded his head in acceptance.

Adam led her to the couch, opposite to Jessie. She leaned in and whispered, "When are we going to go over our items?"

He whispered back, "Soon." They both refocused their attention onto Jessie.

"Last week, when we were at the restaurant, what were some of the things I did right and wrong?" She didn't expect to be revisiting the date again so quickly. "Can you explain which was which?" Eve looked at Adam. She felt like she needed to get permission to talk about their date in front of him.

"Any information you can help him with would be good." Adam seemed to be calm about the subject.

She took a deep breath and held a thumb up. "After setting up the date, showing up is good. You took the time to look nice. When I arrived, you complemented my dress. A plus, when you bought me flowers," she looked in the kitchen where she threw the vase and saw the flowers soaking in the corner of the sink.

"You didn't directly ask, but you said you wanted to touch me before doing so. You moved slowly and gently. If I had disapproved, I could have backed up at that moment. I did blush at the contact. You softly touched my face. And again, let me know your intent to kiss." Eve paused to breathe to ease the flush rising in her neck at the memory.

She shifted her thumbs sideways. "You sat next to me, invading my space. Normally, for the first few dates, you sit across. That way, we can see each other's reaction to the conversation. You explained that way you could whisper answers in my ear so no one else could hear. You placed your hand on my leg, invading my space again. It was not a thumb-down because you had done the same thing on Friday when we sat at the table."

She moved her thumb up. "We had a great conversation. We took turns asking questions and answering. From there, I knew I wanted a second date." She turned her thumb down. "Since I arranged the first date, I was waiting for you, but you never asked me. By the end of dessert, either make plans for the next date or discuss not being compatible and end the date." She put her hand down in her lap.

"I needed to get you to return home for the party. I should have worded it differently, but I'm still learning English. Plus, I didn't want to spoil the surprise. By the time we got to the door, my excitement was spilling over, plus I wanted another kiss before the chaos erupted. That was as far as it should have gone."

Adam leaned forward as he fisted his hands. "What about this miscommunication you guys had?" Eve instantly started to tear up.

"I don't want to talk about it anymore. It's done and can't be changed. Only Jessie can learn to be better for the future. Learn boundaries and when and how to ask for permission. If you had listened, I said no."

She grabbed her satchel and reached for the two boxes she brought with her. She turned to face Adam. "I made an error on Saturday. A friend makes up for it." She handed Adam the larger box. She then looked at Jessie for a moment and then back to Adam. "And my apology." She then kissed Adam on the cheek and handed him the second smaller box.

She started to shake again while thinking about what happened in Jessie's room and needed space to think. "I need a minute to calm down before we start on the budget." She got up, turned, and went into Adam's room and shut the door.

Adam

Adam looked at Jessie. "I know what's in this box. Even though I told her not to, she did it anyway." He opened the box and was not surprised to see a beautiful cut crystal vase with a gold rim. He showed

Jessie the replacement vase. "You see. She did this because she's a woman, not a girl, and claimed her mistake."

He got up and went to the kitchen, filled it with water, put the flowers into the vase, and placed it back on the island. He walked back over to the couch and picked up the small box. "I have no idea what this could be." He opened the box and started laughing. "It's perfect." He laughed a bit more. "Remember the list? A gift that has meaning goes further." He held up a green mug with the Hulk printed on it.

"I don't get it," Jessie responded as he shook his head.

"That's right. Because it's between us. However, I'll explain it to you anyway. She wanted to see the video of me hitting you. Afterwards, she said my muscles look like the Hulk. And then on Sunday when we were talking, I was working out. I teased her and said I was making my Hulk muscles stronger."

Jessie slowly nodded. "You're right. Understanding the reason makes it better."

Adam smiled. "She took the time to find something that was meaningful. A ten-dollar mug has more impact than a hundred-dollar vase."

They were quiet for a minute as Adam watched Jessie think. "When did you install cameras?" Jessie had a blank look on his face, which made Adam smile.

"Wouldn't you like to know? That's how I keep an eye on the place." Adam walked back to the kitchen and let out a chuckle as he set the mug by the coffee maker, then went to his room.

Eve

Eve sat at his desk, just breathing to calm down. She saw a couple of cards there with her name on them. She didn't touch them. 'He will give them to me when he's ready,' she thought to herself. She started to set up her displays, drawing and pictures anywhere she could find a surface. On the dresser, bed, desk, and chair held all her work for the last few days.

Adam walked in, closing the door behind him. She turned after propping up the last board. He held his arms open for her, and she stepped into him. They held onto each other for a long while until she was ready to talk. "I wasn't expecting an intervention," she spoke softly.

"He's been studying ever since Saturday. I hope it's a turning point for him, and that he doesn't go back to the old ways."

She took a deep breath. "That's his journey. For now, we have several things to discuss."

He leaned back. "We sure do. Like I said, you didn't have to replace the vase."

She rested her forehead on his chest. "I know, but I felt it was the right thing to do."

He smiled. "And I really love the mug. It's going to be my official go-to mug from now on."

"I'm glad you liked it." She squeezed a little harder and then let go. "Ready to get started?" she asked with a smile.

"Yes, but I forgot something." He leaned down and gave her a kiss on both of her cheeks. She was shocked because she completely forgot her normal greeting at the front door.

They chatted for another couple of hours before they needed a break. Adam turned on some music and started to hum along. "Adam?"

"Yes, Beautiful." He softly swayed as he was studying one of her concept drawings.

"Would you be interested in doing a duet at the next karaoke night?" He turned and reached for her hand and kissed it.

"I would love to. You did an awesome job singing Rihanna. How's your alto section?" Eve was confused for a second.

"You mean my mid-range?" Adam nodded his head yes. "I think I do okay with it."

Adam smiled. "That's good. I know a song that may be a challenge. Have you heard the one with Bradley Cooper and Lady Gaga?"

She thought for a moment. "I think so?" she responded. Adam picked up his phone and turned off the radio. He then searched his song list and tapped the screen to play. The melody came on, and she instantly recognized it.

"Oh my! This will be a challenge." And they started singing along. By the end of the song, Jessie knocked on the door. Adam walked over and opened it.

"Are you guys doing another karaoke night soon?" Eve leaned around Adam.

"My group of friends normally goes once or twice a month," Eve answered quickly, and then hid behind Adam again.

"I had never done that before, and I really enjoyed it. Can I come next time?"

Adam turned and looked at Eve. "Up to you." Suddenly, she had a wonderfully wicked idea. She took a couple of steps back, then started to pace back and forth.

"Easy, Beautiful," Adam said softly while holding his arms open.

She turned to Adam and smiled. She hugged him and whispered, "Would you be willing to do a trio also? I know a song that I've always wanted to do, but no one can do the lower notes like you." Her eyes sparkled.

"Yes," he answered without delay. She then turned to Jessie with a hopeful smile.

"Tell you what. If you agree to do this, it will be your apology to me and part of the steps to earn my trust back. Your first song will be my choice. Your second will be in a trio with us. Your third song is your choice."

He thought for a moment. "Okay. I'll do it." Eve squealed, bounced for a moment, and then sat at Adam's desk. She pulled out her phone and grabbed blank pieces of paper. She started to write names and songs on the pages.

Adam looked at Jessie with wide eyes. "You made her squeal. I think you may just regret this." Adam devilishly laughed. Eve gave Adam a swat on the back of the leg.

After finishing, she turned. "Is there somewhere in the building we can go? We will want to practice before going on stage." She handed them each a piece of paper. "It's not a hard song, but when timed right, they are powerful notes."

"I know this song. Fairly easy to remember. Simple lyrics also," Adam added.

Eve smirked. "I'll take high range, Adam gets low, and Jessie is middle. It's normally a five-part harmony, but it will still sound good as a three-part." She tapped on the page. "Don't know if the other song is in your normal wheelhouse. But like I said, that will be a step in the right direction. You boys have just over a week until the next gathering. Let me know when you want to practice." Eve smiled, and her body wasn't trembling anymore.

Entry 5: Sharing Drawings, Practicing Singing, Dancing

It had been a week since Eve was at the condo last. She wasn't as worried as she was last week. Adam kept updating her on Jessie's progress in manners otherwise, their texts were mostly about the office. They originally planned on a Wednesday to go over her sketches, then, later, the three of them would go down to the movie room and practice their songs. However, the boys had a last-minute study group arise for the upcoming Friday exam. That left just tonight to practice together before Friday's gathering.

She brought teriyaki for everyone so they wouldn't have to worry about making dinner. She knocked on the door, and Jessie answered. She automatically went defensive and took a step back. He softly smiled. "It's great to see you. I've been practicing my songs. I can't wait to sing with you."

She took an easier breath and forced a smile. He held out his hand. She knew what was coming. She accepted the offer and slowly placed her hand in his. He lifted and softly kissed her hand and then led her inside.

"You didn't have to bring dinner. We could have ordered something to be delivered." He smiled as she held up the enticing-smelling food. He took the bag to the kitchen. "Do you want to eat now or after your meeting?"

She was ready but didn't see Adam. "I'm hungry now, but we can wait for Adam." She felt glued to the floor. She knew he had been working on his behavior, but the fear was flooding her again. He pulled out three plates and started serving up dinner.

"Adam is showering. He should be done soon. Can I get you something to drink? We have water, milk, and a couple of types of pop."

She noticed that alcohol was not on the list. "Do you have a root beer?"

He smiled. "Yes." He grabbed a glass, put some ice in, and then grabbed a can from the fridge. A wave of ease was starting to relax her. She started to feel lighter. She took a couple of steps into the condo, then set her drawings down at the coffee table as she watched Jessie.

He was busy placing the food on the dining table. Jessie sat on one side. Her choice was to sit next to him or across from him.

"Hello, Beautiful." She turned to see Adam standing in the doorway. He had pants on but no shirt and damp hair. His massive muscular torso and arms were on full display.

Her heart instantly started to race, and she felt her face blush as she smiled. "Hello." He closed the distance, and they kissed cheeks hello.

He slowly let his fingers travel down her arms and lifted both her hands to kiss. He leaned in and whispered, "I've missed you," and softly lingered a kiss on her cheek again, setting her body on fire while her stomach fluttered with excitement.

She closed her eyes and whispered, "I've missed you too." She reached her arms around his shoulders and pulled him into a long-needed hug. She could hear his heart was racing like hers was.

Jessie cleared his throat. "Dinner is on the table."

Adam looked up and saw the meal on the table then looked back down at her and leaned back enough to see her face. "You didn't have to bring food."

"I know. I just thought it would be nice to not have to stop."

He softly brushed his fingers along the side of her face. "Thank you." She didn't know why, but her heart sped up even more.

She released the hug. "You're welcome." She held his hand and started to lead him to the table, but his resistance stopped them.

"Let me get a shirt on first, and then I'll join you guys." She smiled but didn't want to let go of his hand.

"Okay." She released her hold and he took a couple of steps into his room, then she turned.

She chose to sit across from Jessie but turned her legs towards where Adam would be sitting so she did not accidentally bump her legs with Jessie. The thought made her giggle a little. Normally, on a date, she would have wanted to accidentally 'on purpose' bump legs together. Just goes to show how much things can change so quickly.

She glanced at Jessie and noticed that he was looking at her. She felt nerves growing again and concentrated on her plate. She jumped when she felt a touch on her shoulder.

"I'm sorry. I didn't mean to scare you." Adam softly stroked his thumb.

She shook her head no and placed her hand on his. "It's okay. Just me." She looked at Jessie. "You are working on learning manners. I'm still working on my nerves. But please don't stare at me. It does make me uneasy." She forced a smile and nodded.

Jessie leaned back. "I'm sorry. I didn't realize I was doing it. You giggled, and I was curious as to why."

Eve blushed, looked at Adam and smiled, then back at Jessie. She didn't want to be rude and talk about it, so she looked at her plate.

"Jessie, can't you read her body language yet? She doesn't want to talk about it," he said as he sat down at the head of the table.

Eve nodded again. "Thank you."

Adam smiled. "Of course. I see you brought some of your drawings for me to look at." He glanced over at the coffee table.

"I did. I think I have most of everything we talked about in concept art." She got up and grabbed the smaller artwork. "I still wanted to be able to see the office with the full staff, so I could see the flow. Plus, I can ask the employees questions." She handed half to Adam, the other half to Jessie, and then sat down to keep eating.

Jessie's face shifted. "These are great. Is this what the inside of your work looks like?"

Adam chuckled. "This is what it could look like," he said as he switched pictures around.

"The larger ones we can pass around after we are done eating," Eve added.

Adam looked at the coffee table again. "When do you have time to do all these drawings?"

Eve laughed and waved her hand at him. "I'm sure it's much like you when you start drawing on the computer. You know where everything goes, you get into the zone, and before you know it, the object in your mind is now on paper." She started giggling.

"Plus, I don't sleep much at night so, I have a few more extra hours per day." She took a bite of her food and noticed that they were both staring at her. She gulped her food down hard. "What?"

They looked at each other, and then Adam asked, "How much sleep do you get per night?"

She tapped her finger to her mouth and thought for a moment. "Anywhere between..." She looked at them as they continued to stare at her. "Two to four hours. Depends on how active I've been. But it also has an effect on how fast my body processes, well... everything. For example," she smirked her lips as she paused to think again, "on Friday evening when my friends drugged me, the nurse was surprised I woke up so soon. I had about six hours of sleep that night. My body processed it faster than normal."

"Wait, wait, wait a minute." Jessie cut in with hands swinging back and forth. "What are you talking about being drugged on Friday? Which Friday?"

She paused and looked at Adam. "You didn't tell him?"

"No, I didn't. He left early and was asleep when I got home. I was so worried, I stayed up all night. When we talked, I finally went to sleep. He was gone when I woke up. And then life was busy with planning his party, I forgot. Plus, I'm not a busybody and talk about someone else's bad day. So really, I haven't told anyone." He shrugged his shoulders and frowned a little.

He put his hand on her leg and she put her hand on top of his. "I figured you would discuss it with Jessie on the date. Please forgive me."

She pondered for a moment. "It depends. What is a busybody?"

Adam chuckled. "A person who gossips about other people without them knowing."

She half smiled. "I see it from your point of view. Thank you for not being a 'busybody' and thinking about my feelings," Eve said as she made finger quotes with her free hand.

Just then, Eve's phone rang. "Please excuse me." She got up and looked at the phone, then let out a heavy sigh and shook her head. "I'm sorry. I need to take this." She walked into Adam's room to answer the phone.

Adam

"Dude! Why didn't you tell me about her being drugged?" Jessie asked as he shook his head. He really did not look happy.

"Sorry. It's like I said to Eve, I figured she would have talked about it with you. And then I didn't want to drag up the bad feelings she was having about her friends."

Adam felt bad for not including him in the evening's ordeal. But it played in his favor to put him on Eve's good side and build trust. Why would he share information with Jessie that could help him in the battle for her heart? He could hear Eve's voice getting louder and they both looked at the bedroom door.

She clearly was getting mad but, that wasn't French she was speaking. Adam got up and took his empty plate to the dishwasher. He turned and looked at Jessie. "Is that Spanish?"

Jessie nodded his head yes and got up with his empty plate. "That's the formal Spanish. The Spanish I know is slang compared to Spain's Spanish language. Like how there is French and Canadian French." Then it was quiet in the bedroom and they both watched the door for a second.

Adam walked over to the couch, sat down, and he started looking at the larger drawings. "These are so impressive. She really listened and made my thoughts come to life." He may be good at making buildings, but she was excellent at finishing the look.

Then he got a thought. A perfectly wonderful thought that could change everything.

Eve

Eve took a moment to calm down before returning to the living room. She hated getting phone calls to deal with issues when she was so far away from home. Eventually, she was going to need to make a trip just to get things back on track. 'Just breathe,' she reminded herself, and she could feel her blood pressure resuming to normal.

On the desk, she noticed four new envelopes with her name on them. She picked one up and peeked inside. There was a card inside. She closed it and put it back. 'He will give them to me when he's ready,' she reminded herself. She took another breath and got up.

"Sorry about that interruption," she said as she came out of the bedroom. She walked around the couch and sat next to Adam. He leaned back and wrapped his arm around her.

"That sounded intense for a bit. Everything okay?" Adam smiled at her. She took another deep breath, and then leaned into him.

"It's a snowball effect from post-COVID. Everyone was home working on projects." Adam nodded his head in agreement. "Most of all, the stockpile of inventory is running out. Anything that requires being handmade is now hard to find. So, an order I put in months ago is now delayed. That means some projects back home are going to be delayed." She took another deep breath and crossed her arms.

"If you can't change the outcome, then there is no use in stressing over it," Adam said softly. "So, you also speak Spanish?"

She looked at him. "French, Italian, Spanish, Japanese, and English."

They both had a shocked look on their faces. "Five languages?" they said in unison.

She smiled. "Well, four and a half. I'm still working on my English. That's part of why I'm here. Immersion learning. When I was younger, I did quiet activities while everyone was asleep. Learning a language just seemed to be an easy way to pass the time."

Adam shook his head. "That's amazing. Speaking of amazing…" Adam picked up a large drawing. "These are wonderful. It's like you took what was in my mind and put it on paper." He set one down and then held the next up. After looking for a few minutes, he put them all back on the table and turned slightly toward her again.

"I had a thought and wanted to get your opinion." He now had her curiosity. "The whole downstairs of our building, we use it as storage. I could have it cleaned out, and you could set it up to have a design studio there. Plenty of room for you and twenty other designers. We could work together on projects. I draw the buildings, you collaborate on materials and details, I build, and you decorate the finishing details. We could be great together." He looked at her with big hopeful eyes.

She really liked the idea. She was completely giddy for a moment with a smile from ear to ear. And then her emotions sunk and her smile faded as reality took over. "That sounds wonderful. I would absolutely love to. But unfortunately, I'm here on a student visa. I'm not allowed to work or earn money." She rested her shoulder behind his.

Adam reached for her hand and laced his fingers with hers. He then leaned in and whispered, "Then I'll have to marry you. As my wife, and as an American citizen, you can work. Plus, I don't think my heart could take you leaving." He then kissed her cheek. She blushed and put her hand on her cheek, over his kiss.

"Adam, don't tease me," she whispered her reply and took a deep breath.

"Hey you two. Are we going to go downstairs and practice together? I've been practicing all week. I can't wait to hear what it sounds like with all of us," Jessie interrupted their little moment on the couch. Eve almost forgot for a moment that Jessie was even there.

She looked up at Adam and he had a big smile on his face. "Ready to get going? We only have tonight to practice." She watched as his smile lessened a little.

"I'm ready." He got up and held his hand out to help her up. Once she was up, he kissed her hand again, sending waves of warmth and goosebumps up her arm. He pulled her in for a hug and whispered again. "Maybe we can put the idea on a back burner for now and discuss it again later."

Eve was stunned for a moment. Was he actually serious? He couldn't be. They have only known each other for a few weeks. He is a wonderful man. Kind, thoughtful, and gives her feelings like she hasn't felt in a long time. She remembered the erotic dream she had after woken up from the night he brought her home. Her heart raced again. It can't be. He has to be teasing. It's too soon. She shrugged off the thought as he collected her drawings into a neat pile.

The movie room downstairs in the common area had a stage and five rows of five seats for twenty-five people. 'We could host parties right here,' she thought to herself. 'But none of us girls had any of the equipment,' she continued thinking.

Adam pulled out his phone and queued the song they would sing as a trio. At first, she stood to the far side, so Adam would be between her and Jessie. "Beautiful. Jessie singing in my ear will make it hard for me to stay on my notes. Do you mind being in the middle?"

She understood the need to separate the sounds. "I can do that," she answered as they switched places. Their voices started softly as the music started and then their voices grew as they relaxed. They repeated a few times, each time getting better, more comfortable.

"Let's run through one, just us, no music. That way we only hear our voices," Adam suggested.

"That's a good idea," Jessie seconded.

Eve bobbed her head yes. "However, we should stand in a circle. That way we can see our movements and sing at the same time." They all agreed and they made the adjustment. "1, 2, 3." After they belted through the song, they all agreed that they had it down.

"Jessie, would you mind giving us some privacy so we can practice our duet?" Eve lightly blushed as Adam was politely trying to get Jessie to leave. She was glad that Jessie would be gone, but mostly she could finally be alone with Adam.

"Sure. Right. I understand. Have fun you guys." He walked out of the room as Adam was making the next selection on his phone.

A slow song came on, but it was not the one they were singing. She was confused for a moment. Then he walked up to her and lifted both her hands and placed them on his shoulders. Her heart started pounding. "I don't recognize this song. What is it?" She blushed as he traced his fingers up her arms and down her sides until they came to a stop on her hips. Goosebumps covered her arms, and there was a hot trail where he had touched her.

"*I Wanna Know What Love Is*. It's sung by Foreigner." He leaned in and softly locked lips with her. He then pulled her closer, and she tightened her arms around him. All her thoughts were gone, and she loved it. The kiss continued as they started moving to the song.

I wanna feel what love is. I know you can show me.

The words played over and over until the song finished. He released the kiss and rested his forehead onto hers. A whimper of disapproval escaped her when he ended the kiss. Adam broke the silence. "I wanted to kiss you the moment I saw you, I just didn't want Jessie to see."

She smiled because she felt the same way. "It feels like forever since I last saw you. Would it be okay if we visited more frequently?" She gave a half-smile and started blushing again. "That came out odd, but I hope you know what I mean."

He smiled. "Yes. I would like to see you more often, also." He leaned back. "But right now, we should practice our song." She pulled him in for another quick kiss before getting back to practicing.

Entry 6: Karaoke – Apology, Trio & Duo

Eve and Adam had arranged to meet at 6, that way they could visit before Jessie got there at 7 p.m. She arrived with two of her friends 15 minutes early, so she signed Jessie up for the 7:15 slot for his apology song. She also claimed the 7:30 for the trio. That way they could regroup and have a couple of songs in between. Then she marked down the 7:40 for the duet. At the last minute, she decided to pick up the 8:00 for a single song. She hoped Adam would like it. It helped her to say what was in her heart when she got too nervous to speak.

She came off the stage and saw her security detail at the door watching her. She walked up to him with a bit of a huff. "Why are you inside? You're supposed to stay out of sight." She tapped her foot impatiently. She very rarely got angry, but she only tolerated being watched over for her aunt's peace of mind.

"Pardon my presence, Madame de Vogues. After the last time you were here, we felt it was more prudent to keep a closer eye on activities inside as well as outside. We were grateful that Mr. Stratford was able to step in when you needed help. We have already let the owner know about our required presence and he understands. Please be mindful of your drink tonight. When you leave to go up on stage, you always get a new one when you return." He stood at attention.

"That was a screw-up that my friends made. I forgave them. I don't feel threatened here. The only thing that's gonna be bad is an occasional off-key note. Keep your distance or I'll make you go up on stage and sing." She barked her frustration out and left.

She returned to the table where one of her friends now sat. Her anger must have been clearly written on her face. "What's wrong?" Stephanie asked. Eve took a deep breath and slowly let it out to calm herself.

"My aunt is being controlling. Sometimes, it just makes my life miserable. Family stuff, you know how that goes." She felt calmer having voiced her complaint but didn't want to go into details. "I'm going to get a water to drink. Do you want something?" Eve asked.

"No. Not yet. Thank you," Stephanie responded. Eve got up and went to the bar for her water.

As she waited, she heard a distinctive walk coming closer and she knew Adam was there. Her heart quickened in anticipation. She turned just in time for him to reach an arm around her and they locked into a deep kiss.

His other hand slowly followed her jawline and then entangled in her hair at the base of her head, pulling her in a bit more. Her hands reached up and pulled at his sides. Her cool body suddenly became a blaze of fire. Then he pulled back, leaving her wanting more. "Hello, Beautiful."

She gasped for breath, like it was her first in life and her heart pounded wildly in her chest. "Bonjour, Héros." She blushed and covered her face for a moment at calling him a pet name for the first time.

He leaned his head in and whispered into her ear, "I like it when you say it that way. I'll always be your hero." He then kissed her cheek. "You look so amazing in your long black dress. The large red flowers complement your hair."

She held his hands. "Thank you. You look stunning in your suit as well." He smiled. After a couple of moments of staring into each other's eyes, she said, "I was about to get a glass of water. You want anything?"

He nodded his head yes, held up his hand, and the bartender came over. "For the table, we need a round of waters, please."

They walked over to the table where Eve's other friends were arriving and Adam set down a tray of glasses. "I have already signed us up for our songs."

"Sounds good." He smirked at her. "I think I'll go sign up for one more." He lifted her hand and gave it a soft kiss. She blushed again at his touch. She watched as he walked away, enjoying the view of his backside. She then remembered her dream and started to wonder if they would get to that point sometime soon. Her skin felt hot, so she sat down and took a sip of water to cool off.

"Hey, Babe." She heard from behind her, and she knew the sound of Jessie's voice. She froze, and all her hair stood on end for a moment. She took in a quick breath, put on a smile, and turned to see him.

"Hello, Jessie. You're also early. Adam is on stage signing up for a song." She pointed to the stage. "I have already marked you down for your first two, but you still need one more." She paused. "Per our agreement." He held out his hand for her. She followed suit and allowed him to make the gesture. "Thank you, Jessie, for being gentle. It makes all of this easier." She sighed.

She felt her face smile, for real this time. "Of course. You look very nice tonight. The dress you're wearing makes your legs look so long." He smiled. "I'll catch up to Adam and sign up for my next song." He let go of her hand and she slowly lowered it back to her lap.

As he walked away, she wondered how much of his training would go beyond public manners and influence private behaviors. She took a deep breath in and slowly let it out. She knew deep down that it would take time to be able to trust him again without having the knee-jerk reaction to freeze.

Now that Jessie was here early, she also figured that Adam would probably show less public affection. She could understand how he would not want to rub it in. She blushed again, thinking of the kiss he just surprised her with. She didn't want to get stuck between them again, so she sat down next to Stephanie.

The group of girls was going on and on about patterns and colors, and all she could do was watch the guys on stage. Jessie stayed and Adam returned to sit next to her. Without a word, she leaned in as he wrapped his arm around her shoulder. She felt at peace. She laced her fingers with his and rested her other hand on his leg. She felt a tired wave and decided to rest her eyes for a moment. The sounds of music playing in one ear and his steady heartbeat in the other swirled in her brain before she fell asleep.

Adam

Adam arrived earlier than planned. He stood at the door, scanning the room as people were arriving. He noticed the added security inside as the bouncer nodded his head at him. He returned the gesture and continued to look around. Then he saw Eve's long red hair flowing with her long black dress. She was at a table but was getting up and walked to the counter. Adam was taken by surprise when the bouncer started talking to him.

"Hello. Nice to see you again." The man politely smiled.

"Hello. I didn't realize there was a need for extra security," Adam responded. The man frowned a bit as he continued to survey the room.

"Sometimes there needs to be more and sometimes less. Now is just one of those times we feel there needs to be more since we had a problem last time." Adam thought about the last time he was here. It seemed mostly peaceful.

"Was there a fight or something? That's not normal for a place like this." The man turned his head and looked at him. For a brief moment, there was a flash of something else in his appearance. Was it confusion?

"Our client was hurt. However, they love attending these kinds of activities, so our presence will be more visible here." Adam thought of Eve and her friends. She wasn't in mortal danger, but his heart pulled for a moment. The bouncer held out his hand and Adam shook it. "Have a good night, Mr. Stratford."

Adam smiled again. "You too." He walked a few steps away when it dawned on him. How did he know his name? He hadn't introduced himself. He stopped and looked back at the man. He was still surveying the crowd. Hmmm. He must be part of a private security team that had done work for one of his sites.

Adam continued to the counter. He didn't want to surprise and scare her, but he was determined to kiss her hello—the way he always wanted to. He had an hour of giving his undivided attention to her before Jessie should arrive, and then he would need to dial it back. She turned around as he arrived, and he didn't hesitate.

His heart was in his throat as he took her mouth with his. Now that he had started, he wanted more. He pulled her in, and her body responded to his touch by pulling him closer. He pulled back while he could. "Hello, Beautiful." He tried to calm his heart. She had a peaceful look on her face.

"Bonjour, Héros." She blushed and covered her face for a moment, then peeked at him over her fingertips. His heart raced again. She had claimed him with a personal name. He leaned his head in and whispered.

"I like it when you say it that way. I'll always be your hero." He then kissed her cheek. "You look so amazing in your long black dress. The large red flowers complement your hair." She moved her hands from his sides and held his hands.

"Thank you," she replied. "You look stunning in your suit as well." He smiled. He could see that she was calming down also.

"I was about to get a water. Do you want anything?"

He agreed with that. He would need to cool down also. He summoned the bartender. "For the table, we need a round of waters, please." He recognized some of the girls from last time when they arrived at the table. Stacy? Natalie? Amanda? Not like he was going to date them, but he really needed to be better with names.

"I already signed us up for our songs." He really liked how efficient she was.

"Sounds good. Think I'll go sign up for one more." He lifted her hand and gave it a soft kiss. He loved watching her blush at his slightest touch. He turned and went to the stage. Now he would be able to get a better time spot.

While onstage, he saw that she had signed up for an upbeat song. So, he followed suit and made his selection. After he finished writing, he stood up to look at Eve. Jessie arrived early and was approaching Eve. She looked nervous for a moment but then eased. He knew Jessie would not do anything stupid in front of all these people.

He then decided to sign up for one more later in the evening. A song to drive home the point. He was scrolling through songs on his phone and asked the technician if they had a specific version. He was happy that they did and marked his final choice as Jessie came up to the stage.

"Hey dude," Jessie greeted him.

"Good evening. It is going to be a busy night for us three. Are you ready?" Adam asked and handed him the pages for the open time spots.

"I guess as ready as I'm going to be. I'm nervous as hell. The song she picked is way out of my normal. But I understand why she picked it." Jessie smiled at him.

"Well, I'm heading down. See ya in a few." Adam excused himself so he could snag the spot next to Eve before someone else did. He slid into the seat, and she instantly snuggled into him as he wrapped his arm around her. God, she felt good to hold. She was testing his resolve when she entwined her fingers with his and rested her other hand on his leg. Dangerously close to getting a feel for his size, but she held still.

After a few minutes, he felt her body completely relax and her full weight leaned on him. He looked down and saw she was sleeping. This made him smile. She felt safe and comfortable enough to let her guard down and sleep. He knew she needed as much as she could get since she was an insomniac. He adjusted his position a little so her head wouldn't fall down.

One of Eve's friends got up to go on stage. That left an opening next to Eve, and sure enough, Jessie was coming down the steps, then walked directly to the open spot. Adam wouldn't be able to do anything about it for fear of waking his sleeping beauty. Adam held up his finger to his lips to indicate his silence was needed. Jessie nodded his head that he understood and quietly sat down.

It wasn't the hour he had envisioned spending with her, but he wouldn't trade it for the world. He relaxed and enjoyed all the performances while he had his arm around the girl he was deeply in love with.

"Beautiful. Can you hear me? It's time to wake up." She stirred a little. "You need to wake up, Honey. Jessie's going on stage to sing the song you chose." Adam felt a warm glow. He had always called her beautiful, but calling her honey just now felt right.

He pulled her hair back and softly kissed her lips. Her hands squeezed firmly where they had been resting for the last hour. And then she... 'Oh shit! God, please. Let me keep some control.' His brain cried out for mercy.

Eve

Eve heard Adam talking to her, but it felt like it was part of her dream. She was coming out of a wonderful music-filled sleep when she felt Adam kiss her. She loved waking up this way. His lips on hers, like that's where they belonged all along.

Her hands tightened on him and instinctively, she opened her mouth then licked his lip. Instantly, he dove his tongue into her mouth as the kiss went deeper. His weight shifted, and he was pushing his body onto hers as his free hand was pulling her body against his.

He leaned up and with both arms, he scooped her onto his lap without breaking the kiss. Both his hands now freely explored her back as she learned his. He pulled his head back and rested his forehead to hers. He was breathing heavily, and she could feel the rush of air against her face.

"I want to keep going," he gasped. "But we can't." He gasped again. "I can't," he said, out of breath.

She was breathing hard also as her body was getting ready for more. She could feel her undercarriage pulse in anticipation. He was right. This was not the time or place. She nodded her head and stood up. She stretched her arms out and then sat back down on his lap, but turned so she could see the stage.

"How long was I out?" she looked up at him. She could have kept on sleeping safely in his arms, she thought as his arms tightened around her.

"You were out for a solid hour. I only woke you up because Jessie is on next."

She smiled. "Thank you for not letting me miss this." She kissed his cheek and then wrapped her hands around his, which were now resting on her abdomen.

The group cheered as Jessie walked up, microphone in hand. He looked nervous and wasn't smiling.

She stood up and yelled, "You got this!" Jessie looked at her and smiled. "*When I Was Your Man,*" by Bruno Mars was displayed.

Same bed but it feels just a little bit bigger now

Our song on the radio but it doesn't sound the same

When our friends talk about you, all it does is just tear me down

'Cause my heart breaks a little, when I hear your name

Eve turned to Adam and held out her hand. "May I have this dance?" Adam popped up in a flash without a word, and together they were moving to the beat.

That I should've bought you flowers

And held your hand

Should've gave you all my hours

When I had the chance

Take you to every party

'Cause all you wanted to do was dance

Now my baby's dancing

But she's dancing with another man

"I picked this song on purpose to make a point to him. I hope you don't mind." Eve smiled as she rested her head on his chest. He just squeezed her tighter.

My pride, my ego, my needs, and my selfish ways

Caused a good, strong woman like you to walk out my life

Now I never, never get to clean up the mess I made

And it haunts me every time I close my eyes

It all just sounds like ooh-ooh, ooh-ooh

Mmmm, too young, too dumb to realize

That I should've bought you flowers

And held your hand

Should've gave you all my hours

When I had the chance

Take you to every party

'Cause all you wanted to do was dance

Now my baby's dancing

But she's dancing with another man

Although it hurts

I'll be the first to say that I was wrong

Oh, I know I'm probably much too late

To try and apologize for my mistakes

But I just want you to know

I hope he buys you flowers

I hope he holds your hand

Give you all his hours

When he has the chance

Takes you to every party

Because I remember how much you loved to dance

Do all the things I should have done

When I was your man

Do all the things I should have done

When I was your man

Eve stood up tall and pulled Adam into another soft kiss, but she knew to keep it under control. He then gave her a dip as she clung to his strong shoulders and then came back up. They ended their dance, and they both started clapping and cheering with the audience.

She walked over to the stairs. When Jessie came down, she smiled. "Thank you. As promised," she held her arms open for a hug.

He stepped in to close the distance and wrapped both his arms around her. She squeezed him for a couple of seconds and then gave him a kiss on the cheek before letting go. She grabbed his hand and led him back to Adam and then also grabbed Adam's hand. "Are we all good now?"

She looked back and forth between the two guys. They both nodded their heads yes and did a typical guy's fist bump. "Good! Now that's past us, I need to go talk to Mother Nature." She let go of both their hands and left them standing there.

Adam

Adam watched as she made her way to the restrooms. Jessie sat down, and he sat down next to him. He then saw the bouncer move in her direction. He said something to her, causing her to stop for a moment and then keep on going.

He didn't follow her to the restroom, but he didn't go back to his spot by the door; rather, he stayed right there. Glued to the floor again with his head constantly watching the room.

"Do you think she has forgiven me?" Jessie asked, breaking Adam's concentration.

"That hug was a big step in the right direction. I wouldn't be pushy, but I'd say you're on the right track." Adam was still watching. After a minute, the bouncer returned to the spot by the door and talked to an older gentleman.

Adam thought he might have been the owner, but he wasn't sure. Shortly after, Eve was on her way back. She looked happy. She leaned over both of them as she hugged them. "I'm gonna grab a new cold water. You guys want anything?" she asked as she picked up empty glasses.

They both looked at each other, then back at her and replied in unison, "Water, please."

She laughed. "Okay," she said and then walked over to the counter.

"I hope so. I've been such a fuck-up for too long. Thank you for your help," Jessie added.

"You're welcome. Why not try out your new skills on a new lady here tonight?" Jessie had a look of fear on his face. "What's wrong?" Adam had no idea what was rolling through Jessie's mind.

"I don't know how to start a conversation," Jessie smirked.

Adam laughed. "You're the king of starting conversations and getting a girl to join you. That stays the same. That part doesn't need any work." Adam looked at Jessie, and his stress started to ease.

Eve

Eve relaxed at the counter as she ordered four glasses, a pitcher of water and a large order of doughnut holes. She knew a little sweet treat would help with energy for the late night ahead. She leaned her back against the counter and watched the two men chat. She hoped that they would repair the rift that was in their friendship. It killed her a little to think that it was there because of her in the first place. That definitely was not her intention.

The bartender slid a tray her way. In a flash, she munched one down, then she was on her way back to the table. She set the tray in the middle and sat next to Adam. She picked up the cold glass and took several big sips. It felt good going down.

They sat in silence while listening to the music. Eventually, their group was called. She suddenly got butterflies bouncing around her belly. Perhaps she shouldn't have eaten the doughnuts. She kept reminding herself to breathe as her chest went up and down. She got up as the guys did, and they made their way up the stairs.

When they got to the staging area, she grabbed both their hands. "Thank you for making a dream come true." She wasn't lying. She had been wanting to sing this song since she heard it as a kid. She pulled both of them into a group hug. Oddly enough, after everything that had happened, this moment felt… great.

She let go, and they all took a step back. "Let's have some fun and kick this song's ass!" She bounced a little with excitement.

"For sure," Jessie said.

"Yes, we will," Adam added.

They were handed their microphones and were ready.

"Seven Bridges Road," by the Eagles displayed on the screen, and the crowd went wild. Several people were already jumping out of their seats and clapping. 'No pressure, right. Just breathe.'

There are stars in the southern sky.

Southward as you go

There is moonlight and moss in the trees

Down the seven bridges road

So far, their harmony was on point. The crowd was singing along with them. She was feeling good and getting into the song. Fortunately, it's a repeating note sequence. Now for the closing a cappella section...

There are stars in the southern sky

And if ever you decide you should go

There is a taste of thyme sweetened honey

Down the seven bridges road

The crowd exploded. They did awesome! She felt herself lose a higher note but came back on the next one strong. She handed her mic back to the stage manager and grabbed Adam's hand. Jessie walked down the stairs, but Eve held Adam back.

"We might as well stay here. There is one song break before our duet. Are you ready?"

He pulled her close and whispered in her ear. "For you, I'm always ready." He then lifted her chin and started kissing her. She felt her face heat up as she blushed hard. Was that meant to be a sexual comment? Or was he saying that he was just always ready to sing? Because sexually was how her body and mind received it.

'Oh lord, help me. I could see myself falling for him.' She pulled back this time, gasping and breathing hard. She reached up and touched his face. "Héros, if you keep kissing me...," She paused to breathe, "I'm not going to have the breath to sing." She let out a slow, steady breath. He lowered his head, and she placed hers against his. She could see him take a deep breath also.

"You're right. We need to concentrate." The stage manager came back to them with their microphones again.

"Okay. Let's have fun." She took a few more deep breaths herself and was preparing to belt this one out.

"At least I didn't have to learn to play the guitar," Adam said, making her laugh.

He took her by the hand, and they walked out. She couldn't stop staring at him. The music started, and she watched him. He was only there with her. She didn't face the crowd at all, and she couldn't hear anyone else.

"Shallow," by Lady Gaga and Bradly Cooper.

Tell me something, girl

Are you happy in this modern world?

Or do you need more?

Is there something else you're searching for?

I'm falling

In all the good times, I find myself longing for change

And in the bad times, I fear myself

Eve's heart was in her throat as she listened to him sing to her. It's not like it was a surprise. They'd been practicing. But tonight, in front of everyone else, it was like he was making a declaration.

Tell me something, boy

Aren't you tired of trying to fill that void?

Or do you need more?

Ain't it hard keeping it so hardcore?

I'm falling

In all the good times, I find myself longing for change

And in the bad times, I fear myself

I'm off the deep end, watch as I dive in

I'll never meet the ground

Crash through the surface, where they can't hurt us

We're far from the shallow now

Eve felt like her body was on fire singing with, and to him. And it was true. She was falling. Was he falling for her also? She smiled and pulled him in for a quick kiss. She didn't care if everyone saw.

They then made their way back to the table. She sat down, grabbed her glass of water, and held it up. "Ladies." She got everyone's attention from around the table, then held up her drink up higher. "It's safe to drink, right?"

They all laughed nervously and nodded. "Yes. It's safe," they all said. Eve turned and toasted her unwanted chaperone and chugged the water down before turning back to her group.

Damn, that was good for water. After belting out that song, her vocal cords were getting sore. She hoped she had enough for one more song. Fortunately, she had a little gap until her next song, which was more like talking loudly and some singing.

"I'll be right back," she whispered in Adam's ear and gave his arm a squeeze. She got up and walked up to the bar with the tray and empty pitcher. She needed something different to lubricate her cords better.

A moment later, an arm was wrapped around her waist and started pulling her. She turned, expecting to see Adam, but it definitely was not him. It was a scruffy-faced stranger with a foul, liquor-soaked breath, trying to get his hooks into her. She instantly started to push him away. "Get off me, creep!" She yelled loudly and continued to keep him at arm's distance, but he still clung to her arm and hip.

Instinctively, she sent a knee to the stranger's groin. He buckled a little, but his grip only tightened, causing her to wince in pain. All at once, Adam and Jessie tackled the man to the ground. The sudden separation sent her flying backward to land at the feet of onlookers that were standing behind her.

Her guard arrived and pulled her back to her feet and held her close. "Are you okay?" Eve nodded, then he turned and joined the boys. He tapped Jessie out, and he popped up to stand in front of Eve, with arms reaching backward to block her.

Her guard tried to restrain the man's arms and managed to get one cuff on, but the man became squirrely. With the extra room, Adam slipped in behind the stranger, crossed his legs around him, put him in a chokehold, and started to pull. The man suddenly stopped fighting.

"Adam, easy," she exclaimed. Adam looked at her and lessened his pull. Her guard quickly finished cuffing the man and grabbed him by the back of the shirt to haul him off. Jessie reached a hand down and helped to lift Adam up. Eve was no longer in danger but started shivering.

Jessie turned to look at her. "Are you sure you're, okay? You're shaking like a leaf." He wrapped his arms around her and tucked his head down to her shoulder. Adam came around and held her from the other side. Both of their warmth spread through her, and that helped to calm her down.

"Always here for you," Adam whispered.

"Me too," Jessie added.

In that moment, something new ran through Eve. She couldn't put her finger on it, but she knew this feeling was deep in her soul. It may have been odd at first. But now it felt right, to have both the guys holding her at the same time. "Thank you," she replied. They both leaned back when they called her name overhead.

"Jessie. I'm not ready to go up right now. Can you see if they can put me in a song or two later?" He let go of his hold and lifted her hand for a soft kiss.

"I will get it done." She smiled as he took off for the stage. There is hope for him after all.

She turned to face Adam. "You were wonderful. Thank you, Héros. The name fits you perfectly." She smiled and gave him a quick kiss. "I need to talk to the guard for a minute. See if I need to file a report." Her smile faded.

"I'll be right here with you." He kept his arm around her as they walked to the door. Two guards walked in and she stopped to stand taller. They bowed slightly. "Madame de Vogues, this is Martin. He will continue in my place while I process the assailant to jail."

She nodded her head. "Nice to meet you, Martin." He stepped forward and held out his hand. Eve accepted, and he firmly shook it, then stepped back. Eve had a warm wave travel up her arm, and she could feel the blush grow up her neck.

'Try to control the reaction,' she told herself before she asked. "Do I need to fill out some paperwork?"

"You should expect to receive a phone call or even an officer to arrive at your place to get your official statement." She nodded her head. "Mr. Stratford and Mr. Cooper as well."

"Thomas, will you be back, or will Martin follow me home?" She looked at Martin and started to blush again. 'Come on, girl. Get it under control. He works for you, for Christ's sake, and Adam is standing right here.' She mentally yelled at herself.

"Sorry, I do not know how long it will take for me to process the paperwork. So, plan on Martin, since he's your new regular night shift. Please excuse me." He bowed again, then returned to his car with the strange man in the back.

She didn't know why, but she held out her hand again. "Nice to meet you. Normally, everyone stays hidden. I guess tonight was one of those things, right?" He shook her hand again, but held on longer than last time, and his thumb softly rubbed her hand.

"It sure was. Glad we were posted on the inside tonight." He then released her hand and held it out for Adam. "Thank you for your assistance, Mr. Stratford. Also, please extend our thanks to Mr. Cooper." Adam shook his hand and nodded his head. He bowed slightly to Eve but maintained eye contact and smiled.

"Adam, I could really use a drink now." They started to walk back to the bar. "So, they are your security team?" Adam had that look of putting the pieces together.

"They are my aunt's way of keeping an eye on me. They watch from a distance. Good thing they were inside today. You were a pull away from popping that guy's head off his neck." She smiled and giggled.

Jessie caught back up as they were walking. "They moved you down, so now you're the one, right before Adam's song."

Eve smiled and reached a hand out and softly touched the side of his face. "Thank you for your help."

He reached up, lifted her hand, and planted a kiss on her palm. "Anything to protect you, Babe. I hope you know that." She smiled as they walked to the bar. Adam's arm was around her shoulder, and Jessie was still holding her hand.

They got to the counter, and she got the bartender's attention. "Can I get three shots of Jack, please?" She pulled out her card holder from her hidden pocket, and Adam placed his hand down on hers so she couldn't use her card. She looked at him, shocked.

"After everything, the least I could do is buy you guys a drink." Adam shook his head no.

"No way, Beautiful. Not anytime soon will I allow you to pay. You brought us dinner the other day and treats tonight. We owe you." He winked. That's when she noticed that Jessie had already paid.

She stomped her foot. "You guys!" She paused and felt her blush take over again. "Thank you." She gave Jessie a kiss on the cheek and then repeated the kiss for Adam.

They all sat at the table to relax for another half an hour before it would be her turn again. Adam's arm was up high on her back to her shoulder, and Jessie's arm was along the back of her chair and holding her side. She was half tempted to cancel her spot altogether because she was oddly comfortable sandwiched between the two guys. Such a stark contrast from earlier this evening.

Eve heard her name called. She leaned forward and stretched from her seat. Her back suddenly felt cold, and she slightly shivered. "Well, I guess it's time to sing and dance." She smiled. Adam stood up with her and grabbed her hand to hold as he led the way to the stage. She wasn't as nervous as last time. This song was going to be a fun one to sing. Adam gave her a kiss on the cheek and then sat on the bench for his turn.

"Bidi Bidi Bom Bom," by Selena y Los Dinos

She felt great getting to dance and spin on stage. The rhythm moved through her. Her feet shuffled for a solo Tango as she started to sing.

Bidi bidi bom bom

Cada vez

Cada vez que lo veo pasar

Mi corazón se enloquece

Y me empieza a palpitar

Y se emociona

Ya no razona .

No lo puedo controlar

Oh, y se emociona

Ya no razona

Y me empieza a cantar

Me canta así, así, así, así

Bidi bidi bom bom, Bidi bidi bom bom

Cada vez

Cada vez que lo oigo hablar

Me tiemblan hasta las piernas

Y el corazón igual

Y se emociona

Ya no razona

No lo puedo controlar

Y se emociona

Ya no razona

Y me empieza a cantar

Me canta así, así, así, así

Bidi bidi bom bom, Bidi bidi bom bom

Eve swayed her hips to the rhythm as she swung her arms around to Tango dance in circles.

Cuando escucho esta canción

Mi corazón quiere cantar así

Ooh, Bidi bidi bom bom,

Bidi bidi bom bom

Me canta así, me canta así

Cada vez que lo veo pasar, ooh

Mi corazón se enloquece

Cada vez que le veo pasar

Y me empieza a palpitar, así, así

Eve was out of breath from singing while dancing, but she felt great. The extra time to let her voice recover was what she needed. She enjoyed how people clapped along as she danced in the instrumental areas. Now she could sit back and relax. After she handed off the microphone, Adam reached for her hand and led her back on stage.

"What are you doing?" she looked at his grip on her wrist.

"It's my turn to dance," he replied and wiggled his shoulders. "I just need my dance partner." She blushed and joined him.

"Why Don't We Just Dance," by Josh Turner was shown on the monitor, and cheers erupted from the audience.

He spun her around and then held her from behind. She instantly blushed while remembering her intense dream. They started to sway to the rhythm. She loved being held by him. She always feels good in his arms.

Baby, why don't we just turn that TV off?

Three hundred fifteen channels of nothin' but bad news on

Well, it might be me, but the way I see it

The whole wide world has gone crazy

So, baby, why don't we just dance?

His velvet low voice sucked her right in and she loved the way it vibrated against her back.

Guess the little bitty livin' room ain't gonna look like much

When the lights go down and we move the couch

It's gonna be more than enough

For my two left feet and our two hearts beatin'

Nobody's gonna see us go crazy

So, baby, why don't we just dance?

Down the hall, maybe straight up the stairs

Bouncin' off the wall, floatin' on air

Baby, why don't we just dance?

Baby, why don't you go put your best dress on?

And those high-heeled shoes you love to lose

As soon as the tunes come on

On second thought, just the way you are is already drivin' me crazy

So, baby, why don't we just dance?

Down the hall, maybe straight up the stairs

Bouncin' off the wall, floatin' on air

Baby, why don't we just dance?

He would give her a spin and pull her back during the word breaks.

Well, it might be me, but the way I see it

The whole wide world has gone crazy

So, baby, why don't we just dance?

At the end of the song, he gave her a couple of extra spins, pulled her in, and then dipped her. But this time, he lifted one of her legs up, creating a very sensual feeling as their pelvises pressed together. When he pulled her back up, he scooped her up, claimed her lips, and carried her to the back of the stage. She giggled as he set her down. "That was fun. Thank you, Héros."

He smiled and whispered, "Beautiful, I really love the new name."

They started to walk offstage and paused as Jessie was coming up the steps. Eve saw his face was different, and she reached out to hold his arm. "Are you okay?"

He was quiet for a moment. He then looked at Adam. "Can I talk to her alone for a second?"

Adam nodded his head. "Sure." He walked down the steps and returned to the table.

"What's going on?" Eve asked. She could see him take a few deep breaths.

"I know you picked out my apology song that you wanted to hear. But this is the one I chose." She could see tears start to well up in his eyes, and she pulled him in for a hug.

"You don't have to do this. I can see that it's pulling you apart. Just cancel the song and come back to the table. We can talk about this another time when we are not surrounded by a ton of people." She tried to throw him a lifeline and save him some pain.

He shook his head, no. "I want to do this. So, you can understand me a bit better." He wrapped his arms around her, leaned down, and gave her a kiss on the cheek, then went to the waiting area. She watched as he was trying to calm himself. There wasn't anything she could do. She went back to the table with Adam.

"He's a mess. He said that he picked a second apology song. One that fit him better. I tried to convince him not to, but he said he wanted to. I hope he's going to be okay," she said to Adam as she sat down. Today has been a rollercoaster of a day. She wasn't sure if she could handle much more emotion. His song came up, and she heard the crowd say "Ooooh," as he walked up.

"The Reason," by Hoobastank

I'm not a perfect person

There's many things I wish I didn't do

But I continue learning

I never meant to do those things to you

And so, I have to say before I go

That I just want you to know

I've found a reason for me

To change who I used to be

A reason to start over new

And the reason is you

Eve couldn't control the tears, and she kept holding napkins to her eyes to clear her vision. She could see he was crying too, which just made her cry more. Adam moved in closer and rested his arm on her shoulder, and his fingers softly moved back and forth.

I'm sorry that I hurt you

It's something I must live with everyday

And all the pain I put you through

I wish that I could take it all away

And be the one who catches all your tears

That's why I need you to hear

I've found a reason for me

To change who I used to be

A reason to start over new

And the reason is you

Eve got up after her tears were under control and started walking to the front of the stage. Jessie sat down at the edge and held out his hand. She lifted her hand to his, and he bent over to kiss it. She felt hot again. Her heart pounded with a flood of feelings that took over her body. He let go of her hand, and she pulled back to finish watching him.

I'm not a perfect person

I never meant to do those things to you

And so, I have to say before I go

That I just want you to know

I've found a reason for me

To change who I used to be

A reason to start over new

And the reason is you

I've found a reason to show

A side of me you didn't know

A reason for all that I do

And the reason is you

Eve moved to the bottom of the stairs and waited. "Jessie, I can see how hard you are trying. You were already forgiven. But you were right. That song let me feel your side." She leaned in and hugged him, and for the first time in a long time, she didn't want to let go.

He tucked his head into her neck, and they held each other for a long moment.

He then pulled back. "I'm gonna get going. I need some quiet and to recoup." He lifted her hand and kissed it for the last time tonight. He then walked out the door without looking back.

She felt the heavy loss of his presence and started to tear up again. 'Just breathe,' she reminded herself. She blinked and wiped the tears away, then walked back to the table. "I think I'm ready to go home. It's been a heart-pulling day, and I'm feeling… overwhelmed."

Adam stood up and pulled her into a hug. "I'll take you home if that's what you really want. Just so you know, I have one more song to go. I picked it just for you."

She leaned back so she could see his face. "You really signed up for a fourth song?"

He nodded his head yes. She smiled a little more. He sat down and had her sit on his lap again. This time, she just rested her head down as she held onto his shoulders until they called his name twenty minutes later.

She released her hold on him, leaned back as he softly touched her cheek and she blushed at his warm touch. She leaned in for another soft kiss. He helped her up and then stood up himself, as they both stretched. It was getting late, but she was holding out for his last performance. Eve walked over to Martin.

"After his last song, I'll be heading home." He nodded his understanding and smiled. She returned to the table, sat down in Adam's warm chair, and waited.

"Make You Feel My Love," by Garth Brooks displayed on the monitor, and murmurs could be heard around the room. She was no stranger to his songs or having them sung to her.

When the rain's blowin' in your face

And the whole world is on your case

I would offer you a warm embrace

To make you feel my love

Evenin' shadows and the stars appear

And there is no one to dry your tears

I could hold you for a million years

To make you feel my love

I know you haven't made your mind up yet

But I would never do you wrong

I've known it from the moment that we met

No doubt in my mind where you belong

I'd go hungry, I'd go black and blue

I'd go crawlin' down the avenue

There ain't nothin' that I wouldn't do

To make you feel my love

Eve started to cry again. The song was so beautiful. She could tell he was singing right to her heart. He then started to come down the stairs, walked to her, knelt, and held her hand. He started to sing again, without looking at the monitor.

The storms are ragin' on the rollin' sea

Down on the highway of regret

The winds of change are blowin' wild and free

But you ain't seen nothin' like me yet

There ain't nothin' that I wouldn't do

Go to the ends of the earth for you

Make you happy, make your dreams come true

To make you feel my... love

He then slid in between her legs and pulled her into a kiss. It quickly deepened, and she knew what she wanted. She wanted him. Her heart pounded in her ears, so she couldn't hear any of the crowd. She was already soaking wet, and her core throbbed to the beat in her ears in anticipation.

She broke the kiss and whispered in his ear. "Take me home, Héros." She took another quick breath. "Now!"

Entry 7: At Eve's, Adam's Vow?

On the way to her place, the taxi driver got an eye full of them in the back seat. She just couldn't keep her hands off him as they kissed the whole way there. She practically bolted out of the car when it came to her stop. With Adam's hand in hers, she led him to her place.

She was so excited that she was fumbling with her keys. Adam reached for her hand, and she stopped trembling. He took the keys from her and opened the door. Eve stepped through the door, but he didn't enter. She noticed that his smile was gone.

She held her hand out for him, but he lowered his head instead. "Don't you want to come in?" she asked as she was starting to get worried.

"I do want to come in, but we need to talk first." Her heart sank, and she started to think that he didn't want her. A single tear formed and fell, but she couldn't move. She started to breath heavily.

"After all of this, you don't want to be with me?" Her voice cracked as she tried to get the words out. He looked up and placed his hand on her cheek to wipe the tear away with his thumb.

"I want to be with you. More than you could possibly know." He had sorrowful eyes. She was confused again and shook her head.

"You want to be with me… but you can't?" He nodded his head, yes. She took a step back. "I don't understand why. Please explain." She took a calming breath, stared at him, and held her ground until he spoke.

He leaned against the door frame. "I had some difficulties growing up." He paused. She could see he was searching for the words. "I decided to pull back from that part of my life until I was older." He looked at her. "Then later, I made a vow with God to wait."

Eve leaned back and tried to concentrate on what he was saying. She wasn't quite sure what he meant, but she understood the word vow, a promise to God. "I understand you have a promise to God. What does that mean for us?"

She took two steps forward to close the gap. "Can you come in and have something to drink? Water, coffee, or pop?"

His smile made her feel better. "Yes." She looked around and then back to him.

"Can you sit and talk or watch a movie?" His smile got bigger, and his hazel eyes pierced through her.

"Yes." She felt so warm when he looked at her that way.

She took a step back and pulled the door all the way open. "Please take off your coat and have a seat. We can keep on talking." He stood up straight and walked in. She knew he had been here before, but suddenly, her heart picked up again. "What can I get you to drink?" she asked as she walked into the kitchen.

"Water is fine, thank you." When she came back with the two glasses, he was standing in the middle of her tiny living room. He held his arms open for her. She set the glasses down on the coffee table and hugged him. "Thank you for understanding. I was so worried that it would scare you away."

She leaned back. "I'm still right here with my Héros." She wanted to kiss him, but at this point, she wasn't sure what to do. He lifted her chin, and she saw something amazing in his face and eyes. Was that… love?

Her heart raced again. She smiled and felt a blush roll up her neck. He leaned down and kissed her. There was so much heat; she thought her face might melt. She let out a small whimper as he pulled away and then set her head onto his shoulder.

"Please have a seat. I'll be right back." She pulled away from him, walked to her room and shut the door. Then a bad thought ran through her mind. Perhaps she should have left the door open and he could have watched her change. She giggled and shook her head.

That may be against his vow. She needed to get to the bottom of this and figure out where to go from here. She paused as she thought. She didn't want to lose him. She hung up the dress to get it dry-cleaned and noticed it was torn. The slit that went to her knee was now a foot longer. She would have to get that mended after it's shown to the officer.

Eve turned on the soft rock station and then exited the bedroom in her yoga pants and a long t-shirt. Adam got up and held out his hand for her to join him. She paused and looked up at him. He suddenly seemed so much taller without her platform heels on.

She recognized that he was being open about himself, so she was brave enough to come out with no makeup on. "Your freckles are beautiful. Just like you are." He kissed her hand and sat back down.

She stood there, still confused. "I need to know your boundaries. That way, I don't hurt your feelings by making you say no. And mine for expecting more and feeling rejected." She slowly sat down next to him.

He nodded his head. "In all my years, I haven't met a woman like you before. There is just something about you that gets my heart pounding. An almost uncontrollable need for more. But I fear that I won't be able to stop myself. And then end up hurting you in the process." He lowered his head a little and reached for the water for a sip.

"That's why we are talking now. To work this out. Open up our communication." She smiled. She could feel this tension in the room. "So, we can hold hands?" She asked as she placed her hand open on her leg. He intertwined his fingers with hers.

"Yes, and we can touch." He lifted his other hand and touched her face with his fingers, traced along her jaw and then into her hair. She got goosebumps all over.

"Mmmm, your hands on me always make me feel good. Even when I'm scared, mad, or sad. My body had never reacted this way before." She smiled and could feel her pulse quicken. "Can I sit closer if I want to?" She asked as she turned her body on the couch.

He placed her legs over his lap, and she leaned into his chest. He let go of her hand and wrapped it around her while the other softly moved up and down her legs. She tucked her arm around his back. "Yes. I love being close to you. It can speed my heart up or help calm it down."

She then rested her loose hand on his chest. "Can I touch you here?" His heat transferred to her hand.

He closed his eyes. "Yes, but I can't touch you there." She nodded and then stood up.

"Scoot over to the center." He slid over and smiled. She then rested one knee on each side and sat down on his lap, resting her arms around his shoulders. "Soft kissing is okay?" He reached his hands up her back.

"And deeper is okay." He pulled her in. She let herself melt into him while enjoying his mouth and tongue dancing with hers.

She pulled back this time, breathing heavily. After calming for a minute, she continued. "This we have all done before. How long do we stay here before progressing to more?"

He closed his eyes. "It's more about my self-control and being able to stop before I go too far. When we decide to take the next step, we will define new boundaries." He opened his eyes. "Time is up to us."

She leaned back a little. "What if I want all of you now?"

He quickly leaned up so they were face to face. "Are you ready to be my wife, now?" His eyes got big and he smiled.

Eve's mouth dropped open, but nothing came out. Did he really just say that, again? He said something the other day. Was he really asking, or was she just thinking he was kidding? He has to be kidding her. He can't tease her about these things. It's too confusing.

"That's how I know you're not ready for all of me." He placed one hand on her ass and one on her upper back and started kissing her neck. She felt wave after wave of heat as he made his way along her neck.

"Oh," she let out a soft moan and dug her fingers into him.

He pulled his head back and rested his back on the couch. "When I saw that man grabbing at you and you fighting him," Adam paused. "I saw red. It was reactive that I got him away from you." He leaned up and looked at her again. "I knew that if he hurt you, I would not forgive myself."

She touched his face softly, gave him a kiss, and leaned back for him to continue. "I was about to kill him, just for touching you. You called my name, and I instantly calmed down. Just your voice has that kind of effect on me."

She smiled, rested her head on his shoulder, and kissed his neck for a moment. "You have the same effect on me. I can feel your voice vibrate to my core. Plus, I know the sound of your walk. I heard you coming into the room today from the front door. That is how I knew when to turn around."

She got to thinking about the what-ifs. What if, by the end of her time here, she had to leave him behind? What if he decides that he doesn't want her? What if, in a few months, she's head over heels for him and he no longer even likes her? Shit. She's already falling for him. She sat up, and her heart and smile started to sink.

"What else should I know?"

He took a deep breath. "I think we covered all the basics." Her smile faded as her heart sank to her stomach. "So, we see each other a couple of times a week?" She leaned further back, and her throat clenched as she felt a sad wave swell inside her. "Keep our touching, holding, and kissing under control." Her heart thumped in her ears as she started to pant for air. "I don't have much time here." She squeezed her eyes shut. "So, at some unknown time in the future, we decide to get married or walk away from each other?"

She felt her whole body deflate at the thought, and tears started to prickle her eyes. She gasped for air, and she choked out her words. "I don't want to lose you." Her tears started flowing, and she stood up. "But if we are going to date for over a year just to go separate ways," she gasped and took a step back as she started to breathe heavier.

"I'd rather just end it now and save myself a worse heartache later." She took another step back. "I can return home in a couple of months instead. Because staying, knowing you are here, would be too hard for me to endure." She turned and walked to the kitchen, pressed her hands on the edge of the counter as she hung her head. Tears freely flowed down her face. She struggled to breathe and gasped and blew out her breath as she could.

She felt Adam softly place both his hands on her shoulders, then slide down her arms. He pulled her up and leaned her back against him. He wrapped his arms around her. She resisted the flow of tears, but she couldn't hold them back, even if she wanted to.

"I don't want to lose you either," he whispered. She could hear him breathing heavily, like she was. "I feel like I'm being ripped apart." He continued slowly. "Seeing you cry and walk away because of me is not something I ever want to see again." He squeezed her tighter and then eased up to turn her to face him, but she couldn't look him in the eyes, so she just kept her head down and eyes closed.

"We were talking about a future together, and then you became sad." She couldn't look at him and see the hurt, even though the pain isn't all about him. But losing him later would just kill her. "Are you hurting because of something I said?" She couldn't talk, so she shook her head 'no'.

"Hmmm, does it have to do with the feeling of love?" She breathed harder, and her tears fell faster. She nodded her head, 'yes'.

"Okay." He was quiet for a moment. "Do you feel love for me?" She paused as her heart jumped into her throat, then nodded, 'yes'.

"That's good. I've been in love with you since the first day I saw you. That was the reason why Jessie and I were fighting. I wanted to talk to you and get to know you, but he kept you busy, away from me, and kept on…, well, you were there. I don't need to re-live it. That's why I asked Jake for help."

Her tears stopped as she listened to him. Then she figured it out. Adam was the shy one Jake was talking about, not Jessie. She took a big breath in and slowly blew it out as her heart returned to mostly normal.

"Are you afraid or have a fear of being in a relationship?" She shook, 'no'. "Hmmmm." The room was so silent, she could hear his heartbeat. "Are you afraid of losing me because you love me?" Her tears instantly started falling again.

"Ah, I see now." He held her tighter. "Have you lost someone you loved?" She leaned into him but managed to nod her head 'yes'. In an instant, he scooped her up and carried her to her bedroom. He set her down on the bed and then came back with a tissue. He lifted her face and softly wiped her tears.

She finally opened her eyes and could see that he had been crying also. That pulled on her heart more, and tears started to well up again. This time she blotted her own eyes as he sat next to her.

"I think it's time for me to tell you about my sister. Elizabeth was my half-sister from my mom's first marriage. When I was 10, she was 20 years old and in college. There was a car chase. They had flattened his tires with spikes, but he kept on going."

Eve started bawling again because she already knew where this was going.

"The guy ended up crashing into a telephone pole. Well, the pole snapped and landed on the car Beth was in. She lived just long enough to call mom and say good-bye." Eve felt her throat clench again, and she held her breath. She wished she could have said goodbye, but was glad that Elizabeth had the opportunity to do so.

She looked up at him and was thankful that he had shared the story with her, but she couldn't stop the tears. "So, I spent several years in counseling. But, for me, what helped the most was writing notes or letters to her. Anything and everything. Good days and bad days. Eventually, I wrote less. Until one day I stopped. My grief process lasted about two years, but I was younger." Eve's breathing slowed, and the tears eased up also.

It was quiet again. Suddenly, he wrapped his arms around her and they flopped back on the bed. He wiggled a little and pulled her half onto him. "Let's not talk about going our separate ways again." He reached up and brushed her hair behind her ear.

"You just about killed me tonight. Let's agree to say that we are working towards marriage." She didn't know what to say. Was that his way of asking, again? "Can you say it?"

She looked at him for a moment, then whispered, "We are working towards marriage."

"Aw, Beautiful? I can barely hear you." She cleared her throat and leaned on him a bit more.

"We are working towards marriage," she replied louder.

He smiled. "That's music to my ears." They were quiet for a bit longer. She enjoyed having his arms wrapped around her as they just held each other. "I know opening up and talking can be painful. Just remember, we are here for each other." She smiled again as she buried her face in his chest. His hands were softly moving up and down her arm and back.

"Do you have any siblings?" Eve quickly pulled back, and her heart stopped. Tears instantly started to drip again. He reached up and pulled her into a bear hug. "Ah, the source of your pain. Can you tell me?" Eve nodded her head, 'yes'.

She then buried her face into his chest and took a few breaths to calm down. She moved so she could hear his heart and closed her eyes so she could let it out and not see his reaction.

"Nicolas, my brother." She took another deep, calming breath, but the tears fell onto his shirt. "He was always my protector. It was hard growing up an aristocrat since France became a democracy. I was always picked on, or I was just easy to pick on. But he was always there."

All she could do was breathe and listen to his heart. Strong and steady. "This next week is the anniversary. Plus, with everything else, I've been trying to control the emotional overflow." She kept on listening to Adam's heart. "It was a drunk driver going the wrong way on the autoroute."

Her breathing was heavy again as the tears flowed down her face. "My 16th birthday party became a memorial and I haven't wanted to celebrate my birthday ever since."

Adam leaned his head up. "Sorry to cut in, but your birthday is coming up in a few days?" Adam asked.

She nodded her head, yes. "Next Saturday is my 23rd." He stroked her hair.

"Clear your schedule for Saturday. I'm changing how we celebrate from now on. But please, continue," he asked. She took another deep breath and listened to his heart again.

"He was groomed since he was little to take over from our mother, to become the next Monsieur. He was trained in everything and even shadowed her to the required meetings. Then everything was dropped on me."

She wiped her face before continuing. "I moved in with my Aunt Sophia. My mother's younger sister and then changed schools. Most of my formal training changed to economics, land management, and so on. I found that I enjoyed re-designing homes."

She let out a frustrated sigh. "I took an academic gap, so my first year of university was when Covid shut everything down. I did all my training from home. When everything opened up, I could finally study here." She listened to Adam's breathing. It was steady. She looked up at him and noticed that he had fallen asleep.

She watched as he slept soundly with her in his arms. She decided to let it all out. She returned her ear to his chest to listen to Adam's heartbeat, then closed her eyes. "My parents also died in the same crash as Nic." She started to tear again. "I was afraid of being alone. An old spinster, like my aunt who never got married or had children. The de Vogues line would end because of my decisions."

She rested her chin next to his ear and whispered. "That's not going to happen because I'm in love with you, and I know you love me too." She smiled, then carefully got up and covered him with a light blanket. She gently untied his shoes and placed them next to his coat. She changed into pajamas, turned off the music and lights, then climbed back into his arms for the night.

Adam

The entire cab ride, Adam knew he would have to stop and tell her before it went too far. The thought was difficult since she hadn't stopped kissing him since he sang his song. Damn, it was too strong of a song. And then pulling her in, spread eagle, was the wrong move. Wrong message. But it felt so right being there between her legs. Shit, she makes me feel so good.

When they arrived at her place, she pulled him the whole way to her door. This must stop here. If I go in and she's this revved up, it will be all over. I hope she understands and won't be angry.

He braced his arms on the door frame and saw she was shaking. He held her hand steady and felt her arm shaking. It may be better if he opened the door and took the keys. After he unlocked the door, she swung it open and reached back for him, but he stayed planted where he was. His heart was sinking. Please don't hate me.

"Don't you want to come in?" She asked. He could feel the weight of the world crushing him.

"I do want to come in, but we have to talk first." He started breathing heavily. He had been trying to think of ways to start this conversation without hurting her feelings. He could see her expression changing, and he dropped his head.

"After all this, you don't want to be with me?" He looked up and saw a tear falling down her beautiful face. Shit, too late. She's already hurting. He placed his hand on her cheek and wiped the tear away with his thumb. Come on man. Like dad said. Be brave and honest. She's not psychic.

"I want to be with you. More than you could possibly know," he replied.

"You want to be with me, but you can't?" He could see the confusion in her eyes and her body shifted to a defensive position. He nodded his head, yes. She took a step back, and it felt like a stab to his already hurting heart. "I don't understand why. Please explain." She took a big breath and then stared at him.

He leaned his shoulder against the door, trying to figure out where to start. He pressed his lips flat. The beginning is probably the best. "I had some difficulties growing up." He paused and saw that she was still staring at him. She doesn't need to know his sexual history right now.

"I decided to pull back from that part of my life until I was older." He watched her to make sure she was understanding. "I then later, made a vow with God to wait." Adam took a deep breath and slowly blew it out. It's done. It's now all out there. The rest is up to her.

"I understand you have a promise with God. What does that mean for us?" She still looked confused but closed the gap. "Can you come in and have something to drink? Water, milk, or coffee?"

He could see that she was trying. That made him smile. "Yes."

She looked around and then back to him. "Can you sit and talk or watch a movie?"

He felt better knowing that she was not angry. "Yes."

She backed up and made room for him to come in. "Please take off your coat and have a seat. We can keep on talking." He stood up straight and walked in. His heart felt lighter and the weight of the world was lifting off his shoulders. "What can I get you to drink?" She asked as she walked into the kitchen.

"Water is fine, thank you." He hung his blazer on the hook but didn't sit down. He decided to wait for her. When she came back with the two glasses, he wanted to hold her again. He held his arms open for her to join him. She set the glasses down on the coffee table and hugged him. "Thank you for understanding. I was worried that it would scare you away."

She leaned back. "I'm still right here with my Héros." He could see the longing in her; however, she restrained herself. He didn't want that. He lifted her chin up and could see her blush was growing. He leaned down and kissed her. Everything was right again and his heart started to race again with the contact. She groaned as he pulled away and then set her head onto him. "Please have a seat. I'll be right back." She pulled from him and walked to her room and shut the door.

She was only gone for a few minutes, but it felt like forever without her touch. He could hear soft music playing and then Eve exited the bedroom in casual clothes. Adam got up and held out his hand for her to join him. He then noticed that she had also removed all her makeup. All her natural beauty was out for him to see. "Your freckles are beautiful. Just like you are." He kissed her hand and sat back down.

"I need to know your boundaries. That way I don't hurt your feelings by making you say no. And mine for expecting more and feeling rejected." She sat down next to him and all his nerves excited on that side. He understood what she was needing.

"In all my years, I haven't met a woman like you before. There is just something about you that gets my heart pounding. An almost uncontrollable need for more. But I fear that I won't be able to stop. And then end up hurting you in the process." He let the truth flow. His throat became dry, and he reached for the water for a sip.

"That's why we are talking now. To work this out. Open communication." She smiled at him, and he melted.

"So, can we hold hands?" She placed her hand on her leg, palm up.

He's always going to need to touch her. He placed his hand on hers and quickly laced his fingers with hers. "Yes, and we can touch." He moved his other hand and touched her face with his fingers. He loved the curves of her face.

"Mmmm, your hands on me always make me feel good. Even when I'm scared, mad, or sad. My body has never reacted this way before." Her smile filled him with joy. He was glad that they were talking this way. Simple and clear. "Can I sit closer if I want to?" She asked, and he moved her legs over his lap.

She rested on his chest, and he moved to wrap an arm around her while his other hand was free to touch. She shifted her body to hug him. "Yes. I love being close to you. It can speed my heart up or help calm it down."

She then pressed a hand on his chest. "Can I touch you here?"

He closed his eyes. We are getting to a real boundary now. "Yes, but I can't touch you there." She nodded and then stood up. "Scoot over to the center." He smirked as he slid over. Now she's going to start pushing his boundaries. Fuck, fuck, fuck. When she straddled him, his body instantly responded to the closeness. She locked her arms around his shoulders.

"Soft kissing is okay?" The look on her face was already driving him nuts. He softly traced his fingers up and down her back.

"And deeper is okay," he added and pulled her in. He claimed her mouth and thrust his tongue in to move with hers.

She pulled back this time, and he fought back against the need for more. He panted for a moment. "It's more about my self-control and being able to stop before I go too far."

She seemed to be taking this all-in good stride. "How long do we stay here before progressing to more?" He closed his eyes, trying to think of the words so she would understand. "When we decide to take the next step, we will define new boundaries." He opened his eyes. "Time is up to us."

She leaned back a little. "What if I want all of you now?" He was shocked, excited, and eagerly leaned up.

"You ready to be my wife, now?" He smiled while pleading inside that she would say yes. But, Eve's mouth opened, and nothing came out. Her lack of words was all he needed to know. "That's how I know you're not ready for all of me."

He placed one hand on her ass and one on her upper back and started kissing her neck. He loved hearing her moan in response to his touches, and then she dug her fingers in, sending a jolt of sexual energy through him.

He started thinking about that man touching her tonight. He pulled his head back and rested on the couch. "When I saw that man grabbing at you and you fighting him…" Adam paused. "I saw red. It was reactive that I got him away from you." He leaned up and looked at her again. "I knew that if he hurt you, I would not forgive myself." She softly touched his face and then gave him a quick kiss. She leaned back and remained silent.

"I was about to kill him, just for touching you. You called my name, and I instantly calmed down. Just your voice has that kind of effect on me." She smiled and rested her head on his shoulder. She placed little kisses on his neck for a moment.

"You have the same effect on me. I can feel your voice vibrate to my core. Plus, I know the sound of your walk. I heard you coming into the room today from the door. That is how I knew when to turn around."

She sat up suddenly. "What else should I know?" He took a deep breath.

"I think we covered all the basics." He saw her smile fade, and he instantly knew something wasn't right.

"So, we see each other a couple of times a week?" She leaned further back. "Keep our touching, holding, and kissing under control." She looked like she was starting to hyperventilate. Was she having a panic attack? Was this too much all at once?

"And at some unknown time in the future, we decide to get married or walk away from each other?" She looked sad, and he could see her tears were growing. She gasped in air, and his heart sunk when she barely whispered. "I don't want to lose you." Her tears started flowing, and she stood up.

'Shit, don't walk away, please don't,' was all he could think for a moment. "But if we are going to date for over a year just to go separate ways…" She took a step back, and his heart was breaking. "I'd rather just end it now and save myself a worse heartache later." She took another step back, and he felt like he was being crushed into the couch. "I can return home in a couple of months instead. Because staying here knowing you are here would be too hard for me to endure."

'Please don't leave me, please don't leave me,' he kept repeating in his mind.

She turned and walked to the kitchen and leaned against the counter.

Tears filled his eyes, and they overflowed, but he couldn't concentrate on that right now. Something isn't right here. Something is wrong. How do we go from talking about a future to walking away from each other? I have to get her to talk to me and figure out what's really going on. It took all his energy to get up off the couch. Just a few steps to her, and he softly placed his hands on her shoulders.

He needed to hold her, so he slid his hands down her arms. He softly pulled her up, leaned her weight onto him, and he wrapped his arms around her. She was crying as much as he was. "I don't want to lose you either," he whispered. She was still breathing heavily. "I feel like I'm being ripped apart."

He continued slowly. "Seeing you cry and walk away because of me is not something I ever want to see again." He squeezed her tighter and needed to see her reaction, so he turned her to face him.

She kept her head down and eyes closed, making it difficult. "We were talking about a future together, and then you became sad." He wasn't getting any response from her. This is going to be harder than he thought. "Are you hurting because of something I said?" She still didn't respond, but she shook her head 'no'. Well, at least she's still communicating.

"Hmmm, does it have to do with the feeling of love?" Her body responded with harder breathing, and her tears fell faster. She nodded her head 'yes'. "Okay." He was thinking for a moment of which direction to ask. "Do you feel love for me?" There was a pause for a moment, and then she nodded 'yes'. The weight of the world lifted from him again.

"That's good. I've been in love with you since the first day I saw you. That was the reason why Jessie and I were fighting. I wanted to talk to you and get to know you, but he kept you busy, away from me, and kept on… well, you were there. I don't need to re-live it. That's why I asked Jake for help." Thinking about the situation again was not the path he wanted to talk about right now.

He started to wonder if a previous boyfriend hurt her ability to love. "Are you afraid or have a fear of being in a relationship?" She shook 'no'. "Hmmmm." About love, but not a boyfriend. Then he wondered if she had recently lost a family member. Someone she really cared about. "Are you afraid of losing me because you love me?" Her tears instantly started falling again.

"Ah, I see now." He held her tighter. "Have you lost someone you love?" She leaned into him but managed to nod her head 'yes'. He needed to get her to sit down. He scooped her up and carried her to her bedroom. He set her down on the foot of the bed. He grabbed the tissues from the living room and then came back to her. He lifted her face and softly wiped her tears. He grabbed a couple for himself and cleared his face. She needs to know that he has experience here so she can open up and talk.

"I think it's time for me to tell you about my sister. Elizabeth was my half-sister from my mom's first marriage. When I was 10, she was 20 years old and in college. There was a car chase. They had flattened his tires with spikes, but he kept on going." Eve started crying again, but he needed to keep going. "Ended up crashing into a telephone pole. Well, the pole fell and landed on the car Beth was in. She lived just long enough to call mom and say goodbye."

He took a couple more deep breaths. "So, I spent several years in counseling. But, for me, what helped the most was writing notes or letters to her. Anything and everything. Good days and bad days. Eventually, I wrote less. Until one day I stopped. My grief process lasted about two years, but I was younger."

Eve's breathing slowed, and the tears slowed again. Of the five stages of grief, she had already moved through denial, anger, and bargaining, but she was stuck in depression. She will need lots of care to move on to acceptance.

He was getting tired and wanted to hold her again and for her to hold him. He wrapped his arms around her and they flopped back on the bed. He scooted up to get his feet on the bed and then pulled her up to him.

"Let's not talk about going our separate ways again." He reached up and brushed her hair behind her ear. "You just about killed me tonight. Let's agree to say that we are working towards marriage," Adam said. She was quiet and not responding. "Can you say it?"

She looked at him for a moment, then she whispered, "We are working towards marriage." Adam wanted her to say it with more conviction.

"Aw, Beautiful? I can barely hear you." She cleared her throat and moved closer.

"We are working towards marriage," she replied. He smiled back at her.

"That's music to my ears." They were quiet for a bit longer. He enjoyed being able to be this close and to be learning about each other. Plus, she felt good to hold in his arms. "I know opening up and talking can be painful. Just remember, we are here for each other." She smiled again as she buried her face in his chest. He softly moved his fingers up and down her arm and back.

He had shared about his sister and was wondering, "Do you have any siblings?" Eve suddenly pulled back, and tears instantly started to drip again. There it is. He reached up and pulled her into a hug. "Ah, the source of your pain. Can you tell me?" Eve nodded her head 'yes'. She then buried her face into his chest and took a few deep breaths. She seemed calmer now and repositioned as Adam had a sleepy wave roll over him. He fought to stay awake since he's not used to staying up this late.

"Nicolas, my brother." She took another deep breath. His shirt was starting to get wet, but he didn't dare move. "He was always my protector. It was hard growing up an aristocrat since France became a democracy. I was always picked on, or I was just easy to pick on. But he was always there." She paused and he waited quietly. "This next week is the anniversary. Plus, with everything else, I've been trying to control the emotional overflow." She paused again. "He was killed by a drunk driver going the wrong way on the autoroute." Her breathing was heavy again. "My 16th birthday party became a funeral and I haven't wanted to celebrate my birthday ever since."

Adam suddenly popped awake. "Sorry to cut in, but your birthday is coming up in a few days?" Adam asked wide-eyed, trying desperately to stay awake.

She nodded her head yes. "Next Saturday is my 23rd."

He yawned and then tucked her hair back. "Clear your schedule for Saturday. I'm changing how we celebrate from now on. But please, continue," he asked as he closed his sleepy eyes.

He listened to how her brother was supposed to take over from his mother. For a moment, he felt bad that sleep was taking him, before she was done talking.

He woke up sometime in the night. It was still dark outside. He still felt Eve in his arms, but she was wearing something silky now. His hand slowly moved up and his finger tips found the straps of what felt like a camisole top. He slowly slid down to her ass and found the same silky bottoms. However, there was a lace border and it felt like a booty-style bottom.

He enjoyed exploring her smoothness when he realized his shoes were no longer on his feet. Did he kick them off or did she take them off? He must have fallen asleep hard. It was a long day, and she was used to being up with less sleep, not him. He moved her to be on him more so he could stretch the arm she had been lying on this whole time. That's going to take some getting used to. If he's going to be sleeping and spooning, he will have to learn not to toss and turn.

But, then again, who would want to move much with beauty sleeping in your arms?

Eve

Eve woke up as the sun was rising. She had forgotten to shut the curtains, so she sneaked out of bed to close them. When she returned, she had a wicked idea. He looked like he was sound asleep and hopefully he wouldn't wake up with her moving.

She climbed back into his arms but faced away. She bent his underarm to hold her, but had lifted her shirt, so his hand was cupping her breast. She slowly moved his upper arm across her belly.

She held still for a minute, just in case he awoke. She listened to his breathing and it stayed even. She then slipped her foot under his leg and had to pull his leg over a bit. She paused and slid her leg through and tucked his ankle back. His leg now held her leg open, completely opening her pelvis. She paused again. Waited and listened.

When she was convinced, he was not going to wake up, she lifted the front of her shorts and slid his hand down onto her bush. She wanted to see what he would do. Would he pull back? Explore? Or just stay still? She closed her eyes and let her body relax. She concentrated on his steady breathing and it helped her to fall back to sleep.

Adam

Adam was having an excellent dream of exploring Eve's soft body. He'd had several before, but this one was more intense. Her silk pajamas rubbing on his skin added to the sensation. His hand slowly rubbed her ample breast. Her body pressed against him in response to his movement. He ran his thumb across her now excited nipple and then gave it a soft pull and twist.

Eve moaned, arched, and placed a hand over his. Her hand felt so silky as he continued. "Adam," she slowly moaned out. That encouraged him to keep going. His other hand had already found its way to her wet needy pussy. He spread his fingers and found her excited clit. He softly stroked his finger back and forth against it, and her body jolted into him.

"Ohhh, yes." Her sounds encouraged him to go farther. He moved his finger lower to get wet, then he dove in and out as he pinched her nipple at the same time. Eve's other hand landed on his. "Oh, Adam," she moaned louder, and then her fingers dug into him. "Adam." Her body arched harder against his chest, and she moaned louder again.

He opened his eyes and realized he wasn't dreaming. He had his hands across the border and stopped. She reached up and twisted her fingers in his hair. "Please, Adam, don't stop. I was about to cum," she begged and pulled him into a kiss.

He didn't know what to do. Stop and let her down, or keep going and risk not being able to stop himself? She felt so good in his hands. So responsive to his touch. Shit, he wanted her so badly that he was molesting her while she was sleeping. But she's not sleeping now, and she's about to cum because of him.

Fuck! He broke the kiss. "Cum for me, Beautiful." He fully squeezed her breast, pinched and twisted her nipple again while he slid his finger in and out faster now.

"Adam!" she moaned again and pushed her hip into his hand to make the thrust harder. Adam's need was taking him as he claimed her neck with his lips. He moved his wrist angle so his thumb could rub her clit and slid three fingers in and out. "Oh God," she exclaimed.

"Cum for me." Her wetness echoed in the room with each thrust of his wrist. She arched hard. "Yes, Adam, yes!" she exclaimed loudly. Her body pulled tight on his fingers for a few seconds, and then her whole body relaxed against him.

'Stop now!' he yelled at himself. He leaned forward and kissed her neck, then moved his leg that had hers pinned open. He removed his hand from under her top and backed his fingers out of her soft, wet core. Her scent filled his senses, and he couldn't resist the urge to taste her. He sucked on his fingers and swirled his tongue to collect all of her juices. "Mmmm. Damn Beautiful, you taste so good first thing in the morning," he said after he finished licking his fingers clean.

She turned to face him. "I know that was past your line, but that was the best wake-up I've ever had. Thank you for not stopping." She gave him a quick kiss, pulled away, and touched her lips. "I've never tasted myself before." She smiled.

He didn't want her to go. He wanted to eat her dry. But it was for the best. She sat up and walked to the closet. That's when he saw the dark marks on her arm.

"What is that?" he pointed to her. She spun around in a circle but didn't see what he was talking about. He got up to take a closer look at her arm and noticed the marks were going all the way around. "That asshole left a hand-shaped bruise all the way around your arm." Adam was getting mad.

"Adam, easy," she said softly. He relaxed a little and sat back down on the corner of the bed. "I'm sure you left an arm-shaped mark all the way around his neck. Take some pictures on my phone, and I'll send them in with the report." He nodded his head yes and was still calming down. "Besides, it doesn't hurt much compared to my hip. Is it bruised also? I can't see back there."

She pulled her shorts halfway down to bare her ass. He probably would have lost control right then, had it not been for the huge bruise that was bigger than his whole hand. "He did this also?" He was getting angry again.

"Well, not really. I was pushing hard to get away. When he finally released, I went backward."

Adam's held his breath as his heart sank. "I did this to you." He breathed out and felt awful for hurting her.

She turned and softly pushed him on the bed and then climbed on top. "You didn't do it to me. Gravity and Newton's third law did. What you did was save me from that creep." She started kissing him, and he could tell she wanted more, but she pulled back. "He did rip my dress, but it can be mended." She smirked with an evil twist to her face.

"It's probably way past your boundary, but I'm gonna take a quick shower." She raised an eyebrow and then leaned in to whisper. "You're more than welcome to join me." She gave him a kiss on the cheek and then backed off the bed and grabbed the clothes she had selected.

As much as he wanted to, that was a hard no. He closed his eyes. Two wet, naked bodies, pressed against each other. Nothing stopping him from pushing her up against the wall, no boundaries… 'Stop, stop, stop,' he reminded himself. Fuck, this was going to be harder than expected. "Adam?" she called from the bathroom.

His body wanted to dive right into hers. His need to dominate her body was overwhelming and his body quivered in anticipation. He refocused his attention. "Yes, Beautiful?"

"Were you going to take some pictures?" Her voice echoed from the bathroom.

Oh. Right. Pictures for her police report. "I'm coming." He didn't know where her phone was, so he grabbed his from his blazer, and look, Eve put his shoes right next to the stand. She's so wonderful.

Then he went back to the bathroom, and she was standing there, naked. "Holy shit!" he exclaimed and closed his eyes.

"Adam, my gentleman. You're here to take pictures, not touch. Right?"

He wanted to do so many things but all his energy was to keep him rooted in this very spot. He bobbed his head. "Yes."

"Then open your eyes and concentrate." He stared at the floor as he got the camera ready. When he slowly looked back up, she had a small towel wrapped around her. That made it easier. He took a good look around but didn't see any other marks. He took several pictures of each deep blue area, some with her hand in for size reference.

She then looked at him with a curious face. "Thank you. But you used your phone. Could you send those to me? Please don't share those images with your friends."

He shook his head. "I wouldn't think of doing something like that to you. I'll send those now and order some breakfast." He smiled and left as she started the water. He wanted something else for breakfast. But he knew, soon enough, she would catch up, and then it would be an all-he-can-eat Eve buffet.

Entry 8: Girl Talk

Eve had been glowing all weekend after Adam stayed the night. She had him on her mind all the time. However, there was a big gap in their school and work schedules until they could see each other on Saturday. There were early morning calls, texts throughout the day, and evening chats. All were basically boiling down to the same conversation.

They missed each other and were looking forward to when they could see each other again. Even though she protested, he had made plans to spend the whole day together for her birthday. She would love to just stay under the covers all day. He agreed but insisted because he already had something planned. At some point, she would need to explain her religious beliefs.

Eve also needed to schedule time away from class for her current project for 'Mr. Stratford's office.' That way she could wrap up and do her presentation. Adam said he would have a ton of the office crew there for the meeting. But for now, she needed to get permission to be gone for the day. It would be weird to be there without Adam; however, Mrs. Ophelia would be there if she needed anything.

Eve knocked on the teacher's door. "Hello, Mrs. Johnston?"

"Come on in," she replied as Eve peeked in. She was looking over display boards from other student submissions. "Oh, Eve. Please come in and sit down. How's it going with your current project?" A courteous look was on her face.

"Well, that's what I've come to talk to you about." Eve swallowed hard as her heart quickened.

Mrs. Johnston set the board down and looked down her nose at her. "You've got a problem that needs our attention?"

Eve shook her head. "Nothing like that. I need to take a day off from class so I can see the office environment at full capacity. This way, I can also get some employee insight on their office needs."

Mrs. Johnston's smile grew again, and she responded with her best British impersonation, "Top notch, Dear Eve." They both laughed a little. "Just fill out the planned absentee form for the day you need and submit it by the end of today for me to approve. When are you looking at doing the presentation?"

"I can visit next Monday, the 3rd of October. After time for adjustments and 3D rendering, that will land the final presentation about the middle of October because he wants to coordinate with some of the staff to be there."

Mrs. Johnston nodded her head. "Sounds good. I look forward to seeing your finished work." They said their goodbyes, and Eve was practically skipping down the hallway.

When she got back to her desk, Stephanie was occupying her chair. "Hey, Stephanie. Can I help you?"

Stephanie spun the chair until she was facing her. "You sure can, because we all want to know. How are you are juggling two guys at one time?" she asked and then laughed.

Eve's eyes went big, and then she started laughing. "Well, to make things clear, Jessie turned out to be a jerk, like you warned me about. After getting his face hit twice in a single evening, he started making changes. So, hopefully, the next girl in his life will get the nice guy that I know is in him." Eve smiled.

"He blew it? Wow, that was fast." She pressed her lips together. "His song choices make more sense now." Stephanie strummed her fingers on her lips.

"You guys were the ones to point it out to me in the first place."

Stephanie tipped her head in confusion. "What happened?" she asked.

"That flop of a date where I was singing a song about making me feel like the only woman."

Stephanie nodded and scratched her head as she thought back, then her eyes went up. "Oh, yeah. Rihanna. That's right." She waved her finger in the air.

"You guys pointed out that Jessie had his face in his phone the whole time and that Adam couldn't take his eyes off of me." Eve shrugged her shoulders. "Well, that's the path I'm taking." They were both quietly smiling.

Eve pulled up another chair. "Stephanie, I have a different question to ask. But please keep it quiet."

"What's up, Girly?" Stephanie whispered as she leaned closer.

Eve paused, trying to find the words. "You know, I sometimes have translation misunderstandings."

"Yes, I understand learning a new language has its challenges."

Eve shook her head as she smirked. "Usually, it's the slang that I don't understand. But Adam and I were talking. Well, we were discussing the future." Eve blushed.

"Well, now you have my full attention." Stephanie leaned even closer.

"It was just a few days ago. The evening of karaoke and everything that crazy evening included. Well, after Adam finished his song, I told him to take me home." Eve raised her eyebrows.

"Oh, yes. I like where this is going." Stephanie wiggled her eyebrows and smiled.

"Anyway, when we got to my place, I was ready, but he put on the brakes."

Stephanie had a shocked look on her face. "What? He did, what?"

"I know. He was telling me he had a vow with God and that he couldn't proceed. What does that mean?"

Stephanie had huge eyes, and her mouth was slightly parted. She cleared her throat before continuing. "It means that he is waiting— saving himself sexually until marriage. That's rare these days for a guy to be celibate who's not a priest. It usually means that he is a virgin."

"Oh." Eve leaned back and absorbed the information. She's going to have to go slower than she thought. She's damn lucky she tricked him. But he was so good at it. She didn't have to coach him at all. He knew just how to move to make her...

"I don't think he's a virgin. His fingers knew how to make me orgasm." Stephanie laughed loud enough for everyone to hear and look at them. "Shhh." Eve held her finger to her mouth.

"It's usually the virgins who are the best at foreplay because, afterwards, that's where they stop. But just expect to be giving him a little guidance down the road." Eve nodded her understanding. This will be the opposite of the Jessie situation.

No wonder he is so shy in the beginning. But once he gets going, he makes her body sing. A quick flashback rolled through her mind. Perhaps that's why he asked if she was ready to be his wife. He *really* wants to be with her.

"And, yeah, Girly. You need to get your mind out of the gutter because we see you blushing all the damn time," Stephanie said with a knowing smile as she pointed to my red face. "Just a piece of advice. Go to an adult store and get a new toy. That way, after visiting with him, you can burn off the pent-up sexual energy." Eve thought about it. That's not a bad idea. She will need to use cash so her aunt can't see the purchase on the card.

Stephanie got up to return to her own desk. "If you want me to take that handsome virgin off your hands, let me know." She laughed as she walked away.

Eve just smiled and shook her head. "No, he's all mine."

Later that evening, she crawled into bed with her new purchases. She pulled out the new journals. On the outside, she wrote in calligraphy, "To My Mother, Father, and Brother." She blew on the ink to make sure it fully dried before continuing. Her mind was going in several directions. How to start? How to recap? She figured, from the beginning would be a good start.

To those I have loved and lost.

It's been almost 7 years to the day since the last time I heard your voices. I miss you three. This week is always the hardest for me. The first couple of years were difficult. Aunt Sophia did her best considering the situation. I don't think she was prepared to take over the responsibility of the house requirements—let alone a sad, lonely, moody teenager.

Moving to her home and changing schools did stop the bullying, and I made friends. I didn't know it at the time, even though I was in weekly counseling, my core friends became my lifeline and support group. Most of them I still chat with to this day.

I took an academic gap before college. That way, I could get some problems that had arisen settled with the estate. I had started my first year of formal training in London. A couple of boyfriends came and went. Well, mostly went, but I'll talk about that later. Just as life started to feel normal again, the whole world went and got sick with COVID.

I then did the rest of my training, isolated again. I finished my program and had the opportunity to come to the United States of America. More or less the same class, but different styling, and I get to work on my English more, since I only spent a few months in England.

Mother, I thought while I was here, I could find a husband like you did with Father. I just wish I had known in more detail how you guys actually met. I had read an article about a plastic and rubber manufacturer, and a small part of the print talked about his son, who was studying to become a lawyer. I basically stalked the guy and organized it so that we would 'bump' into each other. It was successful. We even went out on a couple of dates. But he was a jerk and lost my favor.

His roommate, Adam, turned out to be a wonderful gentleman. I know. I can hear all your Adam and Eve jokes now. But seriously, it has been a crazy few weeks with friends and drunk strangers. Through it all, he has proven himself as my protector. I sure hope it works out well. I think Father would approve of him. He even calls me Beautiful, just like Father always did with you.

Anyway, I'm gonna go for now. I miss and love you.

Chat with you all soon.

Eve

Eve got up and put the journals on the shelf at her desk. She set her hand on the heart-shaped locket around her neck and remembered the day her mother gave it to her. She also remembered when Curtas stole it in third grade, but he returned it at the funeral. She sighed a bit at the memory and then opened the locket to see her parents' pictures on the inside. She smiled and then traced her finger around the two gold hearts.

She closed the locket, then went back to bed for her second purchase. She created a safe area for her new personal toy and cleaner in the nightstand drawer. She hoped it would feel lifelike, as the saleswoman described. Her face started to burn as she wondered how often she would need to use it.

Eve closed her eyes and remembered how she felt in Adam's arms. She got a wave of butterflies, just thinking about it. She smiled at the warm feeling that thinking about Adam brought her. She pulled back the covers and slipped under them.

She opened the cover to her new toy and then turned off the light.

Entry 9: Date with Adam, out on the Town

Adam parked in front of Eve's building and was starting to unload his items when he recognized the guard from last week sitting in the gray car parked across from Eve's building. He walked up and knocked on the trunk before reaching the passenger side window and then he waved.

The guard glared at him for a moment before he unlocked the door, and Adam got in. "Good morning. I'm sorry, I forgot your name." He held his hand out.

"Good morning, Mr. Stratford. My name is Martin," he replied with a stoic look, then shook his hand.

Adam looked at the building, then back to Martin. "Are you guys always watching?" Adam asked.

"There is a normal 4-on-3-off, 3-on-4-off rotation. There are six regular crew members. Always one watching. I normally have the night shift. You also met our Jefe, Thomas. Jefe usually has the second shift. Sometimes we bring extra help for bigger activities or just overlap our shifts like last Friday," he explained.

Adam nodded as he listened. "Is there a number I can contact to advise ahead of time for bigger activities?" Adam was curious about how much warning he should give them.

Martin pulled out a business card from his pocket. "You can call, text, or email Jefe at any time." Adam looked at it for a moment and then added it to his wallet.

"Well, sorry for the short notice, but I have a full day planned for her birthday. Do you have pen and paper?" Adam asked as he pulled out his phone and looked at his itinerary for the day.

Eve

Eve was so excited that she got to see Adam today that she only slept two hours during the night. She had some crazy butterflies going on all week in anticipation. To help pass the time, she prepared for Monday's meeting with Adam's employees. Questionnaires would help guide her to what the group needed and not just the whim of one. Not to say that Adam only thought of himself. He is the opposite, and that's part of what she loves about him. He goes out of his way to take care of others.

Just then, her phone rang. "Adam." She answered immediately.

"Good morning, Beautiful. Sorry for calling so early in the morning, but I figured you would be up anyway."

She laughed. "Bonjour, mon héros. I wasn't expecting a call for a couple more hours."

"I know, but I got notice that part of your birthday gift was arriving early." Just then, her doorbell chimed.

"Someone's at the door," she said. She wondered how they got past the nighttime security door without her buzzing them in.

"Good, that might be it now," he replied. She checked the peephole and saw a vase holding a ton of her favorite flowers.

"You didn't have to do that," she said as her eyes started to water. She opened the door to greet the courier.

"Happy Birthday, Beautiful!" She saw Adam, shrieked, bounced in place for a moment, then wrapped her arms around him and started kissing him. She felt the butterflies again and held her stomach.

She eventually pulled back. "You are so early," she said with a smile.

"Do you want me to leave and come back?" he asked. His face was serious, even though she knew he was kidding.

"No! I want every second I can with you," she replied.

"Good." He then held up the vase again. "Where do you want these?"

"Oh, Adam. They are so pretty. Let's put them on the coffee table. That way, I can see them from everywhere." She smirked. "You were being so sneaky having Mrs. Ophelia ask me all those questions."

He stood up tall. "I thought that was rather smart on my end." He grinned.

She then noticed the big case. "Are you moving in today?" Her smile grew as he pulled his luggage forward.

"Not yet." He then winked at her. "Today is going to be busy. I don't want to give everything away. But I will lay out my clothing so we can coordinate for the day's activities."

She smiled. "Okay. I was going to shower before you got here." She paused, blushed, then took a step back to give him space for his vow.

He took two steps forward and pulled her in. "I want to watch." He then claimed her lips again for a quick kiss.

She broke the kiss, smiled, turned, and sat down on the couch, while reaching for Adam to join her. "I need to apologize for last week. I didn't want to do it over the phone," she said.

He sat next to her. "You have nothing to apologize for. I was the one who went too far." She shook her head.

"No. It was me. I need you to understand something about me. My emotional level is tied directly to my sexual level. Friday night was so emotional that I became overly sexually charged. You clearly explained yourself, and I respect it. But that night, I pushed your boundaries. I'm so sorry." She frowned a little.

"I purposefully chose my outfit so you could have access. When I climbed back into bed, I laid so we were spooning and I placed your hands on my body." She leaned in. "To be clear, I didn't put you in me. That was you. But from here on, I will not tease you like that again. I am ready to jump you at any given time, so for the sake of building our emotional foundation, please don't sexually tease me. You may end up getting more than what you ask for…"

She winked. "I also took a friend's advice and got myself a gift to help me keep my needs under control."

"You gave yourself an early birthday gift?" he asked. She stared him in the eyes, then looked at his lap and then back in the eyes.

"A very personal gift to help me release the built-up energy." She felt her face go red when he started to laugh.

"Good. Everyone needs to know how to take care of themselves. Knowing what makes you feel good and then sharing your likes and dislikes helps me to be better for you." She went even redder as he pulled her into a kiss that quickly went deeper.

His hands then wrapped around her and pulled her closer. She let him know her needs and how she planned to work with her desire. They both broke the kiss, and she leaned against him, breathing hard.

"I would love to watch that also." That shocked her for a second time.

"Adam, that defeats the purpose. To have me lying there in pleasure and you not being able to join in, wouldn't that be torture for you? Besides, I would rather have you than a toy any day." She smiled.

She could hear him take a deep breath and slowly let it out. He pulled his phone from his pocket and picked a soft rock station. He set it on the coffee table, stood up, and held out his hand. "I have breakfast coming soon. Until then, may I have this dance?"

Wow. He sidestepped that question. Perhaps he realized how far he really pushed the boundary. She smiled at him. He's such a wonderful man. How did she get so lucky? She felt all warm and fuzzy inside as she held his hand to stand up. He pulled both her hands to his neck and then slowly traced his fingers along her arms and slowly along her back. He leaned in, claimed her lips, and they slowly danced while locked at the lips.

Her heart was full.

After the food delivery arrived, they sat down and enjoyed breakfast together. "Adam?"

"Yes, Beautiful?" He looked at her with a soft expression.

"This last week has made me realize that I want to see you more often. Here, your place, at the office, or even something quick at Jake's. I know that I can't come to your school and you can't come to mine. But this week in between seeing each other is difficult. If we are going to work on us, we need as much time together as we can. I'm not talking about going on dates, but rather what our lives would be like daily. Would that be okay?"

He nodded his head, yes. "I fully agree. I found it difficult to concentrate on tasks all week because I was thinking of you." He lifted her hand and gave it a kiss. "If we are going to be at my place, we need to keep the hugging and kissing to a minimum. I don't want to upset Jessie or rub it in his face." He made a frown face.

"I see your point. I can be a good girl if you can be a good boy. But when your bedroom door is closed, you can bet my lips will be kissing on yours." She blushed.

Adam

While Eve took a shower, Adam opened his luggage and removed his layers of folded clothes. He grabbed a hanger from her closet and put his dress shirt and coat on it to help keep the wrinkles out. He then laid out his outfits on the bed in order of their activities.

He closed his eyes and listened to her singing along with the new song on the radio and imagined seeing her all wet. Snap out of it. You have things to do. He pulled out a couple of small boxes. The small silver box would be for later tonight, and he tucked it into the coat pocket. But after hearing her confession about self-pleasure, he couldn't resist, and he needed to see for himself.

He found a discreet spot for the little black box and aimed it toward the bed. He was glad that he opted for video with audio this time. He tapped on his phone to activate the image. He made a small angle correction and went back to the matter of outfits.

He went to her closet and pulled out a couple of dresses to go with his suit. Looking at the labels, he didn't recognize the designer. He picked a couple of shirts and pants and then placed them on the bed with his clothing. "Hmmm," more of the label. It must be a French designer, he thought to himself.

Like New York and London, he knew Paris was one of the most important fashion shows, where aspiring designers go to learn and showcase their work. He was looking at her shoes and realized she only had one pair of heels. She is not like the other women he has known. Even his own mother had several for each color alone.

Eve

She was singing along to *"Summertime,"* by Kenny Chesney on the radio when she heard the door click and he joined in to make it a duet.

Two bare feet on the dashboard

Young love and an old Ford

Cheap shades and a tattoo

And a yo-ho bottle rollin' on the floorboard

Perfect song on the radio

Sing along 'cause it's one we know

It's a smile, it's a kiss

It's a sip of wine, it's summertime

Eve froze in place while she listened. "What are you doing?" she asked.

"I said I wanted to watch," he replied. "Not like I haven't seen you naked before." That made her laugh.

"Last time you were here, you covered your eyes and stared at the floor until you had to look me. By then, I had a fluffy towel on me." She giggled at the memory.

"True, I was caught off guard. But I knew what to expect this time." Her shower glass was covered in steam, so she couldn't see him, which meant he couldn't clearly see her either.

"I've got everything laid out. Picked a couple of outfits that I think would go nicely, but by all means, you know your clothing, so pick what you like the best."

He had a melancholy sound in his voice, and Eve wondered if it was the singing just prior that caused it.

"Okay." She would have to see what he's wearing. It's nice that he offered a suggestion. That will give her an idea of the activities that they are heading out to do. "Are you going to give me any hints?"

He laughed. "Can't just wait for the surprise, can you?"

She let out another soft laugh. "You know I don't celebrate my birthday so, you should know that I'm super excited for our date."

"You're right. Well, I'll give you a few clues. There will be times that we are doing a bunch of walking. Sometimes, we will be doing a bunch of sitting. Sometimes we will be in comfy clothes. Sometimes we will be all dressed up. We will be out late, so I brought my own pajamas to stay the night. And a restraint coat to help me keep my hands off you." They both started laughing.

Even in the hot water, she felt her face flush. He'd planned on sleeping over this time instead of falling asleep. She rested both her hands on the wall as a wave of pleasure started to rise. Images of them as they crawled into bed together… clung to each other… kisses… touches… hands exploring… "Oh, God!" She remembered how she felt when his fingers moved in and out. "Shit." She stood still as the orgasmic wave washed over her.

Adam

"Are you okay?" She wasn't responding as he was expecting. He walked to the shower door. He couldn't see her standing upright. "Eve?" His heart pounded as his brain rolled through possible problems. He waited another moment, then he flung the door open and turned off the water. She was leaning away from him so he couldn't see her face. The bruise on her hip and arm had faded to a sickly green color.

Was she in pain? He tugged her arm to get her to turn. Her face was red as she breathed fast. He could see the vein in her neck as it pulsed. "Are you okay?" He was really starting to worry now.

She smiled and closed the distance. "I had a visual." She took a couple of deep breaths. "I warned you about my mental and physical reactions." She took another deep breath and slowly let it out. "Sometimes, things you say or do will send me over my limit and my body will have an orgasm all on its own. The first time was the night you brought me home."

"You're having orgasms without me?" His heart started to race and he became aroused.

"No, they are most definitely with you, on my mind." A smile tugged at her plump lips.

It was amazing how her body responded to him. "What did I say?" He was curious.

She smiled. "You're planning ahead of time to stay the night, with me. And then I thought of the last time and how it felt when you…" She paused, smiled again, and shut the shower door. She pulled him in for a kiss while she started to unbutton his shirt.

Fuck, she feels so good. With both hands planted firmly on her bare ass, now he wanted more. *Stop now before it gets too far.* His brain screamed at him as his heart pounded in his chest. He let go, and he put his hands on top of hers, and she held still.

"You said I could touch your chest." He did, but he didn't mean with her all naked. He rested his head down on hers, and she relaxed her hands and shook her head. "Okay. I understand. It's because you have full access to me right now. But if I was clothed, then I can touch your chest?"

He was speechless, so he nodded his head, yes. He was glad that she understood. "But remember, you came in here with me. I figured you would have stayed in the bedroom." She grinned at him.

Adam took a calming breath and stepped out of the shower to rebutton his shirt. His pants got a little wet, but they would be fine for when he wears them home tomorrow. He needed to change the subject so his raging manhood could relax.

He started humming to the next song. "When is the next karaoke night?" Adam asked.

"I don't know the date, but the last weekend of October is Nicole's birthday. She wants the girls to do a group song together. Halloween themed of course. So, we will have to practice a few times. They all dress up, so, I'll be looking for an outfit." She raised her eyebrows. "Do you want to do something together, like Han Solo and Princess Leia? Or perhaps something darker? Midnight Priest and Priestess?"

He started to laugh. "I would love to. I haven't dressed up since I was a kid, but there are always adult costume parties that I just didn't have time for, before now."

"Oh gosh, yes!" she exclaimed as an idea popped into her head.

"What now?" He had a look of wonderment on his face.

"If you and Jessie did a song together, *Thriller* would be good. Have him do the singing part, but the lower sinister part is so yours."

This made Adam start to laugh uncontrollably. She had no idea as to what was coming.

"What's so funny?" she asked. He waved his hands.

"I can't explain right now, but believe me, when it's time, you'll know why I was laughing."

"That's just fine, Mr. Funny Man. I'm almost done and then I'll get dressed," she warned.

"Okay." Adam went back to the bedroom to change into his first outfit for the day.

Eve

Eve was all done and had her strapless bra and underwear on, but she still came out wrapped up in the towel for his modesty. He had already changed into different casual wear. It was hard to tell by his outfit what he had planned. He turned to see her, and his eyes got bigger and he smiled.

"So beautiful, even in just a towel."

She smiled and blushed. "Thank you." She gave him a look over. "You look very relaxed yourself, handsome." She focused on the bed. "What have you done here, Héros?" She walked to the bed and reached for his hand as they looked at the selections he had chosen.

"We will have casual clothing for the morning until after lunch. We then need to come back and change into our formal wear for a 2 p.m. appointment. Then we have dinner reservations and an appointment after that. That is all I'm going to tell you." Adam moved in behind her and wrapped his arms around her, kissing her neck.

She felt her insides warm up. "Mmmm, Adam." She moaned and reached back with her hand to twist her fingers in his hair. "If you keep that up, we are not going to get out of here."

He spun her around. "That thought crossed my mind also." He pulled her in for a heavy kiss, and her butterflies started again, but then he released her. "But I wouldn't want to rob you of the day I have planned. I'm gonna get my shoes on. All you have to do is pick, and then we can get going."

She smiled. "Do I have time to put some makeup on?" He reached for her hand and kissed it.

"You are beautiful as you are. I would recommend sunscreen instead for the casual wear and save the makeup for later."

He gave her rump a soft spank and then walked into the living room. She stood there and watched him go. Damn, he is a wonderful man. Looking at his evening wear, she picked one of the dresses. A form-fitting crushed red velvet dress would look good tonight. She then hung up the spare.

She took another peek at him again and decided not to use his selections, but to wear her favorite color. She put away his choices and pulled out soft jeans, a white lace top, and her favorite yellow blazer with a sunhat.

The cab pulled up to the Museum of Modern Art, and she was instantly fascinated by the construction angles of the building. She was also excited to see the treasures that were kept inside. They slowly went from one display to another, whispering in each other's ears about what they thought. Some pieces were recognizable, and others were so abstract that neither of them had a clue what to think.

They walked the entire building while holding hands—a first for her in her limited dating history. It probably would have taken an hour to walk the whole exhibit, but it took them two since he kept stopping to kiss her neck or nibble on her lips. She also loved the occasional sneak-in a hug that would also show up. She appreciated that he was not shy to show public affection and would jump at the chance to kiss him off guard also.

From there, he took her to the Loeb Boathouse in Central Park. At the reservation desk, he picked up a picnic basket, and then, before she knew it, they were in a rowboat on the lake. She enjoyed watching Adam flex his Hulk muscles over and over again to move the boat. She felt hot for a moment while watching him, and she had to fan herself to cool down her desire.

"Adam." He paused his rowing for a moment. "How often do you go to the gym and work your muscles?" She felt a blush work up her neck.

He started rowing again. "I usually go two or three times a week to work on different muscle groups. Today counts as working on arms, legs, and the back." He winked.

He had rowed them to somewhere in the middle where there was no one around. They could have rocked the boat with making love motion and no one would have noticed. Eve's blush got hotter at the thought. She opened the picnic basket, spread the tablecloth, and food items out on the bench between them.

They had a wonderful array of meat, cheese, fruit, wine, crackers, and chocolate-covered sweet treats.

They took turns eating and feeding each other as they tried all the different varieties of food. After they were done filling their bellies, she snuggled in his arms as they both lay sideways in the boat to let their feet dangle in the water. She untucked his shirt and finally got her hand on his smooth yet firm muscular chest. They would each take turns singing any song that came to their minds, with rounds of kissing in between.

On the way back, she tried to row, but she was not as successful as Adam was. He started to chuckle as she begun to get frustrated. "Don't laugh at me." She smiled but kept on trying. "I've never done this before. Plus, my arms are not as strong as your Hulk ones." A blush grew as she tried to concentrate.

After about ten minutes of spinning the boat around in circles and going in zigzags around the lake, they switched, and he brought them back to the dock. With a smile glued to her face, Eve watched his muscles the whole time.

After returning their borrowed basket, they slipped right into a taxi. Traffic was light, so they made it back to her place earlier than planned. That was fine with her. They snuggled on the bed for thirty minutes, kissing and holding each other while their tongues softly explored each other's mouths.

Adam

Eventually, it was time to get moving. He went first, changing in the restroom, that way she could stay in longer for her hair and makeup. He wondered how long it would take for them to be comfortable changing in front of each other. When he stepped out, she was just sliding the dress up, giving him a full view of her backside.

Her thin fabric thong underwear hid nothing of her body, and she opted for no bra which made his heart thump in anticipation. Adam kept watching her as she finished sliding the dress on. Damn, that dress fit her like a glove. Almost as if it were made for her curvy body. Adam then picked a song on his phone by Eric Clapton titled *"Wonderful Tonight,"* for her to hear.

She turned and looked at him from the side of her eyes. "Should I change into something different?"

Adam caught his breath after he realized that he was staring at her. "No. Stay just as you are. You do look wonderful tonight. That dress is absolutely perfect for your body." He moved closer. One hand traced his fingers along her arm as the other moved in behind her head. He reclaimed her mouth and pulled her into him. He softly sucked her lower lip in and nibbled.

She gasped and pulled back. "Thought we had to get going?"

Damn, he just wanted to stay here, take her dress off and explore her body, but there she goes, reminding him to be a good boy. Plus, there was so much more left to do today.

Eve

She saw stars as they pulled up to the theater. Adam's next surprise was going to the Michael Jackson Broadway Show. They had taken their seats when it finally clicked in her mind. She looked at him just before the curtains went up. "This is why you were laughing at me this morning." She grinned.

"It was like you were reading my mind." He smiled and wrapped his arm around her shoulders to keep her as close as they could in the theater seats. There wasn't much for talking during this activity, but he kept his warm arm wrapped around her the whole time.

Once the show got going, she sporadically was able to get a kiss. She really enjoyed singing along with the cast and audience. It was one big karaoke set with audience participation. She knew she was going to have to share this day in her journal for her family.

From there, he made a reservation at her favorite restaurant, Dos Casminos. It was just around the corner, so they decided to walk and enjoy the evening breeze. After being seated, Adam got up from sitting across from her and slid in next to her, then pulled her into his arms.

They kept on kissing and smiling at each other until she heard music coming their way. She looked and saw the Mariachi band coming as they sang Cumpleaños Feliz for her birthday song. They had her wear a big sombrero for a picture for their wall. Of course, Adam snapped pictures on his phone. She laughed at the whole experience.

They each ordered different items and shared samples with each other. There was just too much food for her to eat since her stomach seemed much smaller in the tight-fitting dress that seemed to be tighter. Since the evening was getting later, she opted to bring her leftovers home. It would be good if she added it to eggs in the morning.

She couldn't help but smile at him. He had gone way above and beyond for today's activities. She slipped her hand into his and drew hearts on his palm with her fingers. She really wanted to be with him, but she was learning patience and to control her desire. After a little dessert, her tummy wasn't sitting right, so she let him finish her half of the chocolate treat.

At the end of the night, he had one last appointment. He surprised her by taking her to the top of the Empire State Building's viewing platform. Adam grabbed her hand and hip, and they danced all the way around. He would point out different buildings and talk about the architects of the past. They stopped to face west with a group of people to watch the sun set. Adam pulled a small box from his pocket.

"Beautiful Eve. My birthday gift comes with a renewal. Each month for one year, I will add a new piece to chronicle our journey together." She opened the silver box to find a silver bracelet with charms already attached. There was one of a row boat. Another was of a happy and sad theater masks. The third was the Empire State Building with a sapphire in the center.

"Oh, Adam! It's beautiful. After everything today, this is way too much." Her heart swelled with love as she looked into his happy face. "Thank you so much for the wonderful day." She smiled and pulled him in closer to whisper in his ear. "You've changed my birthday forever. I love you." Her nerves were so high, her stomach made flip-flops.

He pulled her in tight and rested his forehead on hers. "I love you too. I've been waiting to hear you say what I've felt since I first saw you sitting in the corner booth at Jake's."

She wrapped her arms around his shoulders. He scooped her up, sat on the bench with her across his lap. They locked into a kiss, and she felt like the rest of the world disappeared for a moment before they rested their foreheads together again.

"It felt so good to say it. I was just so nervous. I don't know why. You are truly wonderful." She gave him another quick kiss.

"It's you and me for as far as I can see. I know that life will have its ups and downs, but together we can work through it all." His smile grew.

She leaned against him as he kept his arms tightly wrapped around her to watch the sun go down. Just after the last bit of the sun was gone, they slow-danced and continued to kiss until 9 p.m.

They walked into Eve's apartment by 10 p.m. "I don't know about you, but my feet are killing me. Men are lucky in so many ways," Eve said as she set her items down on the table then placed her leftovers in the fridge.

"I can only imagine with these torture devices on your feet." Adam scooped her up again and set her down in the middle of the bed. Her heart started to race with the increased intimacy. She leaned back on her arms as he slowly took off each of her heels and started to give her feet a massage.

"Oh, Adam. That feels so good." She fell back onto the bed. Waves of energy flowed through her as "oh's" and "ah's" escaped her. When he was done, he kissed each ankle and helped her back up. "You're full of surprises. Thank you." She smiled at him as he had a content look on his face.

"There is room in here for your shoes." She walked to the closet and put her shoes away. "Do you need to shower?"

Adam leaned against the bedroom door. "I could use a quick rinse off." There was a gleam in his eyes as he smiled.

"I just need a quick rinse and to remove my makeup. Perhaps I can watch you this time." She smirked and then held her stomach as it cinched.

"You okay?" She looked up at him and saw the concern in his face.

"Something about the dessert didn't sit right with me. You basically ate the whole thing. I wonder if I'm developing an allergy to something." The wave passed, and she felt better. She went to the kitchen for a quick glass of water as he went to the bathroom with his pajamas. She came back to the bedroom, took off her dress, set it aside for cleaning, and then turned on the radio. Aerosmith was playing *"I Don't Want to Miss a Thing."* She joined in the chorus and sat on the bed in her undergarment until she heard him go into the shower. She smiled.

Payback time.

She walked into the bathroom still singing along to the song, and she was hoping for a sneak peek, but the glass was already steamed up. He joined in, and they sang in harmony as she removed her makeup and brushed her teeth. She then sat while waiting for the full Monty view, but he was smart and had his towel over the top. He dried off in the shower and had it wrapped around his waist before coming out.

She grinned. "My turn." She stood up and slowly took off her underwear while watching Adam's response. He was frozen in place by the shower door. She could see his towel tent with his erection. She giggled as she tossed the small fabric into the hamper, then walked up to him and placed both her hands on his moist pec muscles and slid them up to his shoulders.

She stood up on her toes and pulled him down for a quick kiss, making sure she applied pressure to his new erection with her lower abdomen before restarting the shower. She got butterflies again at the realization that she rather loved teasing him.

"I'll be in bed soon," she said and then stepped into the shower. Adam was still anchored to one spot for another minute as she continued to sing and rinse off. She was starting to think that Stephanie was right about him being a virgin. She didn't want to always be the aggressor in the relationship or always the teacher. It's fine communicating what she likes or dislikes but, she needed to get him a book or two so he could study. That way, when they do have sex for the first time, she can just enjoy it.

By the time she was done, he was gone without saying a word. She put on her least seductive pajamas this time, as promised, and she came out of the bathroom just as he was climbing into bed. Her heart suddenly raced. She knew that nothing major was going to happen, but her body became excited anyway at seeing him without a shirt, lying in her bed.

She had been looking forward to this all day. She pulled her side of the covers down and leaned over to give him a kiss but suddenly pulled back and stood up. She grabbed her stomach with one hand as her other hand covered her mouth. The butterflies fluttering led to a very distinct nauseous feeling. "Oh no!" she exclaimed and ran into the bathroom while keeping her mouth covered.

Her vomiting led to bad stomach pain, and she felt like she was unable to stop. She gasped for breath where she could. Adam came in and tied her hair up and then later placed a cool towel along her neck. There wasn't much he could do, but knowing he was there helped her feel like she was not alone.

He left for a minute and came back fully dressed and with clothes for her. He didn't take her PJs off but simply layered her clothes over as he could. Shortly after, there was a knock on her door, and he left again. She could hear Adam talking but couldn't make out the other voice.

Adam came back with a pot for her to hold and helped her to stand up. At this point, nothing was coming out anymore, but her stomach just wouldn't stop contracting.

Eve kept her head down in the pot the whole way as Adam guided her to the back seat of a car that Martin was driving. He kept an arm around her for support as the vehicle made corners. The motion of the vehicle didn't help the feeling in the pit of her stomach. They arrived at the hospital, but they had to wait for a while. It felt like forever, but eventually, they got her back to an exam room.

They made Adam and Martin wait outside the room while they collected her fluids. She didn't like the feeling of being alone, not having him there, while it felt like they were violating her to catheterize her for urine. They explained, but she couldn't focus on what they were saying at the moment.

Adam came back in and sat behind her as they took a ton of blood while starting an IV then they gave her fluids with anti-nausea medicine.

It took a few minutes, but the constant need to retch was gone. She leaned back and set her head on Adam's shoulder. His warm arms around her felt so good, and she fell asleep in his embrace.

Adam

Sometime later, there was a knock on her door. "Hello, I'm Dr. Russell," she said as the door shut behind her. She looked at Adam for a moment. "Are you a family member?" He knew what she was asking. "No, ma'am. We are not married yet," he responded.

"Okay. Can you please wait in the hall for a minute?" He gave Eve a kiss on the cheek and then slowly leaned Eve forward to slide out from behind her.

"I'll be just outside the door." He touched her shoulder and placed a kiss on her forehead before he walked out the door. He leaned on the wall opposite the room, next to Martin. There was a small window and he could just see Eve.

"I've never seen anything like that before. Have you?" Adam looked at Martin for a moment before looking back to Eve.

"Norovirus, Rotovirus or simple food poisoning or improperly cooked food. Gringo's coming south for the holidays, drink the water and they get sick." Martin kept a stoic look on his face.

"Hmmm. Right. It may have been dinner. She didn't eat all of it and she hardly touch the dessert." Adam thought back to the picnic on the boat. "Maybe even something from lunch? She did vomit a bunch."

Eve

Eve watched the doctor as she pulled up a seat. "We ran a bunch of tests, but only one thing came back positive." She was quiet for a moment. "When was your last cycle?"

Eve's eyes went wide for a moment. "Oh, shit! Please tell me you're kidding," Eve exclaimed as she felt the blood drain from her face. Tears started to fill her eyes as she grabbed her planner from her bag. She flipped through the pages. Her last cycle was in August. How did she not notice that she was late? Eve placed the planner over her face and started crying when she realized that she was pregnant with Jessie's baby.

"Is the man in the hallway the father?" the doctor asked.

Eve shook her head no. "I wish he was," Eve squeaked out.

The doctor nodded her head in understanding. "Okay, I'm going to get you an appointment with the OB doctor tomorrow and send you home with a prescription for anti-nausea medication and prenatal vitamins. Both will help your stomach settle down." She got up and paused. "Any questions for me?"

Eve shook her head no. "Thank you." The doctor nodded again and left the room.

Adam

As the doctor left the room, Adam entered and sat back down on the bed facing her. He wrapped his arms around her and pulled her into a hug, but she didn't hug him back. He felt her energy had drained as she rested her head on his shoulder.

"I'm sorry. I now know why I've been so up and down with emotions lately." She went quiet and she had a small tremble.

"Whatever it is, we can work through it together." She started to cry.

"After I say this, I understand if you don't want to see me anymore." He pulled her in tighter.

"You're not listening to me. I'm here on this earth for you. I know this to my core. This is part of our journey together. Remember, we are working towards marriage." She lifted her hands and pulled him closer for a second before leaning back from his embrace.

She closed her eyes and lowered her head. "I'm pregnant." Adam gasped and held his breath. His heart was pounding in his chest, but he couldn't show her that he was upset. He wrapped his arms around her and pulled her in again. His mind was going a mile a minute, but then he stopped. Breathe and think of how she's feeling.

"I understand if you don't want to be involved." She instantly started crying again.

Oh shit. She's going to use this to leave him and he just couldn't let that happen. "Remember, I grew up watching my dad raise Elizabeth as his own. He always treated us the same." Her crying was heavier. "So, we are starting a family sooner than planned." She slid her hand up his back and clung to his shoulders.

"It's Jessie's, isn't it?" She nodded her head, yes. Better than a stranger he didn't know. "Our baby will know only love from both of us, their parents. So what if the DNA is not mine? I love you, and the baby is half you and half my best friend."

She let out a big sigh. "I have to let Jessie know. He has the right to know, regardless of everything."

The nurse came back in with paperwork and removed the IV from her arm. Adam let Martin know that they would be leaving, and it was a quiet ride as he drove them back to her apartment. They were back at her place by 4 a.m. Sunday morning, and they both crashed asleep in each other's arms for the night.

October

Entry 1: Confronting Jessie

They didn't talk much in the morning. He had been so worried about her emotional side with everything that had happened over the last few weeks. When they arrived at his place, he hopped out of the car and opened the door for her. His luggage in one hand and her hand in the other, they went up the elevator. Just before they got to the door, he had a thought.

"Wait a second." He pulled her hand. "I know the conversation is going to be difficult. Let me go first and prepare him for a seriousness that needs all his newly found gentleman skills, then you can come in. That way he knows you're not kidding."

She didn't have much of a response other than nodding her head, yes. She let go of his hand and remained still in the hallway with her other hand on her stomach.

Adam opened the door and found Jessie working in his room at the desk. "Jessie, can you come sit with me for a minute?"

Jessie spun around. "Hey man. How's it going?"

Adam stared at him. "Today is a test of all that you have learned so far. What's my body language say?"

Jessie looked him over. "Something is wrong." Adam nodded his head and went to the living room to sit down. Jessie sat across from him. "What's going on?" Adam took a deep breath.

"You need to remember all that you have learned. She's had a very hard few weeks with being drugged and strangers groping and hurting her, and now this. She needs your support because she doesn't know what to do yet. And if you hurt her feelings..." Adam held up a fist, "My punishment will be instant. Do you understand?"

Jessie leaned back. "Yes." he nodded.

Adam pulled his phone from his pocket and sent a text for Eve to come in. A moment later she walked through the door. Jessie popped up and walked to her, but she stopped and took a step back, causing him to stop.

He held out his hand. "Good morning, Eve." She took slow steps forward and accepted his hand as he gave it a quick kiss. "Please come join us."

Adam could see her tears were starting and went to get tissues.

"I have something I need to tell you," Eve softly spoke.

"That's what Adam was saying. Please, I see you're upset. Have a seat so we can talk," he said as he sat back down. Adam sat back down and held an arm open for her. She walked behind the couch and held his hand.

"It feels better to stand for the moment." She gave him a kiss on the cheek and squeezed his hand.

She breathed a few slow breaths. "It's better to just come out with it." She pressed her lips flat. "The night of your birthday." She paused. "Not my gift but your birthday wish." Jessie sat up straight.

She closed her eyes and her tears fell. Adam handed her tissues and she blotted her face. "I'm pregnant." She quickly covered her mouth with the tissue.

Adam stared at Jessie to see his response. But he had a blank face. She then turned, ran for the bathroom, and slammed the door. Adam didn't need to watch, he could hear her retching again.

"You guys were not in your room for long, but obviously long enough." Adam was trying to remain as level-headed as he could. "With the place full of our friends that night, engaging in sex doesn't seem like something she would initiate. So, since we had a gentleman's agreement, I need to know. Did she ask you or did you ask her?"

Jessie lowered his head. "I initiated it. I misunderstood and thought she wanted a quickie."

Adam took a deep breath. "So, you fucked her anyway, knowing how I felt about her."

Jessie raised his head to look at him. "I'm so sorry. I was such a fuck-up. I know this now." Adam leaned back and took calming breaths.

"What's done is done. We can only move forward from here. She knows that I will be there for her. No matter what. The child will know the love of a mother and a father. I will raise your child as mine until the right time comes to tell them the truth. You need to decide your role. How active will you be in your child's life? She's not malicious or vindictive, so you won't have to worry about her coming after you for money. Besides, we can take care of all that on our own."

Jessie shook his head. "I just don't get it. I used a condom."

"They can fail." Adam snapped back as he fisted he hands. Adam glanced back over his shoulder at the bathroom door before he continued. "Once she started throwing up last night, she didn't stop. After fifteen minutes straight, I took her to the hospital and the medicine helped. But she still triggers. She hardly ate yesterday and you know she can put it away. I worry about dehydration and malnutrition. Neither is good for her nor the baby."

Jessie sat up. "Didn't know you were visiting with her yesterday. Would have been nice to see her. It's been a while." Adam swung his head back around to look at Jessie, raised his eyebrows, and pointed to the calendar on the wall.

"Her birthday has been marked." Jessie hung his head again.

"I missed her birthday." He took a deep breath. "I am a piece of shit."

Eve

"No, you're not," Eve spoke up. Jessie's head popped up and Adam spun around. "I feel better now. It comes and goes in waves. I think the car ride with the motion was just too much for me. I'm sorry, Adam, I used your toothbrush. I'll get you a new one."

Adam reached a hand out to her again. She accepted and sat down next to him. The room was so quiet that she could hear Adam's heart beating in his chest before Jessie spoke up.

"I don't want this to come across the wrong way here, but how do we know it's not yours? You two are always with each other," Jessie had a peculiar look in his eyes.

Adam stood up with his fists clenched and Jessie flinched back onto the couch.

"You guys." She reached up and held Adam's wrist. "This is a messed-up situation we are in," Eve said, trying to cool the room. She forced his fingers open with hers and he looked down at her.

"Easy, Héros," she said, and he sat back down. "Adam and I have not had sex. The last time I did, I was 20 years old. I'm not on birth control because I wasn't expecting to have sex while here for school."

She looked at Adam and he was calming down. "Look, Jessie. I wanted to tell you right away so you didn't think we were keeping this a secret from you or trying to prevent you from being a part of the child's life."

She leaned over and gave Adam a hug and kiss on the cheek. "I have to get ready for my follow-up appointment this afternoon. I'm going to walk, so I need to get going." Eve let out a heavy sigh.

"Okay, Beautiful. Are you sure you don't want me to come?"

She smirked. How did she get so lucky to have him? "I'm sure. We will chat soon." He lifted her hand and gave it a soft kiss goodbye.

Adam

After Eve left, the two guys sat there in silence. Adam was wiped out. Being up early, busy all day, and then a late night at the hospital had just taken it out of him. He was about to fall asleep when Jessie spoke up.

"I can't believe that I'm going to be a father and the beautiful, marvelously kind, Eve is going to be the mother. I may have messed this up, but I couldn't have asked for a better woman. Or a better best friend. I want to be involved with everything. Every holiday, camping trip, birthday, you name it, I will be there. I will be the fun uncle, us three musketeers. If that's okay?"

Adam sat up and focused on Jessie. "I would like that. But you need to discuss this with Eve." There was quiet again between them.

"I can see the love between you guys. There is no denying it. I love her too, in my own way. She has changed me. So have you. I haven't gone out or been with anyone since that life-altering day. Now I know why."

Adam leaned back. Perhaps he was taking big steps to being a man after all. "I'm going to go take a nap. I thought I was strong, but she whooped my ass yesterday. How she has all that energy, I have no idea. Like a marathon runner, she just keeps on going."

Adam got up and walked to his room as he emailed the Dean of the school. He was going to miss class on Monday to deal with a family emergency and would return on Tuesday. He wanted to be at the office when Eve was there, just in case she needed his help.

Eve

Eve walked slowly to her next appointment since she left so early. She said what needed to be said, but then wanted to get out of the stress. She was able to watch the neighborhood kids playing in the fire hydrant water and see moms with babies in strollers. Block by block, everywhere she went, she saw life.

It wasn't that long ago that Jessie was who she was interested in. He did force her, which freaked her out and pulled them apart. But if things were different, perhaps they would be celebrating now. He's not an awful guy. He has clearly taken strides to become better. She wanted children but wasn't planning on them so soon, and being unwed, her aunt was going to have a meltdown when she found out.

She blushed. Even though Adam has technically asked her twice now, in his way. Once she learned about his vow, she decided to hold out for him to ask officially. To get down on a knee and say the words that meant so much to her.

Her directions to the clinic took her past the park, so she sat for a few to watch the kids running around the playground. She confessed to Adam her fears. Now is the time to prove that she is no longer afraid and choose her own path. She closed her eyes and listened to the children's happy sounds as they played, and a wave of joy filled her, knowing she had been blessed to become a mother.

Eve's phone rang, pulling her from her peace. She opened her eyes and saw it was Jessie calling. She took a calming breath before answering. "Hello?"

"Hey Babe. I've been doing some deep talking here with Adam, and he told me that we needed to talk."

"You are not required to do anything. I just need you to know that I will be fine." She cut him off and leaned forward to rest her face on her hand.

It was quiet for a second. "But I want to be there." She was surprised and leaned up. "We were getting along just fine. Had I not been so self-centered and expecting more, we would still be dating. You are by far the most interesting woman I have ever met, and I kick myself all the time for messing it up."

Eve started to tear up and took a few deep breaths to calm down. "So, what does it mean that you want to be there?" She was curious.

"Anything and everything. I want to be there for you and our child." She couldn't hold it back anymore and she started to cry. "Oh, Babe. I wasn't trying to make you cry." She wanted to respond but couldn't. After a few moments, she was feeling better and the sad wave had ended.

"I'm sorry. My emotions tend to run crazy on their own right now," she sniffed her nose clear and wiped her eyes.

"You have nothing to apologize for." It was quiet again. "Would it be okay if I came with you to your doctor's appointment?"

Eve was shocked again by his attention. She was unsure if she should have him there. What the hell. It's his child too. "Well, I was planning on going alone. But if you can get there in thirty-five minutes, you can see the ultrasound and listen to what the doctor has to say."

"Shoot me a text with the address. I'm on my way. See you soon, Babe." He hung up the phone and she sent the text with the address to the corner of the park. She then went back to listening to the sounds.

"Eve!" She heard her name being called.

She stood up and waved. "Over here." She yelled back. She saw Jessie jogging her way and she sat back down to continue watching the kids play.

He came up and sat down next to her. "Phew, I thought I was at the wrong location."

She smiled. "It's just up the block, but I had extra time and figured, here in the fresh air was better than a stuffy waiting room."

"Good choice." He was awkwardly quiet for a moment. "I just wanted to say thank you. I was hoping you would let me come. I was serious about being here for you. Anything you need, just ask."

Eve smiled. "Well, right now, it is just the first steps. I'm here to follow the doctor's advice." She looked at Jessie. "It's hard to believe that we created life. Isn't it?" She reached out to rest her hand on his. He spread his fingers apart and threaded hers in with his. She then leaned over and rested her head on his shoulder.

He spoke softly, "It's crazy when you think about it, but I guess the fates had different plans for us."

When it was time, they got up and walked the rest of the way. There wasn't much conversation considering the situation, but they walked hand in hand nonetheless.

The waiting room was crazy as she thought it would be, but they didn't have to wait long before they called her name. After giving a blood and urine sample, she changed her top into a gown and took a seat on the bed. Jessie sat next to her. The assistant covered her with a sheet, then helped to lower her pants and underwear before leaving.

The ultrasound tech came in and introduced herself. "Who do we have here?" she asked.

Eve looked over at him. "This is Jessie, the father." She smiled and held out her hand for him to hold.

"What was the first day of your last cycle?" the tech asked, drawing her attention again.

"Not sure of the exact date, I'd have to look at my calendar, but mid-August," Eve responded as she bit her lower lip.

The tech used a tool from her pocket for a second. "That would put your conception around the 27th to the 1st of—"

"My birthday," Jessie blurted out, cutting off the tech. She smiled as she turned and looked at him. "We used a condom but…" Jessie's face turned red.

The tech smirked. "Well. Happy birthday to you, Daddy." She winked. "That makes you 6 weeks along. We will confirm with the ultrasound for the gestation size and make sure the baby is on track."

The hard wand was uncomfortable going in, but Eve's body adjusted quickly. Instantly, a grayscale image appeared on the screen. The tech pointed to a roundish bubble on the screen. "The black circle is the space in your uterus. There's your peanut." She pointed to a gray bubble in the dark void.

Jessie squeezed her hand. "See this flicker?" The tech continued to point before clicking on a button, and the machine was suddenly making a fast whoosh whoosh whoosh sound. "The baby's heartbeat. Good steady pulse too," she explained.

Jessie lifted her hand and gave it a soft kiss. Eve turned to look at him, and his face was beaming with joy as tears were welling in the bottom of his eyes. She reached up and pulled him down to place a kiss on his cheek.

"I'm glad you were here for this."

Entry 2: Getting Employee Info

Since Adam was playing hooky from school for the day, he got to work early. He didn't want to be seen on the streets by anyone from the school. He hid in his office, looking at the ultrasound image Eve sent of the baby. He was full of mixed feelings about the situation: angry at Jessie for breaking his promise, happy that he was going to be a father, sad that there would forever be a tie between Eve and Jessie, which made him mad at himself for getting angry at something that happened while they were dating.

Now they are not. Adam took a deep, calming breath and slowly let it out then looked at the picture again. Adam wanted a house full of children. He could envision the family's yearly Christmas tree surrounded by six kids. He chuckled—give or take one or two.

He drafted an email to the family lawyer about his future plans for marriage and to prepare the estate for descendants. Adam wasn't about to go into details that they didn't need to know, but sending a word now would prepare them for future possible outcomes that no one wants to really think about. He heard the door announcer and went to let Mrs. Ophelia know about his unexpected presence in today's activities.

Eve

Eve was nervous about being in the office by herself with a bunch of people she didn't know. "Be professional. You're here to do a job," she reminded herself. She arrived at the office and climbed the grand stairs again.

"Good morning, Ms. Eve," she heard Mrs. Ophelia calling from the top.

"Good morning to you, Mrs. Ophelia. How do you know it's me?" she asked as she finished the last few steps.

"I work in an office of men. I know the difference in the sound of your heels on the tile floor." They shook hands as they greeted. "Honey! You are glowing." Ophelia pulled her in and whispered, "How far along are you?"

Eve pulled back in shock and covered her mouth. "We just found out yesterday. How did you know?" Eve asked in disbelief.

Ophelia laughed. "I might be old, but I'm not blind. Over the years, I've seen my fair share of pregnant women."

Eve covered her red face for a moment. "We are not telling anyone yet, so please, shhhh." Eve covered her lips with her finger.

Ophelia motioned that her lips were zippered closed. That made Eve smile. "Please have a seat for a minute."

Eve turned the corner to the waiting room and saw all the new monitors. She stood in amazement as the images rotated exactly as she had described the last time she was here. She had been brainstorming, and that wonderful man made it happen. Each monitor had a different set of images on rotation, and she took turns watching.

There was a new soft scent in the air, and she recognized it as Adam's aftershave. But it couldn't be his. He's in school today. It must be one of the other guys here.

"Good morning, Beautiful." She turned and saw Adam standing there with his arms open.

"Bonjour, Héros." She closed the distance and pulled him in for a kiss as his arms wrapped around her. Her heart raced, and yet she felt so at peace knowing he was here.

"Excuse me," she heard Ophelia say in the background. They turned to see her. "We are fully staffed today," she raised her eyebrows, "and this is not the privacy of your office."

Adam turned and rested his forehead on Eve's. "She's right," he whispered. He took a deep breath and took a step back but kept his hand tangled with hers. "How are you feeling today?"

"I'm doing okay. I took a dose of medicine this morning, so I should be fine for a while." She returned his smile. "Why are you here?" She tilted her head.

"With the craziness of the weekend, I wanted to be here if you needed me." His expression melted her.

She warmed up with the thought of getting extra time with him. She leaned in for another hug. "Thank you." He gave her arm a tug.

"I want to show you something before we get started." She wondered what he was up to as they headed back out the front door and down the side of the building. They came to a large double cargo door. One had a normal doorway inside it. He keyed the door open and turned on the lights.

Eve was filled with wonder. The space had none of the opulence of upstairs, but the room was open the full length as upstairs, without any walls. The ceiling was even taller down here to accommodate a larger truck to load and unload. There were fewer windows, but they all faced south, allowing the lightest in for the size.

"This space is amazing. Is this the area you were talking about before?" She finally spoke up and blushed as she recalled the proposal. He nodded and pulled her in so her back was against his chest then his arms wrapped around her as she continued to look around.

"Wouldn't you still need all these supplies to go somewhere? That means an added cost of storage." She looked over her shoulder at him.

He smiled. "Normally, but I've advised all the contractors to use current supplies and not to bring any more in for safe keeping. It may take up to a year to fully clear this space out. By the time you're done with your training, you could transform this space into a design studio."

She realized that he was still talking about her working with him. Eve felt a warm wave fill her, and she leaned back against him.

"Adam, this space is way too large for me."

He laughed. "You could set it up as a cooperative, LLC, or any way you want. But like I said before, I would like to work on projects together with you."

Eve could feel her heart race with the idea of working with Adam on projects. Her body was suddenly on fire, and she tried to calm herself. She could stay here and still deal with problems back home. Maybe she could fly home for a week here and there.

She pulled from him while holding his hand, turned, and had a huge smile on her face. She could see a future with him.

He shut the door and pulled her back in. Grabbed both her hands with his and leaned her back against the wall. Lifting her arms up above her head and holding with one hand gave him full access to her body. He claimed her lips with his as his hand slowly moved along her arm.

He came to rest his palm under her breast and started to softly squeeze as he pressed his weight into her. He pinched her nipple through the layers, and she gasped.

He jutted his tongue in at the opportunity. His hand continued down her side and slowly grabbed her ass, pulling her pelvis into his. She could feel his hardness straining to escape. His hand continued down, and he started to lift her leg, and she willingly wrapped it around him, wanting more as she continued to grind her pelvis against his.

"Adam," she mumbled against his mouth. He released his hand from hers, and she locked her fingers in his hair as the other clung to his back. His other hand repeated on the other side just as slowly. She arched this time when he reached her breast with both his hands.

"Oh, Adam!" she exclaimed, making her moan loudly on his mouth, breaking their seal. His mouth continued down her neck as his other hand made its way to her leg and started to lift. She pulled herself up and locked her ankles as best as she could, and they both continued to grind on each other. He fully rubbed against her sensitive clit through their clothing.

"Yes." She could feel her climax growing and pulled harder with each grind. Then she felt the fire spread from the inside out.

"Oh, God!" she exclaimed loud enough to make it echo. He ground a little harder and faster, then pulled her in tighter. He broke his kisses and moaned with a little grunt in her ear with a final push. They held each other while she breathed heavily and her fast heart slowed. He leaned his head to hers and kissed her again.

"Sorry, Beautiful. Your pheromones were driving me crazy, and I just couldn't resist you anymore."

She smiled. "Don't be sorry. I'm ready to be open to more when you're ready. Besides, that's how I've been feeling for the last couple of weeks." She slowly let her legs down. "What we just did, would that normally be past the line?"

He lowered his head. "Yes," he breathed out.

She paused. "However, you had enough control to leave your clothes on. I think hard lines should be gray areas depending on what you can control. Since you had restraint to not penetrate, would we be able to add this part to what we can do?" She was hopeful because this felt great.

He took a deep breath. "I'll have to think about that one." He pressed his lips flat. "If we were at your place like the other night, I don't think I would be able to stop. You had me at a disadvantage. Only a towel was in between us. Had you pressed much harder or longer…" He sucked a breath in over his teeth. "Well, you really don't want to know what was going through my mind." He paused and leaned to her ear. "Soon enough, I'll be able to show you. Please be patient with me until then." He then kissed her cheek.

She grabbed his shirt and pulled him closer. "I'm still right here, Héros. I love you." She wanted more and pulled him into another deep kiss.

He placed both his palms on the wall and leaned in, re-pinning her to the wall. He moaned and pulled away. "I love you too."

He leaned back and then took a step back. "Did I get any on you?"

She could feel her underwear was soaked but looked at her pants. "I think I'm good, however, I'll need a restroom." She smiled.

He lifted her hand to his lips and kissed her. "Follow me."

After cleaning up, Adam and Eve walked back up to the office, ready to get down to business. She was so much calmer now than she was at the start of the day. She followed Adam past Mrs. Ophelia, who gave her a wink, making her smile. They entered the main room and Adam announced, "Excuse me, everyone. When you're ready, please join us."

They went to the center table and sat at opposite ends to help keep their needs under control. Ophelia arrived with a cart of beverages and snacks. Damn, she's a good office manager. People started to arrive, grabbed a snack, and sat at the table. Eve felt a butterfly feeling, so she decided to take one more anti-nausea pill, just in case.

Just as she got to the water, Adam was there. "Are you okay? Your cheeks are red."

She looked at him. "Just a small wave." She looked around the table. "Taking something for it now." She winked and walked back to her spot.

After everyone was at the table, Adam started talking to the group. "Hello, everyone. Thanks for taking the time to come into the office today. We have a special guest here who is helping with my idea for refreshing the office space. Everyone, this is Eve."

The group said, "Hello," in unison. Each staff member introduced themselves and their role in the office. There was no way she was going to remember twenty new people's names and job titles, especially since her handouts were meant to be anonymous. She got up and handed out a few pieces of the concept art and her paperwork to everyone.

Besides, standing felt better on her stomach. She started going over a few ideas that were already discussed between her and Adam. Adam jumped in and gave her credit for the monitors in the waiting room. There was an 'ohh' around the group.

She emphasized that the pages were meant to be anonymous, but if anyone had something they wanted to talk about in more detail, then please leave their name and number so Adam and she could discuss their thoughts further in private.

Adam thanked everyone again and dismissed the group, then got up and walked over to Eve. He leaned over and whispered, "I'll be working in my office if you need me. Do you want to have lunch later?"

Eve leaned back. "That sounds good. For now, I'm going to be here so I can watch the flow of traffic and be available if they have any questions or thoughts." Adam nodded and walked to his office.

A few minutes later, Ophelia came up and asked, "What would you like for lunch?"

Eve whispered, "I just took an anti-nausea medicine, so either soft food or soup of some kind, just in case." Eve half-smiled and raised her eyebrows. Ophelia nodded in acknowledgment. Eve reached out and touched her arm. "Thank you."

After a few minutes, Eve walked around to see how work moved from desk to desk. She noticed that not many people worked in a corner of the office. So, she went there to see that point of view and tried to figure out why. There she noticed there was a constant humming sound. She looked out the window and didn't see anything. After walking around, she figured out the water heater on the other side of the wall was older. She looked at the installation date and frowned.

She knocked on Adam's door. He opened it, but he was on the phone, so she stayed by the door to give him some privacy during the call. He walked back over, pulled her in, shut the door, and then led her to sit on his lap. She leaned against him, wrapped her arms around him, and rested her head on his shoulder.

She listened to his voice talking about work. She could feel his voice vibrate against her chest, and she felt completely relaxed. She was only out for a few minutes, but enjoyed waking up to Adam stroking her arm and back with soft kisses on her cheek. She squeezed him as she woke.

"I love you, Beautiful."

She hummed and kissed his cheek. "I love you too." He touched her face softly.

"Did you need to tell me something?" His voice was low and soft as velvet.

Eve suddenly remembered why she came in and sat up. "I think the water heater in the far corner is on its last leg. I noticed that people were avoiding that corner, so I went to investigate. It's very noisy." She stood up, yawned, gave him a quick kiss, and then walked back to the door. "I'm going to keep watching and see if anyone is ready with their pages." She smiled and blew him a kiss before she went out the door.

Eve was taking notes at the center table when Ophelia came back. "Hello, Ms. Eve. I have a ginger tea with a bit of honey to help the tummy." She winked. "Lunch will be here shortly. Where would you like to eat?"

Eve looked around at the guys. "Where do the guys eat?"

Ophelia stood up and straightened her suit. "Almost everyone eats here or at their desk."

Eve smiled. "Then I will eat here. Thank you." Eve was never big on the ginger taste, but was willing to give it a try. By the time the guys started to eat lunch, she had about half the sheets returned. She started to read a few when Ophelia arrived with a bag for her. They both smiled and nodded. Eve pulled out what looked like a container of soup, crackers, and a cut-up apple.

The guys were all politely talking with her when Adam showed up. She smiled at him and saw his bag. "What do you have to eat?"

He sat down next to her and slid the contents out. "I apparently have a sandwich, chips, banana, and a pop." She held up her bag of cut apples.

"I've never been big on the bitter of Granny Smith. Want to trade?" He slid his banana over and she set the apple in front of him.

"Nice doing business with you," she said. They shook hands and she blushed, gaining the attention of the group. 'Oops, the secret's out now,' she thought to herself.

The lunch table was merry with chatter, mostly about work, family antics, and sports. She enjoyed hearing all the banter between them, like the Round Table of King Arthur and his knights. Eve leaned into Adam. "How often do you eat with the guys?" she whispered and sat upright.

Adam tilted his head. "Well, normally I'm here on the weekends when everyone's home. I tend to eat at my desk."

She half-smirked. "That can get messy and could potentially destroy some of your hard work if you had an accident." She winked and felt warm as more blush took over her neck.

He leaned back, shifted his weight in the chair, and placed a foot between hers to pull her leg closer. His hand then casually rested on her leg as his fingers started moving back and forth and then squeezed. He leaned to her and whispered, "Your body is doing it again. It wouldn't be good to take you here on the table in front of the guys, so I'm going back to my office to cool down."

He got up and walked away with his lunch. She hid her face with some of the papers as she felt her pink go dark for a moment, as the visual of having sex with an audience of men filled her mind.

Then the image changed from audience to participants as clothes started coming off of everyone. She got up and walked to the restroom, locking the door behind her. Her body got hot with the thought of all their hands and mouths on her. She leaned against the sink and ran the cold water, splashing her face to attempt to cool down, but her mind continued to spiral.

Cock after cock wanting to get themselves into her. She covered her mouth as her orgasm bolted through her body. She held still for several minutes as the wave subsided.

Just then she thought of Jessie holding her mouth. Was he just trying not to draw attention to them? Was that a misunderstanding on her part? She lowered her hand to her baby. Had she been calmer when talking to him… her brain went back to the day she confronted him. He wasn't trying to restrain her like the stranger was. He was hugging her, trying to apologize, when she freaked.

Oh, shit. Was she the one who hurt Jessie? Tears started to fall. She stood up to wipe her face when she felt the trigger in her belly. She instantly started vomiting. It was too soon to take another pill, so she had to ride this wave until it was done.

Adam

There was a knock on his door. He quickly opened it, hoping that Eve was there. He was surprised when one of the contractors was there with a smirk on his face. "What can I do for you?" Adam asked. He looked back at the now-empty table.

"The designer is in the bathroom getting sick. We were thinking that she should go so we all don't get sick. You know, post-COVID and all." The contractor shrugged his shoulders.

Adam looked over the man's shoulder and saw Ophelia gathering Eve's belongings. "You can't catch what she has because she's pregnant with bad nausea. But thanks for letting me know," he said, and he bolted to the restroom. As he approached, he could hear her retching again.

He knocked on the door and then tried to open it, but the knob would not turn. "Eve, it's me, Adam. Can you open the door, Beautiful?" There were no answer and the door stayed locked. He hated this feeling. He walked over to Ophelia. "Do you have the key to the door?"

She pulled out her key ring, flipped a few over, and held up an old brass key. "I think it's this one." He went back to the door as she finished packing her bag.

He knocked on the door again. "Eve, I'm coming in," he said as he turned the key. She had stopped vomiting and was washing her mouth when he entered. He could see in the mirror that tears had been streaming down her face. He grabbed a paper towel and handed it to her.

She stood up after a minute. "I'm better now. But that one was on you," she said as she shut the door. "You put a very naughty image in my mind of having sex on the table with all the guys watching." She blushed. 'Oops,' Adam thought to himself.

"My daydreams are getting crazier and taking over. I came in here to have an orgasm in private."

"Another one without me? Damn!" He crossed his arms and leaned on the doorframe.

She smirked at him and shook her head. "Then my hormones pull me in different directions, and that wave then triggered me to get sick." She took a deep breath and leaned on him. "I really need to brush my mouth out. I'm packing a toothbrush and paste from now on." That made Adam laugh. He opened the door and they walked out into the office together.

There was chatter, but it got quieter as they came back. Eve whispered, "I'm sorry if I screwed this up."

Adam pulled her closer and whispered, "If anything, I screwed it up. When I was warned about you, I let it slip that you were pregnant, not ill." Eve stopped and glared at him. "I'm sorry. Guess we don't have to keep our relationship a secret here anymore."

"Adam, I didn't want them to think I was here just because we're dating," she said with a huff.

He pulled her closer to him. "Working towards marriage." He kissed her on the cheek. "Ophelia packed your bag. Do you want to stay or go home to rest?" Eve looked around.

"I think I've seen enough. I have about half the pages. After you collect them, we can get together in a couple of days to go over the rest. Would Wednesday for dinner at your place work?"

He loved the idea of visiting more. Perhaps he could get her to stay the night. "Sounds good to me," he responded. "But for now, let's get you a cab."

Eve stopped. "No, I'm going to walk. I don't think I can handle the bouncing of a car right now." She crossed her eyes. "All that stop and go would be too much."

"Then I will walk with you." They smiled and held hands. When they got to Ophelia's desk, Eve stopped.

"Thank you for all your help. I'm sorry my stomach wasn't strong enough today." Eve smiled with sorrowful eyes.

Ophelia nodded. "Don't worry, dear. It will get better in the second trimester."

Eve looked at Adam and grinned. "Yep. She already knows."

Adam just shook his head at the two.

Entry 3: Re-design and Drawing at Adam's

After Eve's realization, she needed to talk with Jessie to air out what happened without anger or fear. They texted and agreed to meet for a bit before Adam normally got home. She decided to make a display box so he could feel what she felt and hopefully help him understand the importance of a woman's preparation before having sex.

One side of the box had a soft piece of velvet. She gave it several small folds so his fingers could slide in and feel surrounded by its smooth silkiness. The other side was a different subject. She attached a rough, sixty-grit coarse sandpaper. She made this side smaller to resemble what it's like to be unprepared.

In her mind, she wanted to go over the key points of touching and kissing but was unsure exactly how to talk about it without getting too personal. Eve shook her head, trying to get the image of being too personal with Jessie out of her mind. "Damn hormones," she said to herself.

She had her bag loaded down with the lasagna she prepped the night before and salad makings that just needed to be tossed together. Along with her drawing boards and pencils, she was wondering if she should get a pull box to lighten her load.

Soon enough, she's going to have a big counterweight in front, and she's not going to want to pick up anything too heavy. She mulled that over as the elevator was going up to the condo. An elevator would be nice at her place. But her building is older and is only four floors.

When the baby comes, will she still stay in her place? It would be super crazy to have all of them under one-bedroom roof. She smirked. Would be nice to be closer to both of them. She needed to think about that some more later. She arrived at their door and knocked.

She could hear footsteps, and Jessie opened the door. "Hey, Babe. It's great to see you." Eve smirk shifted to a smiled.

"Nice to see you too." She noticed that she didn't have any feelings of pulling away. He held out his hand, and she placed hers on his without thinking twice about it. His lips warmed her hand for the brief moment it was there.

"Please come in," he said as he stepped back. Eve nodded, walked to the kitchen, and turned on the oven.

"What are you doing?"

She turned her head. "This is an oven. You use it to bake food." She laughed at her attempt to make a joke and hoped he got it also.

He smiled and waved his hand in a dismissive way. "I'm sorry. What I meant to say was, what are you making?"

She smiled. "I prepped something yummy for our tummies. It will take about forty-five minutes to heat. It should be done by the time Adam gets here. I didn't bring any wine, but if you want or have some, a red will go nicely with it."

Jessie knelt and placed a hand on her stomach. "Sorry baby, no wine for you for another 22 years." They both laughed.

She pulled her dish out of the bag and set it next to the stove. Then pulled the salad makings and put them in the fridge. "You boys need to go shopping. Your fridge is practically empty. Beer, water, and condiments are not food."

Jessie laughed. "We basically eat out for every meal."

Eve was shocked. "Do you not know how to feed yourselves? Man babies, in this house. No wonder you guys needed a woman." She walked up to Jessie and gave him a kiss on the cheek. The oven was ready, so she slid the meal in and set the timer.

"That should give us enough time to talk for a bit." She took a deep breath and sighed. "Can we sit on the couch?"

Jessie nodded his head yes. She started walking over and set her bag on the table. However, he bounded to his room and came right back.

"Before we get started, I wanted to apologize for missing your birthday. It was marked on the calendar, but I missed it," he said as he held out a small black jewelry box.

Eve instantly recognized the Tiffany box and pulled back, covered her mouth with her hand as she gasped. "Jessie, you didn't have to do that," she smiled and stared at him.

"I'm not going to be the bum who couldn't repay the kindness you showed me on my birthday." Eve saw that Jessie was still wearing the bracelet she gave him. She reached out and spun the bracelet around so his initials were on the top. That made her smile more as she enjoyed that he still appreciated her gift. She slowly opened the box and saw a stunning pair of sapphire earrings. She was speechless for a moment and didn't know what to say.

"Do you like them?" He had a hopeful look in his eyes and face.

She looked at him as tears started to grow. "They are beautiful. Thank you."

Jessie reached up and wiped the two tears that escaped her eyes. "No, Babe. You are beautiful."

Eve felt flushed at his compliment, and a happy smile filled her face. She gently removed her earrings and placed them in the lid. Then she put the new ones in her ears. "I love them. Thank you again." She pulled him in for a big hug and kiss on the cheek as he slid his arms around her waist. They held each other for a moment, and it felt wonderful.

A wave of feelings flooded her, so she took a deep breath and then pulled back. "Please have a seat." She gestured toward the couch. He sat down and leaned back, and she remained standing. "Please listen first. Okay?" Jessie nodded his head.

"Last time, I was very upset. I experienced something that no one should have. After watching you grow, it got me thinking that maybe you didn't know the difference. So, in the spirit of helping, you to learn, I made something." She removed her creation from her bag and sat down next to him as she held it in her lap.

"Contrary to what most men think, a woman's body is not ready for sex at any given moment." She felt her face flush. 'Just breathe,' she reminded herself.

"When you surprised me by wanting to engage in sex, my response was that my body was not ready." She paused and looked at the box as she fiddled with her fingers. "It does take a little bit to make sure all the fluids are flowing properly." She felt her blush deepen and looked away.

Jessie set a hand on hers, and she looked back, knowing she was red-faced.

"It's okay. Please continue." She nodded and calmed herself.

"There are a few actions that indicate to a woman's body to prepare for intimacy." Her body was now starting to get hot, and she freed her hand from his, then stood up. She grabbed a page from her bag and handed it to him since she was already feeling overwhelmed.

"Read this out loud, and I'll fill in a bit here and there."

Jessie cleared his throat.

"1. EYE TO BODY. You notice a person across a room – you think you would like to get to know them. There is no action, just a spark of interest. Eyes scrolling over the body but from afar."

Eve pressed her lips before speaking up, "The truth is, I friend requested you a month prior to our first meeting." She breathed a sigh of relief. "So, I had already known a little about you when we met at Jake's." She smiled, glad that she finally got that off her chest.

Jessie smirked, then looked down as he continued.

"2. EYE TO EYE. Your eyes meet – you quickly look away. You look back again. Your eyes lock. It probably means you would like to get to know one another."

"This is when we first properly met. You blocked the door from us going into Jake's." Eve giggled.

"3. VOICE TO VOICE. You talk. You hear the person's voice for the first time. It is like music. Your heart flutters. All your senses are acute. Communication starts via cell phone, dates, letters & messages. You learn as much as you can about this person."

"We had a rough beginning since you forgot about me. But when we did go on our proper date, I thought it went well." She smiled.

"4. HAND TO HAND. It may start with helping you up a staircase, taking your hand while watching a movie, or just walking. The contact is thrilling, sending shivers down your spine. How exciting is it when someone reaches for your hand for the first time?"

"Kissing one's hand is a huge step here. You then skipped to number seven." She felt a flush wave growing again.

Jessie moved his finger as he skipped five and six.

"7. MOUTH TO MOUTH. The first kiss — it can be a fumble or something that races your heart so fast. You have known one another because you have taken it slowly through the previous steps. This is the beginning of deep physical bonding — hugging and kissing."

"On our date, you skipped to this step. I also pulled you in at the door. I was overflowing with excitement about the party and didn't think I'd get a chance later. Kissing is very important. There are so many different levels, from a simple quick kiss to full-body involvement kissing. You watch Adam when he gets home. Even though we agreed to limit our outward expressions around you, I will be able to get him to kiss me because he pays attention to me. You can read the rest of this page for yourself later. But from here you skipped to twelve."

Jessie's finger skipped to the end.

"12. SEXUAL INTERCOURSE. This is a gift you only give once — the ultimate proof that you trust another person. This is the most dangerous physical activity you can engage in when you consider the consequences. You will remember this day for the rest of your life." Jessie sat quietly for a moment.

She watched him as he started to process what he had read. "Touching, hand-holding, kissing is all part of it. Learning to be good at oral sex also makes a difference. Don't let a relationship become a one-way street. Besides, foreplay and oral sex are the biggest turn-on for a girl's body to get ready for penetration. Take this sheet, re-read the whole section, and add it to what you have already learned. Hopefully, it sticks because a woman is telling you and not just another man who may still be learning himself but has managed to publish a book."

Jessie looked up from the page. "I'm not that into kissing or giving oral sex." Eve was shocked for a moment.

"If you want relationships to continue, you're going to need to learn. Adam and I have not had sex, but he loves what I taste like." She went full red with the oversharing and covered her face. She sat back down and placed the box in front of him. "That leads me back to my experiment."

She turned the box so the word 'Prepared' faced him. "When a woman's body is ready, she is prepared for sexual entry." She started to blush again. "Close your eyes and keep them closed." He did as she asked, and she placed his fingers at the opening of the box. 'Breathe, girl. He needs to know.'

"I want you to think of your hand as the head and shaft of your penis. When you're ready, slide in and out like you're having sex." He slowly moved in at first, then he hummed in his pleasure at the softness. He moved in and out a few times and then stopped and pulled his hand out. "Being ready is smooth and very pleasurable for both. You can open your eyes."

He did and looked at her. "Do you remember what you said to me when you entered?" Jessie looked down at the box and shook his head no. Eve turned the box over. The writing said, 'Unprepared. Damn Babe, you're so tight.'

She could see him reading the words, and then he looked at her. "I did say that. I remember that now." She smirked and nodded her head, yes.

"Close your eyes and repeat." He eagerly slid his hand in and stopped. His eyes popped open, and he looked at her. "Think about how you pushed in and out. How fast and hard you thrusted while I was not ready." He moved in a little more and then pulled his hand out. He looked at his hand, and there were several scratches, and a couple of them were starting to bleed.

Eve pulled gauze and ointment from her bag. She cleaned his hand and pressed to stop the bleeding. She was starting to tear up as she remembered that evening. Her throat tightened as she spoke, "This is what you did to me. Not scratches. I was torn in several places," she squeaked out as her tears fell.

She let go of his hand and put everything back into her bag. She got up and walked to the fridge for a bottle of water as she wiped the tears from her face.

He got up and rested on the counter next to her. "You were right. I had no idea. Last time you tried to talk about this, you were so upset and scared of me. When I tried to hug you, you freaked out. I understand now why you reacted the way that you did."

Her tears spilled over again. He pulled a napkin and softly touched her hand. She looked at him, and he reached up to dry her face. He gently pulled her to him and set her hand to his heart. "I'm truly sorry for hurting you."

She nodded her head in acceptance but couldn't speak yet. With his other hand, he softly touched his fingers on her chin, traced her jawline, and took a step closer.

She whispered, "I'm sorry for slapping you and throwing the vase of flowers at you."

He rested his hand on her shoulder and his forehead on hers. "Do you forgive me?" His eyes looked so sad.

She took a slow, deep breath. "I forgave you when you sang your song on stage for me. That's why I felt confident enough to talk to you about it again."

His hand slid down her arm and then tucked in behind her waist. "May I kiss you? The wonderful, patient, kind mother of my baby?"

She looked up at him and smiled. She could see the longing in his eyes. She felt her own longing growing for him. Her fingers tightened on his chest, and she raised her other arm to his elbow and softly pulled. They locked into a well-needed kiss, full of sadness and empathy, heat and desire.

She pulled back when she realized that she wanted more. However, she knew she needed to end the kiss, knowing that Adam had a camera somewhere in the condo, but at that moment, with Jessie, this felt right. "You know Adam's watching, right?"

He nodded his head yes. "I figured as much. I've been casually looking but have not found any inside. The one outside the door is more obvious." They both laughed. "Come over and stand by the couch. I would like to have a conversation with Peanut."

He pulled her hand, and she followed him to the couch. She stood there as Jessie sat down on the couch. He placed his hands on her hips and his ear to her belly. This made her laugh. He was going on and on about everything. Then it occurred to her.

"How is this going to work between the three of us? Are we going to share custody? All live here like 'Three Men and a Baby' style? There are so many questions that lead to more questions." She started to rapid-fire.

Jessie squeezed her hips tighter. "I know it's all confusing. We can tackle one hurdle at a time. For now, we are just enjoying each other." Jessie kept on talking and listening to the sounds of her belly.

Adam burst through the door, causing Eve and Jessie to freeze for a moment. Eve couldn't tell if he was angry or overly excited. Adam stopped and saw Jessie in front of Eve talking to her belly.

"And there is my best friend now. The big strong man who will love and guide you. And if he has any say in it, he will be marrying your mommy sooner than later. I'm okay with that because I know he will take good care of both of you." Jessie turned his head and placed a long kiss on Eve's belly. "We will chat soon."

He then leaned back a little but kept his hands on her hips. "Dude. You want in on this conversation before I hang up the line?"

Adam leaned his head back, took a deep breath, and then focused on Jessie. "I'm good, thanks." He then looked at the kitchen. "Something smells good."

"Oh, I need to get the salad mixed up." She leaned over and kissed Jessie on the top of the head. She then walked over to Adam. "Good evening, Héros." She wrapped her arms around his back and pulled him in as she looked up at him.

Adam looked over at Jessie and then back at her. "Hello, Beautiful." She pulled a little harder, and then he fully leaned down and claimed her mouth. Suddenly, she felt her whole body get hot, pulled away, and started to fan herself.

"Please go get out of your suit and into something comfy before dinner is ready. Should only be a few minutes now." She pointed to his bedroom and gave a firm swat on his rump.

She went back to the kitchen and turned on some soft music. She then started to dance as she got the salad ready while Jessie sat quietly on the couch. He got up and came to stand next to her with the page she had printed.

"I've never really been a big kisser. I think it was my way of keeping girls at a distance so I wouldn't emotionally connect with them." Eve turned and looked at him.

"That's sad. I'm glad you have come to understand your reasoning, and now you can work through it. Women love to kiss. It's one of the main ways we all connect physically. You will have to work on that." She gave him a soft pat on the arm.

He pointed to another step on the printout. She looked and blushed instantly. "I've never been into giving oral either." She was shocked silent for a moment.

"Do you like receiving a blowjob?" He grinned as big as he could and nodded. "Well, so do we. Remember, there are times when to and not to. You have to make sure the girl is clean—no STDs. And cleanliness, like after a shower, helps reduce odor and taste. But if you jump in after she's been at work all day and stopped off at the gym before getting home—well, she's going to be full scent." She made a sour face.

"But I hear that some men really enjoy it that way. So, to each their own, right?" She shrugged her shoulders. "Remember, two-way street. Give and receive." She leaned on the counter. "Do you understand?" She waited for his response.

He nodded his head. "I do. Thank you for explaining all of this to me." He smiled and gave her a kiss on the cheek.

"Good. Please set the table as I get dinner out of the oven," she asked as she handed him the salad bowl.

When she pulled the hot tray out of the oven, Adam crept up behind her and wrapped an arm around her belly as the other pulled back her hair. He leaned in and started kissing her neck. Goosebumps ran down her arm and a small moan escaped her. After she set the baking dish down, she leaned back into him, turned her head, and collided their mouths together.

Just then, Jessie cleared his throat and Adam ended the kiss. Eve let out a sigh because she wanted more but then stood upright again. "Jessie, if you don't like seeing me kiss this beautiful woman, then you can just go to your room." He turned his head to look at him. "Or you can move out, giving us privacy."

Jessie had a look of shock on his face. "I was just trying to say that dinner was ready." Eve turned to face Adam.

"Adam." He looked back at Eve and she raised an eyebrow. "We had a good conversation tonight. Worked a few things out that he needed to learn, and we are good now." She smiled.

"She's saying it politely," Jessie added as he set the hot dish in the center of the table. "We talked about my error in judgment and how it affected her. I apologized from the bottom of my heart. But she's right. I think we are finally moving forward again."

She took a step back and took off the mitts. Before he could say anything, she changed the subject and pointed her finger. "The fridge is a perfect example of a bachelor pad. You will save so much money if you just cooked for yourselves." She smiled and walked to the table.

She sat down in the same spot as last time, but she laughed to herself, thinking that she wouldn't have to worry about whose knees she bumped into under the table. This time, she held out both her hands and waited for them to each hold one. She lowered her head and waited. It was the first time she felt good to pray again.

"Thank you, God, for bringing these two wonderful men into my life," she said.

"Thank you for sending people with compassion to help guide me from the wrong path," Jessie added.

"Thank you for the strength to protect the ones I care about," Adam said as he squeezed her hand.

Dinner went by peacefully as the boys discussed what they covered in school today. Eve talked about textures and how they can change the mood of a room. Afterwards, they all returned to the couches to let dinner settle, and they listened to the music playing in the background. Jessie got up, walked over to Eve, and held out his hand.

"May I have a dance with my baby?" She looked at Adam and he shrugged his shoulders. She turned back to Jessie and accepted his hand as he pulled her up. He gave her a slow turn and then settled in behind her. He placed one hand on her belly as the other moved her hair over, and he rested his chin on her shoulder. Then they started to sway to the beat of the music after he laced his fingers together on her stomach.

She closed her eyes and rested her head back on his shoulder as she placed her hands over his. The song was sad, but the rhythm was nice to slowly dance to. She could hear each breath he took, and he would occasionally squeeze his arms tighter, pulsing his heat into her body. She felt a warm wave roll through her, and her body was heating up.

Suddenly, she felt Adam press into her front side. He softly slid his fingers into her hair to keep her head tilted back, and he placed hot kisses along her neck. She moved her hands from her stomach and embraced Adam's head with one and Jessie's head with the other.

Her heartbeat quickened, and yet she felt calm. Adam's hands slowly made their way down her sides as his kisses worked up her jaw. He firmly cupped her ass when he dove his tongue into her mouth. She let out a deep, throaty moan as her whole body felt like it was burning.

Jessie started to kiss the other side of her neck as his fingers started moving on her abdomen. Her heart now raced in anticipation. She felt Jessie gently thrust his pelvis into her backside, pushing his hardness into her ass as Adam pulled her into a thrust from the front side, effectively creating a sexual Eve sandwich.

That was all she could handle as an orgasm fully consumed her. "Oh God!" she exclaimed as she broke the kiss with Adam and pulled herself from their embrace. Wave after wave sent moans erupting from her lips. Her hands were locked onto the corner of the counter for support as she prevented herself from falling over in ecstasy.

Adam

"Are you okay?" Jessie started to walk towards Eve, but Adam jutted his arm out to prevent him from going any farther.

"Just wait a minute." He shook his head at Jessie. "We are right here for you, Beautiful," he called out as another moan escaped her while she leaned against the counter.

"Please explain what's happening." Jessie looked worried. "Is something wrong with the baby? Do we need to go to the hospital?"

Adam knew Jessie was going to continue to spiral with bad thoughts, so he pulled him aside to explain.

"She's having a spontaneous orgasm. We overloaded her with emotions and her body is reacting." They both looked back at her for a moment.

Jessie faced Adam again. "When I had my hands on her stomach, her abdomen rolled like a belly dancer."

They stood at attention when she walked back up to them. She reached out and held each of their hands. "I have something that needs to be cleared up." She pulled Adam in for a kiss, and this time she demanded his tongue. He dove right in, making his claim to her mouth. She pulled back and stared at Adam for a moment as he tried to calm his breathing. She then turned to Jessie and pulled him in.

'Fuck!' Adam watched in horror as Jessie kissed her with the same ferocity he had. This was spiraling out of control and he had none.

She looked back and forth between the two men. Then she let go and took a couple of steps back. "I need a minute or two to process this."

They both nodded their heads. "We will be over here on the couch when you're ready to talk," Adam said as he motioned to Jessie to sit down.

Adam whispered, "We messed this up big time, seriously crossed the line. What we just did was so wrong, like having sex without permission—wrong. This whole thing could completely blow up in our faces, and she could say that she never wants to see us ever again." Jessie looked worried as they watched her for a moment.

"We just engaged in a throuple activity without prior discussing it nor having her permission to do so," Adam explained.

"Throuple?" Jessie asked as his eyes darted to Eve and back. Adam nodded his head, yes.

"A three-person couple. As a group, we were just making out with our girl. A ménage à trois, without the sex." Adam leaned back to see Eve pacing in the kitchen before whispering again. "Pay attention. In this type of relationship, she is the queen and has all the power and the final say. We agree to her terms. What she says goes, or we go. That is, if she even wants to continue. This could have just sunk all the work done to earn her love."

Adam leaned back and took a deep breath. His heart was pounding. He did not want to lose her over the fact that he was loving on her at the wrong time.

"I didn't realize what I was doing. I had this need to touch her. And then when you joined in and started kissing her, I couldn't resist and needed to feel her on my lips."

She walked up to them and was quiet as she tapped her toes. She opened her mouth, but nothing came out. She blushed deep red and then walked away. They looked at each other, but Adam knew this could go wrong. "At least she's trying to process it in a way she can understand." He needed to help fix his fuck-up. "How about we start the conversation and state our own intentions?"

Jessie nodded his head. "I just wish I knew what my intentions were. I feel like life is on its head, and the only part of my compass that works points directly to Eve."

Adam looked at him in surprise. "That's actually... really good. You should lead with that." They got up and walked over to Eve. "Beautiful. Can we talk for a minute while you're still thinking?" She stopped dead in her tracks but then eventually nodded her head. Adam reached for her hand and pulled her into a hug.

"I'm sorry. I wasn't trying to bombard you. I felt your pheromones and was so turned on that I needed to be a part of it. You know where I stand." He leaned in and whispered in her ear. "I love you. I want to marry you when you're ready. If you need to explore more options before then, I will be supportive. Working towards marriage, right?" He leaned up and placed a kiss on her forehead.

She smiled, nodded yes as her eyes started to tear up. "I love you too, Héros." His heart pounded hard as he gave her a soft kiss.

She rested her head on his chest. "I have these other feelings. I don't know if it's just a residual from before or something that is leading to more, and I honestly don't know where to go from here. Like before, when that creep wouldn't let go. The two of you were there, and when we all hugged, it felt right. I didn't say anything because it's not normal to care this much for two men at the same time. And, if things do progress, I wouldn't want to hurt your feelings because of how I'm feeling." Her tears fell on his shirt.

Adam looked at Jessie and gestured for him to join in. He then lifted her chin and ran his thumb along her cheeks to remove the tears. "If we all choose to go forward with a three-way relationship, honesty is required. No matter how hard or embarrassing it is to say. Secrets lead to distrust and jealousy."

She pulled him into a hug. "How would it work, since you want to wait until marriage for sex, if he's willing sooner than you? Would we have to ask first? Discuss just after, or would you just have to understand that it could happen?"

Adam's heart was pounding with the thought of Jessie being with her again. He honestly didn't want her to have sex with him, but he knew at this point that if they did, there would be no way to stop it without looking like a total jealous jerk.

"We would all understand that we have feelings and needs. We don't need to tell him everything we've done or will do, just as you guys don't need to tell me everything you guys do." He set his hand on the baby. "I have never asked for details. Nor do I need to know."

She smiled. "And what if it's like tonight, where we are all in the mood to be closer? When it comes time for intimacy, will you be able to stop, or would you join in?"

Adam lowered his head. "I would have to fight myself to stop. If you two continue, I would still like to participate. From just watching to partially participating, but not required if the two of you want privacy." She turned her back to Adam, and he wrapped his arms around her.

"Jessie. What do you think?" Adam let out a deep breath as she turned her focus onto Jessie.

"I'm not going to pretend that I'm a good man. I have been messed up for so many years. But since meeting you, getting to know you, and the help in becoming more, you are the only thing I can focus on. There is a pull that keeps me coming back to you. Even school has become easier knowing that I have a goal. I know that the two of you have a strong connection. There is no way I'm going to come in between what you guys have. If you choose this three-way path, I will honor all the guidelines you set forth. I think Adam will agree with me. One of us can find a contract for you to modify to your needs. I think we should sit down, write it all out, and sign it."

Eve leaned forward as she thought. "Can you really put to paper how one feels, or is allowed to feel, before it happens?"

Adam supposed the two lawyers in the room would have her outvoted on that subject. Adam and Jessie stared at each other for a moment.

"Fine. If you can find a contract, I will look it over. I find it difficult to understand how it will help, but I'm sure you guys will help me to understand." She took a deep breath. "Can we shelf this conversation and all this emotion for another time? I think I've had all I can handle." She took a breath and turned to Adam.

"I'm feeling drained. Do you mind if I lie down for a few minutes before we start going over paperwork?"

Without a second thought, Adam scooped her up and took her to his room. He lay down and she snuggled into him. Thoughts of this evening swirled in his mind. Efforts must be doubled. His battle just became a full-scale nuclear war. He softly ran his fingertips up and down her arm, and she was out within a few minutes.

He was hoping she would stay the night but had never thought the evening would take a turn this dramatic. He looked down at her, and he knew she was out because her body became heavy against his. At least she wasn't vomiting. Hopefully, she is getting better. He carefully slid out of bed and covered her with a light blanket.

When he made it out to the living room, Jessie was relaxing on the couch. "We need to have a little chat. I like the idea of a contract, but I think we need to have one just between us. Last time we had a verbal agreement, you broke it and she became pregnant. How am I supposed to trust you in a relationship that deals with more complicated matters of the heart?"

Jessie looked at him. "I wasn't planning on this happening. I was counting myself lucky that she was willing to allow me to be a part of my child's life. Besides, it's not you that has to trust me, but her. The contract of the relationship wouldn't be between you and me since neither of us swing that way. But speaking of trust, how about you remove the cameras from inside the condo?"

"The only reason I had a camera was in case of a break-in. It is video only, no audio," Adam replied, lying through his teeth.

"It doesn't matter. If Eve and I are going to go down this path, I need to know that 'Big Brother' is not watching our every move and then going to question me about it later. Is that why you arrived tonight in such a huff? You were watching us, weren't you?"

Adam leaned forward and rested his face in his hands. "I had been watching. Just in case the two of you started fighting again. When I saw her pull you into a quick kiss..." Adam's blood started to boil. But not being able to hear the conversation left his mind to try and fill in the blanks. Adam stood up. "I was watching for her safety. At this point, I can trust that you won't hurt her. I'm leaving the door camera."

He walked over to the bookshelf and removed a book and set it on the coffee table when he sat down. He opened the book and turned a switch off. The light went out and then he closed the book.

"Really, Adam? You put a camera in the book, The Rear Window by Alfred Hitchcock?" They both chuckled.

"I loved the irony when I picked it," Adam shrugged his shoulders.

They were both quiet for a bit before Jessie spoke, "Dinner was great tonight. She's right. We need to cook more. She called us baby men."

"I can see more dinners at home in our future," Adam added, leaned over and gave Jessie's leg a push. "Come on, bro. She cooked; we clean."

Eve

Eve slowly woke up from her nap and clung to the euphoria of her dream. Now that her feelings for the two men were out in the open, she felt overall better. However, she still worried about hurting them or their friendship in the process. She listened to the noises around her and realized that Adam was still in the room with her. She opened her eyes and saw him working at his desk. "How long have I been out?"

Adam sat up and put his papers away. He came over to the bed and climbed in next to her and pulled her close to him. "It's been a little over an hour. How are you feeling?"

She took a deep breath. "I'm feeling better than I have in a long time." She paused, wanting to tread carefully. This was such a difficult situation she was in.

"I know I'm naive to a lot in the world when it comes to relationships. My past has been difficult, at best," she paused as she blushed. "Jasper is my best mate from secondary school. We both agreed that if we were still virgins, we would be each other's first before going off to college. That way, we would not lose that part of ourselves to someone who didn't care for us as much as we did for them." Eve paused as she collected her thoughts and Adam softly stroked her arm.

"My aunt was away, taking care of business, so we spent the whole weekend learning different positions. What felt good, and what didn't. I learned so much about myself that weekend." She looked up at Adam. "I really enjoy having sex." She blushed and tucked her face back into Adam's chest.

"I think that need interfered with the next selections of who I entered a relationship with. After secondary, I took an academic gap to deal with issues with the estate and some crazy agricultural problems for the community. So, everyone I knew got a year at college before I got there. I started in the winter of 2019. My next sexual interaction was a one-night stand with a boy who I knew from school, before I moved in with my aunt. I helped him to realize that he was in lust, not love." She smirked.

"Suddenly, everyone knew who I was again. I felt popular, but it was all fake. The next boy I was with was trying to get me to buy stuff for him to prove myself worthy of his love. Just because I have access to money doesn't make it mine. I was there for all of a few months before the world shut down and I finished school at home. Isolated and socially inept in the way of life, I had to figure out a way of taking care of my obligations and provide a future for the family name." Eve let out a big sigh.

"My greatest fear was never finding love or being loved for me. That I would have to settle for an arranged marriage." She started to tear up. "I had an opportunity to continue my studies here and I jumped at it for the experience. I came across an article about a man and his company. In the last part, it talked about his son and how he was going to school near where I was. I had this crazy pull towards him. Didn't know how else to explain it but that fate was pulling me that way. That is how I met both of you."

She released the tension from her shoulders. "I no longer have the fear of not being loved because of you guys. But it is clear to me now that I'm connected to both of you guys for some crazy reason." She finished and face-planted into his chest.

"It's insane to me that anyone could treat you so cruelly. You are so kind, patient, smart, and have a warm heart that melts me every time I'm near you. Your capacity for love is amazing, and I'm astonished that you are willing to care for two men at the same time," he smiled.

"I think we all have something we need to learn from each other. That's how and why this group works. It may be a triangle to start, but really, when we share, it all comes full circle. Look at how much Jessie has learned in the last couple of months. He is a different person from when we were all at Jake's. Even you have changed. I can see the changes in myself also. There is no way I could have had this type of conversation with anyone two months ago. But, here I am, starting down a crazy new path and being open and honest about it. Speaking of helping, I have something for you." She gave Adam a quick kiss and then popped up out of bed.

Eve went to the living room, grabbed her bag, and brought it back to Adam's room. She set it down by the desk and then pulled two books from it. "Since I'm not skilled enough to be your teacher, and I don't know your comfort level with asking, I thought I would bring you something to read and learn for when your vow is over and we continue…" Eve blushed and buried her face in the books. She took a deep breath. "I'm looking forward to when we can make love." She peeked her eyes over the books and saw his smile before she handed the books to him.

He read the titles out loud. "Preparing for the Wedding Night and Sex for Dummies." When Adam looked at Eve, he had surprise written all over his face.

"I was looking through the books before I bought them, and these two seemed to be the best." She smiled.

Adam placed a hand on hers. "I'm not a virgin. I can see how you could misunderstand my vow as such." He looked at the books again. "It has been almost six years since I chose to wait for you. I will give them a good read-through so I can be up-to-date and please you in all the ways possible when our time comes."

He leaned forward and kissed her. Then he pulled back and put the books on his desk. He came back to lie with her again, slipped his leg between hers, and pulled her leg up over his hip. He then leaned into her so he could apply pressure on her pelvis with his.

"When I was younger, I didn't know about the size difference. I thought penis sizes were all the same. Mine is a blessing and a curse. My first time was with my high school girlfriend. She was also a virgin. When we had sex, I ended up hurting her. I knew from then on, I would never be anyone's first again."

He paused when he saw Eve blush. He felt a pheromone wave come off her but focused on what he wanted to say. "I had two girlfriends in college. The first only wanted me for money. The son of a successful businessman, I had just become the owner of the family business. Going to architecture and law school, all she saw was what could be bought for her. We never had sex. She said she had a vow with God and wanted to wait until marriage—only to find out that she was having sex with others who gave her gifts and then would dump them." He shook his head. "Kinda like your experience." He smirked as Eve shook her head.

"My third girlfriend somehow found out about my size and only wanted me for sex. Not to be blunt, but we had plenty of sex, yet I never really knew anything about her. Never talked or connected emotionally. I never even knew when her birthday was. That is when I chose to wait and save myself for my wife. To take the time and connect deeper, mentally and emotionally, before moving on to intimacy." They smiled at the same time.

Eve reached up and softly touched his face. "I'm glad now that we are taking the time. I see how learning about someone is important." She blushed deep red and took another deep breath. She was super curious now.

"I didn't know it at the time either, but Jasper is bigger. Since then, everyone else who was average just seemed small. Reflecting back, I like the feeling of..." She paused and tapped her lip to think. She looked back at him. "Being filled in or is it being full?" She shook her head and nervously laughed. "There are a couple of different types. Are you the longer or thicker kind?"

He pulled her into a deep kiss and pressed his pelvis a bit against hers. Then he leaned his forehead to hers. "I'm both," he replied.

Eve was pleasantly surprised. She was not expecting that answer. "Oh my! That will be new." She wasn't sure what to say, so she pulled him in for a tighter hug as her mind started to wander.

"You asked me to be patient with you, and I wholeheartedly agreed. Can you be patient with me while I figure out what's going on with Jessie?" Eve felt her heart sink to her stomach. "I feel like I'm being selfish, asking this of you. Am I being crazy?"

He gave her a squeeze. "I don't think you're crazy. You started with Jessie. It's only logical to see it to its conclusion. I've waited almost six years. What's a little bit longer gonna do but make my longing for you grow? You never know, this throuple may work out. Besides, he's going to want to stay close for the baby. From what he said and has shown so far, he's going to be an active co-parent."

Eve sighed. "You are so amazing, and I'm so lucky to have you in my life," she added and leaned up. "Not to change the subject, but we need to get to work before it gets too late. I brought the pages from Monday. Do you have the remaining pages?"

Adam groaned his disapproval as he stretched and got off the bed. "Yep, I have them sealed in envelopes for you to open without me seeing."

She laughed. "Like I'm not going to share the results with you." She got up, grabbed the papers from her bag, and sat on the bed. He grabbed his from the desk and joined her. They each took turns opening pages and reading the statements. They all said the same thing: Employee break room.

"Was it your father's idea to have the large center round table?" Adam nodded his head yes. "It was his thought to keep everyone equal in the conversation, no matter how much experience they had." She tapped her finger to her lip as she thought of the square footage. "If we relocate the conference area to the SW corner, we could combine it with a kitchenette that ties into the plumbing for the restroom. That way, it would serve a dual purpose."

She bit her lip as she thought. "Beautiful. Don't bite your lip." He reached up, cupped her face, and softly ran his thumb along her lips. Eve blushed. She didn't even realize she was doing it. "That's my job." He leaned forward, sucked her lip into his mouth, and then kissed her. She moaned, and a big smile filled his face. She got to thinking and traced her fingers in little circles along his chest.

"We could put the round table downstairs, and it would be great for collaboration work. There is plenty of room for blueprints and conceptual drawings." She raised her eyebrows at Adam while waiting for his response.

"Does this mean you accept my offer to work together?" Eve smiled and reached to hold his hand.

"Yes."

Entry 4: The Contract

Eve was so excited and nervous that she couldn't keep her vomiting under control, so she ended up not going to school on Thursday or Friday. That gave her extra time to think about the contract that Jessie recommended. She did a deep dive into the lifestyle, and she came to several realizations. Ultimately, she was in control. She got to set the terms. If the guys broke the contract, she could end the relationship right then.

That made her sad, thinking about putting all that energy in just to walk away. Not to mention that this situation was not just about sex. So, she researched a relationship contract. After reading a few, she knew this was the path that she wanted to go and used the other as an addendum. Would she be able to require Adam to have sex with her? Would she want to force him and cause an issue down the line? No. She wouldn't want to be required to have sex if she didn't want to. In fact, she was going to add that to her page.

She printed out several pages and used them as guidelines to create her own. She modified section by section to what she liked. She made sure to leave room for them to be able to add information. Plus, she added requirements before engaging in sexual activities. She filled out the informational section about her likes and dislikes.

After she finished writing out her contract, she typed it all out so there would be no misunderstandings. She was so aroused that she decided that today she would relieve the pent-up feelings before tonight's meeting with the guys. Besides, she had returned to the adult store for a new, larger toy to help her get ready for Adam's size but had not used it yet.

She hoped that both would have more stamina than Jessie did last time.

Adam

Ever since Eve's birthday, Adam had felt guilty about placing the hidden camera in her room. He should have had more control over his desire to watch. Just because she had mentioned getting a toy to help her with her ever-growing needs was no excuse for betraying her trust. He had checked in on her every night since then and was hoping that he would be able to see her pleasure herself, to learn what she liked. And yet, she has not used it. At least not in bed.

She may be satisfying herself in the shower, but he refused to place a camera there, even though he greatly loved to watch her shower. Perhaps she preferred early morning masturbation and he was just missing it.

He pondered the thought for a moment. He purposefully chose not to set the camera to notification since she would be setting it off at all hours of the day and night while he was sleeping and she was not. Finally, he decided, after checking on her for weeks now, that the next time he was at her place, he was going to remove the camera.

He saw that over the last two days, she had spent a lot of time vomiting in the restroom. He hoped that she would be okay for tonight's meeting that she had asked for. He would be extra mindful to keep the path to the restroom clear if she felt the need to run.

As he was driving on his way home, he noticed she was climbing into bed. His little woman was probably worn out. But she wasn't lying flat, and the lights were still on. So, she was not napping. He pulled over and paid closer attention. Was she having stomach pains again or was she drawing with her knees up?

He turned the volume on, and he instantly heard her moaning. The rhythmic, wet sound of her pleasing herself took him over. "Oh, Adam!" Hearing her call out his name sent his cock into overdrive. He quickly grabbed a tissue, knowing he wasn't going to last long. Her in-and-out wet sounds were music to his ears. He kept one hand on the wheel as his other softly moved up and down his pants, over his shaft. With the occasional thump sound of her toy as she fully plunged it in, his climax grew closer.

He watched her body enjoying the pleasure she was experiencing. The wet sounds became faster, and she arched as the moaning got louder. "Oh God! YES!" She screamed her climax, and he ejaculated on the spot. The only sounds left were her heavy breathing. He wished he could be there to sample her climax flavor and clean her dry with his tongue. But for now, he had to get back to the condo and shower before she came over.

Eve

Eve stood at the partially opened door for a moment. She took a deep breath before knocking. Adam opened the door and picked her up for a big hug. "Facile, Héros. Easy, my stomach has not been feeling well."

He gently set her down. "I'm sorry, Beautiful. I was just so glad to see you. I was hoping you were feeling better since you asked for this meeting." He lifted her hand and gave it a kiss. She felt her face heat up and pulled him in for a proper hello kiss. She pulled back, even though she wanted more. She really wanted all of him but was trying hard to wait. Perhaps soon, some of her needs would be fulfilled, hoping Adam sees this as her engagement proposal. But looking forward, she didn't see Jessie conforming to her guidelines.

"We do have a lot to talk about, and since I'm nervous, this may take a bit." She held onto his hand for support as they walked in. "Where is Jessie?" She looked around.

"He's finishing up his shower and will be right out. How about we sit and relax until then?" Eve liked that idea. Hopefully, it would settle her stomach a bit. There was already soft music playing, and the view from the window was a perfect sunset. She nodded her head yes, and they took the few steps to the living room.

He sat down, and she snuggled into him and enjoyed the heat from his body and his arm around her. "I was hoping your tummy would be feeling better. Is the medicine not working?" He reached up and tucked her hair behind her ear.

"I think it would normally be fine, but with my mind going crazy these last couple of days, my body is just trying to keep up." He softly moved his hand back and forth across her back.

"You've been trying to figure out what to say to us?" She nodded her head yes. She leaned in tighter and wrapped her hands around his chest. Pressing her ear to his heart, she instantly felt calmer. She could sleep like this all night.

"Don't you two look cozy." Eve's heart sped up, and she stretched as she looked at Jessie standing in his doorway. He was finishing getting his shirt on, and she saw his slender, muscular frame. She blushed and tried to hide her face, but Adam saw and pulled her in for a quick kiss. Oh man. If Jessie says yes, how is she going to manage the attention of two men?

Jessie turned and grabbed a stack of papers from his desk and then came back and set the bundle on the coffee table. He stepped up to her and held out his hand. "It's good to see you." Eve placed her hand in his, and he gently placed a long kiss on her hand, making her blush again. Then he sat across from them on the opposite couch. She was mostly sure what paper he had, but they were going to need to conform to her needs and requirements or this would all end today.

Eve held her side and slowly pulled herself from Adam's embrace. She felt the loss of his heat, and it saddened her a little, but she knew after she was done, it would return. "I've been doing a ton of thinking these last couple of days. Thank you for not bombarding me and allowing me some space to figure this out." She paused to try and read the guys' faces, but they were both blank.

"In my solitude, it also helped me to realize that I don't want to be alone." She paused again while she fiddled with her fingers. She looked back up at Jessie. "What I'm about to propose breaks away from the normal. You must understand that I'm not just some girl to hang around with and have some fun. There is a short time limit. We had discussed this on our date." She blushed and took a slow breath in and out.

"By the end of this contract date, we are married or married and a commitment ceremony, or I will never see you again. Because the pain of choosing someone to love and walking away only amplifies if you keep running into them." She pulled out a folder and set it on the table.

"What this represents is not just a sex contract, but a relationship guideline that is also a marriage contract." Feeling pressure growing, she took another deep breath and slowly let it out. Looking over at Adam, she knew he was on board. She reached a hand toward him and right away, he entwined his fingers with hers.

She suddenly let go of Adam's hand and stood up while holding her tummy. "Breathe, Beautiful." Adam got up and went to the kitchen and came back with a glass of water.

"Thank you." She smiled, and he was grinning back at her. In a way, this is exactly what he wanted—a commitment, a vow between them. As she sipped on the water, she wondered if, by signing this, he would consider this step a marriage step or if he would truly make her wait until their honeymoon. She guessed that was his part of the contract alone. Jessie stood next to her and softly moved his hand along her back.

"Jessie, I know this is a big decision. If you need more time to think about this before continuing, I fully understand," she nodded. They were all quiet, so she took a step to the side. "I need to lie down for a minute or two." As she turned, she noticed Adam whisper something to Jessie and then followed her to his room. She set her stuff down on the desk, and they both climbed onto the bed. She felt better with his warmth again.

Adam broke the silence. "I bet your anticipation has been going crazy thinking about all of this." He kissed her softly and pulled their hips closer together.

"It sure has been. My mind has been all over the place with possibilities." She buried her face in his chest as his hand lowered to her thigh and he pulled her leg over him.

"Mmmm hmmm. I can only imagine how bad your ache has been. Did you take care of your needs?" His fingers squeezed her ass tightly.

She slid her arm over him and pulled him in for a deeper kiss. "Of course, I did." She smiled and leaned her head to his chest again.

He sucked a breath through his teeth and softly traced his fingers along her arm. "I love how honest you're being with me."

She smiled bigger as she listened to him chuckle. "But I could always go for more. Besides, a toy is never as good as the real thing." She started to slide her hand down his abdomen and he quickly let go of her ass to stopped her hand from traveling any farther.

He made a tsk tsk tsk sound with his tongue. "I wouldn't be able to stop if you did that." She pulled him in and whispered in his ear. "Don't you understand what today is about? I don't want you to stop. I'm ready for more. I'm just waiting for you to-"

There was a knock at the door, and they both looked up and saw Jessie standing in the doorway. "Can I come in and join you?" Eve raised her hand and motioned for him to join them. Jessie slid in behind her and spooned his body to her curves. With his free hand, he tucked her hair back and rested his head on his hand. He leaned forward and gave her a kiss on the cheek. Eve closed her eyes and felt a soft blush grow. The heat from both of their bodies was making her hot again.

"I don't know how long you were going to give me to think. But I've been thinking about you for months now. I don't need any more time. I'm in." Eve blushed deep red and covered her face.

"I thought for sure you were going to say no." He slowly slipped his hand over her waist and rested it on her belly. "The old me would have walked away and left you to figure everything out. Since you woke me up, I took a hard look at my life. Now, I don't see how I could let you escape."

She slowly rotated onto her back so she could see them both, then reached up and held each of their hands before closing her eyes. Her world was about to go crazy. She had to be certifiably insane to even consider trying this. She took a deep breath and slowly let it out.

"Well, we should go over the paperwork I brought. It's the best way I could figure to move forward and keep everything clear."

She laid still as the guys got up. "Are you coming?" they both asked in unison. She rolled to her side and slowly sat up. "Yes. Sitting straight up hurts now. I need to get used to new ways of moving." They both offered their hands to lift her, and she accepted both. She was surprised when they both kissed her hands at the same time. She lowered her face as she blushed again.

Adam lifted her chin. "You have nothing to be embarrassed about with us. We will guard you." She saw Adam shoot Jessie a look. What has she put herself in between? She thought for a moment and then giggled. Two full-grown men, that's what. Not that long ago, she was worried about growing up and becoming an old spinster. Now she had a couple of men going after her.

She took a calming breath. In tonight's conversation, she must tell them about her responsibilities back home. She could do most of the work remotely, but she would need to return home now and then. She moved to the desk and grabbed her folder. There were several pages she brought as references. However, after picking and choosing what to say, her ten pages were enough to make a person's head spin. The first three are for both now.

Adam has a big head start on Jessie, but she was sure he would catch up quickly if he truly wanted to. The next seven were her boundaries, gray areas of learning sexual activities, and her desires. They are for Jessie now, and later when Adam is ready. "Let's have a seat at the table." She claimed the head of the table so she would have them an equal distance on each of her sides, and they could stare at each other.

Eve wrote all three names in the participants' section. "This contract is a tool to communicate as well as a symbol of commitment. This contract is intended to be, and should be thought of as, serious and comparable to marriage. After covering all the topics set here, by signing our names, we freely and of clear minds commit ourselves to this marriage path," Eve clearly spoke.

Both the guys nodded their heads yes. "Legally, I can only marry one. However, I am open to a commitment ceremony." Her heart pounded in her ears, and she was breathing heavily. Even her palms were starting to sweat. She set the papers down so she wouldn't damage them and wiped her hands on her pants. Eve started to read out loud.

"Dating to Marry Contract"

She turned to the last page. "First and foremost, this contract has an expiration date. Because of my visa, I must marry before this date, and anyone who has not committed by that time understands that dating ends." She looked at Adam, who had a stoic face. "If no marriage or commitment ceremony has taken place, I leave to return to France." She tried to keep calm as a tear started to form and glossed over her vision. She turned back to the front page.

"There is room to add additional information and a place to initial after each section." She tried to keep herself calm. "We are treating this as a trial marriage. In marriage, we go to (school/work), and at the end of the day, we come home to each other. We talk about our days, the good and the bad. Listen to each other's concerns. Offer our thoughts or advice. Even though, at this stage, we can't spend every evening together, daily communication is a must."

Eve continued to turn pages. "By either text, call, FaceTime, or in person. Three-way text/chat is reserved for making plans as a group. With our three busy schedules, I am not requiring a minimum of private dates, but they are encouraged to continue the learning phase of our relationship. In this process, we grow together mentally," she winked at Adam.

Eve looked back and forth at the guys, and she could see that she had their full concentration. She took another deep breath, nodded, and continued.

"Physically, this is a closed relationship, including an exclusive sexual relationship and a promise not to be intimate with another outside this contract. No outside dating or actions that could reasonably be deemed as sexual. Outside friendships with the opposite sex are okay. I prefer visits are as a couple and that no emotional feelings or erections are present." She looked back and forth at the guys again to make sure they understood.

"Honesty! If you are asked a question, tell the truth. Even if the answer may bring up hard feelings or the past. Honesty helps to prevent jealousy and helps us to learn more deeply about each other. We do not need to discuss actions between the three of us with the understanding that we will be intimate separately. When talking or discussing intimate details, we will be kind, courteous, and respectful of the others' relationships, knowing that we will each grow in different ways and at different speeds."

Eve was in full blush and used the pages to fan herself. After her heart calmed, she continued. "My family is in France. So, I am good with spending holidays and special occasions with your families. If my family comes here, please allow me time to visit, even if we had prior arrangements, or to include them in the activities if possible."

She looked at them to make sure they were keeping up. "I do have obligations to my community in Sarlat, France. I do most of my work remotely. From time to time, I will be required to return home to take care of business and solve problems."

Eve paused and studied the guys. "You guys should both understand the responsibilities passed on from parent to child better than most. I am no different. Sometimes, I wish I didn't have this burden, and other times I feel so blessed to have the opportunity to make a difference for others." She pressed her lips together. "Any questions so far?" Both the guys shook their heads no.

"This arrangement is not about money. Although in the future, finances will be discussed to determine future events, no one person is required to pay for another. If one volunteers to pay for an item or event, no repayment is required unless repayment is discussed.

Example:

1. We are out to dinner. Person A says to Persons B & C, 'I'll cover dinner.' That means that Person A is agreeing to pay for the amount of the meal. No reimbursement is required.

2. Person A says, 'I'll cover dinner; you can Venmo me or repay me.' That implies that reimbursement is required by legal tender only. Sex is not required nor is it considered currency."

Jessie's hand smacked the table. "Damn, I was looking forward to being repaid with sex." He smiled.

Eve giggled and blushed. "I am used to paying for myself. If someone insists on paying for me, I will do my best and learn to be gracious and say thank you. I do appreciate the gesture, but I have a hard time accepting kindness." She continued to read.

"Income – During the term of this agreement, any income earned shall be their own. After marriage, I am legally required to keep my/our income separate from that of the estate which I manage. We currently have our own living arrangements. In the future, if we decide to all live together, we can visit and agree on an arrangement we can each afford. Since the baby will most likely sleep in my room most of the time, a three-bedroom will be beneficial."

Jessie spoke up. "I would like to amend that if we three move in together, that we share a single room and have separate rooms for children, or for when someone needs time apart. It would also depend on how many children we have together. Would we need to move further away from the city for more space?"

This took Eve by surprise. He was already talking about more children. She nodded her head, yes.

"We can decide all of that as the time comes." She got to thinking about it, and a single bed may not work out. "Just a thought, and think about this, Jessie. Let's say the three of us are sleeping in bed after being intimate." She paused as his eyes got bigger with excitement. "We are all naked." She paused again, and his smile grew.

"Then I wake up after my couple of hours of sleep, get up, and leave to go draw. That leaves the two of you in bed alone, naked." Jessie's smile faded, and he looked at Adam, who was not smiling either. "That would only work if I stayed in bed."

Jessie grabbed her hand. "Then stay in bed with us. Or, better yet, wake us up for another round. No man in his right mind would say no to more sex." Jessie shook his head.

She smiled. "We will get there when we get there," she added before continuing to read. "When it comes to group decisions for outings, we each take a turn. It's part of how we learn about each other's likes and discover our commonalities.

Example: I choose going to karaoke because it helps me to feel closer to my family that I miss. Growing up, we would have regular Friday night singalongs. Then the next two group dates will be determined by each of you guys. Dates and outings do not need to be expensive; however, some things do take planning ahead." She tapped her lip for a second.

"Example: Your favorite band will be in concert. Ticket sales start three months before the show. If someone is unable to go because of cost or scheduling, perhaps plan a dinner, play your music for the evening, and discuss what their music means to you. Then go to the concert separately and enjoy. Afterwards, share your experience." She would love to go to a concert while here.

Eve let out a sigh before she continued. "There will be no illegal drug use. No tobacco products. I'm okay with alcohol, but not intoxication." Eve paused and made sure the guys were still on board.

"When we have a fight or disagreement, we will talk things through as calmly as possible. We will not keep things bottled up or ignore the problem. We improve by solving issues together." Eve set the last of the relationship section down and tapped her finger on it.

"Any questions or issues so far you'd like to add or change?" Jessie raised his hand.

"I'd really like it if you repaid me with sex. Not from Adam though." Jessie had a huge smile fill his face and he winked.

Adam laughed. "Same for me also. Any time you're low on funds, you can just—" Eve thumped her fist on the table.

"You guys! I'm trying my best to be serious here so that we all understand what is expected." She was getting angry and turned on at the same time.

"Sorry, Beautiful. I was just trying to lighten the mood," Adam smiled.

"Sorry, I was trying to do the same," Jessie smirked.

"As far as sex is concerned, you should be thinking about compatibility. Adam and I have already discussed his vow. For him, this part would be valid later. I will try my best to honor your decision and your boundaries. Jessie needs to work on the steps he and I discussed prior, before consent is given. I do not wish to read all of these pages, so please take the time and understand. After reading, there is a separate line to sign at the bottom of this section alone."

She paused as she had a thought. She already knew Adam's answer but was curious as to what Jessie would say. "I have a question that will affect the next section." She held up four fingers and looked at Jessie. "How many people, including me, have you had sex with?" In her peripheral vision, she saw Adam hold up his two fingers.

Jessie leaned back and puckered his lips together. "I honestly don't know. I'd say my average is about two girls a week for four years. That was up until two months ago." Jessie shrugged his shoulders.

Eve gasped and slowly lowered her hand to the table as she tried to do the math in her head.

"Dude, really? You've had sex with over four hundred people?" Adam had wide eyes. Eve's hands shook as she pulled the paper back and stood up. She took a deep breath and held the paperwork tighter to her chest. How could she be feeling this way about someone so careless? Her heart pounded in her chest and her mind spiraled.

"Breathe, beautiful." Adam touched her arm and the air in her lungs rushed out.

"When it gets added up, I have been extremely reckless." Eve started to pace back and forth. Was she just another girl to him in the beginning? Just another conquest for the week? How could she become so interested in someone who obviously didn't care about how people felt?

Adam got up and pulled her into a hug. She smashed her ear to his chest and listened to his heart. Slow, strong, and steady. She could feel her own heart start to sync with his, and she started to calm down. Jessie came up alongside her and wrapped his arms around both of them.

"I know how all this looks. And, yes, I've been an asshole in the past. I'm ready for the next step in life. And I see it with you guys. I know I have a lot to learn still. Please, be patient with me." He squeezed a little harder and then eased up. "Can we keep going with the list? Can I just sign now? I'm ready for what you want to do."

Eve breathed a big sigh and loosened her grip on Adam. She couldn't speak yet, so she just pointed to the table and sat back down. A few calming breaths later, she looked at the guys who gave her their full concentration. She decided to write in an addendum. Specifically for Jessie but they all three might as well show proof. She cleared her throat and then continued.

"Sexual Timeline. Since we are entering this as a group, each of us will be tested for all possible STDs and share our results with the group before engaging in sexual acts." Eve stared at Jessie, making sure it sunk in. He just nodded that he understood.

"Please see sexual contract for what is or is not allowed. Once sex is consented to, at first, slow and gradual is preferred. In the heat, if both want to attack each other and screw our brains out all night, simple communication is needed. At any time, anyone who does not wish to engage in sex will not be pressured by another. Group sex needs to be simply communicated prior to beginning. I will try my best not to pull away if a spontaneous orgasm arises, but rather share the pleasure I'm experiencing." Eve fanned herself as she felt like she was on fire during that whole conversation.

"Birth control. During pregnancy, I will not be on birth control. You guys do not need to use condoms either. It's not like I can get more pregnant. Unless you wish to, for cleanliness." Eve giggled at her little joke and the guys both smiled at each other.

"After pregnancy, birth control resumes for both until we all decide to try for another baby. During cycle/time of the month, there is no sex. I am normally regular, so make plans accordingly. When in doubt, ask me." Her eyes flashed back and forth between them.

"If you wish to add anything, please discuss and write it down before we all sign."

Adam was the first to break the silence. "I talked about this a bit before. I like to watch. Whether it's just you taking a shower, self-pleasuring on the bed, or if the three of us start something before my vow is finished, I would like to watch. If it's the three of us, I would like to participate as much as I can until I reach my boundary, but I don't want to feel pushed out just because I can't finish in you."

Eve nodded her head. "Okay. Please write it down in your section." When he was done, she marked her initial and continued.

"At any time, anyone who wishes to exit the contract only needs to communicate the desire to and sign their name on the exit contract line to terminate their end of the agreement. No one will cause problems for anyone who wishes to leave. If the contract is terminated before the expiration date, we will still remain friends, given that no partner violated the adultery rule. Breaking any rules can end the contract depending on the level of the offense."

Eve felt a nausea wave, held still, and breathed slowly. "Keep reading." She gasped, slid the pages to the center of the table, and then ran to the bathroom.

Adam

Adam sat as still as he could while she covered all the high points. He was going nuts from all the scents coming from her from the moment she arrived. But right now, he was trying his hardest to concentrate on what she was saying. He was surprised at how much research she had done in just a short amount of time. As she continued to talk, it was not just about her needs, but for everyone and the group.

As soon as she slid the papers over, he grabbed it and pulled the bundle to himself. He turned and saw her close the bathroom door behind her. He studied the remaining pages, and it all looked good. He was glad to see that she wasn't a freak in the sheets but willing to explore other pleasure outlets.

But knowing her limited experience, perhaps she would want to explore more later. After all, she is now open to being with two men at the same time. He added his request and signed the last page with their names. He held onto it and looked at Jessie.

"These are her rules of engagement. By signing this, your former player's life is gone." Adam then slid the pages to Jessie. Jessie nodded his head and reached for the pages. He started to read the pages she had not finished reading.

"I think she did a wonderful job. Above and beyond just a sex contract that I mentioned. If she was a paralegal, I'd hire her in a heartbeat. Everything she talked about was either common sense, fair to everyone, or informative about what she likes or dislikes. I mean, I like to have anal, but I know not to even ask. And on the flip side, I've learned that she loves having her clitoris massaged." Jessie smirked.

"And who knew that you two were so inexperienced? Looks like I'll be giving you guys pointers," Jessie chuckled.

Adam leaned back. "Prior to Eve, of all the girls you have fucked, how many of them have you had a relationship with or thought of them as a girlfriend?" Adam smirked, knowing his player ways wouldn't allow it.

Jessie leaned back and slid down in his seat. "One." He said softly. "I was engaged to my high school sweetheart. A couple of months before the wedding, I came home early and heard her moaning. I thought she was pleasing herself, so I thought I'd give her a helping hand." Jessie raised his eyebrow.

"I stripped down and went to join her. When I walked in, her legs were up in the air and a guy was pounding her hard. I was standing there, butt-ass naked, thinking that this was crazy because she never wanted me to go hard on her."

Jessie shook his head. "I tossed a robe on and was standing right next to the guy when she finally noticed me. The guy scrambled for his stuff and fled. Her and I had a huge fight. To find out that she was only marrying me for the inheritance and she was in love with the other guy." Jessie sighed as his head flopped back.

Eve

"That's awful. No one should have to feel the sting of a betrayal," Eve said as she sat back down and put a hand on his arm. She looked at him with empathy in her heart. Adam slid the pages to Jessie. "Are there any changes I should know about?" She raised her eyebrows.

Jessie picked up the pen. "Nope." He signed his name to his spot, then he slid the pages back to Eve.

She couldn't help but smile as she signed her name. She felt a full-body blush wave. "I guess it's official then. Never would I have thought, in a million years, a socially awkward girl like me would be dating two guys at one time." She paused. "Two husbands…" She giggled nervously as she covered her face before putting the pages into the folder.

Jessie placed his hand out to hold hers. "I'm a bit behind where you two are at. May we go out on a date tomorrow? We can try to cover some of the same topics you guys have talked about. And then Sunday would be nice as a group date before the next crazy week starts."

Eve placed her hand in his. "A date sounds nice. I'm good with Sunday also." She reached out to Adam.

"What do you think?" He held her hand.

"I think we are the crazy three musketeers. It's going to have ups and downs, but most of all, an adventure we will never forget." Eve laughed at the reference to the 1800s French historical adventure novel written by Alexandre Dumas.

"Since you planned the last date with me and the other two karaoke nights, leave the details to us," Jessie gave her a serious look.

"Agreed," Adam added. They both looked at each other and nodded like they were reading each other's minds.

"Next weekend is busy with my presentation for school at Adam's office. We could come back here for dinner? And then Saturday is the Halloween karaoke. We still need to pick out costumes. Would it be okay on that Sunday to just stay in for some quiet time? You guys can pick what we do for the activities."

She sighed and put her face in her hands. "I'm sorry. From the get-go, it feels like I was planning everything."

Adam squeezed her arm. "No, it doesn't. Most everything was already planned. You were just communicating the schedule."

"We should set up a bigger calendar so we can all write information on it," Jessie pointed to the small calendar.

Eve started to tear up. "You guys are wonderful. How did I get so lucky?"

Adam stood up and lifted Eve's arm for her to stand. "You should get some rest. The next couple of days may be busy. We will contact you with details as we finalize." They both gave her a hug and a kiss before sending her on her way.

Later that evening, she got a text from Jessie. 'Hello Babe, Saturday, please be prepared for a casual day. You will be picked up by 8:30 a.m. and will return about 10 p.m.'

She was surprised that he was planning on spending so much time with her. 'Wow, all day. Really?'

He responded with a devil emoji. 'I wish I could have your night as well, but I have steps to work on first.'

'Oh my gosh,' she said to herself. He's already expressing more sexual interest. Her insides were starting to get hot and twist on their own. She sent a blushing cheek emoji. She then started researching a location to get tested. She didn't set a time limit, but she wanted to show the boys that she was serious about a clean and healthy relationship.

Entry 5: Dating

Eve didn't get much sleep. Every time she had fallen asleep, her dreams would twist back and forth between Jessie and Adam, taking turns touching, kissing, and pleasuring. She had built up so much sexual energy that she needed a release.

She was so wet and excited, she easily slipped her big toy into herself. She loved the way it felt as it spread her open as she pushed it in. Slowly sliding her toy in and out felt wonderful. "Mmmm, Adam." She could go on for hours at a steady pace. But she wanted—no, she needed—a climax.

She got to a point where she had her toy all the way in, and she started rubbing her clit. She felt her insides clench on her toy, and the fire inside quickly lit to a full blaze. She was so hot that she had to kick the covers off. Slowly plunging again and again, she rubbed her clit a little faster until she felt her climax explode.

"Oh, God!" escaped her as all her muscles reacted to the peak. However, she decided to keep on plunging after her climax, thinking about taking two men, not just one. She rolled in bed to find a new position but kept on sliding her toy in and out. Eventually, she moved to her knees with her ass up in the air.

With her face flat on the bed, she thrust harder and faster. In her mind, the two men were kissing her all over, their hands on her body equally exploring, and both their cocks wanting to be buried deep in her. She thrust as hard as her insides could stand. She leaned up and buried her toy deeply as a second climax wave rolled through her.

"Oh, God, yes!" she exclaimed as she pushed her pelvis against the toy. She breathed heavily with satisfaction and wondered if sex with Adam would feel like that. Then she wondered how it would work with both at the same time. She was going to have to dive into some videos and learn more about this new path she's was on.

She laid back down and softly petted her pussy as the last of the climax wave calmed down. She knew deep to her core that she loved Adam. The way he made her excited and yet how he calmed her, like no other, points the way of their path in love. She closed her eyes and thought about how safe she felt in his arms, the warmth that transferred from him to her as she started moving her toy again.

Jessie was leaning against a car, waiting for her when she came outside her apartment at 8:20 a.m. "Hello, sexy."

Eve wondered how long he had been waiting since she was early. She walked over and gave him a hug. "Good morning." He pulled her back. He then slowly pulled her in for a kiss.

'Oh, shit!' She had forgotten how soft his lips were. 'Why does this feel so good?' she thought to herself. She moaned softly against his lips. She pulled back and was fully blushed. He softly touched her cheek.

"You don't need to be embarrassed around me." She smiled and pulled him in closer to whisper.

"It's not because I'm embarrassed." She stepped back and let her hand slide down his arm until her hand was in his. "What do you have planned for the day? I guess I'm at your beck and call today." Jessie tipped his head forward and moaned loudly as he pulled her hips to his.

He whispered, "If you were at my beck and call, we wouldn't be out in public all day." He leaned into her and started kissing her neck. She got goosebumps down her arms. The heat of his hands warmed her back as she reached her arms around his shoulders. She's not going to have any resolve in making him work through the steps if she jumps him.

"Jessie," she said breathlessly. He pivoted and leaned her against the car as he pushed himself into her. He gently pulled her hair, giving him more access to her neck. His hands moved along her body. One hand rested on her side with his thumb going back and forth across her breast, as the other had a firm hold on her ass.

She started to explore more of him when, suddenly, she lost all contact with him. When she opened her eyes, she saw that Thomas had pulled Jessie off her. Since Thomas had him by the back of the neck, Jessie was not fighting back.

"Sorry, Madame de Vogues. His behavior is unbecoming of a gentleman. Especially in the public eye. I have my orders to maintain your honor along with your safety."

Eve covered her face as real embarrassment colored it. "Thank you, Thomas. We will try and compose ourselves better." He let go of Jessie, and he stretched his neck.

"I see you're not out with Mr. Stratford today. Has there been a change in the guards?"

Eve giggled. "A lady's business is her own, but if you keep it to yourself, I'm dating both during my stay here. Yes, they both know, so there is not an issue there to worry about."

Eve had a sudden feeling of longing, and yet she needed to keep a wall up. She needed to hold back so Jessie could learn and grow. When Eve is pressing Adam, is it the same when Jessie is pressing her? She decided then that she would no longer press Adam's boundaries and wait for him to be ready. She also needed to be more steadfast for Jessie's journey. At least she would try.

Thomas took a step back. "It makes perfect sense the way they both protect you." He handed Jessie a business card. "Next time, pre-warn me of special activities so I can have security in place when and where needed." Jessie looked at the card and placed it in his back pocket.

"Today, we are just sightseeing around town. No dangerous activities today. Please call Adam about tomorrow's schedule. I don't want to ruin any more of the surprise." Jessie raised his eyebrows and then turned and opened the door for Eve to sit down.

After he climbed into his seat, he asked, "Are you hungry? I haven't eaten yet. There's a great diner just down the street."

She smiled and nodded her head, yes. "I can always go for a nibble."

They pulled up to the Applejack Diner. The restaurant reminded her of the typical American street diner. It was just around the corner from Jake's bar. He was probably a frequent patron there since he ate most of his meals out or to-go.

The host sat them down, and he sat opposite her. After the breach in protocol on their first date, this felt like several steps backward, and it didn't feel right. She decided to get up and sit next to him. After sitting down, she smiled and held his hand.

"That feels better." She smiled, and then they both scanned the menu. She was tempted to get something heavier but opted for the softer oatmeal and side fruit. "Do you come here often?" Eve looked over the menu at him.

Jessie nodded his head yes. "We tend to pick up food here on the way to classes."

She tipped her head. "Are you guys in the same classes or different years of study?"

He leaned forward so he could face her better. "Adam is about to finish his third year. He can then take the test for the bar. I'm in my first year. We have different bachelor's degrees. I originally studied English and History to become a teacher. Then my father had me transition to law." Jessie continued as he bit his lip.

"As long as he's paying for everything, I'm stuck on his timetable. Of course, Adam studied business and architecture before starting law. I understand his reason with running the family construction company."

Eve leaned back and tapped her finger to her lip as she thought. "I guess you could become a labor union representative for the teachers. Or maybe work for the school board? I've never researched that type of path before. I'm sure you could put it all to use somewhere."

Jessie smiled at her. "I've been dragging in my studies, but after meeting you, and been woken up. I feel invigorated, like I have a purpose now. A goal, so to speak. And hearing your thoughts that I never would have considered makes absolute sense now."

Eve smiled. "Since you are both in different years, how did you two become roommates?"

He leaned back and stretched his arms behind his head. "It was before my freshman year. My father arranged it. He didn't want me to end up in a frat house or running wild in a dormitory," he explained. "Adams' parents and mine are friends through mutual acquaintances. Not like we had hung out before."

She waited for him to ask her a question, but he kept on eating. She knew they covered a bunch on their first date, but there is always something to learn. "Do you have any siblings?" she continued.

He leaned back again. "Nope. I'm an only child." He swallowed hard. "What about you?" he asked.

Eve felt the tears come but answered honestly as promised. "I had a brother, but he passed away when he was 18."

She paused as he reached a hand out to hold hers, then he made a pouty face. "I'm sorry to hear that."

"There is more. I just don't want to fully discuss it until we are alone." He nodded his understanding, then they were silent again.

He looked at his watch. "Not to be pushy, but we should get going. I have a busy day planned." Eve bobbed her head yes in agreement but felt like the conversation this time was not flowing like last time.

She wondered if it was the whole sexual tension that was getting in the way. She flagged the server down for the check.

"No, darling. Not today," he said. She started to fuss but then remembered.

She took a deep breath. "Thank you. I do appreciate it." She leaned in, and he closed the distance to steal a kiss.

"I kind of like seeing your fire streak come out when you fuss. But, for clarity, I understand why you're keeping calm." He winked at her.

When they were back in the car, she decided to bring up the elephant in the room. She reached over and set her hand on his. "I have an appointment on Monday to get tested. The sooner we get this one of several steps resolved, the better. Don't you think?"

He smiled. "I have my appointment on Tuesday. Do we have to wait for Adams' results before we can be together?" He lifted her hand and gave it a kiss.

"No. But I already know his history, and I'm not worried about his results. I was warned that it could take a couple of weeks for results." He had a grimace look to him. She wondered if that would be long enough to work on the other steps? She knows how she feels now and hopes she can hold out that long.

"I was thinking that our first time should be as a group." She felt a wave start to roll and placed a hand on her belly. Her insides started to heat up at the thought of having both of them. How far would Adam go? Would it be like when they were in bed and he had his fingers in her? Would it be like at the office where he dry-humped her sensitive clit? She started to blush and breathed heavily.

"Even though he can't complete, I will honor his desire to watch. How do you feel about that?" Her heart pounded, and she started to get wet. Perhaps she shouldn't have started this conversation. He pulled her chin to face him and claimed a kiss. She felt like she was melting from the lips down.

"I don't care if he voyeurs our lovemaking. Whatever level he participates in will only amplify the intensity for you. So long as you don't mind being watched. Most people have a difficult time with it."

That never occurred to her. "I'd never been in that situation before, so I don't know how I will feel about it. But I know how I feel about both of you." She leaned over and gave him a kiss on the cheek. She hoped that talking about it would help ease the tension. Or it could have just made it worse...

They arrived at the 9/11 Memorial Museum in Lower Manhattan. She was surprised that he would bring her to a place of such sorrow and healing. After getting out of the car, he pulled her in close so they could walk around hand in hand.

Looking at all the documents about the terrorist attacks on the World Trade Center in 2001 made her feel sad. He would wrap his arms around her for a hug, and sometimes he'd place both his hands on their baby while he rested his chin on her shoulder.

There were artifacts that included first-person accounts of what happened, multimedia displays, and exhibits on history, which commemorate nearly 3,000 people who lost their lives. They were able to explore the museum at their own pace, which was nice to focus on the pieces that meant more to them.

She didn't realize how big the reflecting pools were. They are now in the footprints of the former Twin Towers. The museum remembers and honors the 2,983 people killed in the horrific attacks, along with those who risked their lives to save others and all who demonstrated extraordinary compassion in the aftermath of the attacks.

They had simple conversations about the situation here and there as they walked together. Before she knew it, two hours had passed by.

They decided to grab something quick instead of a regular sit-down meal so they could make it to their next location. He seemed more excited about his next choice. As they approached the street vendors, she couldn't get close because the smell of cooking meat was churning her stomach, giving her bad nausea.

She stood back and held her stomach still. She watched Jessie order lunch to go as she was checking out his ass and admiring his pleasant shape. She was surprised she hadn't done so before. She closed her eyes and imagined reaching around his waist and holding both cheeks with her hands, feeling his firm buttocks flex as he leaned into…

"What are you thinking about that's making you blush so much?"

She opened her eyes and smiled at him. "You."

They made it to Bryant Park by 12:30 p.m., and they walked out to about the middle of the field where there was an open spot. Jessie tossed a blanket out, and they sat for a picnic. She positioned her legs so she would tuck into him as they listened to Terry Waldo play swing-time music on the piano. She enjoyed the wonderful sounds coming from the stage.

After eating, he leaned her up, got up, then he held out his hand. "May I have this dance?"

She smiled. "Of course." She held both hands up for assistance, and he slowly pulled both her arms over his head. His hands traced down her sides, and he pulled her into a long kiss as they swayed to the music.

She felt so happy being in his arms. They danced and kissed for nearly an hour when the program came to a close. The park cleared out quickly after the music ended. He kept an arm held around her as they walked back to the car.

"Jessie." She looked up at him. "I'm a bit tired. Can I ask if the future activity is busy or slower?" He leaned against the car and pulled her into a hug. She rested her head on his shoulder.

"I took that into consideration when I made my plans. Our dancing was the most active event I had planned. From here, we either stand, walk a little, or sit." He turned and kissed her forehead and then leaned her back up. "Let's head to our next stop." He opened the door and held out a hand to help her sit down.

She smiled as she accepted the help. When he sat down next to her, she held her hand out, and they locked fingers. She rested her other hand on her stomach as her eyelids got heavy.

She woke up as Jessie softly moved his thumb back and forth on her cheek. She felt flushed with the heat of his hand under her ear. He kissed her, and she reached up and pulled him in for a deeper kiss. She opened her mouth and softly let her tongue dip into his mouth. He slowly slid his tongue back and forth against hers.

She moaned and opened her eyes. It took a moment to realize that she was dreaming and they were still driving to their next stop. She looked around, and they were still holding hands.

"You have a wonderful snore. It sounds like a kitten purring. Very peaceful and relaxing to listen to you sleep," he chuckled.

"I've never heard that one before. Are you teasing me?" She was curious if this was his humor or just her understanding.

He lifted her hand and kissed it. "Honesty, remember?" He lowered her hand to rest on his leg as he turned the corner. She grasped his leg a little tighter to help with her balance.

"We are almost there." She saw a very tall building standing above all the others. "That's it. The Edge," he pointed out.

When they got up to the observation deck, they were 100 stories up. As one of the newest and tallest outdoor skydecks in the Western Hemisphere, they could see all the way around the building.

"There is our condo," Jessie pointed out their building.

"The Empire State Building," Eve added and smiled at the memory of Adam taking her there.

Jessie pointed. "You can see all the way past the north end of the park and on the opposite side past the Statue of Liberty."

Eve was concentrating. "I don't see it. Can you point it out?" He came up behind her and placed a hand on her stomach, pulled back her hair with the other, and set his chin on her shoulder. He lifted her arm with his hand.

He spoke softly in her ear, "Point your finger." She made a fist and stuck her finger out as her heart quickened. He whispered, "See the One World Trade Center where we were this morning?" His breath on her ear sent a shiver down her body and her insides ached.

"Yes," she whispered as her breath was gone. He moved her arm and body slightly and pulled her closer.

"Hudson River?" Her heart was pounding in her ears, and she was hot all over.

"Yes." He moved ever so slightly and placed his lips to her ear.

"The little island in the river?" Her heart was ready to jump out of her chest and she felt extra heat between her legs.

"Yes," she barely whispered.

"That is Liberty Island, and the statue is our Lady from France." He took a deep breath through his nose. "God, you smell great." His other hand came back to her body as he started to kiss her neck. She leaned her head back as she felt her fire grow and could feel her body wave climbing. She suddenly realized couldn't hide anywhere here.

She spun around and pulled him in as her body quivered. "I'm about to…" her eyes went wide, "self-climax." She gasped. "Hold me, and I'll try to be quiet." He cinched his arms around her and walked her to the glass wall. He feverishly claimed her mouth, and they clashed their tongues wildly together while he started to push his pelvis into hers.

The outside suddenly felt so cold as her body was burning with fever. She pulled him tighter and moaned against his mouth as her body released the energy. She was breathing heavily and was slowly relaxing her grip on him. He ended the kiss and leaned a hand against the glass. "I…" he started.

She looked up at him and could see the desire burning in his eyes. "I do too," she finished his sentence. His hand squeezed her ass to pull her forward, and he pushed his hardness into her. She gasped and put both hands on his flexed chest.

"But we can wait for the results first. Then we can." She smiled, and her face went into a deep blush. She leaned to his ear and whispered, "I wouldn't mind going a few rounds when we do."

He stood upright, took a deep breath, and slowly let out the groan. He stepped back, nodded, and held out his hand. "We have one last stop for dinner." She removed herself from the wall and held his hand.

They arrived at the Hudson Dinner Cruises at the north end of town just as the sun was starting to get low. There were about 50 couples waiting to board the boat, the Spirit on the Hudson. It looked like an old-time paddlewheel boat from New Orleans. Eve smiled because she never knew something like this was even here in the city.

After boarding, she took medicine to prevent nausea from the motion of the boat. They walked around admiring all the details they had put into the design of the boat. Shortly after, everyone took their seats and the boat set sail. She snuggled into Jessie, and he wrapped his arm around her.

After reading over the menu, Jessie ordered the roast beef, and Eve chose the stuffed chicken breast so they could share. As the sun was setting, the lights all around New York City started coming on, and she enjoyed the illuminated landmarks. There was a guide pointing out all the locations as they floated down the river.

The air got cooler as a breeze drifted in off the water. She wished she had brought a sweater. Jessie rubbed his hands up and down her arms, spreading his heat to soothe her goosebumps. She pulled him into a full hug to warm her body. They stayed like that as the full-sweeping views of Manhattan's lights drifted by.

She enjoyed spending the day with Jessie. There were some slow times in the chat, but mostly today was wonderful. And this dinner was a great way to end a day of sightseeing.

After they stopped in front of her building, he got out quickly to open the door for her. She smiled and accepted his help. Her core muscles were already not as strong as they were two months ago. He closed the door and leaned against the car as he pulled her in for another hug. "Tomorrow, you will need to bring layers and a raincoat. An umbrella may be a good idea also."

She was so confused. "It's not supposed to rain tomorrow."

He smirked with a raised eyebrow and a secret behind his eyes. "A change of clothes wouldn't be a bad idea either." He winked. "We will be here at 5 a.m., and we will be back later than tonight." Eve's heart started racing when he placed his fingers in her hair and pulled her in for a kiss. She was thoroughly enjoying the heat from his body when she heard someone clear their throat.

Eve looked up and saw her guard Martin, watching Jessie as he stood next to them, just before he gave her a bow. "Buenas noches, Madame de Vogues and Mr. Cooper." He gave Jessie a side glance. "We made arrangements for guards along your route tomorrow."

Jessie quickly held up his finger to his lips. "Shhhh. Don't spoil the surprise."

Martin nodded his head in understanding. "At the stops listed by Mr. Stratford, we will have someone waiting. If your route changes for any reason, please let us know right away."

Jessie nodded his head yes. "Sure will. Thanks. Good night."

"Adiós, señora." Martin maintained eye contact as he slightly bowed again, then walked away.

Jessie tugged on Eve's elbow. "I understand why your family has security while you're here, but what I don't understand is why they bow."

'Okay, Eve. You promised the truth.' She smiled and blushed. "It's because, once upon a time, in a land where kings made all the decisions for the people, my family was in line for the throne. Now that France has a president and a prime minister, my family line is now called aristocrats."

She paused to calm herself, but the tears pricked the back of her eyes. "They protect me because I'm the last in my line. If I die before having children, my family tree ends." Her tears welled up and fell, then he wiped them away. A smirk lifted on one side of his mouth.

He leaned in and whispered, "So we need to have lots of children. I'm good with that." Eve turned beet red with the thought of how much sex they would have to make lots of children. She clung to him in anticipation and pulled him in for some more of his soft lips on hers.

Jessie pulled back and pressed their lips together. "So, you're what, a princess?" he asked with high eyebrows.

"Louis-Auguste, the last king of France was our cousin. The title Madame would be equal to an English Duchess, if that helps you to understand. Had I sought out to marry and be a royal, my bloodline would have qualified me. But that is not the life I wanted for myself. I already have enough responsibility to my community back home. I don't need to add a whole country to that list."

She crossed her eyes and started laughing, but he was not. "Are you like, stupid crazy rich?" Eve didn't like where this conversation was turning but promised honesty.

"No. It's not like I inherited a cave full of gold coins," she shook her head. "I have access to the accounts which run the town's affairs, but it is not my money. The lawsuit and death benefits from when my family died is the only reason I could afford to study here and have security officers for the short term."

She smirked, wanting to make her point. "My money is what I earn." She chose not to disclose her details until later of how much she actually had. Not like he wasn't doing the same for her.

He pulled her in for a big hug and a kiss. "I'm sorry you lost your family, but I'm glad it brought you to me."

They said their goodbyes, and she watched him pull away in the car as she walked into the building. She was tired tonight. It wasn't like they did anything majorly energetic, but she felt like she could sleep all night without any sleep aid.

She got into her room, sat down, and kicked her shoes off when her phone rang. She saw that Adam was calling. "Hello?"

"Good evening, Beautiful. I hope I'm not interrupting your date."

She smiled and leaned back on her elbow. "Hello, Husband. Nope, Jessie dropped me off at the door a few minutes ago." She laid down on the bed.

"Mmmm, I really like that name better." He paused for a moment. "Did you have a good time?"

She smiled again. "Yes. It was a nice and easy-paced day. How was your day?" She was curious if he worried about her all day.

"It was fine. I worked on payroll today. During my break, I went to the clinic for a blood test. And then I went to the store for snacks for tomorrow."

She rested her head on her hand and sighed. "I forgot to tell you that you didn't need one. That was for Jessie and his busy history. I'm getting one because we connected before I knew. Just in case, you know what I mean?" she asked and pulled the covers over as she rolled on the bed.

"I understand. I got one anyway because I'm not a virgin. Just to prove that when we connect, we will be clean together. Plus, I want to honor the contract you set up because I love and respect you."

She felt warm all over and smiled. "I love you too, Héros. I'm exhausted. I need to get going and pack for tomorrow so I can get some sleep. I'll see you bright and early tomorrow."

"Okay. Good night, Wife."

She blushed. "I like the way that sounded also. Good night, Husband."

Eve got everything packed per Jessie's request. She was wondering what plans they had up their sleeves. She would find out soon enough. After she laid down for what she thought was going to be several hours of rest but it was only a couple of hours. She used that extra time to draw out her plans for Friday's meeting.

Since she decided to surprise Adam with a complete rendering of the downstairs, she was doing twice the work in half the time. For class, she was splitting it into two so she would get credit for the extra work. She labeled it, industrial buildings being used for commercial properties.

She closed her eyes and could see all the clutter disappear. New electrical lines all the way around for several workstations. No closed-in, stuffy offices separating each other. She could have a lunch area similar to upstairs. She didn't want too much color, so she settled on white, light, and medium gray. She opened her eyes and started drawing.

True to form, the guys were waiting for her outside when she came down at 5 in the morning with her loaded bag. They both walked up to her, and she pulled them both in for a hug. "Good morning, husbands." She smiled as they both pulled her in tighter and spoke in unison, one in each of her ears. "Good morning, Wife."

She felt herself turn red. Adam picked up her bag, and they both locked hands with hers as they walked to the car. Adam put her bag in the trunk as Jessie got in and slid over. Eve followed, and then Adam squished in to close the door.

The pressure on her hips was causing pain down her sciatic nerve. She pushed up as she tried to sit on Jessie's lap but bumped her head. She slid back into the center again. "Guys, I'm not going to be able to sit like this for long," she said as she rubbed her head and hip at the same time.

She turned and looked at Jessie. "Where are we going?" Jessie pressed his lips shut and shook his head. "Sorry, Kitten."

She turned to bat her eyes at Adam. "Adam, please tell me." She gave him the biggest sad eyes she could make to beg.

"Beautiful, we will only be in the car for a few minutes. Then we will each have our own seats for the duration. I reserved the whole back row, so we can stretch out and get comfy. That is until we get back into the car to take you home later tonight."

She tilted her head. He didn't answer her question, but at least they would be comfortable soon. That also meant it was going to be a long ride. Good thing she brought her tablet. She could get some work done if needed.

"Plus, I packed games, food, and drinks to help pass the time. And, if we need to take a nap, we can." Adam grinned at her.

She looked back at Jessie. He zipped his mouth and tossed the imaginary key. "So, we are going for a long ride?" Adam nodded his head. She frowned. "I brought my medicine, but what if I get sick?" Her eyes went bigger with worry.

Adam smirked. "I planned for that also. Our seats are the closest to the restroom. And just in case it's busy, I brought travel bags." Her heart was racing with worry, but calming down.

She sighed and leaned over to give him a kiss. "Thank you for planning ahead."

Adam smiled and shook his head. "This trip was Jessie's idea."

She looked back at Jessie and leaned in his direction. "Whatever we are doing, thank you." She pulled him in for a kiss.

Shortly after, they were standing in front of a travel company with a group of people. Jessie came up behind her and rested his hands on her belly.

"How's baby doing?" She tipped her head back and to the side and reached up with her hand to hold his head closer to kiss his soft lips. She quickly demanded his tongue to join in, then she paused the kiss.

"Still growing. Our next 12-week appointment is just around the corner." She reached for Adam, pulled him to her front, and looked up into his eyes. He firmly claimed a kiss, and she kept a hand on each of them. He pulled back, and she saw everyone looking at them. She honestly didn't care if everyone watched. She was going to love her husband's when she wanted to.

A large travel bus arrived and pulled up alongside the group. The door opened, and the announcer stood up on the first step. He called for all passengers on the Niagara Falls trip to come forward. Eve stepped aside and looked at both the guys as her eyes lit up.

"We are going to the falls?" Her voice went up an octave. Both the guys nodded their heads yes. She bounced in excitement. "It's been on my list from the beginning of things to see, but it just seemed too far of a journey."

"That's why it's an early bus. We will see the falls and then make a few stops along the way back," Jessie laughed. The attendant scanned their tickets as they climbed aboard the bus. As Adam described, they claimed the back row seats for themselves.

The guys pulled pillows and blankets from one bag and sat down. They both patted the seat between them for her to sit. She joined, and the three of them got comfy, leaning into each other to rest for the first part of the journey. She loved feeling the heat from both of them as their arms wrapped around her back and front.

She quickly realized that she wasn't going to be able to sit in this position for too long. She rested her hands on each of their legs and shifted her weight to sit and lean more towards Adam so her legs could rest over Jessie. She let her head rest on Adam's chest where she could hear his heartbeat.

She wrapped her left arm around his back to help stabilize her weight, and he rubbed both his hands along her back. She reached out with her right hand to hold Jessie's hand, as his other hand softly moved up and down her legs.

Eve woke up around 6:30 a.m. as the sun was starting to color the sky. The guys were sound asleep. She carefully slipped out of their grasps and tucked their blankets back around them. She found her tablet and a breakfast bar in her bag and utilized the empty seats in front of them to get some work done.

She quickly took a picture of them while they looked so peaceful. Scanning the bus, everyone was asleep except the driver. Around 7:30 a.m. she heard a short buzzing sound that quickly stopped. She looked around the cabin but didn't see anyone moving.

She went back to drawing when a hand softly touched her shoulder. She looked back in Adam's direction just as he closed the distance for a good morning kiss. She reached up and tangled her fingers in his hair. "Come sit on my lap," he whispered.

She got up, put her tablet away, and started to sit across, but he stopped her and pulled her hips square to him so she would straddle him. He wrapped the blanket around them and then placed his finger on her lips.

He whispered, "Shhhh, keep quiet or you'll wake the whole bus." Was he talking about public displays of affection? He pulled her in and claimed her tongue with his. He moved his hand down her core and slid his fingers behind her pants and underwear. She froze in excitement.

He whispered, "Do you want me to continue?" She looked around and saw that no one was looking. She looked back at Adam, smiled, and spread her legs wider to give his big hand better access.

She reclaimed his mouth as he started to massage her clit, and her body instantly flexed and wiggled. She pressed her face into his and moaned into his mouth. He slowed his rubbing and inserted a finger and rubbed the inside and out at the same speed.

She gasped at the new sensation and then reclaimed his mouth. He rotated between rubbing harder and softer, slower and faster. She felt her wave growing, and she lowered her head. Adam whispered again, "Cum for me, Beautiful." Eve opened her eyes when she felt extra movement along her leg.

Jessie was starting to gently move his hand back and forth. Adam slipped a second finger in, increasing the pressure, heightening her pleasure to send her over the top. "Oh God," she exclaimed in a whisper. She crashed her face into his, and her pelvis thrust forward as her body released her climax. Adam slowed, and her heavy breathing slowed to match.

He removed his hand and cleaned his fingers with his mouth. "Mmmm, yummy breakfast appetizer." She leaned back and took a deep breath. Adam lifted her arm and pressed her hip to guide her to move. "Your other husband wants a turn," he whispered.

She started to move when Jessie whispered, "You guys are nuts. We are on the bus." Eve came to a stop on the center seat.

Adam leaned his head over and continued to whisper, "Did you not read her fantasy sections? We can't fulfill it completely until all our results come in, but this is as close as we can get for now." Adam looked back up at Eve. "Did you enjoy that?"

Eve blushed, and her head bobbed, yes. Eve heard a coughing sound and looked forward. "Dude, your window is closing if you're going to try," Adam said to Jessie. Jessie reached his hand up and cupped her face.

"I would rather have you in private first before having everyone watch. You guys should also," Jessie shook his head. Eve went to full blush and covered her face. Adam leaned over and whispered, "We already did."

Eve turned and sat down in between them and covered her and Jessie with the blanket. "It's okay, Jessie. But there is something else I'd like to do with you since I can't with Adam right now." She placed her hand on his thigh and slid to the lump between his legs, then flexed her fingers back and forth. She whispered in his ear, "May I stroke you until you release?" She licked his ear and kissed his neck.

"Mmmm, I would like that." Eve unbuttoned and unzipped his pants. She then freed his shaft through the slit in his underwear. She leaned in to dance her tongue with his as she continued to move her hand up and down his shaft.

She listened to him and felt his body move to figure out what movement she did that he liked and which was less effective. Once she figured it out, she started rotating between the top five. After several minutes, she felt the base of his shaft get extra hard and his balls moved closer, letting her know his climax was coming soon. She broke her kiss and bent over to wrap her mouth around the head of his shaft while still stroking.

"Oh God," Jessie moaned and rested his hand on her head. Just then, Adam's hand pressed her undercarriage as his fingers moved back and forth across her clit. Eve softly moaned on Jessie's shaft, and his eruption started to spurt into her mouth.

She swallowed as fast as he released each climax contraction. After he was done, she leaned up and wiped her face as Jessie tucked himself back into his pants.

She turned to Adam. "Getting a little extra feel? I liked that." She leaned in to kiss him, but he pulled away and shook his head no.

"That's not a taste I wish to know." Eve leaned back and nodded her head in understanding.

She reached into her bag and grabbed her toothbrush and paste. She was glad she brought a locking cup to spit into. She smiled back at him. "Better?" she asked.

He pulled her into a hug. "You are so wonderful. I'm still getting used to all of this. Just give me a little bit to adjust." He pulled back and kissed her forehead. "Let's eat some breakfast before it gets too late." Adam adjusted and pulled food from his bag.

Jessie also shifted and pulled bottled juices from a small cooler in his bag. "You guys are full of surprises. I love it." She kissed Jessie on the cheek and then Adam's cheek. She whispered, "Thank you for the wonderful experience, Héros. I love you." She smiled.

He smiled in return. "I love you too."

The bus made it to the Niagara Falls State Park. When they got off the bus, the smell of street vendors' food filled the air, and Eve's stomach growled loud enough for both the guys to stare at her. She laughed. "Is it too soon to blame that on the baby?" Both of the guys laughed.

"I know her tummy is sensitive to cooking meat, so I can go and get us something to eat for lunch if you two want to get our place in line?" Jessie smiled as he backed away.

Adam nodded his head. "Sounds good." Jessie disappeared into the crowd of food trucks, and Adam was looking around and seemed lost.

"What are you looking for?" Eve quickly scanned the area before looking at him again.

He leaned down and whispered, "Your security, just in case."

Eve stood up straight and looked around again, then she got a wicked idea. "Want me to start kicking and screaming and see who comes running, or should we just keep going knowing that he's out there?"

He looked down at her with a surprised face. Then he relaxed in the next breath. "I see your point. Let's go get in line."

They stood in the short line for the Maid of the Mist boat tour. She was glad the guys were working well together and had arranged it for them to stand in line. By the time Jessie got back to them with food, at least another hundred people were now standing in line behind them. They managed to eat the chili dogs and chips by the time it was their turn to load.

Since they were near the front of the line, they were able to get a great spot near the front of the lower level of the boat. The view was truly amazing. She didn't realize how big it was until she was staring up at it. The waterfall was easily 50 meters tall and the mist raised up twice as high. The boat brought them right up to the edge of the mist falling down. Had she not been wearing her rain gear, she would have been soaked through to her skin.

Eve also didn't realize how loud it was going to be. She was yelling at the guys to take a picture, but they couldn't hear her. She tapped a nearby gal on the shoulder and held up her camera to ask if she would take their picture. The gal smiled and nodded her understanding to help.

Eve grabbed both the guys and pointed. When they saw the gal holding the camera, they both squeezed in and smiled. The gal held up her thumb when she was done. Eve went back to her and did the same favor for the gal and her friends. Eve returned her camera and then backed up as she waved. Suddenly, she felt the world spinning around.

Eve felt cold and something heavy was on top of her. She was able to partially open her eyes for a moment before being blinded by the light. In that moment, she saw someone she didn't recognize holding her head. She peeked again and glanced around to see Adam and Jessie next to her, talking to what looked like medics.

Her eyes still felt heavy, so she closed them but moved her hand towards them as her body started to shiver. "Cold," she managed to squeak out.

Her right hand was instantly picked up. Right here, Beautiful."

She felt her other hand picked up and held. "Right here, Kitten."

"What happened?" Eve kept her eyes closed.

"Ma'am, can you open your eyes and look at me?" The man's demanding voice set her nerves on end.

Eve didn't know why, but she became frustrated. "It's Madame de Vogues or Eve," she barked out at the strange man.

"Easy, Beautiful. He's just doing his job. Please open your eyes." Eve could hear the concern in Adam's voice.

"Just open them slowly and adjust to the light," Jessie added. She slowly opened her eyes but was having a hard time focusing.

"It's giving me a headache, but mostly my back hurts, and I can't stop shivering." She looked up at the man above her. "This is not the angle I was planning on seeing the waterfall. What happened?" she asked again.

"Eve, my name is Evan, and I'm the ship's onboard medic. I'm going to shine a light and look at your eyes and ask a few questions," he replied without answering her question. "Do you know what day it is?"

She sighed. "It's Sunday, October 21st." He moved the light past her eyes.

"Where are we at?" His voice remained stoic.

She groaned as her frustration grew. "Niagara Falls, vessel Maid of the Mist."

"Good short-term memory. Where are you from?" he continued.

She had enough and blew up. "This is getting fucking ridiculous. Like you can't tell by my accent that I'm from France? I don't need some guy trying to pick me up while my husbands are standing right here. And why hasn't anyone told me what happened?" Eve let out a frustrated huff.

Adam let go of her hand and came in for a quick kiss. He stared her in the eyes. "Easy, Beautiful. He's not flirting, just checking your memory. There was an accident. You and someone else collided, and you both fell down. You have been out for a few minutes." Adam leaned back up and picked her hand up again.

"Your... husbands told me you're pregnant. How far along are you?"

She closed her eyes to think of the calendar as she tried to calm herself. "Nine weeks. Can I get up now? This ground is really getting to my back."

"I just want to check your mobility and sense of touch first. Then you can slowly sit up. Okay?"

"Okay," Eve sighed. Evan's eyes shifted and then he nodded. "Ouch!" She pulled her hands from the guys after they pinched her. "That wasn't nice." She crossed her arms under the heavy warm blanket.

"Last one, can you wiggle your feet for me and let me know if they feel normal?" The guys moved the blanket up and she wiggled her feet, ankles, knees, and hips.

"That all feels fine, but my back is now killing me." She turned over without warning and saw someone next to her covered with a sheet. She covered her face and rolled the other way into a ball and started crying. "What happened? You didn't tell me everything."

Adam scooped her up, walked with her to the shore, and sat down on the bench. The heat from his body felt hotter than normal. Jessie laid a warmed blanket over her and slid in next to Adam and hugged them both. After she stopped crying, she wiped her face. "Please tell me," she asked again.

Jessie spoke up this time. "You both collided. You fell straight to the deck. When he fell, he hit his head on the railing first before landing on the deck. They were doing CPR and shocks when the ambulance arrived. They kept going before the doctor on the phone ended CPR. We stayed with you the whole time while they worked on him. They were just discussing with us about taking you to the hospital since you were still unconscious when you woke up," Jessie finished.

"There are a couple of different views of what happened. Some say you bumped into him, while others say he bumped into you. We are getting the videos to help determine what really happened," Adam added.

"You know we couldn't take our eyes off of you once you started to walk away. We saw him stumble and then crash into you. Plus, if an issue arises, you have two capable lawyers at the ready to defend you." Adam lifted her chin and softly kissed her.

"Excuse me, Madame de Vogues." Eve looked at the stranger and figured it was her guard since he used her proper name. "I reviewed and made a copy of all the videos on board the ship. It clearly shows the man stumbling into you. Going back further in the video and watching him, he was most likely having a massive heart attack." He bowed his head for a moment, but remained standing with them.

Eve started to tear up again. "It's sad that he was having a problem and no one noticed. Then again, it was so dang loud, he could have been screaming for help and no one could have heard him." Eve saw the medic walking up to them.

"Hello again. Nice to not be staring up your nose." Eve smiled as he handed her a pamphlet.

"I can't force you to go to the hospital, but I do urge you to, or at least make a follow-up appointment. Take it easy for a few weeks. In this pamphlet, they talk about the signs and symptoms of a concussion and recovery. If you are experiencing any complications, please seek help right away. Also, advise your OB about the accident. They may want to get you in sooner."

Eve held out her hand. "Thank you so much. I'm sorry for being so cross earlier."

He smiled. "It's okay. I truly hope you feel better soon," he said, and then parted ways.

Jessie broke the odd silence. "We are supposed to go to the observation tower from here, but I don't think climbing several flights of stairs is on the approved list of taking it easy." Jessie tapped the pamphlet. "I think we should just slowly walk around for a bit and enjoy the sights," Jessie softly suggested.

"Later we can find some dinner before heading back to the bus. Does that sound okay?" Adam added as he looked down at her.

Eve frowned. "Did we have other things planned for today?"

Adam shook his head. "Spending time with you was the plan. On the way back, the tour guide will talk about Northern New York. But for now, we can learn some fun and interesting facts about the mighty waters here." Adam laughed a little.

"Maybe find a souvenir shop for some special memento," Jessie added.

She hugged both of them. "I could just as easily snuggle in bed with you guys right now, but all our beds are really far away. I guess we will walk slowly and pay attention to the signs." She held up the pamphlet.

The car service pulled up to her apartment. They all piled out and walked Eve up to her door so she wouldn't have to carry her bag. They both hugged and kissed her good night. "Remember, if you need anything, don't hesitate to ask. No matter what time it is," Jessie smiled.

"Hey, that's my line," Adam laughed and put his fists on his hips. Eve pulled them both in for another hug.

"I love you guys. Thank you for the wonderful day. Chat with you tomorrow." They waved good night as she closed the door. She leaned back on the couch and sent a message to the school about her accident, concussion, pregnancy, and tomorrow's follow-up appointments. That also gave her some extra time for getting tested.

She started going over the pamphlet again about what she could and should avoid when a soft knock sounded on her door. Which one will it be? Romeo one, Romeo two or both of them? She knocked on the door in response to see what he'd do.

"Open the door, Madame de Vogues." That was not Adam's or Jessie's voice. She refocused, not recognizing the man's voice. She opened the peephole and saw Martin.

"Oh. Hello, Martin. Just one second," she said as she unlocked and opened the door.

"Good evening. I got word earlier that you had an accident and are on concussion protocols. With your permission, may I stay here to keep a closer eye on you tonight?" He had a very serious look to his face.

She giggled and side-smirked. "Do you snore?" she asked, trying to lighten the mood.

He cracked a small smile and his eyes lightened up. "I will be awake all night."

She laughed. "I hope you know that I only sleep for a couple of hours. So, what are you going to be doing? Playing gin rummy with me?" She shook her head. "I don't mind you out here while I'm asleep, but once I'm up, you can head back down."

He shook his head. "The reason I asked is to make sure you don't need help faster. So I'll keep the door open and be in and out." He held out his hand, and she set her hand on it. He then turned it over and put two fingers on her wrist to check her pulse. After a moment of counting, he spoke again.

"If you could, please sleep with the covers partly down. That way, I can count your respirations and keep an arm out, so I can check your pulse like I just did." He lowered his hand. "If you're fully covered, it makes it more difficult to check without waking you. After we're done, I'll head back downstairs." His face slowly shifted as his smile grew.

She pressed her lips together as she thought. "I will be okay with that. Just keep the noise down." She turned and grabbed her pajamas and changed in the bathroom. When she climbed into bed for the night, he was at the bedroom door. He smiled again as he bowed and then turned off the light.

Eve woke up to the sound of someone banging on the door. "Ugh." She groaned and placed a hand to her forehead as a headache took over her brain.

"I've got it, Mi Reina. You can stay in bed." She looked over and Martin was sitting on the foot of her bed, then he got up to answer the door.

Eve heard the door fly open and slam the wall behind it. By all the thudding sounds, it was obvious that there was a fight happening in her living room. God, was someone trying to attack her? She popped out of bed to grab her robe but felt a dizzy wave, then she stumbled sideways to the wall instead.

There was a large crash that sounded like furniture breaking. She managed to get her robe on and then carefully made her way to her bedroom door. Her eyes popped out of her head when she saw Adam and Thomas on top of Martin.

"What in the hell is going on?" she demanded as she stomped her foot.

Adam turned his head. "I'll explain everything. Please go to your room and shut the door. I'll be back in a few minutes."

Thomas finished putting cuffs on Martin. "UP!" Her whole body shook at his command. She had never heard Thomas yell so loudly before. It reminded her of a military commander barking orders. Adam got up, and Thomas pulled up on Martin. Martin flipped his head up and looked at her as if he were begging for her help.

Adam pointed to her room. "Please go, Beautiful." She backed up and closed the door. She heard a little more commotion as another thud landed, then she heard Adam, "That's for touching my wife."

Eve looked around the bedroom. Nothing seemed out of place. Then she noticed some wet marks on her bed cover. She moved closer to look. It looked like snot. She pulled the cover straight and saw several clusters. There was too much here for it to be that. Plus, the repeated sound of someone blowing their nose would have woken her up. It then dawned on her. Martin called her 'his Queen' and not her proper name.

There was a soft knock at the entry door. Eve tiptoed out and saw her living room was destroyed. The coffee table was smashed flat, and the couch was broken. She peeked through the opening and saw Adam. Her heart started racing as she opened the door.

He shut and locked the door, then pulled her into a deep kiss, slipped his tongue in, and demanded hers. He held her tight and slowly walked her to the wall, then pressed himself against her. He released her mouth and started kissing her neck and then suddenly stopped and pulled back.

She pouted a little with the sudden loss of his touch. He lifted her chin and looked closer. "Fuck!" he muttered just loud enough to be heard. He then kept looking at her clothing and hair. He let out a long deep growl in anger. "No one's allowed to touch you but me or Jessie."

He softly grabbed her hand and led her to the bedroom. "Take everything off and put it on the bed." She wasn't sure what was going on, but after what she just saw, she wasn't about to start arguing now. She removed her robe, pajamas, and underwear and placed it all on the bed.

She stood there naked and watched as Adam had also removed his clothing except his underwear. He had set all his clothing on the desk. Eve stared at Adam's physique and started to get excited as her breath hitched. He then grabbed her hand and led her to the bathroom.

He started the shower, and when the water was warm enough, he stepped in, pulling her with. "Let's get you clean. You don't need his sperm all over you."

She looked up at him. "Is that what's on my bed cover?" He nodded his head yes and closed the door. She hadn't been bathed since she was a small child. Adam washing her felt so sensual and erotic, but she knew now was not the time to press his boundaries. So, she just enjoyed every moment of every touch.

A moan of pleasure escaped her lips as he scrubbed her hair and scalp with his strong fingers before rinsing. Eventually, Adam turned off the water and wrapped a towel around her and then one around himself.

"Finish drying off. I'm going to send your clothes and bed linen down the laundry chute. We can make the bed when I get back."

She quickly dried off her body and she tried to get her hair as dry as she could, but left her towel on. When she came out of the bathroom, she saw the other towel and his underwear on the chair however, his clothes were gone. He sure is a fast dresser. She got dressed in her only other nightgown, which was the silky two-piece from before. She grabbed new linen from the closet, but she only had the one quilt. She should look into getting another.

Adam returned and helped her to make the bed. He looked around and then back at her. "I only have one bed cover." He nodded and returned to the living room. He came back with a couple of throw blankets that were on the couch. Eve picked one and placed it on the side where she wanted to sleep. Adam did the same for the other side.

He came back to her and then sat down on the bed. She gave him a soft kiss and then turned and picked up his towel and underwear. He looked confused for a moment. She then took them to the bathroom and hung them up to dry. She looked back at him and smiled. She removed the towel from her hair and hung it up also. She walked back and stood in front of him.

"Are you staying the night?" He nodded his head yes, and she pulled his shirt up and over his head. She started with the belt, but he stopped her hand. She looked at him in the eyes. "Only the belt so you can be comfortable." He released his hand, and she unthreaded the belt from the loops, then set it all on the desk.

"You said you would explain. I'm not a psychic, and I can't read your thoughts. What happened tonight?" He reached up and wrapped his arms around her and then leaned back, slowly pulling her onto the bed.

"Why was Martin in the apartment?" Adam asked. Eve rested her head on his shoulder.

"He was concerned about me having a concussion and asked to be able to monitor me while I slept, just in case I needed medical help." Eve shrugged her shoulders. "I didn't see any harm in that. Just in case." She set her hand on her stomach.

Adam took a deep breath in and slowly let it out, then turned to face her. "Have you heard the term Somnophilia before?"

Eve smirked. "Latin word somnus, meaning sleep, and the Greek word philia, meaning friendship. So, a sleeping friend?" She shrugged her shoulders. "What does that have to do with what happened tonight?"

"In modern times, it means a person who becomes sexually aroused by seeing someone sleeping. It usually leads to the girl being raped. That's Martin." Eve gasped and covered her mouth. "There is no way of knowing that type of problem is there unless the opportunity presents itself and he acts on his impulse. Like tonight."

Eve shook her head. "I don't understand. How did Thomas know I was in trouble. I didn't push any of the panic button." Eve furrowed her eyebrows.

Adam reached up and softly touched her face. "He didn't. I did. I then called Thomas, and we both arrived at the same time."

Eve leaned away in confusion. "And how did you know?" He grabbed onto her and rolled over so he was on top. He started to kiss her, but she placed her hands on his chest and pushed him away. "Now is not the time for distractions. Otherwise, I would have pressed on you in the shower."

He lowered his head. "Please don't be mad at me." He had a worried look to his face.

She reached up and slid her fingers over the stubble on his face. "Just be honest, as we agreed, and then explain it to me. Let me decide if I'm going to be mad or not." Adam slowly nodded his head yes and leaned back to stand and pulled her arms to sit her up.

Adam took a deep breath. "I explained last time when we showered and during our meeting that I like to watch."

Eve nodded her head. "Voyeurism," she added. Adam nodded his head and then hung his head again.

"I've lived with this shame for as long as I can remember. I'm not that much different from Martin. Only, I like you to be awake." Eve reached her hand out.

"You are nothing like Martin, and I don't think it's shameful. You clearly explained yourself and your desire. Did you see us get offended? No. You know yourself, and there is nothing wrong with that. I'm currently into loving two men at the same time. The world would see that as being shameful, but I don't give a shit what everyone else thinks. Only you guys."

She squeezed his hand and pulled herself up, wrapped her arms around his shoulders, and kissed his chin. "How did you know?" she asked softly.

He rested his forehead on hers. "You know the home security video I showed you when I hit Jessie after your fight?" She nodded again. "On the day of your birthday outing, I placed a camera in the apartment."

She pressed her lips together as she thought back. It's been here for a few weeks now. "Where in the apartment?" she asked while trying to keep calm.

He looked her in the eyes. "Bedroom."

Eve blushed when she thought of everything she had done during that time. "And how often have you been watching?"

"Off and on, usually during the evenings as I'm relaxing to go to sleep. Seeing you helps me to calm down from a stressful day, and I have slept better in the last couple of weeks than I have in years."

Knowing that she was helping him made her happy, and she smiled. "See anything else interesting?" She was very curious now.

"I did see you satisfy yourself, the day of the meeting, and I loved every moment of it." She covered her mouth, and a little squeal came out. Then she decided to have a little fun with this.

She walked him to the chair and pointed. "Sit." He did as she instructed. She went back to the foot of the bed and sat down. "Thank you for your honesty about your needs. I'm not happy that you placed a camera without my approval, but I couldn't imagine what could have…." She paused and shook her head as her eyes went wide.

"These last few months have been crazier than I think I could have managed, but knowing you're here for me makes all of it easier to deal with. I don't mind the camera here, so long as I know when you are watching me. When we are talking and making plans, I may ask which dress to wear? That means I want you to look. You understand me?"

Adam bobbed his head, yes. "You may watch me any time before going to sleep, since it helps you to rest." Adam's smile grew. "Where is it?" Without taking his eyes off her, he pointed to the shelf above her desk. "Okay. Leave it there."

She took a deep breath and pressed her lips. "Let me see the video. I need to understand fully what he was doing." Adam picked up the phone from the desk, patted his leg, and held his arm open for her to sit on his lap. She went to him, sat down, and wrapped an arm around his shoulder as he held onto her waist.

She leaned in, gave him a kiss on the cheek, and then held a hug until the video was ready. He gave her a soft pat on the butt. "Ready. Are you sure you want to see this?"

"Yes." She sat up, turned her hips to straddle his legs, and placed her back on his chest.

"I had been watching all evening, not liking that he was there while you were trying to sleep. He paced back and forth like a caged animal until…" He held her tighter, then pressed play.

She had a moment of déjà vu watching herself climb into bed. Adam moved the video forward thirty minutes. Eve was in the same spot when Martin came to the door. He then slowly entered her room and touched her foot through the cover. After a moment, Martin walked up to her nightstand, leaned over, and touched her shoulder.

After holding still for another moment, he stood up and reached into his pants and moved his hand up and down. After another minute, he unzipped his pants, and she could just glimpse his hardened cock as his hand continued to move up and down. Eve tensed up and pushed into Adam. Martin was fully stroking with one hand, and he started to run his fingers along her body.

Adam let out a short, low growl. Eve covered her mouth. "I had no clue he was doing this." She watched as Martin ejaculated on the bed. Eve felt disgusted, but she couldn't stop watching. He kept jerking his shaft and walked to the other side of the bed. He reached over, tucked her hair back and ran his fingers along her neck. He slowly pulled her covers down, and he ran his fingers along her breast and played with her nipple.

Unlike his previous growl, Adam moaned, and his fingers clenched at her clothing. Eve was disturbed and turned on at the same time. She felt her inside start to heat up, and she clenched her legs against Adam as she started to breathe heavily. She placed her hand on Adam's hand and wove her fingers into his. Then she had a very naughty thought. She tapped the screen to stop the video.

"I don't need to see any more." She got up and turned on the radio and sat down on the side of the bed but turned to face him. "You were super strong for me as my vulnerability wall was coming down. I almost walked away because of fear. I want to show you that I'm not mad and what being honest does to me. Because I love and trust you, I have no fear in doing this."

She giggled as he had a confused look on his face. She then turned over and reached into the drawer for her toy. She leaned back, slid her bottoms down to her ankles, spread her legs open to expose her wet desire for him to see, unobstructed. She looked at him, and he had both hands firmly gripped on the arms of the chair as he stared at her private invitation.

She smiled and closed her eyes, moved her toy around her wetness then slowly moved it in and out. Wave after wave of pure enjoyment moved through her. She didn't need a climax, so she took her time. Knowing that Adam was watching gave the pleasure a different edge, where she would normally fantasize to reach that high. After a while, she felt the bed compress around her, then his lips were softly on hers so, she halted her toy movement.

"You are so amazing. I now know why we were meant to meet. You are so perfect for me. I just want to know how you can keep going for so long?"

She leaned her head to the side. "What do you mean?"

"You've been going for forty-five minutes now. I've climaxed a couple of times already, and I don't think you have yet." He smiled as he softly ran his hand over her wild hair.

Eve blushed as she thought about him reaching his peak. "I was thinking about what our first time could be like. Slow, passionate, kissing, and touching," she answered. "I wasn't going for a climax, just pleasure. Had you not stopped me, I would have kept on going, like the Energizer Bunny," she winked.

He leaned his weight onto his elbow and kissed her. "Let me take control." Her heart started to race as he placed his hand over hers.

She suddenly became nervous. "Be gentle, it's not like the real thing," she said as she let go.

"I saw how hard you took it the other day. I know what your body can handle. You can always tell me to stop at any time." While he started moving the toy in and out, he started pressing kisses against her lips again. A loud moan escaped her as her body reacted differently this time since she wasn't in control.

He would change angles, plunge depth and speed faster than her brain could keep up. He let go of the kiss and changed position to move her leg up to his shoulder. He moved his other hand to her core and started rubbing her clit.

"Adam!" she exclaimed as her body arched in pleasure. Her body wiggled and flexed with each movement he made on her sweet spot.

"Cum for me, Beautiful. I want to see your pleasure released." He started plunging faster and harder as he rubbed faster and harder. Her body contracted and flexed with the pleasure rolling through her. Her toes curled as she pushed her pelvis into his thrusts.

"Oh God, Husband." Her hands gripped the bedding as her body arched again. This time, her body's fire exploded from within. Her pelvis pushed hard against his hand as her climax released. "Yes!" she moaned loudly.

He held the toy all the way in for a few seconds, and then he slowly thrusted as her climax settled.

He pulled out the toy and returned it to the tray, then placed himself between her legs as they started kissing. Her breathing was still heavy, but she had to ask.

"Husband, how much longer are you going to make me wait until I get to feel you for real? I'm ready when you are. My answer is yes."

His hand squeezed her ass. "At this rate, I won't be able to hold out much longer. God will just have to forgive me."

Entry 6: Post-Fall Concussion - OB Follow-Up

Eve woke up in Adam's warm arms and snuggled further into him as her drowsiness was clearing. He reacted by pulling her closer. She loved the feeling of belonging in his arms and slowly moved her hand back and forth along his smooth, muscular back. She thought about it some more. She really loved being with him and him with her.

She moved her leg over his and pushed her pelvis to his hip. "My husband," she whispered. He turned and rolled on top of her, splitting her legs open. Her heart started to race as he stared down at her with longing in his eyes.

"My wife," he said before kissing her. She wrapped her legs around him and reached her arms up his strong back to his shoulders. She felt the heat wave start as his kisses steadily went lower. "Take me, husband. Make me yours." Her body twisted in pleasure.

Adam leaned up, unbuttoned and unzipped his pants, then lowered them before he laid back over her. "I think we waited long enough. I can't hold back anymore." He reached down and started to tickle her clit.

Her body instantly reacted and moans escaped her mouth. "Adam, that feels so good, but I want you in me." He moved himself to her opening, sliding his tip up and down between her soaking wet lips.

"Are you ready for me?" She could see he was already breathing heavily and hers matched in the anticipation.

"Yes, Adam. Please!" Eve begged in excitement as she cinched her legs tighter around him.

"Here I come, Beautiful." Adam's tall body arched over hers, then he thrust his full length into her.

She gasped with the increased pressure as his manhood forced her open. "Yes..." Eve's eyes flew open. "Ouch." Eve sat up and held her head with both hands. The pounding feeling was worse than before, when Adam and Thomas showed up. She reached over and found Adam's sleeping body warming the bed. These damn vivid dreams were driving her nuts.

She got up to take some Tylenol and stumbled again, but this time, instead of going to the wall, she fell through the bathroom door and landed on the floor. The door made a horrible crash sound and the pictures rattled on the wall. She laid on the floor for a moment, trying to figure out which way was up.

The lights turned on and they seemed intensely bright, so she covered her eyes.

"I'm right here, Beautiful." He slowly helped her to lean up and kneeled in front of her. "Do we need to go to the hospital right now? I can have a car here in just a few minutes."

She took a deep breath and shook her head. "The damage is done. I'm following the instructions for post-care. The headache is a bit worse. I was just dizzy upon standing, like last time."

Adam took her hand. "What last time?" he asked with worry in his tone.

She looked at him and raised her eyebrow. "When two burly men came crashing through my door as I was asleep and saved me." She held her head again. "I need some Tylenol. Not Aspirin or Motrin per the instructions on the pamphlet." She pointed to a cabinet in the bathroom.

He got up and started to shuffle through her drawers. Then he came back with two Tylenol and a glass of water. She slowly started to open her eyes. It wasn't as bright as it was before. "Thank you." She swallowed all of it before she gave the glass back to him.

"Why didn't you say you were having symptoms?" he asked as he set the glass on the counter and then came back.

She looked up at him and smirked. "We got to talking about other stuff and…" She shrugged her shoulders. "I guess I was more focused on you and making a new, fantastic connection that I forgot." A blush creeped up her neck.

He scooped her up. "Come on, Wife. Let's get back to bed and get a little more shut-eye." He paused. "Unless you need to release some more energy? I wouldn't mind watching again." She laughed, patted him on the shoulder, and rested her head on him.

"I don't think my brain can handle the extra pressure right now." He set her down on her side, then went around and climbed on the bed. She instantly pulled herself into his arms and got comfortable in his embrace.

Eve

Eve sat nervously in the waiting room for her turn to be seen. She didn't want the guys fussing over her, so she told them not to come this time. However, Thomas was hovering by the door. All the surrounding women had very large stomachs and looked like they could pop at any time. She set her hand on her small bump and wondered, with all the vomiting, if her body was going to tolerate stretching that far.

"Eve?" She heard her name called and looked up.

"Here." She got up and started to walk to the nurse, but her body decided to go left instead. She stumbled and fell to the ground, sending the contents of her purse scattering on the floor. She held still for a moment, holding her head as the room spun around. When she opened her eyes, she saw all the women helping to pick up her items.

She felt so embarrassed and yet so loved that pregnant strangers would help her when she needed it. "Thank you, ladies. I appreciate the help." Thomas came around, kneeled in front of her and helped her to stand. They held still until she had her balance and then proceeded to the exam room with the nurse.

Thomas waited outside the room as they entered. It was different from the ultrasound rooms in that it looked more like an emergency room. Perhaps they had urgent deliveries here. "The doctor will be in shortly," the nurse said before leaving.

Eve looked around the room at what she figured was equipment for procedures and wondered what their functions were. "Hello, Eve?" There was a knock on the door as the doctor entered the room.

"That's me." She suddenly felt very nervous.

"Hello, I'm Dr. Patterson. Sorry for having you meet in this room. We are full for the day but wanted to check on your condition since your accident yesterday."

Eve smiled. "I didn't know you had a delivery room here." She looked around again.

"Sadly, we use it more than expected. Sometimes babies come out faster than planned," the doctor smiled.

She walked around and stopped by the table. "Well, let's take a look at you," the doctor said while pointing to the table. Eve got on and lifted her shirt a little and lowered her pants a bit. The doctor brought out a tape measure and then felt and pressed in here and there.

"Ouwwch. It's tender on the side." The doctor smirked her face.

"Okay. You're in line for an ultrasound. Normally, for a head injury, a CT is ordered, but since you're pregnant, I've ordered an MRI. It will take a bit longer but will still show if there is an injury." The doctor pulled up a seat. "I watched the video of the accident. You were out for thirty minutes. That's a long time, considering. Any problems since then?" Dr. Patterson asked as she sat on a wheeled chair next to her.

Eve nodded her head. "The headache comes and goes, but it's increasing in pain. I lose my balance when I stand up and I fall to the ground. It's happened a few times. Twice last night and then again in the waiting room," Eve responded as she pressed her lips flat.

"Any change in how often you vomit or its intensity?" Eve put her finger to her lip as she thought. "I wasn't paying much attention to that since it happens on such a regular basis."

"Even with the medication?" The doctor raised their eyebrows. Eve nodded again. The doctor smirked. "Okay, I'm gonna mark you down for lab work also and see about diagnosing for Hyperemesis Gravidarum. If it continues for too long or with intensity, you may need to be admitted overnight for fluids. We really want to keep an eye on that."

Eve didn't like the sound of that. She's gonna have a lot to tell the guys tonight. There was another knock on the door. "Ultrasound is ready," the voice from the other side said.

"Thank you," Dr. Patterson replied. "We will get some images and will come back here for blood work before going on to the MRI."

Eve sat in the small report room after having all her tests done and was waiting for the doctor. Looking at the clock, she realized she wasn't going to make her other appointment on time. The MRI took forever and was very loud. With earplugs and headphones, it was still loud.

Then she wondered if the test could be added to the blood she just had drawn. She was pondering that when the doctor came in. Eve smiled. She liked the friendly disposition she always had. "Hi, Eve."

"Hello, Dr. Patterson." She sat down with a folder and opened it up and started looking over the notes. "Before we get started, I have a question—well, something I was wondering if it could be done?" Eve blushed and she covered her face for a moment.

"What's your question?" the doctor asked as her face became stoic. Eve paused as she collected her thoughts.

"I have another appointment I'm not going to be able to make and was wondering if the test could be added to the blood that was collected today?"

Dr. Patterson leaned back. "Depends on the test. Different test tubes run specific tests. What are you needing done?"

Eve blushed again. "I was wondering if I could add STD testing. It turns out that the father of the baby has had several partners in the past." Eve looked down and spun her fingers around themselves.

"Is that who's standing in the hallway?" Dr. Patterson pressed her lips flat.

Eve sat up straight as her eyes just about popped out of her head. "No, that is Thomas. He's in charge of my security from the French embassy while I'm here."

Dr. Patterson eyes went wide for a moment and then she flipped through a few pages. She pulled out a single page. "STD testing is standard for all first-time pregnancies." She handed the paperwork to Eve. "You're negative in everything."

Eve smiled and breathed a sigh of relief. "Can I have a copy of this?"

She nodded. "You can have that one. We have it on file."

"Thank you," Eve was grateful that she didn't need another blood draw today.

"Well, now that's done. Let's cover the rest of what we did today. The MRI does show some swelling. It's pushing on your cerebellum, which helps control motor function. There is no bleeding that we can see. As the swelling goes down, your symptoms will improve. Keep your stress down, limit screen, TV, computer time, and physical activities that increase your blood pressure." The doctor smirked.

"This could take a week or two. I'll get you a note for work or school. Your blood work does show you going down the Hyperemesis Gravidarum path. I want you back in a week for another round of blood work to compare. If your numbers keep falling, you can expect to stay next week for your first of many overnights for fluids. This is also something to keep in mind for future pregnancies."

She turned to the recent ultrasound, then pressed her mouth, and her friendly disposition suddenly was gone. "I think your baby may be in stress from a partial placental abruption. This is a condition where the placenta separates from the uterus. Normally, it is something that can be dealt with in the third trimester, usually by delivering early or performing a C-section. However, during the first two trimesters, there isn't anything we can do for the fetus because it's not viable for it to survive on its own."

Eve instantly developed tears in the bottom of her eyes but fought them back as best as she could. "From your last check to now, the baby's heart rate has significantly dropped. It could be from the fall or several possibilities. Babies at this stage can still recover and develop as scheduled. But I want you to be prepared for the possibility that this pregnancy may not survive."

Eve's heart dropped and so did all her tears. The doctor got up and came around to sit next to her. She wrapped her arm around her and handed her tissues. "Following the guidelines for concussion is very similar to what you need to do to help your baby's outcome. Rest, reduce stress, limit physical activity, and now add no heavy lifting. Nothing over ten pounds. That's just a little heavier than a gallon of milk."

After Eve calmed down a bit, she asked, "Can I get a copy of all this to help explain later tonight when everyone gets home?"

"Sure thing." She grabbed the file and pulled out the paperwork and added it to the other copy she was leaving with. "Remember, try not to stress. I know that is difficult. Take a hot shower. Have your man give you a back and foot rub. Lots of rest. Make him cook or order in. Just take it easy."

"Thank you for your time, Dr. Patterson. I'll see you next week." The doctor nodded and went back to her office. Eve sent a group text to the guys.

'Done at the doctor's office. On my way to your place. We need to chat about a few things.' She picked up all her paperwork and slowly stood up. When she was stable, she went to get Thomas.

Her phone chirped with Jessie's response, 'I'm already home. See you soon.' She knew Adam still had an hour left before he could respond. But that way he knew he could expect to see her.

Eve made it to the condo and knocked on the door. Jessie pulled the door open and gave her a soft kiss and hug. "Hello, Kitten. I figured something was going on for an unscheduled group visit." Eve started to cry and he pulled her in harder. "Come on in. Let's set your stuff down." She had so much to say, but the words were stuck in her throat.

She set the pages down for the boys to read and placed her copy of the STD report on the counter with the contract. She decided to leave it there just in case one of the guys wished to read it. As Jessie was reading the findings from today's check-up, she laid down on his bed.

She closed her eyes and breathed in his scent. In with good and out with bad. She felt her body relax. After today, she needed it.

Adam

Adam saw the text from Eve and opened the camera monitor. He didn't see anything. Only new papers on the counter. He sent the group a message. 'On my way now. Be home soon.'

Jessie responded with a sad face, 'We are lying down in my room. Rough day.' Adam looked at the monitor again and zoomed in. Jessie's door was open and he could see their feet, but it didn't look like they were moving. Adam opted to take a taxi for the faster ride home. It would be quicker and he wanted to see her after last night's shenanigans.

As Adam approached the front door, he saw Thomas standing there waiting. "Good evening, Mr. Stratford," he said as he got within talking distance.

"Hello, Thomas. Bit of a late day for you, isn't it?" He nodded his head yes. "We are still trying to find a suitable replacement. Our other evening shift is currently out of town. If Eve stays the night here, I'll feel comfortable leaving for the evening knowing that you both are watching out for her."

Adam nodded his head. "I'll convince her to stay, one way or another." Adam smiled, liking that idea more and more.

"Sounds good. I'll be back in the morning. Have a good evening," Thomas said, and then turned to walk away.

Adam came through the door and set his stuff down and walked to Jessie's room. "You guys making out without me?"

Jessie looked up and held his finger to his lips. Oops, he forgot to pay attention to what they were doing first before he opened his mouth and stuffed his foot in it. Jessie picked up his phone, typed, and then nodded for him to read. "Go read paperwork on counter. Whole bunch going on. Figure out what you want to do for dinner and then come back, quietly. She needs the rest."

Adam nodded his head in acknowledgment. He walked back out, sat down, and started reading. Looks like she has been busy today. MRI – brain swelling, rest, relaxation, and no exercise. Hyperemesis gravidarum – may need overnight care from time to time for fluids. Ultrasound report – low heart rate, fetal stress was highlighted, placental abruption. No heavy lifting over ten pounds.

Adam lowered his head. Shit, she's had a hard day and it may be harder in the near future. He pulled out his key ring, removed the spare key and set it on the counter. He was going to make a grand gesture out of giving her a key, but now it seems like the wrong thing to do.

He got up and found her keys and placed his own on her ring. He found a permanent marker in the drawer and wrote "A&J" on the key.

After putting the keys back in her bag, he gathered up her paperwork to put away.

He then saw her result and contract on the other end of the counter. If she lost the baby, is she thinking of exiting the contract? Or would she continue as if after a normal delivery? He turned to the back page and ran his thumb over the signatures. If she did exit, it would be easier for him to have her all to himself.

But now that she's on this path, would she ever want to go back to monogamy? He set the pages back on the corner and felt his stomach rumble. On a rough day like today, he ordered her favorite food: six soft tacos with rice, beans, and chips for delivery.

He went to his room and changed into a comfortable shirt and shorts, then went back to Jessie's room. He slowly laid down behind her and rested his hand on her hip so he wouldn't accidentally press on her abdomen.

Jessie whispered, "She needs to be here with us so we can watch her better."

Adam nodded. "I just put the spare key to the condo on her keychain."

Jessie smiled. "Perfect. We can take turns on whose room she sleeps in, so the other can get some rest," Jessie added.

"We won't have to worry about her being here alone during the day. Her security will be here if she needs help," Adam said.

"Even if we lose the baby, we should really look into getting a bigger place. Is there a three-bedroom available in this building?" Jessie asked, raising his eyebrows.

"I've already looked. It's out of my budget. We would have to look farther from the city. Plus, with adding kids, rural areas would be better." They both nodded at the same time.

Eve

As Eve woke up she felt a bit foggy, but it slowly lifted as the smell of food filled her senses. She stretched, sat up, and held still until the room stopped spinning. She felt pressure in her head and placed a hand to her forehead. She slowly got up and walked to the door. Both guys were at the table as they chatted and ate their meal.

She quietly snuck up behind them and grabbed an ass cheek of both and squeezed. "Mmmm, husbands, I wouldn't mind some of that, and the food smells good too." She giggled as she let go of her grip. She kissed Adam on the cheek and then Jessie's cheek.

"Hello, Beautiful. How are you feeling?" Adam smirked at her.

She raised her hand to her head. "The headache is back. Do you guys have any Tylenol?"

Jessie popped up. "I have some. I'll be right back." He took off to his bathroom, and Adam got up and went to the kitchen. Eve moved over and sat down next to where Jessie was eating and set her head in her hands.

"It only hurts when I sit up." Jessie set the Tylenol down next to her.

"Then we just need to keep you horizontal," Jessie said as he leaned her back on the bench and kissed placed kisses on her neck.

Adam set a glass of water down on the table. "Your doctor did say for your concussion and the baby to rest and keep stress down. That sounds like bed rest to me."

Jessie popped his hand up. "I second that motion." They both grinned, and then Jessie helped her to sit up.

"While you were sleeping, we were doing some talking, and Thomas agreed that, for the time being, you need to stay here with us at night," Adam said firmly, leaving no room to argue.

"You can take turns on whom to sleep with or keep awake in your insomniac state," Jessie added.

"You're not a prisoner here, you're free to come and go. I placed a spare key to the condo on your key ring," Adam smiled.

Eve opened her mouth and then closed it. She thought about it for a moment. There would be no guard at night at her place, and she would love to spend more time with the guys.

"I did send all the information to the school about the accident and the baby. They understand that I will be out for the week and will return next Monday. My teacher knew that I was still going to the meeting on Friday and to expect my submission. But otherwise, I would just be resting and drawing."

She paused and looked down at herself. "I can't wear the same outfit for seven days, so I'll need to get a few items." She looked back up. "Are you sure you guys want me here?"

"Yes," they said in unison without hesitation. "We all can go tonight after dinner and gather what you need. Plus, I have yet to see the inside of your apartment," Jessie volunteered. Eve smiled and hugged Jessie. Adam came around and sat behind her and hugged both of them.

The three of them made it to her place by 9 p.m. after playing several rounds of tonsil tennis with lots of fondling with the guys. She was hoping that Jessie's results would come in sooner rather than later or else she'd have to pack her personal toy also. She opened a bag and tossed in several undergarments, comfy pants, shirts, and then grabbed her small travel bag of toiletries.

She stopped and looked at Adam, smiled, and then grabbed her black suit for Friday's meeting and placed it on the bed. She grabbed her Halloween outfit and placed it on top of her suit. She opted for her low heels for comfort and placed them in the bag. She turned to grab her case of drawing materials.

"Tsk, tsk, tsk," Adam sounded as he took the case before she could pick it up. "Nothing heavy, Beautiful." Eve smiled and pulled him into a kiss.

Jessie came up behind her and whispered, "Let's take this back home where we have a bigger bed." Eve felt the desire flow from both of them, and she felt so loved.

It was a strange idea at first, sleeping in Jessie's bed one night and then Adam's the next. But she saw the logic in only keeping one of the guys up per evening. Each had different benefits and disadvantages to the level of pleasure.

Being with Jessie sometimes felt like class was in session. Helping him to learn how to make her body sing was proving more daunting than she originally thought it was going to be. However, he is more than ready to penetrate her at any given moment. Where Adam was a master at making her body peak and beg for more, him holding back only makes her want him more.

No matter who she was sleeping with, she still woke up after a few hours of sleep, but felt more rested having someone to hold onto. She was long since done with everything for Friday's meeting, so she decided to start drawing the guys as they slept. By all means, she was no Lucas Cranach painting the iconic painting of Adam and Eve, but she created what she was capable of with her limited skills.

Thursday morning, after the guys had left for school, Eve noticed a new page on the counter with the contract. Adam had added his results to the stack. Suddenly, her urge was overflowing, and she needed to self-satisfy her growing needs. She took off to her apartment with her goal in mind.

When she got there, she turned on the music to love songs and mounted her toy in the shower to the desired height to give her maximum pleasure. Then she went to change in front of the camera, into something a little more sexually appealing. She had purchased a new La Perla two-piece and wanted to show it off. Then, she moved the camera to the bathroom counter and faced it toward the shower.

She picked up her phone and lay on the bed to send Adam a text message. She knew he was at school and would get it later, but wanted a time stamp so he'd know when to rewind and watch. "I saw you got your results. It got me thinking that we are one step closer. So, I thought I'd share my excitement with you. For your viewing pleasure, check out my bedroom camera. Love and Kisses."

She sent the message and walked into the bathroom. Then slowly moved in front of the camera to the beat of the music while touching and slowly undressing to what was left of the Stevie Wonder song:

I just called to say I love you

I just called to say how much I care, I do

I just called to say I love you

And I mean it from the bottom of my heart

Of my heart

After seductively getting her garments off, she then climbed into the shower. This time she left the door open so he would have a full view. She was glad that tonight was her evening with him. She'd get him all wound up before he got home. She was curious what he would do in response to a normal, not-in-person voyeur show.

When she was done, she returned the camera to the spot on the shelf where she had found it. She hoped it was facing the correct direction. If not, he could fix it later. Then she stopped and thought for a moment, then purposefully moved it in the wrong direction so he would have to come back and fix it.

That made her laugh deep down inside. She picked up her shopping list and headed out the door for food for the evening and weekend.

Eve spent the rest of the afternoon cooking up the sausage and hamburger and softened the noodles to construct the lasagna she loved to make, but it was always too much for just herself. She diced up the veggies she picked out to roast.

She hoped that there would be enough leftovers for Friday because she didn't think she would have time after her final presentation to make something new. She could just cut it in half and put it into the refrigerator, but she would need a storage container. She started looking in cupboards when she was swept up, giving her a queasy feeling. "Easy," she said and covered her mouth.

"Oh, my. I'm sorry, Kitten. I was gonna take you to go lay down because it's obvious that you have not rested today." He gave her a quick kiss on the forehead and then slowly set her down.

"Hello, Husband. I'm almost done here and then it takes almost an hour to cook. We can lay down and chat about your day during that time?" she smiled.

"I would love that. What were you looking for in the cabinets?" Jessie fidgeted with her hands.

She looked around. "I was looking for a container for leftovers for tomorrow's dinner."

He started laughing. "We very rarely have leftovers. Normally, we just leave extras on a plate in the fridge."

Eve took a step back. "Well, when I cook, there will be good food with plenty of leftovers to be eaten for lunch the next day or a following dinner for all of us. So I'll look into getting some containers." She gave him a full hug and kiss this time. "How about you go change? I'll come join you in just a few." She pointed to his room.

He turned and gave her a soft spank as he walked away. She arranged the final layers together and placed the lasagna in the oven. She was crawling into bed for a short rest when Jessie came out of the bathroom.

"Hold still right there." She froze her movement and blushed. "Now that is a gorgeous sight for the eyes." He kneeled behind her, placed her legs between his, and ground his hard member on her entrance. A moan escaped her and then he leaned her up so his hands could freely roam the front of her body.

She turned her head towards him to gain his lips as her arms went up to pull him in, opening her body further to his roaming hands as they found her breasts and nipples. Her body flexed to the added attention and he groaned. "God, I want more of you," he said while his breathing was heavy in her ears. She turned and wrapped her arms around him.

"Adam's results came back today. Hopefully, yours will be soon," she whispered. "Maybe even this weekend." She raised and wiggled her eyebrows.

He slowly laid her down on her back and started to unbutton her shirt, kissing each new area that was exposed. She moaned and gripped her fingers on his backside as he explored her with his soft lips.

His hands squeezed her ass and pulled her legs open for him to push his hardened cock on her sensitive bud in between. She arched and moaned louder as he ground harder while his hand unclasped her bra. Her upper half was now bare for him to enjoy. His mouth claimed one nipple, flickered, twirled, and nipped as his fingers twisted, strummed, and pulled at the other.

"Jessie!" she moaned loudly as her fingers tangled in his hair, encouraging him to keep going as her climax grew. She wrapped her legs around his buttocks and squeezed with his motion to pull herself harder against his grind. She dug her fingers in and her toes curled. "Yes. YES! Oh God!" she exclaimed and arched as her orgasm exploded freely.

He continued to grind through her climax as he was reaching his. "Yes, Jessie." She reached down with her hands and pulled them across his back as she squeezed his muscles. He grabbed her ass and pulled hard, then let out a grunt and a moan as he held, flexed against her body. He pushed a couple more times and then relaxed his thrusts as they lay together, breathing heavily.

"It's insane how good that felt without being in you." He pulled her in for a kiss and they held each other for another minute. Then there was a break in the silence.

"Thank you for leaving the door open so I could watch. That was amazing to see." Adam stepped in and kneeled behind Eve. "I need to chat with Wifey about the message she sent me earlier." Eve blushed because she had forgotten about playing in front of the camera.

"It was the perfect pick-me-up for my horrible day." He scooped her up and then paused. He looked at Jessie for a moment. "In private. Besides, tonight's my night." He winked at Jessie, looked at Eve, and grinned before he carried her to his room.

He whispered in her ear as he shut the bedroom door. "I'm gonna make you squeal and moan so loud, the neighbors will be jealous." Eve blushed deep red in excitement.

Entry 7: Stratford Presentation

Eve was up bright and early as usual, but decided to stay warm and snuggled in bed until Adam's alarm went off. She enjoyed seeing his growing morning masculinity as part of his routine. Hopefully, someday soon, she would be able to change his morning to include a workout to get the circulation going. Her face blushed at the thought of morning sex.

Adam rolled over and watched her." Morning, Beautiful. What's got you blushing so early?"

She smiled and pointed to his bulge. "Someday we will have to set your alarm clock fifteen minutes earlier for some morning exercise." She leaned in and gave him a good morning kiss.

He smiled. "If I have my way with you, it's gonna be more like an hour." He gave her ass a firm pat. She gasped and then stretched out and watched him get dressed. A real view of what married life would be like.

She got up and went to the kitchen to make coffee and breakfast burritos for the guys. While that was heating up, she pulled out sandwich makings, fruit, and chips and packed two lunches for her husbands. She drew hearts on each of the bags and wrote 'Love you' on them.

Jessie came up behind her and slowly slid his hands around her waist. "Good morning, Kitten. I was thinking of ditching class today. What do you think?"

Eve turned around and shook her head. "No, you will not. I know you have a test today, and I will not let you risk all you have been working toward just to spend a few extra hours with me when we have our future together."

He pulled her into a kiss. "Already taking care of me for my best interests." He smiled.

"Plus, I will be gone for the presentation anyway." She shrugged her shoulders. He looked at the bag and then back at her and smiled.

"I love you." He lifted her up, set her on the counter, and pressed in between her legs.

"I love you too," she replied, and they started kissing deeply.

"Okay, kids," Adam teased in a parental tone. "We have to get to school now," Adam said as he entered the living room. Eve ended the kiss and then pouted. Jessie leaned back and helped her down, but not without getting two handfuls of her ass with his fingertips tickling at her privates. She gasped and then playfully swatted his shoulder before turning to get breakfast from the microwave.

Adam closed the distance. "Mmmm, that smells good. Remind me to thank you properly later." He smiled.

"Hey, tonight's my night," Jessie interrupted.

"Yes. Doesn't mean I can't have my way with her first. Like you did yesterday," Adam continued.

Jessie smirked and shrugged his shoulders. "Good point." He looked back over at Eve. "I sure hope you're good with having lots of sex. Because once this floodgate opens, you're gonna have two horny guys after you all the time."

She giggled. "Perhaps we should put it into the contract for a minimum of one day of rest per week." She winked and handed out bags. Jessie gave her a kiss goodbye and headed to the door.

Adam came over for his bag and gave her a kiss as well. "Remember, I have a special employee coming to the meeting that you have not met yet. Just be your usual self to win them over." He winked.

Like she wasn't already nervous about seeing the guys today. "Okay." The image swirled in her mind of the last time, and she was sure she left a lasting impression of her throwing up in the bathroom. She smiled and sent them on their way so she could go shower and get dressed for the meeting.

Eve

"Good morning, Mrs. Ophelia," Eve announced herself as she started climbing the stairs.

"Good morning, Ms. Eve." She could hear her voice echoing down the stairs. Wow, Eve thought to herself. It's only been a few weeks, and now these stairs seem so much taller and longer to climb. She was winded and needed to catch her breath when she reached Ophelia's desk. She looked back down the steps and then back at Ophelia.

"Did you guys install a few more since the last time I was here?" Eve asked as she took a couple of deep breaths.

"Ah, I see the baby is now pushing up into your organs. How far along are you now?" Her eyes got bigger.

"I'll be ten weeks in a couple of days," Eve responded. Ophelia held out her hand. Eve set her bag down and reached for her hand. Ophelia pulled her in closer and put her hand up to her mouth to whisper in Eve's ear.

"Are you secretly Mrs. Stratford now? Because once the family finds out, they are going to want the family name to continue," she asked quietly. Eve pulled back in shock, covered her mouth, and giggled while shaking her head, no.

"He did kinda ask several weeks ago, but I was in so much shock that the words wouldn't come out. I would have eventually said yes, but he took my silence as a no." Eve blushed and saddened a little.

"Oh, don't you worry about it. I'll be working on him from this side." She winked, got up, and opened the door to the offices. "Adam should be here after lunch." Suddenly, she had an oops look on her face. "I wasn't supposed to tell you."

Eve set her hand on her arm and winked. "It's our little secret." Eve smiled and continued through the door and headed to the center table, where she started setting up the extra tablets. She laid out her larger design boards and floor plans, knowing the guys would be able to understand those images.

Eve stopped and admired the table for a moment. "I absolutely love this table." Eve spoke to herself and smiled as she softly ran her hand along the grain.

"I'm glad you like it." Eve gasped in surprise and turned around. "Oh, I'm sorry. I didn't mean to startle you. But I love the table also." In front of her stood an older woman with strawberry blondish-red hair.

Eve smiled. "It's nice to have everyone equal at the table. Not a common thing you see today in business," Eve added.

"My husband made it when he first opened the doors. You see, when he was growing up, he came from a family with limited means.

He went into carpentry to earn money and help the family, like his father. However, it wasn't his passion. He studied on his own and got his hands on every architecture book he could find." She reached over and softly touched the table also.

Adam looked so much like her. "It's nice to meet you, Mrs. Stratford. I'm Madame de Vogues, but please, call me Eve."

Eve held out her hand. "Oh, my. So formal. Call me Sharon." Eve blushed.

"Perhaps after we have gotten to know each other better." They shook hands, but she pulled Eve in and put an arm around her.

"I can see why he likes you so much," she whispered, then stepped back and smiled. Eve's blush deepened.

"Oh, Lord have mercy. I used to blush like that too." Mrs. Stratford waved her palm in the air. "Once you experience the world, you'll see that you won't blush as much." She winked at her. "Well, are you ready to get this meeting going?" Eve smiled and nodded yes. Then, without warning, Mrs. Stratford pulled up her two fingers and whistled loudly.

"The secret to life is that, with all these men, you've got to take command," she whispered. Eve could not contain her laughter. If Mrs. Stratford only knew how she had two wonderful men under her spell.

Eve spent the better part of an hour going over all the designs, including the added break room that everyone requested. She sat next to Mrs. Stratford and made sure she was the first to see each image, along with the multiple possibilities of color varieties.

At the end, Eve handed out new blank slips and asked everyone to anonymously write down which one they liked the best and their second choice. When they were done, they were to return the slips by the end of lunch. She placed a collection box on the table for the slips.

She giggled to herself, knowing that Adam was coming but wasn't supposed to know. She decided to play a little trick on his sneakiness. "Mrs. Stratford, would it be okay if I treated you and Mrs. Ophelia to a lunch break?"

Sharon's face lit up. "I don't know. Let's include Mrs. Ophelia in this conversation." They both walked over to the front desk, and

Sharon spoke up. "Ms. Eve wanted to take both of us ladies out for lunch. Would that be okay with you?" Ophelia looked as guilty as a cat with a canary.

"I promise to have you back by the end of the lunch break. Just figured us ladies could use a little time away from all the testosterone." Eve winked at her.

"I would be most honored to join you ladies. Let me just transfer the phones to go right to voicemail, and we can be right on our way." They let the group know that they were heading out and would be back soon. Between the two of them, they picked a smaller delicatessen that carried artisan wines and spirits.

Mrs. Stratford ordered a bottle for the table. "You must simply try this Merlot with the roast beef. The pairing is wonderful."

Eve looked at Mrs. Ophelia and then back at Mrs. Stratford. "I'm sorry. I am unable to drink alcohol at this time." Eve gave her really big eyes and then looked back at Mrs. Ophelia.

"I'm more than willing to be her stand-in drinker, but you will need to order me a cab home." Mrs. Ophelia spoke up. Sharon put her hands over her mouth, popped up, sending her chair backward to the ground.

"You guys are expecting? I get to be a grandmother? I'm getting a daughter? Oh, my good God. This is the best day ever!" she exclaimed and started dancing as she lifted Eve's arms up to stand. "How did I not notice? You even have a bump going." Eve lowered her hand to her stomach.

Then Mrs. Stratford leaned in and whispered, "I raised that boy, so I know what gift he was bestowed. I've been without for so many years, so please tell me. How is the sex?"

Eve was in momentary shock and sat back down, then leaned back with a guilty look. She covered her mouth in surprise, then the reality of all the questions hit her.

"Please have a seat," Eve said to Mrs. Stratford. She fixed her chair and sat back down. "It's a bit more complicated than that." Eve blushed and paused, trying to find the words as she twiddled her fingers in her lap.

"I'm gonna be honest with you ladies. I've had some trying times these last few months. But the only reason it's been manageable is Adam." She looked Mrs. Stratford in the eyes. "I don't know what he is like in bed because of his vow to God. The child is not his, but Jessie's. That in itself is a long story, but everyone knows. Both are being so supportive, and I see this being absolutely crazy but wonderful at the same time."

Sharon leaned back. "You love Adam?" Eve cracked a big grin and nodded her head yes. "He is so in love with you. Every time we talk, you are all he talks about. So, I see no problems at all."

Eve smile grew. "You don't think it's weird that he wants to be the father of his best friend's baby?" Mrs. Stratford kept on smiling.

"I don't see anything wrong with wanting to be a father. So long as everyone knows what's happening, there's no issues." She leaned forward. "Did he talk to you about Elizabeth?"

Eve pouted her lips a little. "He was a small boy when she passed and that she was from your first marriage. Mr. Stratford raised Elizabeth as his," Eve answered.

"Yes, but what I never discussed with him was that my ex-husband was an asshole. Straight-up mean when it came to her. No matter what she did, she could never please him. I saw that journey becoming very bad, so I removed us from the situation. Just goes to show that just because you're blood-related doesn't mean that you'll be a good parent." She pressed her lips flat.

"Sometimes in life, we have to make those hard choices. Not that it's good or bad, but just choosing the path your life will go. It sounds like Adam made that choice to love you and the baby as his."

Eve smiled and placed a hand onto Sharon's hand. "At one point, I was ready to go home to France. But then Adam was there for me during my lowest point, and he stood fast to watch over me. He's been there several times, unquestionably. That is how I know he will be a good husband and father." They all nodded in agreement.

"He has not asked you to marry him yet?" Sharon's questions continued.

Eve shook her head. "I'm not worried about it. I know how he feels, and yes, there is a deadline for me to return to France."

Sharon raised her eyebrows again. "Are you here on a visa?"

Eve nodded her head. "Both the guys know. Like I said, everything has been on the table with them. Complete honesty, which is the building block of a strong relationship, right?" Eve smirked.

"Geez, I admire you kids. You are starting out on the right foot. I didn't figure that out until I was in my forties." Eve smiled, thinking that they were on the right track. It may be difficult with all the wanting, but working on their solid foundation is just as important.

An hour and a half later, the three of them walked back to the office arm in arm, while chatting the whole time. Eve loved having older and wiser friends for help and their opinions. In a sense, it was like she adopted two extra moms. They staggered through the main door, and their conversation echoed up the stairs. Adam was standing and smiling at the top of the stairs as they made it to the top.

"Did you ladies have a good time?" They all grinned at him as he stood up straight. "And what have you all been doing?" They all giggled. Eve took a couple of steps forward and gave him a big kiss.

"We've been talking about you, Héros. As you say, the cat's out of the bag." She smiled and gave him a hug.

"You talked about... everything?" He had a concerned look on his face. She started to giggle and looked back at the ladies and then back at him.

"No, not everything. But your mom knows I'm pregnant and that it's Jessie's, and that we are working on the whole situation." She smiled, and the other two started giggling again.

"I don't get what's so funny." He had a serious look to his face, but the corner of his lips started to curl.

She smiled and pulled him in to whisper in his ear. "They each had a bottle of wine with lunch. They are so cute when their filters are gone." She laughed again and let go of Adam. "Come on, ladies. Let's go hold down the couches and drink some water." Eve guided them around the corner of the waiting room.

Adam nodded his head. "I'll go get some water and something to snack on as well." Eve smiled and mouthed 'thank you' as she led them to the couches. After the two ladies landed with a laugh, Eve went to follow Adam. She packed all her items into her bag along with the collection box and then headed back to sit with the ladies. Adam came out of his office with a few bottles of water and some bags of chips.

"I'm glad to see that you two are getting along," Adam smiled.

"You could have warned me that the special person was your mother. But nonetheless, we had a wonderful time. She is so proud of all your accomplishments." She leaned in and gave him another kiss.

"Whoop, whoop." A bunch of cheers came from the guys as they kissed, and Eve blushed just before walking through the door. Adam turned and waved like there were paparazzi in the room.

Eve sat down on the arm of the couch and opened the box with the comments.

"Let's see what they voted on, shall we?" Eve asked as Adam handed them each a bottle of water and a bag of chips. The gals kept on chattering as Eve tallied up the votes. After her final count, she got up and gave Adam the result. She held up a picture to share. "Light and bright with blue accents won by a landslide."

Adam smiled. "Sounds good. Now we just need to figure out what to do with everything as we remodel."

Eve smirked. "I have a thought on that as well."

Adam looked intrigued. "Really?" She smiled as she handed the tablet back to him and pressed play. A short video played of the downstairs emptying out, transforming into a blank slate. Walls grew into place, drywall, paint, then all their desks filled in. Then the video shifted and showed the upstairs emptying out and the remodel progressing to completion, then all the needed furniture moved back into the freshly remodeled space.

"You created a second video presentation?" Adam asked, and Eve smiled and nodded.

"I figured, since you had the space, it would only make sense to utilize it for the remodel upstairs. Then when done, the downstairs would be mostly ready for the next phase. Kinda two remodels for the price of one. When you compare the value of usable space, you are doubling the building's square footage. Plus, with all the strong men at your disposal, the movement of furniture should be quick."

He took another step closer. "You are so amazing. You did two presentations for me." Eve smiled, her hands pulled on his waist as she stood up. He bent down and locked her into a kiss as he walked her to the wall. His arm moved behind her back and pulled her into him as he pushed into her.

"Excuse you." Adam and Eve both looked at his mother, who was gawking at them.

"See the heat I was talking about," Mrs. Ophelia said with a big smile.

"You need to marry her, then you can go get a room," Sharon said, and then they started laughing again.

"Are we starting an office pool on when he's going to finally get down on a knee and ask?" Mrs. Ophelia asked.

"Oh my gosh. I want in on that." Then they both started laughing again.

Sharon staggered up and composed herself for a moment as she brushed her outfit off. "But seriously now. Eve, darling. You did a wonderful job here. I was impressed with the work you put in. How do I go about getting you to come out to the house and help me with a project there?"

Eve walked to her and gave her a hug. "I'll get you a card. You can call and schedule for me to come. If you have any questions, ask Adam. He did the same thing." Eve smiled.

Adam called the car service to have Mrs. Ophelia and his mother returned home. Adam then carried Eve's bag with his briefcase while they walked the few blocks hand in hand, back to the condo. At this rate, they would have the place to themselves for a few hours. She wondered if that is why he came so early instead of staying in class all day. Then a sad wave washed over her.

"What's on your mind, Beautiful, to make you frown?" Adam asked.

"I had so much fun with your mother today. I'm just... missing my parents. I'll write to them and keep them updated." She tugged her frown to a partial smile.

"I'm sure they would love to hear from you," Adam added. Eve had forgotten until now that she had talked about them while he was sleeping. She felt a little guilty and decided that she needed to have that conversation again with him tonight.

While standing at the light, he pulled her so she would stand in front of him. He tucked her hair back and slowly kissed her neck. She felt her insides heat up and kept her hands on his, at her abdomen, while fighting the urge to venture out and explore while surrounded by strangers. When the light turned, Eve pulled Adam to walk a little faster. She was looking forward to being horizontal with him.

By the time they made it to the condo, Eve was already wound up, ready to go. Adam set her bag on the table and she leaned into him as she placed all her heat into the kiss. She pulled back and looked at him for a moment and then stepped back. "Husband?"

Adam smiled at her. "Yes, Wife." Eve removed her blazer and set it onto the arm of the couch.

"After talking to the ladies, I came to realize something." Adam set his case down and removed his blazer and set it on top of his case.

"What's that, Beautiful?" She kicked off her shoes, started to unbutton her shirt, and then turned and walked to his room.

"I want to make love with you." She held out her hand for him. "Come make love with me," she said and turned to lean against the door while still holding out her arm for him. She then saw that he wasn't walking towards her.

She came back to him and reached for his hand and gave him a soft pull. However, he stayed anchored in place. "Adam?" She tilted her head. "I need you to be honest. I can't read your mind. Do you want to be with me?"

He looked at her and smiled. "I really do," he replied.

"Great. Then let's seal this union." He let go of her hand and sat down at the table. She stood upright and tucked her shirt back in. "I don't understand. What are you waiting for? Do you need me to put a ring on your finger? Do you want us to go to court and sign papers today?" Eve was starting to get annoyed. She was hoping the contract would help him to see how serious she was about him.

Adam looked back at her. "I'm waiting for you to decide." Eve was confused. She had already decided and had made her intentions clear.

"I'm confused. I thought you realized that the marriage contract was for you, to show you, that I did decide." He shook his head no. "Decide on what? Please explain." She took a step back and leaned against the door frame.

He slowly looked up to her eyes. "For you to decide on whether you want me or Jessie."

Eve was dumbfounded for a moment as she thought about what he said. And then anger took over and she could feel it in every ounce of her being. She tried to speak calmly, but her anger took over.

"Je n'arrive pas à te croire! Adam, weeks ago, I answered your question and said I was ready. You didn't say or do anything. And then this whole, both are interested in me situation started and you said nothing. For the days after, nothing." Eve stomped her foot.

"I did a deep dive into a world that I knew was there but didn't pay much attention to until that day. I came to realize that is where I fit. My love is not singular. With the world shut down, it was hard to learn and explore this feeling inside me."

She fisted her hands wanting to hit him. "This crazy ball of emotions I have for you, I also have for Jessie. And I don't want either to go away."

Eve started to pace to calm down and took several deep breaths. She then stopped and faced him. "You love your mom, right?"

He smirked at her. "Of course, I do," he replied. She put her hands on her hips and stared at him with big eyes.

"So, does that mean you don't love your father?" She raised her hands and lifted her shoulders.

He had a harsh look on his face. "You know I love my dad."

Eve started to pace again. "If…" She paused for a moment, tapped her finger to her lip and then looked back at him. "If we have six children, will you only love the first one?" She took a deep breath and slowly let it out.

"Now you're just being ridiculous. Of course, I'd love all my kids."

"I'm not being ridiculous, Adam. I'm trying to explain how I feel for both of you. I can see having children with both of you. Being married to both of you at the same time. A life together, we three and a football team of kids."

She started to pace again and then halted. "You were open and honest about your desire to watch. I accepted you for who you are and even allowed myself to open up further than I ever could imagine before, for you. I would have never played with myself in front of someone before or on camera. But for you, I allowed myself to."

She paused to breathe. Her anger was decreasing, but sadness was taking over. It was getting more difficult to keep her emotions under control now. "I was open about what I needed." Eve started to tear up and her voice cracked. Her breathing became sporadic.

"You entered into this with your eyes open and I thought your heart too." Eve walked over to the counter to grab the contract. On top, she saw that Jessie had placed his results out for everyone to see. He must have done that this morning. That's why he wanted to skip school.

She shuffled the results to the back and opened the contract to the exit page. She then grabbed a pen from her purse and brought it back with her. She set it down next to Adam on the table. Eve's tears were falling now, but she had to say what she needed to before she couldn't at all.

"If you can't see yourself in this type of relationship, then sign to exit. I will not hold any grudge or be angry with you. I'd rather you did it now and not a year from now."

She started bawling, took a few steps away to wipe her face. She was hoping he would have a response or react to her emotions, but he didn't. Now she was beyond talking. She turned and walked to Jessie's room and slammed the door shut. She flopped on his bed and didn't even try to hold anything back. She just let all the crying out. This was not how she saw the evening going just a few minutes ago.

Adam

Jessie breezed in the door at his usual time. "Hey there. You're home early. How did class go today?" Adam remained quiet in his thoughts. Jessie walked into the kitchen and set his stuff down on the counter and grabbed a couple of bottled waters from the fridge. "Dude, you gonna talk to me?" He sat down next to him at the table and handed him a water. There was still silence. Then Jessie's tone changed. "Why is the contract here and open to the exit page?"

Adam hung his head. "I think I fucked up."

Jessie leaned back. "Explain." Adam paused for a few and then turned to Jessie.

"I'm having difficulty with the group dynamic and told her that I want to be with her, monogamously. She got furious at me and has been crying ever since." Adam pointed his finger to Jessie's room.

Jessie got up and stood in front of him. "It wasn't that long ago that you told me to get on board or get out. Whether it's monogamous or polyamorous, she sets the rules. I know you remember what you said to me. There is something magical, even spiritual, happening here." Jessie paused to stare at him.

"When the three of us are in the same room, I feel the cords pulling us together. Now, it's your turn to get on board or get out. You need to decide if you want to be with her or not. You already signed. If you're not sure," Jessie tapped the page. "Sign the exit and we can all figure it out later."

Jessie looked over his shoulder to his room and then back at the contract. He turned the pages back over so his results were back on top. "I'm going to go cheer her up and make her feel better any way I can. Leftover dinner is in the fridge when you're hungry." Jessie got up and walked to his room, shut, and locked the door.

Eve

Eve had fallen asleep for a bit after crying but awoke sometime after. She was in no mood to continue talking with Adam, so she just remained lying still on Jessie's bed. She could hear when Jessie came in the door and could just hear them talking but couldn't understand the words they were saying. Eve had replayed the conversation in her mind over and over since she came into the room, but it didn't get any easier.

Why would Adam enter this contract if he wasn't willing to be a part of it? Perhaps she should just exit and end the contract and date them as individuals. Her heart dropped a little. Going as individuals would still be the same. If one or the other did propose, he would want her to walk away from the other man. She took another deep breath and let it out.

It would hurt her, but perhaps Adam is the one who needs to walk away after all. She started to cry again, feeling the pain of losing love.

Jessie came into the room and shut the door behind him. "Oh Kitten," he said in a sorrowful tone. He lay on the bed and used tissues to dry her face. "Please don't stress over this. He has issues to work on, not you. You clearly said what you wanted. He needs to decide to be a part of it. Crying isn't going to change his mind one way or the other. So, take a deep breath."

Eve wrapped her arms around him and took a deep breath. His aftershave was still just as strong as it was this morning. "I know I'm being overdramatic about this, but my heart was preparing for a bigger life for all of us and as many children as we would all have together."

Jessie rolled her onto her back and slowly pulled up her shirt. He softly kissed her baby bump. Heat started to grow in her. "We're on our way. One day at a time. One baby at a time."

A soft moan escaped her lips and she ran her fingers through his hair as his kisses moved around her belly. "Jessie?" she softly spoke.

"Hmmmm." He responded without taking his lips off her.

"I know I said before that I wanted our first to be a group."

"Mmm hmmm." He responded again, sending vibrations through her stomach. She lifted his head with both her hands to have him look at her.

"After the events of today, I changed my mind." A smile grew on her face. "I saw you placed your report with the contract." He nodded without a word. "Do you want to… make love?" She was nervous asking him to have sex with her.

He rolled up to his knees and slowly lifted her to a seated position. He then stood up and lifted her to a standing position. He finished unbuttoning her shirt and slowly slid it off her shoulders. She unbuttoned his shirt and slowly let it fall to the floor. His slim, muscular frame overshadowed hers.

Her trembling fingers unfastened his belt and button, then unzipped his fly. His slacks slid down his legs to the floor, then he kicked them off. His member was standing at full attention as it protruded from the fabric of his underwear. She wanted to touch him, and this time she didn't hold back.

She softly moved her fingers along his shaft while he released her slacks from her body. He pulled her in for a kiss as his hands wrapped around to unfasten her bra clips. Once her bra was free, he kneeled in front of her, pressed both breasts together, and took both nipples into his mouth with suction and his swirling tongue.

"Oh my God. That feels so good." She moaned loudly as she became instantly wet. His hands now slowly slid her panties down until gravity took over and they fell to the ground. Her hands fumbled along his back because she didn't want to move and break the suction he had on her nipples. He gave them a soft nip and then released. "Ah." She moaned again.

He stood up and her hands went to his underwear to slide them down. Once down far enough, his cock stood straight out at full attention and his briefs dropped to the floor.

He led her back to the bed, and after she laid down, he started to rub her clit. Her body arched with the attention. "Oh, look at you. You're already soaking wet," Jessie groaned.

She smiled and pulled him to be on top of her. She spread her legs wide open to give him full access as he positioned himself in between her legs. This would be her first time having sex without a condom. With someone she was in love with, and they were in love with her also. The father of her unborn child making love together. She pulled him in for a kiss as he lined himself with her wet invitation.

She instantly let go of his mouth and moaned loudly as he slowly pushed into her, filling the room with her joyful noise. Her legs wrapped around his hips to encourage his thrusts, and her hands gripped the back of his shoulders so she could lift her pelvis with each following thrust to take him deeper.

He leaned his head back. "Jesus Christ, this feels so good," he moaned as he continued to thrust all of him into her. He leaned his head forward, resting his forehead onto hers and looked her in the eyes. "God, I love you," he said, and then their mouths and tongues joined in the lovemaking.

The fire inside her burned as bright as it ever had. After a while of being slow and steady, he released her mouth and leaned back. He grabbed her hips and changed his speed to double time. She started continuously moaning loudly, and their bodies started clapping with each thrust.

"Oh God, Jessie, yes! Keep going," she exclaimed. After a couple of minutes, she realized what she was missing. She slowly reached down and softly touched her clit. Boom, her body exploded, and she felt all her muscles tighten on his shaft. "Oh, God!" she exclaimed again.

"Holy shit, Kitten." He plunged a few more times, and she felt the added warmth and fluid fill her. She tightened her legs to keep him deep in her and pulled him back in for another round of breathless kisses.

He slowly rolled to the side, but she kept firm with her upper leg and didn't want to let go. They held onto each other with heavy breathing and hands softly exploring. She tucked her face under his chin and gave him soft kisses on the neck. He slowly reached up and ran his fingers through her hair.

"That was by far the best sex I've ever had." His voice was sultry. She looked up at him and smiled.

"So far," she giggled. "There are so many different positions to try." He pulled her tighter.

"Mmmm, I love you. We can go again in a few minutes. I need to recoup some energy first," he let out a slow happy moan.

"I love you too. Take all the time you need. We have all night." They simply held each other and fell asleep in their post-sex position.

Later that evening, Eve woke up and came out of the bedroom with her shirt loosely on, but her whole body was still exposed to be seen. She paused when she saw Adam was still sitting in the same spot. She looked at the table and saw the contract. She turned it to the back page and saw that it had not been signed.

"You guys were loud. I couldn't help but listen." Eve went to the kitchen and grabbed a bottle of water from the fridge and rolled it across her forehead and down her body.

"That could have been you and me, and then all of us together, since all the reports came back negative," she said, took a sip as she walked back to him. She waited for a response. "I hope that this behavior isn't how you wanted to properly 'thank me later' for breakfast and lunch that I made for you." She made air quotes and then leaned against the table.

"You gonna say anything else?" She waited again as the silence became deafening. "Do you just want to be in this relationship so you can hear or watch Jessie and me have sex?" Her tears started to well again. "You know how I feel about you and what I want." Her breathing became heavy again. "I'm not going to ask you for your hand again." She walked in front of him and lifted his face.

"Either you want me as I am or you don't. So help me God, Adam. If you wait until the end and break my heart," she shook her head as her tears started to fall again, "I will never talk to you again." Her voice choked and she gasped for air before she gave him a quick kiss on his forehead. Her tears streamed down her cheeks again as she went back to Jessie's room.

Eve softly closed the door and leaned her arm on it until her crying was under control. After wiping her face dry with her shirt, she walked over to Jessie and sat on his lap, then she started rubbing his chest to wake him up. His eyes slowly flickered open.

"Hello, my sexy Kitten. Are you in need of more love?" He moved his hands up and squeezed her hips.

Her face soured a little. "I actually have something else in mind."

He leaned up and pulled her down for a kiss. "What's on your mind, Babe?"

She took a breath to concentrate. "Monday, I can move my appointment back to a later time. Would you come with me for the check-up?"

Jessie sat all the way up. "Name the time and I'll be there." He smiled and pulled her in for another kiss.

She leaned back. "I want to take my stuff back to my apartment tonight. Then you and I can stay the night there. That way, Adam can't listen and still get his jollies, while sitting outside of the door. If I'm going to honor his needs, he needs to honor mine. Until then, I'm stepping back from him until he figures it out."

Jessie had a shocked look on his face. "Wow. I mean, yes to taking your stuff back and staying the night, but..." he paused. "You're cutting him off?"

Eve nodded her head, yes. "I don't want to be here waiting while he thinks about what he wants or doesn't want. I made it clear. I think he needs to see what it's like when I'm gone. So, I have a plan..."

They came out of Jessie's room together. Neither of them said a word to Adam as he continued to just sit there. She placed the condo key on the contract and then she went to Adam's room and packed up her clothes and toiletries from his bathroom. Through the reflection of the window, she noticed that he was watching her as she collected her things.

She then picked up her outfit for Saturday's karaoke and carefully placed it on top of her luggage. Jessie had all her art supplies handled and had opened the door. She turned to face Adam. She was thinking of saying something snarky but at the last second she decided not to. "Goodbye."

He stood up as she turned and rolled her luggage out the front door, not giving him a chance to argue.

*

Eve was surprised that they were able to find a taxi so quickly at that time of the night. They arrived at her place not that long after they had left the condo. The moment they entered her bedroom, her phone rang. She looked and saw Adam was calling. She slid the red X to

307

decline the call and walked to the camera on the shelf. She picked it up and walked to the bathroom.

She dangled it over the toilet as she moved some clothing in her laundry basket to make room to hide the camera. She then flushed the toilet, spun the camera around in circles, then covered the lens with a dark shirt and placed the camera in the bottom of her hamper. She made sure all her laundry covered it, so no sounds would get to it. As a last measure, she placed several books on top to help squish the material tight around it.

She wiped her hands clean of that task and went back to the bedroom. Her phone rang again. She looked and it was Adam, again. She slid the red X again as she took a deep breath and slowly let it out.

Then Jessie's phone rang and he looked at it. "Should I answer?" he asked.

"He's your friend. It's up to you," she shrugged her shoulders. Jessie answered, but put it on speaker.

"Hello?" Jessie pressed his lips flat.

"What the fuck is happening?" Adam demanded loudly.

"What do you mean? Eve wanted to spend the evening with me, in private. Plus, it would give you some space to think," Jessie replied. It was quiet for a moment.

"That's fine wanting privacy, but to pack up and leave without discussing any plans? She still doesn't have any nighttime security."

"Don't worry. I'll be here all night and the next day keeping her whole body safe and cared for." Eve blushed and blew him a kiss.

A bit of a huff could be heard over the phone. "Are we still meeting for tomorrow night's karaoke?"

Eve nodded her head, yes. "That's the plan," Jessie replied.

"Ok, well, let her know that she flushed a thousand-dollar camera down the toilet." Eve covered her face so her laugh couldn't be heard. Then she raised her shoulders and hands and smushed her face as she shook her head.

"Dude, at this point in time, I don't think she really cares. If it's that important to you, you shouldn't have made her cry. She was saying earlier that she will honor your needs if you honor her needs. Anyway, dude, I'm going to let you go so that I can have sex with MY wife." Jessie hung up before Adam could say anything else.

Jessie looked up at her and smiled. "Well, I think that just put a bee in his bonnet."

Eve looked at him funny. "Jessie, men don't wear bonnets. So, what did you mean to say?"

He looked at her and laughed. "It means that he has something to think about or talk about. Hopefully he figures it out soon. Are you and I coming back here after karaoke?"

Eve took a breath. "I guess it depends on how Adam behaves. If he is standoffish and distant, then yes. If he has accepted and agrees to being us three again, then we can go back to the condo." Eve shrugged her shoulders again.

"Well, we left all your wonderful lasagna at the condo. What do you want for dinner?" Jessie traced his fingers along her arm, sending goosebumps all over the arm.

"Oh, my favorite teriyaki place is just around the corner. They stay open late. There is also a 24-hour grocery store for snacks and drinks for in-between sex breaks." Eve pulled him into bed for another round, and he didn't complain or resist at all.

Entry 8: Halloween Karaoke

Eve didn't realize how much she needed emotional and intimate contact until they started having sex. She felt bad for waking him up in the night for another round, but he didn't complain and he took his time. So far, she was loving being taken from behind. There was something about the angle and depth that felt so good as he moved in and out. But she missed the ability to claim kisses when she wanted one.

Now, it was 4 a.m. and she decided to let him sleep before she made some breakfast for them to eat. She pulled out her art supplies and her new tracing prism to help her with drawing portraits. She got comfortable and drew several images of Jessie sleeping from different angles. She even pulled back the sheets just far enough to capture his manliness.

One of her future drawings would have to be when his body was fully awake. She giggled to herself. If she could keep her hands off him or his hands off her long enough to get the drawing done. Eve felt the blush spread up her neck and it made her cheeks hot. With each picture she drew, she felt she was getting better. Guess it's true: practice makes perfect.

She was starting her sixth picture when Jessie started to stir. "Come back to bed, Kitten. I sleep better when you're in my arms." Now, how could she resist?

"Ok, I'll just put my art supplies away and be right back." She was in the living room when her phone chirped, signaling that she had gotten a new text message. She looked and saw Adam had sent it. She tapped to open.

"Good morning, Beautiful. I'm sorry for being such an idiot. You were right and I'm still learning to navigate my own feelings about our group dynamic. I think you being so honest with my mother sent me for a bit of a loop. You were open and honest about what you needed and I was not being flexible, even after you were flexible to my needs. I can't wait to see you and show you. I still want to wait for sex, at least until I put a ring on your finger. I hope you understand. I love you. Please call or text me when you're ready to talk."

Eve closed the message and finished putting her supplies away. She was glad that he finally understood her. But she was going to make him wait. Right now, she was going to concentrate on Jessie.

"Mmmm." He moaned a little as she climbed back into bed. She pulled the covers up and tucked her body into his arms and warmed her face on his chest. Her arm felt cool against the warmth of his back, and he slid his palm along her back, then tucked under the silk top and slid along her shoulder blades.

"When did you put your jammies on?" he asked, opened his eyes, and leaned up.

She smiled as he pressed his excitement into her. "A couple of hours ago when I woke up." He sat up and lifted her to join him.

"Tonight is not a night for jammies." He lifted her top up and over and let it fall to the floor. He worked her shorts down, but they only made it to her hips. Eve got up and slid her shorts off as he laid back down. "Do you need to be warmed up?"

He reached out a hand to her. "Just a little," Eve responded.

"Mmmm. Come sit on my lap. When you're ready, you can take me in and ride at your speed, cowgirl style."

Eve decided on a slightly different direction. She placed herself between his legs and started picking up and down his shaft.

"Oh fuck, Kitten. Your tongue feels so good." She watched as his chest raised and fell.

One hand grabbed his ass cheek and would squeeze as she took him deep in her throat. Her other hand slid up and down his abdomen and chest.

When he was rock hard, she positioned herself on his lap with his hardness just in front of her. He reached down and started grinding her clit along his shaft. Instantly, her body was hot and moans escaped her. She grabbed onto his cock and slowly stroked up and down as her pleasure waves moved through her. His other hand reached up and grasped a breast as his fingers teased her nipple.

"Easy, Kitten. I'm not used to not wearing a condom. I'm more sensitive now. You're gonna make me blow early," Jessie warned. Eve released her hand and pressed her pelvis into his thumb for another moment and then leaned forward. "Ready?"

Eve nodded yes, gave him a kiss as she moved a little forward. She kneeled all the way up and he angled his shaft vertically. His length dragged along her clit before finding her entrance, sending another quick shock, causing her to gasp.

She slowly took him in a little farther with each plunge until she had him all the way in. Her body was on fire again and she could feel the pleasure growing. She leaned forward and rested her hands on his chest for support as both his hands went back to tantalizing her breasts and nipples. She rotated between plunging up and down his shaft and grinding forward and backward. They both felt great and had different effects on the inside.

She reached up and grabbed one of his hands and guided it back to her core. Once he touched her clit, her body seized up and her climax released. "Oh, God, Yes! That feels good," she cried out.

He started lunging his pelvis upwards and a moment later he released. "Jesus, you're so amazing. I'm so thankful to be with you."

She grinned as he pulled her down for a kiss and then she rested her head and listened to his racing heart and deep breathing.

"I know the situation is messy with the three of us, but I'm thankful to be doing this with you also. I don't care about what is proper. All I know is that this feels right. I can see us three, years from now, clinging to each other and our brood of kids running around."

Eve could smell the aroma of coffee in the air long before she opened her eyes. She stretched an arm out and could not feel Jessie next to her. She turned over, opened her eyes, and looked at her bedroom door.

"Good morning, Kitten. You were asleep for a while, considering. Guess I worked the energy out of you." He winked.

She stretched her legs out and arms up, pulling the covers from her top half. He walked over and set the cup down on the end table then leaned over the bed and started sucking a nipple.

Eve moaned, her body arched, and her fingers gripped the sheets in response to the stimulation. He placed his hands next to her and pulled her nipple as far as it would go until suction released with a 'pop' sound. Eve moaned again as her breast recoiled.

"Good morning to you too, husband. I was thinking of taking a shower. Wash all this sex off my body." She reached up and ran her fingers through his hair. "Do you want to join me?"

He leaned in and gave her a soft kiss. "I would love to. Since I don't have anything planned until this evening with you, we could even just stay in bed all day." He wiggled his eyebrows.

Eve giggled and blushed. "That sounds like a great plan to me. I just need the restroom for a moment and then you can join me."

Eve turned on the shower and then the radio. She picked her favorite love songs channel and softly swayed to the beat. Once the water was at a pleasing temperature, she climbed in. The warm water felt like a dance as it flowed in a downward pattern along her body.

The steam filled the air, giving a glisten of moisture to everything. She swayed her hips to the music as she lathered herself. After rinsing, she felt extra fluid, slightly sticky and slippery. She ran her finger along and then followed the substance inside her. She then realized that Jessie's semen was slowly spilling out. With how much sex they had had, it's no wonder it's not coming out in a tsunami wave.

She began to wonder where Jessie was. Perhaps he was finishing his cup of coffee or eating breakfast. She got out of the shower and was done drying when a knock sounded on the door.

Eve flung the door open, wondering why Jessie would be knocking. Eve saw Thomas standing there and his eyes went huge as he covered his face and turned.

She screeched and slammed the door shut since she was standing there buck ass naked. She turned off the music and screamed, "What the hell, Thomas?" She scrambled to put a towel around her and then slowly opened the door. He still had his face covered.

"I'm sorry, Madame de Vogues." Eve slipped her robe on as Jessie was at the foot of the bed with his pants on.

"He wouldn't believe me that you were fine," Jessie shook his head.

"When Mr. Stratford left this morning, he informed me that you had left late last night. I then tracked your phone to here and I had to verify that you were safe and sound before I took guard downstairs. Please, next time you have a change to your location, a text will work."

Even thought about it. She should have notified him directly. "I'm sorry, Thomas. You're right. I should have notified you myself. I will be here all day until tonight's karaoke as planned. Then we may return here or to the condo for the night. Jessie will be with me all day and night, so if you need to take a break for a nap, I understand. Adam didn't tell you I was here with Jessie?"

Thomas shook his head. "No, Madame." Eve let out a sigh.

"That's quite odd, because he knew we were here together, the same way he knew Martin was here." She paused in her questions and smirked. "How goes finding a replacement?" Eve asked as she lowered his hands from his face.

Thomas bowed. "I have found someone. She will be there tonight training. I hope you like her. If you do, she will take over on Sunday evening."

Eve was surprised. She must be a badass to keep up with the bulky men.

After breakfast, Eve sent Adam a text message when she knew he would already be in class and wouldn't be able to call her back.

"Good morning, Héros. You have the right to feel how you feel. It worried me when you stopped communicating with me. Then it scared me to think that you might leave me. But I had to make sure you didn't feel like you were backed into a corner. That is why I had to leave and give you space to figure it out. I understand that you want to wait to have sex. I am a sexual person and have come to realize it more lately. I will try my best to back off on making advances towards you and let you lead for what you are comfortable with. I meant what I said. I can see all of us growing old together. Jessie and I will be dressed up and at karaoke at six. Hope you have a good day. Looking forward to seeing you. Love you too."

Adam

Adam had been dreaming of Eve non-stop since he first saw her that first day at Jake's. He knew down to his core that they would be together. Their emotional and physical connection had been growing ever since. Seeing her so happy, visiting with his mom, he knew she would be a good fit with the family. And with both their growing desires, he needed to marry her sooner rather than later.

It did shock him how much Eve had told his mom, but she seemed to be accepting of the situation so far. He had been drawing and planning wedding rings since the day he and Eve kissed in his office for their first meeting. Since high school, he set money aside each month for rings.

Now, after saving for nearly ten years, he was going to be able to make a wonderful pair of matching rings that she would love for all their years together.

After last night, and the thought of losing her to his stupidity, he decided to head around the corner to Tiffany's on Fifth and get the concept from his mind into a real design.

"Good morning. Are you Mr. Stratford?" the sales clerk asked as he entered the jewelry store.

"Yes, I am." He looked around and saw so many pieces of wonderful sparkle trying to get his attention.

"I'm Veronica. I'll be assisting you today. You were saying that you had an idea of what you wanted a set of rings to look like?" she asked.

"Yes." He opened his case and brought out a page that had three rings on it. One for him, and a wedding set for her. "Since we both work with our hands, I was thinking that our eternity rings should be a channel set. I do want all the diamonds and sapphires to be the same size and clarity. That way no one stone stands out among the others," he tapped on the page.

"Except, of course, her center engagement diamond. I would like it to be about three to four times the size of the other ones."

Veronica was taking notes on the drawing page he brought in. "Now, the most important question. What is your budget for all three rings?" Adam wrote a number down on the page and handed it back to her. Her eyes and smile lit up at the number.

"Okay. That budget will get you a beautiful matching set of his and her rings. I will get started on a rendering and figure out how many stones of the different sizes and see which you like. Once you approve a stone size, I'll get a hold of our gemologist to pull stones for your approval. I do need to warn you that there is a significant backup in custom work for our jeweler. Your rings may be completed around the end of February to mid-March."

Adam smirked. "So no, for a New Year's or a Valentine's Day proposal," he stated.

"If everything goes well, you may get lucky for Valentine's Day, but at this point, I cannot make any guarantees. The other thing we need is both your sizes for the renderings. We can do yours right now. However, you will need to figure out her size and let us know right away." He nodded his head.

She brought out a key ring of circles from her pocket, slid a few aside and slid one on his finger. It stopped on his knuckle and she pulled it off, then changed it to a different size. "Whatever we are now, I want to make sure that it's loose. Especially as baby weight comes and goes and age fills us in. Do you have any suggestions on how to figure out her size?" he asked.

"There are a couple of ways. If she has rings that she wears, 'borrow' it and bring it in to get measured," Veronica used air quotes. "If not, you can use a string and mark with a pen where the end meets. Or you could enlist the help of someone else and have her try on their rings."

Adam tapped his finger on his lips as he thought. "I will figure it out. Thank you for your help."

Eve

Jessie and Eve walked into the cabaret, hand in hand, for some karaoke fun. He was in his blue musketeer tabard, and she was in a sexier version of the same. When Adam would get there, he and Jessie would be matching.

After their fight yesterday, Eve was feeling less like a three musketeer and more like the rope in a rope-pulling contest. She truly hoped Adam was serious about his apology and that the three of them could move forward. She knew sex was out of the question, but there was nothing saying that the three of them couldn't play together.

Looking around, it was busier tonight than the last time they were here. She could see all the different types of costumes walking around. "Looks like it's going to be busy tonight with the costume contest. Do you want to wait for Adam to sign up?" She turned to face Jessie and saw Thomas at the door.

"Yep, I'll wait." Jessie turned to see what Eve was staring at and saw Thomas. "Wonder who the new trainee is?" Jessie asked.

She looked back at Jessie. "Don't know, and don't really care. So long as they don't masturbate while watching me sleep," she shivered in disgust at the thought. "I'm going to sign us girls up for our group song. I'll be right back." She pulled him in for a slow kiss. She slipped her hands under his outer tabard and squeezed his back.

"Mmmm." Jessie pulled away. "You keep doing that and we are not going to stay here long," he whispered, and then softly sucked her lower lip in for a soft nibble. She got goosebumps as his teeth let go and her heart started to race. She then fanned herself to cool off. Fully blushed, she turned to walk to the sign-up sheet. He spanked her ass, causing her to gasp and blush deeper.

Eve got to the top of the stairs, as Stephanie, along with a couple of her other gal pals, was there waiting for her. "What gives? Last we knew, Jessie was out and Adam was in. Now Jessie is all over you?" Stephanie asked.

Eve blushed, looked back at Jessie before looking back at the girls. "It's not a secret that I'm dating both. Plus, you know Jessie's the father." There were shocked faces among the group. "You didn't tell them?" Eve asked.

"Didn't think it was my place. But now they know." Stephanie giggled. The rest of the girls joined in the circle.

Adam

Adam walked in and saw Thomas at the door monitoring the room. "How's it going tonight, Thomas?" He kept on watching the room.

"Good evening, Mr. Stratford. It's busy tonight. Glad I have the extra help keeping a closer eye on her." Adam looked around to try and figure out who the new officer was. "Mr. Cooper is directly ahead, and Madame de Vogues is on stage with her friends. Have a good evening."

Adam gave Thomas a pat on the shoulder before heading to Jessie. Adam saw Eve among the giggling girls on stage as he approached Jessie, who was also watching Eve. "It's hard not to stare at her, isn't it?" he said as he bumped a shoulder with him.

"It's like a drug. When she's with me, I have a hard time controlling my hands, and when she's away, all I want to do is get my hands on her." A smile pulled at the corner of his mouth. "Such a wonderful drug too."

Adam took a deep breath and sighed. "I know exactly how you feel. That's part of my struggle. I want her all to myself." Adam held up his fist to bump. "But I'm working on it. I'm sorry about last night."

Jessie gave him a tap. "We both have things to work on. Come on. Let's go sign up for our songs and get this show on the road." They walked up to the stage, and all the chatter came to a sudden stop.

"What are you ladies talking about?" Adam asked as his eyes darted around the different girls who all looked very guilty.

"Nothing," all the girls said in unison. Most of them were blushing and several started to giggle again.

"Sure. Like I believe that," Jessie added as all the girls started to giggle. "Well, let's get our songs on the schedule before the contest, so everyone can see our outfits," Jessie suggested as he jutted his thumb towards the sign-up page.

"Sounds good to me," Adam agreed and kissed Eve as she blushed in return. Just as they were out of earshot, their chatter continued. He looked over his shoulder at the group and shook his head. "Girls will be girls." He nudged Jessie.

Eve

As Eve came down the steps, she saw Adam and Jessie sitting next to each other. She would have to choose who to sit next to but would rather sit in between them. Adam held his arms open as she got closer, and she decided to sit on his lap for the meantime. "Hello, Beautiful. How's wifey feeling today?" Adam asked as he pulled her into a hug with his hands softly moving back and forth along her back.

Eve could feel herself relax, and she reached her arms around him and clung to his back. "Hello, Héros. I'm actually feeling better overall. I'm even less nauseous today." She smiled.

"That's good to hear." He softly rubbed his cheek along hers. She took a deep breath, took his scent in, and she fully calmed as she closed her eyes for a moment.

"How's Hubby today? I was worried about you." Eve leaned back up to look him in the eyes.

"I'm also better. I got stuck for a moment, but I'm looking forward to later tonight." He devilishly smiled as his hand went up to her neck and pulled her into a deep kiss. He claimed her tongue to dance with his.

"Ohhh! Shame, shame, know your name." All the girls cackled, causing Eve to blush and cover her face.

Stephanie came up to them. "Hey everyone. This is my cousin, Jamie. She just transferred in from Chicago." Eve held out her hand.

"Nice to meet you. Are you going to join us in our group song?"

Jamie eyes went wide and she looked back at Stephanie. "I haven't rehearsed anything."

Stephanie laughed. "We'll put you in the second row so you can just sing along. Being on the stage is the rush. With a group, it just makes it that much easier." Stephanie tugged on her arm. "Come on, let's leave the lovebird and her men alone for now." Stephanie winked, and then they walked to the other side of the table.

Eve stood up and stretched. "I'm gonna go get a water. Be right back."

Adam grabbed her wrist and stopped her from going. "Sorry, Beautiful. You can stay here with the group where we can all keep an eye on you. I'll go and get drinks."

Eve was about to protest, but then she remembered the last time she was at the counter alone. After Adam stood up, she gave him a quick thank-you kiss and sat down on his warm chair. Jessie reached over and slid her chair closer.

"Did you put some perfume on, Kitten? Because you smell wonderful." He pulled her into a kiss before she could answer, and his hands started to explore her back and leg.

"Okay, seriously. Now you guys are just rubbing it in." They ended their kiss and looked to see Stephanie and Jamie standing there. "You three need a room or something? Jeez. Anyway, our spot is coming up soon. We were thinking of a quick run-through."

Adam came back with a tray of glasses that had ice and a pitcher of water. He poured two waters and slid Eve one and took one for himself. He slid another seat over that had become available so they could all sit together. Eve shrugged. "I guess I could leave all this special attention for a moment." She leaned over and gave Jessie a kiss, then stood up and gave Adam a kiss before going with the girls.

Stephanie and Jamie each linked an arm with Eve as they walked to the other girls who had already migrated to the corner to practice. "I've got to ask, so forgive me. What is it like openly dating both of them at the same time?" Jamie had a look of pure innocent curiosity.

Eve blushed and covered her mouth. "I've only been with Jessie." Eve raised her eyebrows. "Adam has a vow until marriage. But he is very experienced in other pleasures."

Jamie was shocked quiet for a moment. "Okay, yes, but are you with them together or just separately?" Then it dawned on Eve what she was asking about.

"Even though we are a throuple, we have yet to experience a ménage à trois. That's primarily because of the level of Adam's participation. I won't push him past his comfort zone." Eve winked. "But someday, I would love to experience two men at the same time." Eve smiled as she felt her face turn dark red.

"Right at the very beginning, we experienced a group kissing. That shocked the hell out of me, but it led us to become a group and helped me to realize that I'm polyamorous," Eve explained.

"Well, nowadays, there is more than just monogamy. When you take into account all the swinger groups, polygamists, BDSM, impact play, and so on, there is just more out there to experience than just a couple of generations ago," Stephanie added.

Eve thought for a moment. "For me, it's not just about sex. It's more about love and the connection between us." She looked over her shoulder and saw the guys talking to each other and smiled. "I don't think this would have worked had they not been friends first." Eve silenced as the other girls started in on the song.

Adam

Adam watched Eve walk away to the group of girls in the corner. Some of them were already belting out notes. He turned to Jessie. "So. How was it?"

Jessie had a confused look. "What?" Adam leaned in and whispered.

"How was it? Making love instead of just sex?" Adam leaned back, raised an eyebrow, and then grinned.

Jessie smiled, sat up straight, and took in a deep breath. "It was amazing. Better than anything I have ever felt before. And her body is so reactive. Plus, when she climaxes, it triggers mine." Jessie smiled. "Without a condom, it's on a whole new pleasure level. It's going to suck having to go back when we are currently not trying." He smirked.

Adam leaned in again. "In the contract, she said she wanted slow at first. But last night, after a while, it sounded like you guys were going hard. What do you think she likes best?" Adam leaned back and waited for his response.

After a minute, Jessie turned to face him. "I think she likes it all. There is a time for slow, passionate, and fast with crazy energy. I didn't even mind being woken up for a midnight round. And I think I actually wore her out because I was up for breakfast before she was awake." Adam was shocked to hear that she slept for so long. "Maybe that's why she needs both of us. To wear her out so she can sleep." Jessie gave Adam a friendly punch on the shoulder.

They sat quietly while watching the first performance of the evening. Afterward, Jessie spoke up. "Thomas said you left this morning. Didn't know you had to work today?"

Adam looked at Jessie and turned to face him. "I went to Tiffany's to pick up a charm and custom-ordered rings for Eve."

Jessie's mouth dropped open in obvious shock. "Dude, really?" Adam nodded his head yes.

"Unfortunately, the jeweler is backed up, so it will be several months before I can properly ask her to marry me." Adam took a deep breath. "I sure hope she can be patient with me," Adam added.

"From what she was saying last night, she's gonna let you go at your pace. She doesn't want to lose either of us." Jessie took a slow breath in and out. "When are you thinking of asking her?"

"They said the rings could be done at the end of February to mid-month of March. So, I was thinking of asking on my birthday. My parents usually have a big party and all the family and friends are there." Adam cracked a smile as he thought about everyone around them as he got down on one knee to ask for her hand in marriage.

Jessie nodded. "Your parents do have epic parties. How's your dad doing?" Jessie's face shifted to a concerned look.

"The MS is progressing. He is basically fully immobile now. His mind is still sharp as a tack and full of wisdom. I do miss throwing a football or baseball with him. Seeing him command a room by simply walking in is another thing I didn't know I'd miss until it was gone. He still keeps an eye on everything from the monitors. Guess that's where I get my urge to watch from." Adam laughed.

"Do you think your dad gets off watching the staff doing their work?" Jessie smirked.

Adam turned and grinned. "Most likely not, but probably while watching Mom do yoga or her workouts." They both laughed. The announcer called their names. "Well, ready to creep out the audience?" Adam asked.

"As good as I'll ever be," Jessie replied.

Eve

Eve heard the guys' names called, turned, and saw them get up, then walk to the stage. She tugged on Stephanie's arm. "I don't want to miss them singing." Stephanie and Jamie walked with her back to the table, and they chose seats closer to the stage. The other girls followed and sat nearby. They all chatted quietly among themselves during the intermission.

When it was their turn, they approached center stage and waited for the cue. The display showed *"Thriller,"* by Michael Jackson, and the music started to play. Eve started clapping and admired them for looking so good as her two favorite musketeers. She could feel her heat growing inside as she watched them sing together.

Eve placed her hand under her sexy musketeer tabard and softly touched herself as she remembered the conversation she had with the girls about wanting to be with both of them at the same time. Adam's deeper octave complemented Jessie's mid-range and it teased Eve's senses. Then Adam finished with the evil solo and laughed that gave her goosebumps all over her body.

Eve clapped and cheered along with the group of friends as they finished. She popped up and went to the bottom of the stairs. As soon as they came down, she pulled both of them into a hug. "That was wonderful, you guys." Then she gave each a kiss as they both pulled her in tighter.

Suddenly, her body became hotter by the second, and then she felt the same pleasure wave as before when she and Jessie were at the viewing platform. Her face became red, her breathing became labored, her grip became tight, and her smile shifted.

"Are you about to——" Adam started to ask as a soft moan escaped her lips; her eyes closed as her head leaned back.

"Hide me." Adam wrapped his arms fully around her and claimed her lips, feverishly searching her mouth with his tongue. He gently lifted her and the three of them went to a nearby corner. The two guys fully blocked any view of her as Jessie leaned in and started kissing her available neck as her hands explored both of them. Her spontaneous orgasm ripped through her and she vented all her sound into Adam's mouth.

Damn it! Why do they affect her this way? She was going to give Adam space, and here she was pulling him right back in. She eased up her grip and broke the kiss from Adam. Jessie, on the other hand, was going in for more. He slipped in where she released Adam and took her the rest of the way into the wall.

"You smell so good." He pushed his hardness into her, causing her to gasp. "We could leave now and I'd be good with that." He claimed her mouth before she could answer, and Adam now stood guard to block their activities.

Behind them, someone cleared their throat. "Excuse me. We are going to need her in a minute." Jessie ended the kiss and rested his chin on her shoulder. They were both breathing heavily and still clung to each other. Eve opened her eyes and saw Jamie standing there, grinning from ear to ear. "Come on, girly. The group is circling before heading up."

Eve nodded her head and took a couple more deep breaths to calm herself before letting go of Jessie. "Damn, you guys. The two of you together get me wound up so fast." She took a deep breath and slowly blew it out.

Adam started laughing. "The pheromones coming off you get us wound up fast." He let out a heavy sigh.

Jessie looked at Adam. "Is that what I'm smelling? It's a sweet yet erotic scent. It gets me hard in a heartbeat."

Adam nodded his head. "It drives a man to do what he knows he shouldn't."

Jessie took a deep breath, placed both hands on the wall, and leaned his head back. "I was about to take you right here, Kitten. I didn't care who was watching." He stepped back, put both hands behind his head, and gave her space.

Jamie pushed in and extended a hand to Eve. "Come on. I see I've got to help keep these men under control." Eve smiled. It was herself that needed to be kept under control.

Eve put a hand on each of the guys' chests. "Let's finish this conversation back at the condo tonight." She smiled and fully blushed, then grabbed Jamie's hand and giggled as she walked past them.

Adam

"That smell gave me the energy to keep on going, time and time again throughout the evening, night, and all day today," Jessie smiled.

Adam turned and saw Jessie watching Eve walking away while adjusting himself to make room in his pants. He also needed to adjust to compensate for the added size. "How much sex did you guys have?" Adam asked.

Jessie looked at him and shook his head. "I lost count," he said with a straight face. "At one point, it would roll from one to another as we would just keep going and taking turns with who was giving and receiving. Even when I was soft, the kissing, touching, and pleasing almost never stopped." Jessie looked back at Eve and let out a slow, long sigh. "I've never been so deep in love before. It feels good."

Adam looked at Eve and took a deep breath. "Same here." Adam wished she hadn't flushed the camera. He would have given just about anything to watch her. "The feeling you're having now is what I felt from the beginning. That's why I got so angry at you for putting your hands all over her in your player ways."

Jessie looked at Adam again. "Had the roles been reversed, I would have reacted the same." He patted Adam on the back and then looked back at Eve. "Now, there's nothing I wouldn't do to protect her."

They remained in the corner until the girls took the stage.

"Come on, let's get a good seat," Adam suggested.

They moved to where Eve was sitting before. Since they had all vacated their seats and no one else had claimed them yet, they got center view seats.

The group on stage was more like a small choir. *"I Put a Spell on You,"* by Screamin' Jay Hawkins played, and there were tons of cheers already. Regardless of what the group was doing with their motion and dancing, Adam kept his eyes glued to Eve with a permanent smile on his face. After the group was done, they all came down except Eve, who got back in line. She waved and blew kisses at them. Both Adam and Jessie motioned to catch them, and she blushed in return. She sat on the bench and waited her turn.

Two of their guy friends were on stage singing *"The Monster Mash."* One was dressed as a vampire and the other as Frankenstein. Adam was surprised to see so many of their friends returning regularly, since none of them had expressed interest in karaoke before. It was just another way Eve's friendship pulled people together, which he loved about her.

Jessie was talking to some of the other guys nearby when Eve stood up. Adam reached over and tapped him on the shoulder but never stopped watching her.

*

"At Last," by Etta James was displayed, and the audience became quiet. Eve felt a wave of nerves again and took another last deep breath. She had chosen this song because it was simple but had a powerful message that she could make fit for her situation.

At last,

My loves have come along

My lonely days are over

And life is like a song

Ooh yeah, yeah

At last,

The skies above are blue

My heart was wrapped up in clover

The night I looked at you, two

I found a dream, that I could speak to

A dream that I can call my own

I found a thrill to rest my cheek to

A thrill that I have never known

Ohh yeah yeah

You smile

And you smile

Oh, and then the spell was cast

And here we are in heaven

For you are mine

At last

She may have altered or added a few words slightly, but she knew that Adam and Jessie would figure out that the song was directed at them both. She covered her mouth with both hands and blew kisses again and then turned to walk off the stage. Both the guys were standing when she came back to her seat. Jessie moved one over and she sat in between them.

Jessie leaned in. "My offer still stands. We can leave now and just have a quiet evening." He smirked and then slid his hand on her leg under her tabard while his fingers started moving back and forth, slowly getting closer to her hot spot. As tempting as that was, she still wanted to visit with friends in the meantime. She smiled, placed a hand on his, and gave him a quick kiss on the cheek.

Adam picked up her other hand and gave it a kiss. Eve turned to Adam. "That was a wonderful song. I have my song coming up soon, but I agree with Jessie on getting out of here." He then leaned closer and kissed her cheek. Eve blushed as he stood up because his bulge was at her eye level. He turned to head to the stairs and she fanned herself. Oh shit, she's in for a hell of a night.

Jessie wrapped his arm around her back, scooped her legs, and slid them over his lap. "My song is on shortly after Adam's. From there, I think we should high-tail it out of here." Jessie reached up and pulled her in for a soft kiss. She wrapped her arms around his shoulders and just simply enjoyed the attention.

Jessie leaned back, breaking the kiss, and tucked her hair back behind her ear. "Adam is on stage." He pointed. She turned her body to face the stage and leaned her body against his. The screen displayed *"I Knew I Loved You,"* by Savage Garden. Instantly, her heart started pounding, knowing the song. Adam started to sing, and she couldn't help but tear up a little.

Maybe it's intuition

But some things you just don't question

Like in your eyes, I see my future in an instant

And there it goes, I think I've found my best friend

Even though Adam's voice wasn't in his normal low range when he was singing this song, it was just as sultry, and it gave Eve goosebumps. Jessie wrapped his arms tighter around her and tucked his head into her neck and placed soft kisses from the edge of her shoulder all the way up to her ear.

"I think Adam sings for both of us on this song," Jessie whispered.

I knew I loved you before I met you

I have been waiting all my life

There's just no rhyme or reason

Only a sense of completion

And in your eyes, I see the missing pieces

I'm searching for, I think I've found my way home

I know that it might sound more than a little crazy, but I believe

Eve was loving the dual attention. Both visual and audio, combined with touch, were taking over all her willpower.

I knew I loved you before I met you

I think I dreamed you into life

I knew I loved you before I met you

I have been waiting all my life

As Adam walked to the chairs, Jessie slid Eve over and stood up to stretch. He bent down and gave her a firm kiss. "I'll be back in a few." Eve smiled and watched the two cross paths for a moment while exchanging fist bumps. Adam sat back down and she turned and sat on Adam's lap then hugged him.

"That was such a great song choice. I always love your serenades, and you have a wonderful falsetto. I love you, Husband." She leaned in for the beginning of a deep kiss, but Adam pulled her back. She stuck her lip out in a little pout. He gave it a soft pinch and then started to laugh.

"It's hard to believe that it's been another month. It has gone by so fast. But I made you a promise." He pulled her arm down to be in between them and he brought out a small bag from his pocket. The bright orange pumpkin practically glowed in the low light. His thumb stroked the underside of her wrist as he attached the new charm. He then gave her hand a soft kiss. "Ten to go."

He smiled as she held it up to see closer. "I love it. Thank you." Then she claimed the deep kiss she was going for. After the current song was over, Adam ended the kiss and turned her around to sit next to him.

"He said he picked out something special." Eve looked on stage and saw Jessie. He looked nervous.

"Breathe, Jessie," she whispered under her breath. Jessie looked in their direction, and Eve put her hands to her face and whooped loud enough for him to hear her, and he smiled. "*Arms Wide Open,*" by Creed played. She turned to Adam. "I don't know this one," she whispered. Adam pulled her to him and wrapped his arms around her.

"That song is making an announcement. Just listen," he told her and placed a kiss on her cheek.

Well, I just heard the news today

It seems my life is going to change

I closed my eyes, begin to pray

Then tears of joy stream down my face

With arms wide open under the sunlight

Welcome to this place, I'll show you everything

With arms wide open

With arms wide open

Well, I don't know if I'm ready

To be the man I have to be

I'll take a breath, I'll take her by my side

We stand in awe, we created life

Eve covered her mouth and looked at Adam. "Did he just tell everyone?" Adam nodded his head, yes.

With arms wide open, now everything has changed

I'll show you love, I'll show you everything

With arms wide open

With arms wide open

I'll show you everything, oh yeah

With arms wide open

Wide open

Eve could feel her desire growing, and she knew right then that she wasn't going to stay later to visit with her friends.

If I had just one wish, only one demand

I hope he's not like me, I hope he understands

That he can take this life and hold it by the hand

And he can greet the world with arms wide open

With arms wide open under the sunlight

Welcome to this place, I'll show you everything

With arms wide open, now everything has changed

I'll show you love, I'll show you everything

With arms wide open

Eve leaned forward and whispered to Stephanie, "We are taking off. You ladies have a good night." Stephanie and Jamie turned around. "It was nice to meet you. I hope to see you again soon." She smiled and waved goodbye. Eve clenched Adam's hand, and they got up to walk to the stairs. Eve held both of her arms open as Jessie came down.

Just as he got to her, he swooped down and lifted her up, and her legs wrapped around him as her arms clung around his neck. He claimed her mouth for a hot minute before setting her back down. She leaned her forehead to his. "Time to go home."

Jessie pulled back. "Oh, thank God." Jessie grabbed Eve's hand, and Eve grabbed Adam's hand, and they took off for the door.

Just as they approached Thomas, Eve spoke up. "Condo." Thomas nodded as they were heading out.

Eve found the taxi ride to be a bit of a challenge. It was only three blocks until they got to the condo, but with the effort the guys were putting forth, it might as well have been three miles. With the guys sitting on each side, her two hands were trying and failing to hold off their four hands from advancing.

Adam was kissing her lips, and Jessie was kissing her neck. Adam got her legs to separate as Jessie got her skirt slid up. She gave up when they both found her hot, wet center, and both her hands went to the backs of their heads. Her fishnet stockings and the thin sliver of underwear offered no deterrence as their fingers rubbed and probed.

Adam's mouth on hers helped to stifle her continual moans. With her eyes closed, she couldn't tell who was doing which motion, but their dual effort made her climax quickly. She pushed her back hard against the seat as the wave exploded from her. She felt an immense amount of heat release from her.

Before she knew it, the three of them were clumsily making their way to the condo. Adam turned, opened the door, and the three pushed in at the same time, eager for the next step. Jessie shut and locked the door, while Adam had already claimed Eve's lips, and his hands were working her Halloween outfit off as she was starting with his. He broke the kiss and pulled her tabard over her head, then she pulled his tabard off.

Jessie spun her around, pulled her in as his tongue started to explore her mouth. His hands started to unbutton her shirt as she tugged his tabard up. Adam had her skirt unzipped, and he pulled her skirt to the floor. He pulled her hair back and placed kisses on her neck as his hands started working her stockings and underwear down.

She released Jessie's mouth and pulled his outfit the rest of the way over his head. Adam had rolled everything down to her knees but ran into friction. The rest would have to be slid down. Jessie had her shirt undone and slid it off her shoulders, and it dropped to the floor. Adam reached up and unclipped her bra, and down it went. Her hands were feverishly trying to keep up with trying to undress two but were not very successful.

"Time out," she whispered. She tried to step aside, but they still had her blocked in. "Time out," she said louder. Suddenly, they halted in their movements. She was breathing heavily and sat on the arm of the couch. She slid her stocking down one leg.

Adam kneeled in front of her and continued sliding them down and placed kisses on her legs as he pulled. "I can't keep up. You guys will have to help me catch up." She sat there naked, staring at her dressed men. She stood up and continued to unbutton Adam's shirt, then let it fall to the floor as he worked off his pants.

She turned to Jessie, who already had his shirt off, and she started on his pants. As she was slightly bent over, Adam came up behind her. His left hand reached around and cupped a breast, and his right hand went in between her legs, forcing her to spread them farther open. Jessie's pants fell to the floor as Adam started plunging a finger in and out, and a loud moan escaped her.

Adam slowly lifted her to a standing position. "Which room, Beautiful?" Jessie stepped closer and rubbed her clit from the front as he sucked on her other nipple.

"Oh, God!" Their teamwork was on point. Eve's body was about to explode again. She reached behind Jessie's underwear and wrapped her hand on his hard cock as her head leaned back onto Adam's firm chest. Then her climax released. "Oh, yes." As the wave subsided, she thought about going to Adam's room. But since he's not going to penetrate, he probably wouldn't want Jessie's mess all over his bed.

She took a step towards Jessie's room, and their momentum continued. After a couple of awkward steps, Adam pulled his finger from her and scooped her up. He placed her in the center of the bed at an angle, then placed himself at her head. He started kissing her upside down while both his hands claimed her breasts and nipples. Jessie slid her legs open and started teasing her with his tongue.

"Ohhh." It's been forever since someone had gone down on her. Of all her previous relations, she had given plenty of blow jobs but had not received much in return. She marveled at how soft his tongue was also, compared to his lips and fingers. All the information she had given to him prior was now being put to good use. She moaned as he plunged his tongue in and his thumb started rubbing her clit again. "Jesus Christ," she muttered against Adam's mouth.

Her body was now in a full roll, one hand gripped the covers, and she placed the other hand on Jessie's head. Her body arched and her toes curled as her climax gradually climbed to another peak. Her body quivered as the pleasure rolled through her.

After a minute, her body was starting to relax, but they were still going. How many times are they going to do that this evening? Adam broke their kiss. "Switch." And like a choreographed movement, they traded places. Eve was trying to catch her breath in between their direct attention. Did they plan this out ahead of time? They work so well together.

This time, instead of Jessie's mouth, as she thought was going to happen, his hard cock showed up next to her face. She turned her head so she could suck on him, and he softly moved his hips forward and back. Adam placed both hands on her bush and peeled her lips open for him to have full access that Jessie didn't have.

His tongue was so much firmer and did wonders on her clit as he started sliding fingers in and out. Her body instantly responded to his stimulation. She slid one hand behind Jessie and grabbed hold of his ass, and she softly rested her other hand on Adam's head as she swirled her fingers in his thick hair while he swirled his tongue around her hot center.

At some point, he had switched, and she didn't notice. His tongue dived in and out, and then he sucked her juices. His thumb started going crazy on her sensitive nub, and her body jolted in response. She wasn't going to last long. She moaned on Jessie's member, and she squeezed her nails into his ass cheek as Adam feverishly rubbed her. Eve released Jessie from her mouth and grabbed him with her hand.

"Oh God, Adam," she screamed and pushed her pelvis into Adam as her next climax exploded from her. Her insides were drenched now in anticipation. He dragged his tongue the whole length of her slit.

"Damn, Beautiful. Your climax tastes so good!" He moved up slightly and placed soft kisses on her bump. Adam softly grabbed her hand and sat her up. He leaned back and laid down while he pulled her on top of him. She looked at Jessie as she had to release him. Jessie had a huge smile on his face. Eve centered herself over Adam's hardness and leaned down to kiss him. Her juices were still on his lips.

She leaned up a little and licked her lips. She had never tasted herself before. It was different for sure. Jessie positioned himself behind her and softly pushed her down so her ass would rise up again. She instantly knew he was going to take her from behind and bit her lip in anticipation.

"Don't bite your lip. That's my job." Adam pulled her down and claimed her mouth in a soft kiss and then gave her lower lip a little nip, causing her to gasp. Her hair cascaded around them like a private room just for them. She then felt the pressure of Jessie's hard cock. He placed both hands on her hips and guided her forward, and he closed the distance. Adam's hands claimed her breasts that were now dangling in his face, and he took turns sucking on them.

Jessie pushed in and pulled her hips back at the same time. The first plunge was his full length, forcing her body to adjust to all of him all at once, while Adam's bulge rubbed her sensitive nub from the front. "Oh merde!" she exclaimed as Jessie repeated his full-length drive into her. Adam started pinching her nipples, and then Jessie started into a rhythm.

Each time, their bodies would clap at the impact, her clit would rub, and an "oh" moan repeatedly escaped her. This felt so good. She couldn't have asked for more. She opened her eyes and saw Adam watching her with amazement. She leaned forward and halted herself so she could kiss him; her tongue dove into his mouth. Jessie adjusted and did his full-depth plunge on his own. Now it was perfect.

She felt her core get hot again as her next climax grew. She started pushing against Jessie to take him in deeper while she ground herself on Adam. Suddenly, her body seized on Jessie's shaft as her body's buildup came to a peak. She leaned up from Adam's mouth. "Yes!" she exclaimed.

"Jesus Christ, Kitten." He plunged hard and let out a couple of soft grunting moans. He plunged hard again, which caused her to gasp. He then rubbed his hands over her back and sides. Eve rested her weight on Adam, breathing heavily as her body completely relaxed from its high. "Damn, Kitten, your body is amazing. Your climax feels so good on my shaft."

He started to give her a back massage, rubbing his thumbs into her back muscles. "Oh, that feels good too," she responded.

"I still have more to go. Come ride me," Jessie said as he withdrew from her and laid down. Eve leaned up and gave Adam a quick kiss before shifting off him to sit on top of Jessie. She positioned herself over his pelvis and lifted up. He angled his shaft up, and then she slowly lowered herself down to take him in. "Mmmm," Jessie moaned, and his hands held her hips.

She leaned forward to brace her arms on his chest and moaned as she slowly moved up and down and back and forth. Adam came up behind her and pulled her upright. She could feel his bulge on her backside as she moved on Jessie. He tucked her hair to one side and started kissing her neck. His hands started exploring her body before one claimed a nipple and the other migrated to her hot spot.

Her body reacted to his touch. "Ahhhh." She relaxed her head back as he synchronized both finger movements together, restarting the fire within. Jessie's hands helped guide her hips as he also thrust up. Her one hand rested on Adam's at her core, she reached back to hold his head with the other and turned her head for a heavy kiss.

She increased her speed on Jessie, and Adam matched her speed with his fingers. Her fire turned into a white-hot burn fast. Suddenly, Adam's fingers went crazy, and her body was quickly going full tilt. Adam broke the kiss, ground hard on her ass as he moaned in her ear, which triggered the rest of her climax. "Yes, yes. Oh God, yes," she moaned out as pleasure waves rolled through her. Jessie reached up and placed his hands on top of her shoulders and pressed her down as he repeated his thrusts up.

"Oh, Babe," Jessie said. His fluids felt warm and made her insides extra slippery. She softly moved up and down as her climax cooled off. All three of them were breathing fast and heavy.

She turned to face Adam again. "Lay down with me." Adam didn't say a word; he just started to shift over. She lifted off of Jessie, and they crashed onto the bed together. Eve spooned to Jessie's side, and Adam spooned behind her.

She felt so happy and content in their arms.

Entry 9: Lazy Day in Bed

Eve woke up feeling a bit cold. The guys had pulled away, but they each still had a hand on her. She looked at the clock and figured out that she had been asleep for about six hours, give or take, depending on how long their lovemaking actually took. She quietly got up to use the restroom and then made it to the kitchen for a drink of water. She saw the mess of clothes scattered in the living room and picked them up.

"Can't stay in bed, can you?" Adam whispered in her ear. Eve gasped in surprise and dropped all the clothes when she covered her mouth. Adam held his finger up. "Shhh, Beautiful, or you'll wake Jessie."

She giggled and reached out and held his arm. "You startled me," she whispered back. She started picking the items back up. "I was getting some water and was gonna come back with a blanket because I was getting cold. Then I saw our mess."

Adam squatted and helped pick up the other articles of clothing. "Let's just leave these here on the counter for now," he whispered and pulled her closer. "I want more of you." He pulled her in for a kiss.

"Mmmm, that sounds nice," Eve said and then set all the clothing down. "Let me just toss a blanket over Jessie and then I'll meet you in your room." Eve smiled, and then he gave her a pat on the butt.

"Don't make me wait too long." Adam winked and headed to his room. Eve grabbed the blanket from the couch and then went into Jessie's room. He was still stretched out on the bed. Poor guy. She wore him out all last night, and this morning, and the night before. She softly covered his nakedness and gave him a kiss on the cheek. He didn't even stir.

Adam was already in bed and had the covers pulled back for her when she came back to his room. She leaned on the doorframe and admired the view. He tapped the bed. "Come here, Wifey. I'll warm you up." Eve felt flush, knowing just how warm he could make her.

"Do you want me to put something on and reduce temptation?" She didn't want to push his boundaries, and she knew that her purposefully being naked alone with him was pushing it. He leaned up on his elbow. "It would only be in the way." She walked over to the bed and sat down on the side.

"After yesterday…" She pressed her lips as she thought. "I just don't want you to feel pressured. I do understand you wanting to wait, and I'm going to be patient and not push you." She reached out a hand to him. "After opening yourself up to this possibility, I feel comfortable having a camera in my apartment again. Do you have another one?" she asked.

"I don't think I'll send you home with another camera. The last one was a bit expensive to flush." He pouted his lower lip. Eve giggled and covered her mouth.

"You really thought I flushed it, didn't you?" She shook her head. "No. I know better than that. I only dangled it over the toilet and spun it around to make a point. I then covered the camera with my shirt and left it in the laundry hamper. I was thinking of putting that one back on the shelf and having another one in the front room. That way, you can see me there if I'm drawing or in the kitchen cooking when we are talking."

He fully sat up, wrapped his arms around her, and pulled her into bed with him. With a swoosh, he had the covers over them, and he adjusted his position in bed to match hers.

"You are so amazing. I'll have one sent to you. Being open and honest is difficult. Yesterday was my difficult day. I'm sorry for making you cry. Seeing you walk out the door made me realize how easily I could lose you. And I never want to see that again. So, what if you love two men at the same time? I'm just glad that it's with someone I know, and now I can trust him with your heart and safety."

Eve processed his comments and wondered. "Now you can trust him?" she wondered what he meant by that. Adam's hand slowly moved back and forth along her body, giving her pleasurable goosebumps.

"He was such a player before. I understand being jilted by his ex, but he chose to continue that way instead of growing and moving on. After meeting you, and with help, he completely changed. The only reason I didn't stop you from leaving was because you were with him. Because I now trust that he will take care of you."

Eve smiled at his answer. It was all true, and she knew it. "It's amazing what giving love and accepting love can do for a person." She paused, and her face smirked. "It also hurts to lose love, or think you're losing love. In Jessie's case, I think he really and truly loved her. Which is why he blocked out the possibility of loving someone, so he wouldn't hurt like that again." She paused and smiled to herself.

"The good man has always been there, just like you." She then tucked her face into Adam's chest and wrapped her arm around his back. Her fingers expanded to feel his muscles as she slowly moved her hand back and forth. Adam lifted her chin and placed soft kisses on her lips. She instantly felt her desire grow, and her insides lit up again.

He halted and stared at her for a moment. "He still has a long way to go. He admitted tonight, he was going to take you at the cabaret. He still needs to learn self-control, especially when your body is giving off these crazy hormones. There is a time and place for stopping action." He closed his eyes and inhaled deeply, then refocused on her. "And a time to take action."

He rolled with her onto her back and attacked her neck with his mouth and tongue. "Your scent is so damn irresistible." His foot pushed her leg open for him to kneel between her legs. Her hands clung to his back, and he pressed his hardened member along her sensitive nub. She pulled him in close as she moaned. Reactively, she bent her legs up and out for him to have more access.

He pressed his mouth to hers and teased her tongue with his as he ground his cotton-covered cock harder against her. Her body flexed under his weight, her fingers dug in, and she placed her heels behind his ass to encourage his thrusts as she pressed her hips up to increase the pressure. She could feel all his muscles flex and relax with each thrust from his legs all the way up to his neck.

He curled one hand behind her shoulder to prevent her from sliding up, and his other landed on the headboard. He was grinding so hard now, she feared he was going to bust through the fabric. She broke the kiss and arched her head back. "Adam," she moaned loudly as her insides peaked. She then felt her wave crash over her, time and time again, as he continued to grind on her.

She moaned louder with each thrust until she couldn't handle being kept at peak any longer. "Adam!" she said firmly and was breathing heavily.

He halted and eased into a rested position. "Are you okay?" he whispered. "Did I hurt you?" She reached up and pulled him into a kiss.

"I may be in danger of a rug burn, but my body couldn't hold the climax any longer. I needed a break," she smirked. He took a deep breath and rested his head down on hers.

"I didn't realize you climaxed. I thought you still needed a little more to get there. I climaxed almost at the beginning when you first moaned in my ear." He took a deep breath and slowly let it out. Eve giggled and covered her face for a moment.

"I have found that the external stimulation feels way different from the internal. And, when they get mixed, the combination is on its own level."

Adam moved his leg to the outside of hers and lay down next to her. "So, you're saying you have different types of climaxes?"

She nodded her head. "Yes. But right now, I can't help but feel that this is all one-sided. Are you sure you don't want me to touch, lick, or suck on you?"

He moved his hand down past her soft pubic hair and plunged a finger into her wetness. She instantly flexed in pleasure. "I get my pleasure by pleasing you." Then he pressed his thumb on her clit. Her body engaged, and she rolled a leg over his, getting her core closer to him.

She squirmed and moaned as he changed the speed of his rubbing and plunging. "Besides, I'm not strong enough to stop myself if there are no barriers between us," he whispered in her ear and plunged three fingers deep to massage her G-spot and clit at the same time. Her insides squeezed on his fingers, her body arched, and her fingers gripped him.

"Oh yes, Adam!" Her head thrashed back, and she pushed hard against his thrusting hand. "Yes, yes!" she exclaimed as she peaked again. He stopped moving, and her body started to relax as she breathed heavily. He leaned over, softly kissed her lips, and plunged hard, causing her to gasp. He sucked her lower lip, then gave a soft nip and plunged hard at the same time. "Ah," she gasped.

She put her hand on his wrist. "Enough," she said as she tried to catch her breath again. "I can only handle so many hard thrusts. Plus, I need to keep it more gentle for the baby."

He softly claimed her lips again and slowly slid in and out. "Sorry, Beautiful. I was exploring what else you might like. I got wrapped up and forgot for a moment."

She smiled. "I also think that, if you're going to grind, I need a layer on to prevent a rug burn." She reached down and softly applied pressure.

"Let me kiss you and make it better." He softly rolled her back again and slid down between her legs. He placed both hands on her lower lips as he swirled, licked, and sucked on her undercarriage. Her body tightened and squirmed again with each of his movements. She rested a hand on his head, swirling her fingers in his hair. Her other hand locked fingers with his.

She moaned loudly with each change of movement. He slipped two fingers in and started rubbing her G-spot again along with the licking. Her body pressed into his face. "Ahhhhhh!" escaped loudly. "Yes, Adam!" she exclaimed again as her body curled up through yet another climax peak. She collapsed on the bed, not realizing she had lifted that far up, and lay there panting.

"Jeez, you guys are loud." Eve leaned up and saw Jessie wrapped in the blanket she had covered him with. She smiled and raised her eyebrows at him.

"That's all her noises," Adam added as he came up from under the covers. Eve raised her hand and curled her finger to signal Jessie to come closer and join in the fun.

"I can see why you like to watch. It's like a dedicated porno, for your eyes only." He laughed as he removed the blanket and laid it on the foot of the bed, showing his nakedness and that his member was at the ready. "Wow, it's so much warmer in here. I can see you're already having a good morning." Jessie leaned over and placed a soft kiss on her cheek.

Eve smiled and blushed. "I don't have anything planned, so we can just spend all day here for all I care," Eve started. "But there is something we need to discuss first." She rotated to face Jessie, and he closed the distance, pressing his hard member between her legs.

"Last night, in the beginning, you were thrusting too hard. Don't get me wrong, it felt great and you only did it a few times, but we need to halt the jarring movements for the baby's sake."

He reached up and pulled her forehead in for a kiss. "I'm sorry, Kitten. I was so into your body that I lost control for a moment. This whole situation is next-level hot."

Eve smiled. "This has been insanely pleasurable. But now that you have brought it up, let's talk about control." She started running her fingers up and down his chest. "I know my hormones are crazy, and I don't even know when they're doing it. You need to keep control when we are in public. You admitted at the club that you were going to take me and you didn't care who saw us."

Eve shook her head. "It's one thing to be in the back corner of the bus as everyone was sleeping and be making out. Completely another to have sex with an audience." Eve felt a hot wave and then leaned in and kissed him.

"You're right. I have been out of touch with dating rules. I need to relearn and respect you better," Jessie replied. Eve leaned up and pulled part of the covers back. She repositioned herself on top of Adam, started kissing him, then sat back up and started rocking her pelvis on his.

"Mmmm." Adam closed his eyes, and his hands gripped her legs. She looked back at Jessie and held out her hand, motioning for him to join her.

"Let's try it again, but with control this time." She smiled and leaned forward to start kissing Adam as Jessie pressed in again.

Entry 10: OB Check

Eve sat at her desk for the first time in what felt like forever. Really, it was only one week. She was able to keep in contact with her instructor while the guys were in school to keep her updated on her assignment progress. Also, for when she submitted her presentation on Friday. So, it was no surprise when Eve was called into her office.

"Hello, Mrs. Johnston. You called for me?" Eve asked as she knocked on the open door.

"Eve. Please come in, shut the door, and sit down." Eve suddenly felt the weight of the world on her shoulders.

"Did I do something wrong?" Eve nervously asked.

Mrs. Johnston started laughing. "If what you are doing is wrong, I want you to do more of it." Eve looked at her confused, and Mrs. Johnston waved her hand.

"We will get there in just a minute." She pulled out a folder, opened it, then lifted a couple of pages up. Eve recognized the emails that she had sent to the school.

"How are you feeling after your accident? I want to know if you came back too early or if you are truly feeling better." Mrs. Johnston had a worried look on her face.

Eve smiled, and her spirit lifted as she felt the concern her teacher was now showing. "I am feeling much better. Plus, I have a follow-up appointment later today."

Mrs. Johnston leaned back in her chair. "That's good to hear. Concussions are no joke. As a mother of a footballer, I'm always watching for signs." She leaned forward and looked at the second page, and her expression shifted. "Also. Congratulations, but I need to know if Mr. Stratford is the father."

Eve blushed. This was not the conversation she thought was coming. "I just need to know if our people are safe at their sites or not." Eve took a calming breath and shook her head.

"No, Jessie Cooper is the father of my baby. However, they are acquaintances. I've been friends online with Jessie for months, and when we met for the first time, Mr. Stratford was there, but I only knew him as Adam. He did see my presentation at Jake's Bar and Grill, and then he made the call."

She nodded her head. "Okay. And how did the presentation go?"

Eve smiled. "I think it went well. Mr. Stratford wasn't there, but the whole crew and his mother, who is the other co-owner, were there. I think most of the esthetics will be up to her anyway. I hope I made a good impression on her. She seemed very nice." Eve thought of the girls' lunch and smiled.

"Well, it seems you did just that." Mrs. Johnston held up another slip of paper, and Eve recognized it as a call-in slip. "She has asked to have you come out to her home and help redesign a wing of the house."

Eve covered her mouth in surprise. She wasn't sure if she would remember after drinking so much. "I'm already working on another project for the downstairs neighbor at the Stratford building. It will be a quick project since I already have the building plans. It's similar to the upstairs layout, minus the side offices and none of the tile details. It's basically being switched over from a storage facility to a commercial business front. Then I can start in on her project."

Her teacher leaned forward, set her elbows on her desk, and rested her chin on her hands. "I really like your drive to get more work. That will be important when you are out on your own. I wish most of the other students had your work ethics." She slid the paper over, and Eve looked over the details.

"If you need time away to view the property, presentation, etc., or even to just lay down for a headache, morning sickness, whatever, doesn't matter, just let me know." Mrs. Johnston smiled.

Eve returned the smile. "I will do. Thank you very much. This house address is not local. Do you know where this is?" Eve handed the page back for her instructor to look at.

"Hmmm. It looks like it's out on Long Island," said Mrs. Johnston. Eve nodded as the page came back to her.

"I will have to figure out if a bus route can get me there or close. I may need a few full days just to include the travel time." Eve smiled.

Mrs. Johnston waved her hand. "Whatever you need, dear. You're doing a wonderful job."

When Eve got back to her desk, she noticed that there was not much chatter today when, normally, the class was abuzz from the weekend. Everyone seemed engrossed in their own projects. She started to wonder if maybe some of the other students were having a hard time finding locations. She was glad to already have the next one done. It gave her a little leeway in her work.

She sat down and sent Adam a text. 'Bonjour Héros. Your wonderful mother called the school and asked for me to come to the house to work on a wing of a building.'

'Hello Beautiful. She said she would. I think she's already in love with you too. Now, we have something else to talk about when I check in.' That made Eve smile.

'I'll give her a quick call after school today before going to my doctor's appointment. What type of rooms do you think she'll want to update?' She was curious.

'Probably the wing with the most bedrooms. It's the older part of the house.'

Eve smiled. 'Okay. I'll also check in with you on camera placement. Love you.'

'Sounds perfect to me. Love you too.' She programmed the new contact number into her phone.

She sat there in a daze, thinking about Saturday evening and Sunday as they continued to love and play all day. Sometimes taking turns and sometimes all together. They only took a few needed rests for fun; naked meal breaks until she had to return home last night. Even then, they were trying to convince her to stay the night. As tempting as that was, she needed rest for her undercarriage.

She shook her head to focus and started pulling images of bedrooms in different styles and color themes.

While walking back to her apartment, she called Mrs. Stratford. They talked for about thirty minutes and made plans to meet for the following weekend since the guys already had plans with Eve for this weekend. Eve got upstairs and placed her bags down so she could work on them later.

She opened the box that arrived and put the new camera in the living room corner where it could see from the front door all the way into the kitchen. She then returned the original camera to the shelf. She removed her school outfit and opted for something warmer for the evening, since it was getting colder at night.

Her phone rang, and she saw Adam was calling. She laid down on the bed and then answered the phone. "Hello husband." She smiled and slowly ran her fingers along her body.

"Hello wife. I was waiting for your text but then got an alert on camera activity."

Eve smiled. "So, you just had to watch, huh? Well, I can't stay long. I have to leave in a few minutes, so watching me dress is the best I can do for now." She sat up and faced the camera. "Is it angled correctly?"

"They are angled perfectly," he replied.

"Good. I love you, and I'll let you know what the doctor says later," she added.

"Okay. Love you too."

They said their goodbyes, and she finished getting dressed, then was out the door.

Eve sat on the park bench as she waited for Jessie and watched the kids playing. She set her hand on her stomach and softly moved it back and forth as she was lost in thought.

"How far along are you?" Eve looked up at a strange gal's face.

"Excuse me?" Eve asked.

"No one sits at the playground alone, watching kids playing while petting their stomachs, who are not pregnant. So, how far along are you?" the gal asked again as she sat down and watched the kids.

Eve smiled. "Ten weeks now." The gal turned to face her.

"One quarter of the way there. Enjoy the glow while you can, because once they come, it's hardly ever quiet again. And when they are quiet, you start to worry that something is wrong. It's exhausting." The gal rolled her eyes.

Eve started to laugh. "What's so funny, Kitten?" Eve looked up and saw Jessie coming in for a kiss. She held onto him as their lips collided.

"She was telling me to enjoy the silence while I can." She smiled at the gal as she got up. "Have a nice day." Eve waved goodbye to the gal and they walked off holding hands.

Jessie pulled her in and wrapped his arms around her. "How was my wife's day, back at school today?" She looked up at him and smiled.

"It was a good day. I really like my teacher. She's very understanding." Eve looked down as he set a hand on her stomach.

"It's good to have as many friends in your corner as you can gather." He suddenly stopped, lifted her chin and kissed her again as she pulled him in tighter. "I'm here for you regardless of the news we get today."

Eve's smile faded with the thought of bad news. "No, babe. Don't go there. Only think positively. You have been careful all week with plenty of rest." Eve took a deep breath and looked him in the eyes seeing his love for her. "Whatever happens, we will do it together," he added. They embraced in a hug and then went inside the OB office.

After all her many follow-up examinations, they were called back into the small report room. Eve was so nervous that she was squeezing Jessie's hand while sitting and waiting for the doctor. After a few minutes of anxiously waiting, the knock on the door finally came. Eve instantly noticed that it was not the doctor from last week. Her heart sank and tears started to form as her breathing quickened.

Jessie turned and hugged her while holding her head to his shoulder. "Easy now, Kitten." She clung to him as the tears started falling.

"Oh my. I have not even gotten to say hi and you are already crying." Jessie picked up the box of tissues and moved them closer to Eve.

"Sorry, doctor. As you can see, Eve is very worried about losing the baby. I'm Jessie, the father." He held out his hand and they shook.

"Hello, you two. I'm Dr. James Mickels. I'm a Perinatologist. That's a fancy word for a doctor who specializes in prenatal care for women who are at high risk of having a complicated pregnancy. We will be working together from now on." Eve started to calm down and Jessie helped dry her face.

"Little better now?" Jessie asked and Eve nodded her head, then slowly turned to face the new doctor.

"Your results from today compared to last week are much better and I'd say the baby's viability has gone way up. But," the doctor paused to turn the monitor and displayed an image, "as you can see here, the damage to the placenta has been done and that can't be fixed. So, it's up to the baby and your body to continue on the slightly limited connection," he explained.

"Baby is doing better?" Eve's voice squeaked out the question as Jessie squeezed her hand.

"Yes, the baby is doing better. I just need to warn you and prepare you. No horseback riding, rollercoasters, jet boats, skydiving, or anything that would give your body a sudden jolt." He pointed a finger at them. "And I say this to everyone: no rough sex."

Jessie tossed his hands in the air. "Well, I guess that means no sex for me, 'cuz that's the only kind I like." Eve smirked as she started laughing and Jessie hugged her again. "There she is. It took a sex joke to get you out of your shell." He lifted her chin and placed a soft kiss on her lips. Her body flushed in response, making her hot in the seat. He whispered in her ear, "I can smell you. Your body just turned on." Eve nodded, held his hand and refocused on the doctor.

"So, continue with being calm, keeping stress down, relaxing, get your man here to give you a regular full massage, and so on," Dr. Mickels continued to explain. "Since you are now high risk, we will see you every week now up until delivery."

Eve smiled as a thought filled her mind. "Since I will be in more often, can I bring a friend to see the ultrasound or is it only just for fathers?"

The doctor smiled. "There is only room for one guest. It's up to you who comes. So, same time next week?"

Eve smiled and nodded. "Yes, this time slot works well with my schedule." They said their goodbyes and they were out the door. As soon as they were outside, Jessie scooped her up to carry her.

"Jessie!" Eve squealed in excitement.

"What? Adam can't be the only one who gets to carry you away." He laughed as he walked them to a bench and sat down with her in his lap. Then they started kissing like no one was around.

"Do you guys ever stop?" They broke their kiss to see who was talking.

"Jamie!" Eve's happiness came through as she was looking at her clothing. "What are you wearing?"

"I'm taking over from Thomas for the evening." Jamie had a big grin on her face.

Eve looked at Jamie for a moment as she processed what was said, then her mouth dropped open. "You're my new guard?" Eve was sure shock was written all over her face.

Jamie smiled and waved both her hands. "Surprise."

Eve bounced out of Jessie's lap and hugged Jamie, then looked around. "That Thomas sure is a sneaky man. I haven't noticed him at all today. I know I said to keep some distance, but I didn't mean for him to be invisible," Eve shook her head.

Jamie nodded in agreement. "That was part of why I was hired. The ability to blend in when needed."

Jessie reached for Eve's hand. "Well, Jamie, we just got good news and I'm going to take Eve back to the apartment. We will be having our own private celebration." He looked back at Jamie, raised an eyebrow, then winked at her.

Jamie covered her ears and shook her head, "La la la la la. TMI, Jessie." Eve laughed at Jamie's antics.

"What? Isn't it your job to know what she's doing at all times?" Jessie started laughing.

"NO. Just where she is at and that she is safe." Jamie stood tall as she nodded to Eve.

Jessie started rubbing his thumb on the back of her hand. "She's safe with me." Eve sat back down on Jessie's lap and gave him another hug.

Then Eve reached out and grabbed Jamie's wrist. "Are you on shift tomorrow night? I have a few girls coming over. It would be nice if you could join in. Your cousin Stephanie will be there."

Jamie nodded. "I would love that. Want me to bring something?"

Eve's face lit up. "In fact, yes, there is. I want you to bring a full dose of your charm and personality. Does 6 p.m. work for you?"

"That would be wonderful. Thank you." Jamie smiled.

Eve got up from Jessie's lap and gave Jamie a hug. "I think we are going to be good friends. What do you think?"

Jamie firmly squeezed her. "I do too."

Jessie stood up and softly started kissing her neck. "Let's get you home so we can start to celebrate." Eve smiled and nodded. Eve tucked into Jessie and Jamie followed closely behind as the three of them walked to Eve's place.

On the way home, Eve sent Adam a quick rundown of the meeting and that the baby is stable and doing better. Now she is in the high-risk group with a new doctor and will be having a weekly appointment. 'Would you like to come to the next ultrasound?'

'I would be honored to see our baby growing.' Seeing Adam claim the child as his made her heart flutter with joy.

Eve paused in front of her door and turned to Jessie. "Before we go inside, I need to know if you are alright that Adam watches. If you don't want him to see us, I'll cover the cameras."

Jessie smiled. "If Adam wants to see my ass as I'm taking my wife, so be it." He smirked. He picked her up and she wrapped her legs around him and they started kissing in the hallway. His hands were all over her body, slipping under her clothes, and he leaned her into the corner of the frame as he tried to unlock the door.

Eve laughed as he fumbled for a minute. She got down and got the door open. The moment they walked through the door, they were like wild tigers, pulling clothes off each other in a fury. Jessie lifted her up with her legs around him again, and her arms clung around his neck as their lips sealed together. He carried her to the kitchen counter. "Do you need a warm-up?" he whispered.

Eve shook her head no. "I've been wet since the doctor's office." Jessie started kissing her neck as he positioned himself better between her soaking-wet lips.

"Mmmm, that's when you started smelling good. It took all my effort to keep my hands under control." He slid his hard member up and down until she felt his tip start to enter. "Ahhh." He moaned, then he grabbed her ass to pull as he slowly pushed in.

Adam

After getting Eve's text message, he got the announcement for movement and opened the video of her front room. He watched in anger as he saw Eve and Jessie kissing and removing each other's clothing. His hands were in a fist, and he was breathing hard. She knows the camera is there and is not trying to hide their actions.

As they continued, he calmed down, and excitement took over. He reached into his pants, watched, and listened to their sounds of pleasure as he softly stroked himself. He closed his eyes and visualized himself taking her, thrusting his raging hard cock into her, and he matched the strokes on his shaft to the sounds in the video.

Hearing her exclaim at her climax caused his own eruption. "Oh, yes, EVE! I can't hardly wait to get into you." He spoke out loud as he breathed heavily for a minute and then turned the notification alarm off for 12 hours. He didn't need to see any more for today, nor did he need the continuous announcements alarming his phone.

Eve

Eve woke up in bed; all tangled with Jessie in their post-sex position. She had an unsettling feeling in her stomach. She touched her belly and then looked around the room. There was a coldness, like a soft breeze had come through her apartment. She looked up at the bedroom window, but everything still looked to be locked.

She let out a soft sigh. Perhaps Adam was watching from afar and she's just picked up on it. She pulled the covers higher and then tucked back into Jessie's chest. He pulled her closer in response to her motion.

"I was thinking about something, Kitten." Jessie's soft talk was just above a whisper.

Eve gently reached up and softly touched his face. "Sorry if I woke you. What's on your mind, husband?"

"I think part of why I don't like to go down on you is all the hair." Jessie moved his hand to cover her undercarriage as his fingers started to rub around. "It tickles my face when I'm trying to concentrate on what I'm doing to please you." He moved his hand up and down her soft patch of hair. "Would you allow me to shave you? I promise to be very careful."

Eve smirked as she thought. "I've never really given it much thought. Plus, no one has explained it that way either. I noticed you were hairless, but now knowing, shaved. And you're right, the hair does tickle me also. I normally just hold it back."

Jessie leaned up on his elbow. "Want me to shave you in the shower, or do you want to lay down on the bed?"

She leaned up to match his angle. "Which would be easier for you?" He softly placed a kiss on her nose.

"Shower. Plus, then we can have shower sex." He grinned and wiggled his eyebrows. That made Eve giggle. Jessie got up and held Eve's hand as he led her to the shower.

She was as nervous as she could be, having Jessie slowly move the razor on her most precious area, but she had total trust in his ability. It was nerve-racking and erotic at the same time, trusting and letting someone else take control.

He would have one of her legs out to the side and then he'd switch to the other. "Are there any cameras in here?"

Eve kept her eyes closed as he worked. "No. Complete privacy in here."

"I was thinking about our privacy. Without Adam, that is." He paused in his movements. "If Adam asks about details, could you be vague in your answers unless it is important? But if he just wants to know how things are between us, I think those details should be kept between us. That is all that I'm saying."

She looked down to see him return to work. Swipe by swipe, her hair was removed. "You are asking me to keep secrets from him?" He paused and looked up again.

"Not really a secret, just a lack of the full truth. For example, if he asks if being together was good or bad. He doesn't need to know. If he asked if we had sex, then yes." Eve finally understood what he was trying to say.

He then ran his hand along the newly exposed skin, and it was so sensitive to every bit of his touch. "So soft now. Here, feel this." He guided her hand as if she didn't know where to go. Her skin was so smooth to the touch now.

She wondered how long it would stay that way or how often she would need to shave to maintain the smoothness. Would it be every few days, like her armpits, or would she need to every day, like a man's face? Would Jessie keep on shaving her?

Then, Jessie lifted her leg to rest on his shoulder and dove into her wetness. "MMMM, this is so much better," he mumbled as he spoke with his mouth in her wet lips.

"Oh my! You're right, so much better." She pressed her arms to the walls for support as her hot urges begged for more of his touch. The water was wonderful as Jessie's hands were all over her ass while his mouth worked its magic.

The combination of everything sent her body over the edge. "Oh, Jessie! Yessss." Her orgasm exploded, and she pushed herself harder into his face. He pushed back harder with his tongue. "Oh God!" He kept on flicking and swirling. She pulled her pelvis back and lowered her leg to get a moment's rest, but Jessie popped up and turned her around and bent her forward.

She braced both hands on the wall and gasped for air as she felt his hardness push into her. He plunged hard a couple of times, which made her moan each time, and then paused. "I'm sorry. I lost focus for a moment." He then started moving at a slightly slower, less pounding speed. His cock felt wonderful moving in and out, rubbing her g-spot as they counter-moved together.

She was still high from her previous peak and was climbing quickly again. "Jessie." Was all she could say as a warning before she climaxed hard again. She slightly leaned up, and he countered his positioning to thrust up through her release on his shaft. He pushed harder a couple more times, groaned, and grunted as he released his own climax.

After a couple of short lunges, he wrapped his arms around her. "It's crazy how different it feels for me without hair. How does it feel for you?" She wasn't sure if it was the lack of hair, the water from the shower, or all together.

She turned to face him. "It all felt amazing. You are amazing." Eve grinned in pleasure as she claimed him for a deep kiss. Her hands squeezed his back muscles as she lifted her legs to straddle him. He clung onto her and pushed her to the wall, then re-plunged into her depths.

Entry 11: Girls' Night

Eve was so excited about hosting her first house party. Their group of art friends had met several times for girls' karaoke or at a coffee shop for caffeine jolts, but this was all new territory for Eve. Not quite the margarita-and-shots kind of evening she would have imagined just a few months ago, but there would still be lots of laughs and fun to go around.

Back home, other than a few close friends, there was no way she could have pulled this kind of party off. Everything would have been too formal, with everyone dressed up and on their best behavior.

Eve had enlisted the help of a few friends to help lighten the workload with different assignments, especially since it was a school night and she was limited on time. She had reserved the common room because they wouldn't all fit in her apartment. It was nicely decorated with fall colors and a few spooky details here and there.

Eve brought out her decorations and spread them out among the different tables. She had a selection of movies to choose from and picked *Jason* to get started. She had tons of popcorn made but had several extra types if the gals wanted a different kind. Some of the others were bringing pop to drink, but she had a cooler filled with ice and plastic cups ready to be used.

Games were ready to be played in a corner. She set them out all around the kitchenette island. And, of course, the pool table was set up for the girls to play. But, of everything, Eve knew that most of the conversation would be spent talking about guys. And most likely about 'her' two guys. She was prepared to answer a few basic questions, but nothing too deep in the gossip.

She walked over to Thomas, who was standing like a statue in the corner. "Most of these girls won't be used to a guy hovering over them during a girls' party. It's the only time they can let their hair down and vent about men. So, whatever you may hear, you need to keep it in confidence."

Thomas nodded. "Madame, I don't care what the girls will chat about tonight. I'm just worried. Martin has been released on bail, and no one knows where he is. There is a restraining order against him to stay away, but a piece of paper won't stop someone who is determined to commit a crime."

Eve could see concern on his face, and she nodded her head in understanding as he let out a sigh. "When Jamie arrives, I will quietly leave so as not to disturb the party. Then, I'll return to my post downstairs. I will leave for the night when our night shift arrives."

Eve nodded again. "Thank you, Thomas, for watching out for me." She smiled and rested her hand on his arm.

Just then, a group of six girls from her design school were the first to arrive. They all hugged each other before they spread out. They each brought a new friend to join in tonight's fun. And just like that, the area had become noisy. Shortly after their arrival, Stephanie and Jamie arrived.

"Hey Girly," the cousins said in unison, and then laughed while pointing fingers at each other. They all three screeched as they bounced into each other's arms for a well-needed hug. "I can't believe how many people are here for a Tuesday night," Stephanie smiled as she looked around at the crowd.

Eve looked around. "I'm glad for the turnout. I have to admit that I was worried that no one would come."

"Are you kidding? We were all looking for a reason to blow off some steam," Jamie responded.

By the time everyone arrived, there were a total of twenty giggling girls mingling around and chatting. Eve looked over and noticed that Thomas was gone. "He sure is quiet for a big man," she shook her head as she mumbled to herself. One of her classmates came up, grabbed her wrist, and pulled her over to sit down on one of the couches.

"You simply have to tell us how you managed to wrangle two men to fight for your attention? And how are you dating both at the same time?"

Well, shit, Eve thought as she looked around and everyone else was staring at her with wide, hopeful eyes. She took a deep breath and smiled. Eve sat down and told the girls about her story.

She started with how she read an article and the last paragraph was about Jessie going to school here in town, near the art school. She discussed how she 'stalked' him online and orchestrated a meeting. Both guys were there when she 'bumped' into them. How she started to date Jessie, but discussed how he became a jerk and she ended up slapping him. All the girls gasped at learning that bit of information.

She continued her story about how she never officially broke up with him when she started to unofficially date Adam. Adam was helping Jessie with behavior, which led to more feelings between her and Jessie as he transitioned back to being a good man. Then she found out she was pregnant with Jessie's child. Since they are best friends, they agreed to be co-parents. She spilled more than she wanted but still didn't tell them everything.

The girls broke apart into groups again as they started playing games, and some watched the movie. Eve didn't notice, but at some point, alcohol arrived and was being passed around. Eve was worried about intoxication for the girls since there was no bartender to cut people off. Eve walked up to Jamie.

"I don't want to be the bad guy and ruin everyone's fun, but I just want to make sure that everyone makes it home safe. Can you help me arrange rides if people need them?"

She bounced her head. "I got it. I have a taxi cab number to call for a ride that they can pay for instead of using my own Uber account. That way, I'm not trying to get people to pay me back."

Eve smiled. "That sounds like a wonderful plan. Wish I had thought of that ahead of time."

As Eve feared, some girls were trying to leave intoxicated. But Eve and Jamie would tag-team them and only allow girls to go if they had arranged rides or a designated driver was among the group.

By the end of the evening, everyone else had left except for Katie, who had passed out and was left behind.

Eve decided to have her sleep it off on her couch as Stephanie and Jamie joined in the clean-up before returning to her apartment for the evening. When they returned, Katie was still out cold, and they laughed. They made new popcorn and had their favorite snacks ready, then they curled up in her bed to watch another movie. By the middle of the movie, Stephanie and Jamie were out, so Eve cleaned up the bed and put away all the food. She then climbed back into bed to rest for the night.

Adam

Adam got a motion alert and opened the camera to Eve's front room. He watched as Eve's friends carried a third girl into the living room and set her down on the couch.

Is she injured? He zoomed in to watch as they straightened her out, and Eve covered her up with a blanket, then placed a pillow under the girl's head. They talked for a moment and then they all left together.

"Okay, another crazy girls' night," he laughed to himself. About 30 minutes later, he got another motion alert, and he watched again as the three girls came back with boxes and a cooler. Then, they were clearly getting ready to stay up and watch another movie, so he turned off the alarm for another 12 hours. He didn't need to spy on any of their crazy antics.

He laughed to himself. And there's no way she's going to do anything private for him to watch while they are there.

Entry 12: Panic button

"Bonjour, husband."

"Hello, beautiful. How's your day going?" Adam asked as she answered the phone.

"Class was fine today. But I was looking at the weather report for this weekend and wanted your opinion on what to wear. Can you take a look at what I've got set out?" she looked over her selection.

"Sure thing." There was a moment of quiet as she waited. "Those do look nice. Are you going to model them for me or just hold them up?" he asked, and Eve giggled.

"It would take forever if I were to change in and out of all the clothing."

"Mmmm, this is true, but then I'd get to see you undress and then dress again. Maybe just one outfit change? Do you have that sexy matching black two-piece on?"

Eve giggled again. "No. I was saving that little number for this weekend for you to take it off of me." She could hear him suck a breath in.

"Damn, you're teasing me," he said in his low tone.

She laughed again. "No, this is teasing you." She set the phone down on the bed and slowly took her top off, then set it on the chair. She turned to face the camera and played with her nipples through the bra. "Mmmm." She then slid her fingers behind her bra and pinched. She gasped and let go. She walked back over to the chair, put her shirt back on, and then picked the phone back up.

"You are so wonderful and evil at the same time. I love you," he moaned over the phone. "Door notification?" he mumbled.

She giggled, not knowing what he meant. "I love you too and I do what I can. So, which one do you like?" She held up both and turned back to the camera for him to see. There was quiet on his end. "Adam? What do you think?" she asked again.

"I want you to listen to me and do exactly as I say." His voice changed to a serious harsh tone.

"Okay?" she replied, now worried since he never talks this way.

"I want you to go to the nearest panic button and push it now." Eve froze in her spot. "Go now, Beautiful," he said more firmly.

She tossed the clothes on the bed, sat next to her side table, pulled the drawer open, and pushed the button under the lip. She knew her security officer would be on their way. "I don't understand?" she said as she could hear him breathing heavy as he was running.

"I'm on my way. I want you to hang up and call 911. After they answer, let them know where you are and just place the phone face down so the screen can't be seen. Then arm yourself with anything and get ready to fight."

Eve could hear anger and fear in his voice. "Okay, love you," she said, then the line went dead.

Her heart was pounding in her ears and her body quivered; she was so freaked out. She called for help just as she heard the door open to her bedroom. She turned and was surprised at who was walking through her door. She yelled, "Martin! What are you doing here?" She set the phone face down.

"I had to come see you," he responded breathlessly, like he ran up the flights of stairs. Eve was taken aback. Think, girl, think.

"You're breaking and entering, trespassing, harassment, breaking a court order, and I'm sure there's more that I can't think of. You are not welcome here and you need to leave," she said angrily but was frozen in her spot.

He had a smirk on his face. "It's not when I have a key." He shut the door behind him.

"So, you illegally had my key copied when you were a guard. You're still here without my permission and against court orders. Set my key down and leave now before you get yourself into more trouble," she said with a huff.

His smirk grew to a smile. "No chance, Mi Reina. I've come to claim you and make you mine. I've had this deep-down feeling from the day we met," he responded, closed his eyes, took a deep smell, and then refocused on her.

How dare he talk to her in such a familiar way. She was so angry but had a flashback of her many years of instructions before traveling.

She shook her head in confusion. "What are you talking about? If you haven't figured out from the last time you were here, you are no longer allowed to be here. You crossed the line. Charges are pending. Just because you posted bail doesn't mean you are clear."

He took a couple of steps in, rested his knee on the corner of the bed, and she was trying to think of anything substantial to grab. There was nothing big enough within reach she could hit him with. He leaned his head to the side, then took off his coat and tossed it on the chair with a thump.

"I've come to put my baby in your belly. Now that Roe vs. Wade has been repealed, you can't get rid of it. Even if I must put my seed in you every day for a year, I'm going to fill you up until we are pregnant." Eve's mind cringed, and her body twinged on the inside with excitement while the thought of that much sex sunk into her mind.

He had a grin on his face, and she knew he was serious about his intention. Stay calm, Eve. "Just curious about how you see this going to happen." She remembered her training and tried to keep him calm and talking.

He unbuttoned his shirt. "It would be more pleasant for you if you allowed me to show you how good of a man I can be." He removed his shirt, exposing his massive muscular chest, abs, and arm muscles, then he tossed his shirt with his coat. If he wasn't being a total creep, she could see how any girl would want to be with him. He's even easy on the eyes, but Eve only kind of noticed before. She wasn't sure how much of it was body armor.

He took another step closer to her. Her heart began to race out of her chest. She lowered her eyes so she wasn't staring at his muscles. Stay calm, keep him calm, she kept saying to herself.

"Otherwise, I came prepared to tie you up and take you forcefully. That will hurt you a whole lot more." He lifted her chin to make her look at him, and he smiled again. "I'm good with either way and they both have their own advantages." Eve's nerves went into overdrive hearing his warning.

He placed his other hand behind her head and leaned in, kissed her hard, and forced his tongue into her mouth, demanding space as his tongue moved around hers, trying to get her tongue to dance with his, and then it changed to something softer and sensual. Eve felt herself lean into him for more and then remembered her situation.

"Martin," she exclaimed, mumbling against his mouth. She put two hands on his chest to push and she removed her chin from his hand. He had a scowl on his face and his hand gripped her hair tightly. She was breathing hard and took a couple of calming breaths and looked him in the eyes. "Martin, I choose gentle."

He let go of her hair and leaned back to compose himself and then placed both his hands on hers, still pressed against his chest. He smiled. "I knew you'd be the one." He took a deep inhalation through his nose. "You smell different, more alluring than everyone else." He took the last step and put his legs between hers. Eve's body reacted to the closeness and she started to heat up.

Why does she attract men like this? Men who know nothing about her, who think they are fated to her because of her scent. She could see the lust in his eyes. The same look she's seen time and again from previous men. "Martin, if you are gentle with me, I won't fight you." She looked down again and spoke softly. "But you are mistaken. I can just go home and get rid of the unwanted pregnancy in France."

He placed a hand on top of her head and softly ran his fingers through her hair. "Not if I keep you here."

Eve sighed. "And you can't impregnate me because I'm already almost three months pregnant." He jerked her face back up and she saw his face had turned red in anger.

"You slut. It's the guy from Monday night, isn't it?" he demanded loudly. "I saw you two sleeping when I came in." She was offended at the name-calling and scared that he was here, in her room, the other night.

"Not just a guy. My husband." She raised her voice. He punched her in the face, sending her sideways on the bed, and then he held her down. Her hand held her face at the impact, her ear still ringing. Her eye felt like it was going to pop. Her brain pounded with each heartbeat, but she could hardly think, let alone move.

"I also came back on Tuesday, but you had a bunch of girls sleeping over and I wasn't looking for an orgy. I only want you.

Anyway, I'll get that baby out of you and then I'll keep you so you can't leave. But I'll have my way with you tonight."

He leaned forward and ground himself on her backside. "Martin, get off me!" she screamed.

He used his free hand, grabbed her pants and underwear, then pulled them down hard. They only came down partway on her cheeks, and her body slid closer to the edge so she was bent over. "No, Martin! Please don't." She screamed and started to kick and push herself away by swinging her arms at him in any way she could to break his hold.

He re-grabbed her, held her up, and started connecting hard punches to her face and body. It caused pain all over while making her dizzy. He bent her over and started kneeing her abdomen and chest. "Stop! Please stop." She tried to block as best she could, but one connected hard, sending her back onto the bed. He leaped on top of her and started pulling on her pants again.

"No, Martin! Please stop." She started swinging punches at his face and landed one or two solid hits. He picked her up like she weighed nothing and threw her hard onto the wall. She felt and heard pops like she had never experienced before. A massive pain wave swept all over her body, and she fell, crumpled to the ground.

He walked around the bed and stared at her for a moment. He reached into his pants and started to rub himself. "Your fighting has made my dick rock hard, and I know you're gonna love every bit of it when I bury my cock balls deep inside you."

He kneeled down and pulled her body straight. "Ouch." She whimpered and seized in pain as her body shifted positions. She didn't have much left in her to fight. She managed to hold up her hand up, to say stop, like that was going to make him change his mind.

He leaned over her and placed a hand next to her head. "Are you really hurt?" She nodded her head, yes. "You made your choice to fight." A devilish grin spread across his face and eyes.

She shook her head, no and moved her hand to touch his chest. "I was holding still. I agreed not to fight if you would be gentle." She then moved her hand to his neck and slowly pulled him in for a soft kiss and then pushed him back. "Like that. But at the first test, you hit me. You were going to force me." She bit her lip, then moved her hand back to his chest and softly pushed him farther back.

"That was a test?" His question bounced in her brain as her pain had reached her maximum tolerance. Tears were pooled in her eyes, draining to her ears, making it difficult to see.

"You broke your own rules. I wasn't fighting you. I was trying to stop your aggression. But you hurt me anyway. If you truly care about me, please get help. I have broken bones and I'm in a ton of pain."

Her arm slowly rested to the floor as the last of her energy was leaving her. Pain had completely taken over and her eyes fully overflowed. At this point, it would be better to just submit so he wouldn't hurt her further. He leaned in closer again, softly kissed her lips, neck, and then her collarbone, sending another wave of pain through her chest.

"Don't worry, Mi Reina. I'm gonna make you feel good again." He ran his fingers down her face, along her neck, down her breast, and he started twisting her nipple through her shirt. She gasped and then winced in pain. Her body lit on fire at the sensual touch and her fingers dug into the carpet. "Before you know it, you'll be screaming my name in pleasure."

Oddly, she was wet and could feel moisture slowly dripping from her body. He stood up and Eve watched as he unzipped his pants, exposing his enormously large member. "God. Please help me," she cried out and closed her eyes. He's gonna rip her apart from the inside also.

There was a loud crash and Eve opened her eyes just enough to see someone she recognized. Jamie was taking Martin down to the ground. Eve watched as she lay as still as she could, since she hurt all over. It even hurt to just breathe. She watched the commotion between them as Jamie quickly had Martin cuffed to the radiator, then she placed his shirt and coat over him to cover his erection.

Jamie then came over to check on her. Eve flinched in pain when Jamie touched her. "Key," Eve whispered.

"What about a key?" Jamie asked with a confused look on her face.

"He made a copy of mine," Eve whispered again.

Jamie nodded. "I'll take care of it." Jamie got back up and found the copied key on the floor. She then punched him in the stomach. "Real men don't hurt women." He didn't say anything. He just wiggled in place a bit. Jamie returned to Eve. "Where does it hurt?"

Eve closed her eyes. "Everywhere." She continued to whisper. She looked back at her again. "End table, phone, talk to them."

Jamie stood up and went to the other side of the bed and picked up her phone and started talking while she monitored Martin's behavior. Eve closed her eyes again and listened to her chat with the emergency operator. A couple of minutes later she heard Jamie say, "Don't move her. She's hurt. Medic is coming." Eve cracked her eyes open and she saw someone stand up and stand back at the door.

"I'm here, Beautiful." Eve fully opened her eyes to Adam's voice. She shifted her head back to watch Martin as he started to twist and wiggle. She wondered what he was doing.

"She's mine. You can't have her," Martin said angrily. Suddenly, his arms moved free, and she saw a glint of silver that was tucked away in his coat.

Eve jutted her arm up. "Gun!" she screamed as Martin pulled the weapon from his pocket.

Adam quickly grabbed Martin's wrist and landed a punch across his face. Martin fell to the ground and the gun tumbled to Jamie's feet. Adam pulled him back up and reached back to strike again.

"Ouch!" Eve let out a cry. She closed her eyes again as a new pain took over her abdomen. It felt like she soiled herself. "Jamie." Eve cried out for her.

A moment later she was next to her. "You need something?" Eve opened her eyes and looked down as she slowly opened her legs. Adam returned next to her and had a look of horror on his face. That's when she knew that she was leaking amniotic fluids. That asshole did what he said he was going to do.

She closed her legs and could feel a sad wave take her. Her tears started endlessly streaming to her ears again. "Call Jessie. He needs to know." She couldn't let out and cry like she wanted because her chest hurt so much.

"I'll be right back," she heard Adam say. Then she could hear the sound of pounding feet down the hallway, getting louder as it got closer. Suddenly, there were a ton of voices in the room and Eve chose to keep her eyes closed and concentrate on not moving to control the pain. There was a bit of noise and they moved her bed to make room.

"Hello. My name is Eric. I'm the lead medic."

She opened her eyes a little. "Eve," she whispered.

"Can you tell me where you hurt so we can figure out how to move you?" She closed her eyes and started mentally checking her body. Slowly she went over what hurt. She would need to document everything for the reports.

She fully opened her eyes and looked at him. "Recovering from a previous concussion. Worsening headache. Left wrist, hand. Left face, ear. Center chest. Left and right ribs. Right is worse. Upper stomach. Lower abdomen. 10 weeks pregnant. Leaking fluids."

Eve closed her eyes and tears streamed faster than before. She listened to the conversation in the room and could tell something was wrong but couldn't put her finger on it. She was so glad that she had set up the cameras. That asshole needed to be locked away forever and all the videos would cement his sentence.

"Okay, I got all that down. I'm going to give you an IV and get some meds started to help with pain and for you to rest."

She looked at him again. "I'm also a chronic insomniac. Sleep meds usually don't work well. Thomas, my lead security officer, should have a copy of my medical charts."

"I have already contacted Thomas. He will meet us at the hospital," Adam's voice sounded from somewhere around her bedroom door. There was a small pinch in her right arm and then cold fluid flowed in, making her arm cold as well as her head and body feel heavy.

"You did a good job fighting him off. Now, just relax, Eve. Slowly count back from ten."

She closed her eyes and felt them roll around her head. "Ten…, nineee…, eeeeiiiiight…sssssss"

Adam

"She's out for now. For how much she listed and how she looks, I gave her the full dose. You can go back to the police officer," the medic advised him.

Adam nodded. "Thank you for your help." He gave Eric a pat on the shoulder and then walked over to the officer who was examining Martin's dead body. He pulled out his phone and re-opened the video from the beginning. Then, he advanced it to when Martin entered the apartment and handed it to the officer.

"I didn't touch him until he broke free from his restraints and pulled a gun. Then, I hit him once. I was going to hit him again, but he was already out and Eve screamed in pain, so I set him back down. I can forward this video for your evidence." He tapped play for the officer to watch the horror scene.

Adam then kept his eyes on Eve as they carefully moved her to a backboard and then onto the gurney. They started cutting her clothes off and he walked back to them. Eric held up his hand.

"Sorry, we have to, so we can properly assess. We leave the undergarments on, but they will be cut at the hospital. You may want to pack a change of clothes for her." Adam nodded and turned to get a bag from the closet. He pulled a pair of soft pants, a matching t-shirt, and a sweater from the closet.

He opened the top drawer and saw the matching set of underwear he was talking about earlier with her. She's not going to want to wear that one for a while. He then picked a more comfortable undergarment, knowing she was going to lose the baby. He closed his eyes and lowered his head as tears started to fall. He was looking forward to being a dad.

He took a calming breath and wiped his face. Hopefully, that asshole didn't permanently damage her and they can try again. He opened his eyes and placed a bra, underwear, socks, and step-in running shoes into the bag. "Where are you taking her?"

"Lenex Hill," Eric answered. Adam picked up her wallet and placed it in the bag of clothing, then handed it to Eric.

"Thanks again for your help," Adam said as they wheeled Eve out of the apartment with Jamie closely shadowing. Adam sent Jessie an update on where to go and that he would be following shortly.

The officer in the living room was tagging and collecting Martin's items he had brought with him.

"He had an agenda and was ready." He opened the bag to show Adam the contents. All sorts of different restraints were in there, along with an assortment of sexual items for pain and pleasure. Adam was speechless and just shook his head. He turned back to the officer in the bedroom who looked sick to his stomach.

"It's hard to believe that there are men out there that are this disgusting. To purposefully rape someone so they would have their baby. From what I see, this case is open and shut. It's just so sad that she was hurt during this." Adam didn't know what to say, so he just shook his head again.

"She clearly had training. She kept calm and that helped to keep him calm, until he snapped." The officer handed the phone back to Adam as another gurney rolled into the room.

Everyone stepped aside, then it came to a stop next to Martin. They did a last-minute check for vitals, then everyone helped load him, and then the medics wheeled him out.

Adam looked around and didn't want her to return to a mess, so he put her clothes away, straightened her bed to the wall, and fixed the items on the end table. He placed the extra key Martin made on his key ring and gave the room one last look. When he was satisfied, he checked back in with the officers in the living room. The officer handed him a business card with his contact information.

"We will be contacting you and Eve for your statements along with the security officer."

Adam picked up a piece of paper and wrote down three numbers. "The top two are mine and Eve's. The third is Thomas, who is the lead security officer. He can get you the guard Jamie's number." They said their goodbyes and Adam locked up before heading to the hospital where Jessie should be waiting.

When Adam arrived at Eve's hospital room, Jessie was there with his arms and head on the end table, but Eve was gone.

"Hey there. Where's our wife at?" Jessie sat up and stretched as Adam pulled up a chair alongside him.

"They took her to radiology for imaging. Said it would be a while with the number of images that were ordered. Jamie's also with her."

Adam reached out his hand and set it on Jessie's. "I don't know if they said anything to you, but she's going to lose the baby. We have to be strong for her."

Jessie jerked his head and focused on Adam. "How do you know that?" Jessie had a worried look on his face.

Adam leaned back in the chair and crossed his arms. "At the apartment, her water broke. It wasn't clear water, but bloody." Jessie lowered his head as a tear fell, then he wiped it away.

"I know you and I were both looking forward to being dads, and the pain we feel is only part of what she's going to go through. We need to be patient, gentle, helpful, and supportive for anything she may need. It's not just a physical loss, but a mental struggle as well. She may have anger, guilt, and sadness for not being able to protect the baby." Adam pressed his lips together. "She put up a hell of a fight."

Jessie sat up straight and his eyes went big. "You still have a camera there."

Adam smirked. "Good thing too. We were on the phone talking when I saw him walk into the apartment. I was able to get her to push the panic button and call for help before he even got to the bedroom." He shook his head. "It could have been worse. He could have killed her."

Adam pressed his lips together again to prevent himself from crying. "But I killed him instead. With one punch. I didn't think about it until now, but I may be expelled from school. I may go to jail while they investigate. Doesn't matter if it was in self-defense."

Jessie leaned forward and held out his hand. "Let me see the video." Adam didn't move. He knew the video was disturbing to watch. Jessie hit his hand on the table with a thump and then held it up again.

"Are you sure you want to see her that way? It's the type of thing they make movies about. It's that bad."

"I have to know. Plus, then I can see how your actions were to help you with school. If anything, don't hide it. Be upfront about it and show them the video ahead of time and bring them to your side before they get word from the police."

Adam smirked. That would be the smart thing to do. Adam nodded his head and pulled out his phone and got it ready. "Prepare yourself, this hurts the soul to watch. Even I'm a changed person because of it." He then slid the phone over.

Jessie started watching at the part where Eve was teasing Adam. He looked at Adam and shook his head with a smile. After a couple of moments, his face changed as the happiness left and anger, fear, and sadness took over.

Entry 13: Miscarriage and Surgeries

Eve opened her eyes and saw that she was surrounded by tall flowers. The ground she laid upon was warm under her body as if it was radiating the heat back up at her. She sat up and recognized the hill overlooking her family home. The sweet smell of wild flowers filled her nose. It's been many years since she last visited here. "Finaly, I've come home."

She sighed and looked around, but no one was there. She brought her hands up to her face. "Mama, Papa, Nicolas," she called out for them but no one responded. She felt a pain in her stomach, then she heard a baby crying in the distance. She knew it was her baby, so she tried to stand up, but struggled to get her footing.

"It's not your time, little one." The thunderous voice vibrated the air around her. "You still have lots of spirit left to live."

Eve was sad that she couldn't at least see her child. "No. Please. Let me see my child. Just for a moment, then I'll go back."

"It's not your time." The voice spoke with more conviction. Suddenly, the clouds sunk and pushed her back down to the ground.

"Please," she begged, as she struggled against the air. A wave of pain took over her whole body and she started to wake up. Coming out of what felt like a deep sleep, she started to cry and moan out loud. Her memory of the fight replayed in her mind. She opened her eyes and was looking at a white ceiling in a darkened room. She tried to listen to the voices, but the rhythmic sounds of beeps and clicks as machines hummed as they worked were very distracting.

After falling asleep on the floor in her apartment, she figured she was in the hospital. Her body was stiff from not moving, so she started with her toes and worked her way up. She stopped at her hips because it put extra pressure on her ribs, and that caused pain around her body. She moved her right hand, elbow, and shoulder slowly.

She found a hard object and lifted it up to her face to see. She saw the button for the nurse and pressed it. Her left hand was still hurting from earlier. She slowly lifted the heavy hand and saw a bloody bandage wrapped around it. There was a gentle knock on the door. Eve raised her good hand and waved.

"You are not supposed to be awake yet. How are you feeling?" A man's voice filled the small space.

Eve was trying to be serious, but... "I feel like I was being used as a punching bag. Oh, wait. I was." She smiled a little at her well-placed joke. She pointed to herself. "This is what happens when a big strong man punches and kicks." She frowned a bit.

"Oh my gosh! That is awful. I'm going to push some more pain relief. You'll feel it in a minute." A smiling face appeared in her view. "Hello, I'm Tony."

Eve weakly smiled. "I'm Eve."

"Nice to meet you. Wish it was on better terms. Like in the park on a nice summer's day would have worked." He smiled again, which made her smile. Another face appeared in her view.

"Jamie! Thank God for you." Jamie smiled, and Tony laughed.

"Your shadow has been everywhere with you. After a very angry phone call from the French embassy, who threatened to have SWAT sent in if she was not present, the surgical crew finally allowed her to scrub up and be in surgery with you."

Jamie giggled. "I've seen your insides. I can't say that about anyone else."

Tony smirked. "Well, after everything you've been through, I'm glad to see you are in good spirits."

Eve looked at Tony funny. "What do you mean, everything I have been through?"

Tony picked up the chart. "Do you want me to tell you all the procedures that you have undergone in the last four hours?"

She shifted her head to get a better view. "Might as well get the bad news out first. Right?" Tony nodded his head and opened to the front page as Jamie sat down next to her on the bed.

"After the medics sedated you to move, they determined that you had lost most of your amniotic fluid already." Tony rested his hand on hers. "There was no saving the baby at such an early gestation. I'm so sorry." He squeezed her hand. She already knew that was coming, but the tears still came anyway.

"So they did a D&C. You will have a cycle for about six weeks as everything returns back to normal."

Eve made an icky face. "Guess I need to stock up on pads." Tony smiled.

"Can I still have children?" Eve really wanted the answer to that question. Tony paused, and Jamie softly moved her hand on her shoulder.

"That's a question that will be best for your OB. They may do some more tests." He read a little more and flipped pages.

"Medics noticed a lack of movement as you lay on the floor, so the doctor ordered a ton of images. A CT of your head, neck, and spine. You are still going to want to follow the concussion protocol again, just in case from your last injury."

He turned a few more pages. "Also, before and after x-rays of your hand, sternum, and rib surgeries." He held up a couple of images to a small light.

"Wow. He really did a number on you. Do you want to see these?"

Eve thought about it for a moment. "Maybe later. But not right now."

He returned the images to the file and turned to another page. "I can understand that. Take a little time to process before seeing the images. What was his name? The guy who hurt you?" Tony had a sorrowful look in his eyes.

Eve looked at Jamie, then back to Tony. "I only knew him as Martin. He was part of my security detail, like Jamie here." Eve turned her head and smiled at Jamie. "Guess one day he got the wrong idea in his head. He crossed the line and ended up in jail. Details are too gross to talk about." Eve waved her hand.

Jamie shook her head. "Thomas told me. It's fucking disturbing."

Eve looked back at Tony. "Anyway, guess he posted bail and came back to finish what he wanted to do. I'm afraid I could have been more diplomatic about it and followed my training better, but I angered him instead. Thus, being the punching bag." Eve frowned a bit.

Tony held up a page that read, Martin Jose Julius Evola.

"Why is his medical stuff in my file?" Eve was getting angry.

"Oh, dear. No. This is your copy of his death certificate." Eve just stared at Tony for a moment in shock. Then she looked at Jamie.

"What? How?" Jamie lowered her head, breaking eye contact. Eve looked back at Tony, who shrugged his shoulders.

"I don't have his file. It would most likely be with him in the morgue." He smirked and shrugged his shoulders.

Eve closed her eyes and could feel the medicine working to pull her under. She thought back and remembered how Martin broke free and pulled the gun. He and Adam struggled for a moment, and Adam hit him. Did Adam continue to hit him until he was dead? Did the gun fire and she just couldn't remember hearing it? "I wish I had my phone."

"Sorry, dear. No electronics in recovery." Tony's voice was soft, yet firm.

She opened her eyes for a moment before the heavy lids sunk closed again. "It's not like I wanted to surf. There is a security camera in my apartment. I wanted to see how he died. I'm sure my husbands will tell me."

Tony giggled. "I can tell you're getting a little loopy. You said husbands, plural."

Eve opened her eyes and looked at Tony. "I do have two husbandsssss." She emphasized the 's' sound.

Jamie giggled and nodded while holding up two fingers. "Present tense. Not one ex and one current."

Tony's mouth dropped open. "Wow. I would love to hear this story, but you need to get some rest."

She was feeling tired again as her pain level was decreasing.

"I'll be just outside your door," Jamie added.

Eve nodded and then thought of the last Saturday evening and all day Sunday about how everything fit together just right.

Unfortunately, everything feels wrong now.

November

Entry 1: Adam discloses Eve's attack

Eve took a deep breath, rolled over onto her side, then locked her fingers with the warm hand next to her. "Buenos días, Mi Reina. Last night was wonderful." Eve opened her eyes and saw Martin lying naked with her. He reached his hand up and the heat of his fingers warmed her face as they slid along her cheek.

"You sucked my big cock like it was going to be your last meal. Plus, you know, I love taking your tight pussy from behind and pounding you hard, just how you like it." Eve felt her body twinge in excitement. He stretched and yawned, then turned to face her. "Mmmm, I'm getting super hard just thinking about it." He wrapped his arm around her and leaned in to kiss her, but she pulled back, and he squinted his eyes in confusion.

"Don't start fighting me now, after all this time. We have an agreement." He softly pulled her leg over his and pressed his hardness to her wetness. Eve moaned at the pressure, and he traced his hand up her body. "I'll be gentle if you don't resist me. Unless you want it rough, like last night."

He brushed his lips on hers, then he took her mouth and pushed his tongue in, but then softly stroked his tongue on hers, and she felt her resolve fade. Eve slid her hand up Martin's arm. "You remember what happened the last time you fought me." He pushed her over onto her back, kneeled between her legs, and then he started rubbing her huge baby belly.

"I made love to you two times a day for three months as you were tied up. I showed you the different levels of hard and rough versus soft and gentle, and I learned just how you liked it." He started rubbing his finger back and forth on her nub.

Eve gasped in excitement, moaned, and arched to the pleasure. "Oh, Martin." Eve felt a pleasure wave roll through her body.

"Only after I knew you were pregnant with my child and we came to our agreement, was I able to trust you to remove the restraints." He started to rub faster and harder. She reached for his other hand and they entangled fingers. "Now we make love three or more times a day because you want me to." Eve's body was burning from the inside out.

"We have been happy this whole time. I knew we fit together from the beginning. I just had to wait for you to figure it out."

Eve lifted her free hand and waved. "I'm sorry. I wasn't trying to resist. I was just temporarily stuck in waking up."

He softly held her wrist and kissed the palm of her hand before bringing it to his face. "Your scent gives you away, Mi Amor, Mi Reina." He lifted her hips and pressed at her opening, making her body expand to his size. "Oh, Mi Amor, Mi Rey," Eve exclaimed as he began thrusting himself into her and her burn quickly turned into a fire.

"Ohh, Martin." Eve started to moan as a pleasure wave rolled through her. "Ouch." She cried out loud in pain as her muscles flexed as she tried to move. She held both arms up to push back on his chest. "Martin, NO! You're hurting me." She screamed out loud. Her eyes popped open to realize it was just a dream. What a fucked-up dream it was.

"Easy, Beautiful. We are right here." She slowly lowered her arms to the bed. Her tears started draining from the sides as she felt Adam take her hand in his. His low voice sounded like a warm hug. Then she felt movement on her other arm.

"Morning, Kitten. We've been with you all night." For the first time, she felt okay enough to let her cry loose, and she started bawling.

"Everything okay in here?" Eve could hear Jamie's voice in the distance. She wanted to hold everyone, but it hurt to even flex her muscles. They both reached up and dried her face.

"Whoa, now. What's going on in here?" She recognized Tony's voice and was glad he was still on shift.

"She's waking up." She heard Adam respond for her.

"Waking up in pain?" Eve's sobbing subsided a bit, and she re-opened her eyes, noticing that things were a bit blury.

"It's all just hitting me at once. All the different areas of broken bones and the emotions of everything. I'd like to move a little, but then the pain spikes." She frowned a little but her face hurt to move.

"Okay, then. I can help with that part." Tony paused and looked back and forth between the two guys. "These two men must be your husbands you were talking about earlier." Tony laughed. Eve blushed because she had forgotten about that conversation. "How do I get me one like you?" He growled like a tiger and curled his fingers at Jessie. Eve held up her arm.

"Sorry, he's taken." Eve laughed and then winced in pain as she slowly set her arm back down. She looked outside, and the sun was starting to come up. "Is it Thursday? It feels like I've been asleep for a few days."

Adam squeezed her hand. "Yes, Beautiful. You had your surgery during the evening, Wednesday." He lifted her hand and gave it a kiss.

"Oh, my. Now I can see why you have him also." Tony laughed and winked. "Your medicine is set to go off at specific times. If the pain gets intolerable, you can ask for more. I'm heading off shift soon. I do hope you recover well, but I suspect with these two handsome husbands, you will have a peaceful recovery and heal fast." Tony waved goodbye just before closing the door.

Shortly after Tony left, she felt a wave of reduced pain and she breathed easier. Eve had sad news to discuss, so she started to take a deep breath and winced again. "Slow and short breathing until your body gets used to the new hardware." Eve had a hard time controlling her tears. They just wouldn't stop.

"Can you guys stand up so I can see you and not just hear your voices?" They both got up and sat next to her on the bed then leaned forward. She rested her arms on their legs. It's the closest she will get to a hug for now. "I need to let you know…" She paused as she choked up and tears streamed down her cheeks again.

"We already know everything that's happened," Jessie spoke up.

"The baby, surgeries, and recovery to come," Adam added.

Eve started bawling again. Her voice hitched as she whispered, "I tried my best to keep him calm and away, then to just protect the baby once he started hitting me."

"We don't blame you for what happened." Jessie squeezed her arm.

"You did your best to survive, and that's what we are most concerned with," Adam added. They both reached dried her face again.

"Why does this keep happening to me? I've heard that God only sends challenges that he knows we can handle. But you have to admit, even this one is really hard." She lifted both arms to their sides. Jessie softly placed his hand on her stomach.

"Life will dish out horrendous things. People find themselves in despair and crying out. Have faith, Eve. God is the source of love and blessing. And we are here because we love you," Jessie softly said. She smiled and softly touched Jessie's face with her good hand and then Adam's face before resting both arms.

"I know I can handle this because I have both of your love and support. I love you both very much." They both smiled and each took turns softly placing kisses on her sore lips.

She smirked at them. "I guess my body will never be beach-ready again with all these new scars," she said as she pointed to the big bandage down the center of her chest. She lifted her knee and rubbed her scar along the side.

"You will still turn our heads even if you're wearing a burlap bag. Everyone else can just keep their eyes and hands to themselves," Adam nodded firmly.

"And if they have something bad to say," Jessie pointed to Adam, "he will respond with his killer punch. I can attest that it's a doozy from when he clocked me. And from what I saw, I got nothing compared to what he gave that Martin guy."

Eve's amusement left, and she looked at Adam. "Did you really kill him?" Adam demeanor changed as he nodded. His shoulders slumped and he looked sad.

"In one punch," Jessie filled in.

Eve's mouth opened in shock. "Well, I guess I won't have to worry about him coming back to the apartment again. Though, I wish I knew the building was a little safer.

Adam reached up and softly brushed the hair from her face. "We were talking about the next few weeks of your recovery. Originally, we were thinking of having you at the condo with us, each taking turns in your care. But we didn't want you switching rooms every night. If it's okay with you, after discharge, we'll take you back to your apartment, and we can switch on who stays the night."

Eve pursed her lips together in thought. "I think that would be fine. I will be more comfortable, but when I feel better, it would be nice to come back to the three of us." She smiled again. "After I have recovered and we are all ready, we can try again for children." Both guys smiled and nodded.

"We can talk about that, months from now," Jessie smiled as his thumb rubbed back and forth on her arm.

"You'll have to be checked out before trying again. We want to make sure it will be safe for you," Adam added. "Let's just concentrate on one day at a time." He softly stroked his fingers along her hand. Eve closed her eyes and smiled. The heat from them spread through her and warmed her spirit.

"Okay." She opened her eyes and refocused out the window. "I'm not going to pass class this semester with all the time I'm missing." A frown settled on her face.

"No, that's not how it works here. You did your work and even did a presentation," Adam interrupted.

She smirked. "I set up the downstairs as a separate project. I can turn that in, and it will buy me another bit of time." Adam picked up her hand again.

"If you will allow me to represent you, I'll talk to the school on your behalf and explain the medical situation. They then can't take action against you. But from what you say about your instructor, they are nice to work with. So, you shouldn't have much trouble."

Eve smiled. "Thank you. That would be nice." Then she thought about them both being here. "I don't want you guys missing classes just to be with me. If you guys insist, at least take turns, draw straws or something."

They both looked at each other and shook their heads. "We've been up all night. There's no way I can go to school and concentrate. If anything, I'm going to get some sleep, then come back to see you before visiting hours are over. I can go back to school tomorrow," Jessie chimed in.

Adam nodded his head. "Same here, Beautiful. But I'll talk to your school when they open first." He smiled. "Plus, it's up to the hospital when they discharge you. One of us may be sleeping here or at your place tonight," he added with a half-smile.

She smiled and nodded. "It would be nice to be in my comfortable bed. Not to say that theirs isn't, it just… not home."

There was a knock on the door just before it opened. "Hello, I'm taking over from Tony. My name is Jessica." Both the guys got up and sat back down in the chairs to make room. She walked closer and faced Eve. "Good morning. Are you hungry?"

Eve nodded her head yes. "I could go for something. Do I have to eat lying down?"

Jessica laughed. "Didn't Tony show you how to lift the bed?" Eve shook her head. "Shame on him." Jessica picked up the controller that was near her hand and explained the buttons. She pushed the head-up button, and the bed instantly started to move.

Eve grimaced, "Ouch," and her tears instantly started pouring down.

The bed halted. "Where does it hurt?" Jessica had a worried look.

Eve continued to wince as she slowly adjusted her position. "Center chest and right ribs," Eve slowly pointed.

"It's going to continue to hurt there until one day it just doesn't hurt as much. Don't be mistaken—you are broken. There is a plate holding your sternum and seven ribs together. Also, two in your hand," she said as she pointed her finger to Eve's left hand. "You have control here. You can go a little at a time or all at once, just get to an upright position—the speed is up to you. I'll go and get breakfast ordered for you. Do you have any questions?"

Eve nodded. "How long will I be admitted?"

The nurse smirked to one side. "It kinda depends on you. Today for sure. We need to make sure your bowels are moving again, and if you can show that you can safely move around, then you can go home tonight. If you're still struggling, tomorrow sometime." Jessica raised her eyebrows like she laid down a challenge.

Adam

Adam arrived at E 73rd x Park Ave by taxi and looked out to see the New York School for Interior Design where Eve attends. He was surprised at how close her apartment and hospital were to her school. Perhaps that's part of the reason for her choice of location. As he entered the main hallway, he saw several before-and-after drawings on the wall and thought to himself, 'These would be better in video, like Eve's idea for their office.'

He found the main office and took a deep breath before entering. He walked up to the front desk and cleared his throat. "Morning. My name is Christian Adam Stratford. I'm here to represent Madame Amanda Evelyn de Vogues. I need to speak to the school administrator and her teacher, Mrs. Johnston."

The secretary had a confused expression on her face. "That's a request I've never heard before. May I tell them what it's about?" She had a perky nose and thick glasses that reminded him of a librarian he once knew.

"Respectfully, I'm not allowed to discuss the situation with you. I was only given permission to speak to the administrator and her teacher. To reduce possible communication errors, it's best to speak with both at the same time. Thank you."

She still looked confused but got up and walked around the desk. "The side office is currently not being used. I will have them join you." She held her arm up for Adam to enter.

Adam nodded his head. "Thank you." After entering the side office, he chose to sit in the seat facing the door. That way he could see who was coming into the room. He set out his identification and the page for representation for them to view first. He also pulled out the documentation of Martin's last attack with the no-contact order.

On his tablet, he accessed the video of the current attack for them to view and brought copies of Eve's current police and hospital reports.

He took a deep breath to calm himself as he walked through his planned speech. As he was finishing setting up, the door flew open.

"Is she okay?" Adam leaned up from the table, not knowing which person had just entered the room. He put his hand out to shake.

"Hello, I'm Christian Adam Stratford." She grabbed his hand to shake but didn't let go.

"From Community Construction?" Her eyes drilled into him as if he was on the witness stand.

He nodded his head. "Yes, Ma'am. And you are?" It was a fifty, fifty guess on who she was.

"I'm her instructor, Mrs. Johnston. She wasn't in class. It's not like her to just miss without a notification." She pressed her lips flat. "And then you're here. Is she okay?" She finally let go of his hand.

"She has been hurt, but I'd like to go through this just once, if that's okay with you?" She sat down at the table and then looked at his identification card.

"You're in construction. Why are you representing Eve?" she started asking questions again that he wanted to do just once. Adam sat down with her. He took a deep breath.

"The expansion of Rule 138-A states that a law student must be at least in the second year of law school. Allowed cases are civil, criminal, and administrative. I'm at the end of my third year of law. I'm not being compensated for this, so there are no complications," Adam replied curtly.

She leaned back in the chair and crossed her arms. "Okay. Did Jessie do something to her? I know you two are friends," she glared into his soul like he or Jessie were both guilty.

"No, he did not. He is with her right now as we speak." She let out a bit of a huff, and then sadness rolled over her face.

"Is the baby okay?" Adam didn't know what to say. He wanted to explain all of this just once. She stood up. "What happened? She was so happy just yesterday."

Adam lowered his head. "Please, let's wait for the administrator."

"Can't get any damn answers around here." She flung the door open and left the office. "Douglas!" she screamed as she was going down the hallway. "Douglas Chapman." He heard her one more time as she stomped down the hallway. There was a bit of a commotion, then she and a man he presumed was the administrator, Douglas Chapman, walked into the room.

"Please, shut the door and have a seat," Adam spoke softly so the people who started to congregate couldn't hear their conversation.

"Now you can explain," Mrs. Johnston demanded as she sat back down. Her body language had changed, and she looked furious.

Adam's heart dropped because he knew he had to relive the experience again and crush someone else's soul. "Do you know she's a diplomat from France?" Mrs. Johnston shook her head no, while Mr. Chapman nodded, yes.

She hit Mr. Chapman on the shoulder. "How could you keep that from me?"

Mr. Chapman frowned. "Sorry, Maggie. It was in the stipulation for her attendance so she would be treated equally. Sometimes royals just want to be normal for a while."

Adam nodded his head. "As part of her being here, she has a security detail twenty-four hours a day. One of her guards crossed the line and became too friendly." He handed the report to Mrs. Johnston and the no-contact order to Mr. Chapman. After a minute, they exchanged papers.

"This report was from a while ago. Why are you bringing this to us now?" Mrs. Johnston shrugged her shoulders.

"Martin used the excuse to monitor her post-concussion to get closer. He didn't know about the hidden camera. He was caught starting to violate her while she slept and was arrested."

"That's disgusting," she said, with a scowl on her face. "But again, this was over a week ago. Why now?"

Adam took a deep breath as he put the pages back in the file. "He posted bail on Monday and hadn't been seen until last night." Mrs. Johnston gasped, and Mr. Chapman looked worried. "I'm sorry to be the bearer of bad news." Adam handed out the second police report and the hospital file. "He came back and beat her up. He was about to rape her when her current officer busted in and stopped him."

Adam was getting choked up and started breathing heavily. He took a few deep breaths to control himself. "Because of this attack, she lost the baby, is back on concussion protocol, and had surgery on her left hand, sternum, and seven of her right ribs."

Mrs. Johnston started to cry, and Adam also started to tear up himself. He reached out to touch her arm. "She will be okay but needs time to recover. Because of everything going on, she was worried about letting you down and failing because of missing classes."

Mrs. Johnston waved her hand. "She is so far ahead, she could skip next semester and graduate right now. I just want her to be okay." Adam pulled back the tablet after deciding that they didn't need to see the video. They fully understand what she's going through, and they don't need the visuals to haunt them.

"Do we need to worry about him coming here? Is that part of why you are telling us?" Mr. Chapman looked nervous.

Adam shook his head no. He pulled the copy of the death certificate to show them. "Martin died at the scene last night."

They were both stunned into silence for a moment. "Wow. That's some security officer," Mr. Chapman responded.

"Actually, we are not exactly sure why he died. We should have answers soon after his autopsy. But, when I got there, the guard had him tied up. He broke free from his restraints and pulled a gun. I disarmed him and punched him once. We thought he was knocked out, but actually, he was dead." Adam looked up at them.

"Well, sounds like you're a good man to have around in a pinch," Mr. Chapman said as he nodded.

"I'm sure Eve was glad you were there also," said Mrs. Johnston, as she stood up. "I need to go compose myself before going back to class. Thank you, Mr. Stratford, for taking the time to come and explain the situation." Adam nodded as they shook his hand before leaving the room. After they left, he packed away all the paperwork. Before heading home, he sat there quietly for a few moments as the weight of the day pressed down on him.

Entry 2: Visit from Teacher

Dozing in and out while listening to daytime drama shows was not how she saw her day going. Jamie had left and Thomas had taken over. He sat in the chair next to her instead of standing in the hallway. She appreciated being able to talk when she felt the need to. He wasn't much of a conversationalist like Jamie was, but then again, it's hard to talk about guys with a guy. Eve giggled softly.

If only Thomas were gay like Tony clearly was, then their working relationship would be way different. Perhaps that's why Martin went bonkers. He thought there was something between them. Eve pondered that for a bit, trying to think back to all their prior interactions. They had never had any private conversations, and he always spoke formally when they did talk.

There was a knock on the door, and Eve thought that lunch was arriving.

"May I come in?" Eve instantly recognized Mrs. Johnston's voice.

"Yes. Please, come in," Eve responded, and Thomas put his feet on the floor to sit more upright.

Mrs. Johnston came around the edge of the curtain, and she instantly grimaced. "Jesus Christ!" She covered her mouth, and started crying before closing her eyes. No one had said anything to her prior, and she had yet to see a mirror. Does it really look that bad?

"I'm so sorry. I knew you were hurt, I just wasn't expecting…" She made eye contact again, and her face cringed. Thomas was now on his feet, walking toward Mrs. Johnston like a protective pit bull.

"It's okay, Thomas. This is my teacher." Eve waved her hand at Thomas. "Please have a seat, Mrs. Johnston." She motioned to the empty chair next to her. "Thomas, can you please see that we are not disturbed for a few?"

Thomas turned and bowed. "Yes, Madame." He left the room and closed the door behind him.

Mrs. Johnston let out a heavy sigh. "Oh, my dear girl. No one should have to go through this." Eve held out her hand, and Mrs. Johnston held on as she sat down.

"No one has had your reaction. Please tell me. How bad do I look?" Eve grimaced, feeling the extra pressure in her skin.

She paused, and her face frowned. "It looks like you went two rounds with a heavyweight boxer." Eve rested her head back a little.

"I went one round with an MMA fighter. And he was strong as hell. After he was done punching and kicking, he picked me up like I weighed nothing and threw me." Mrs. Johnston covered her mouth again, and Eve could see her eyes filled with tears again. "I think that is when I broke the ribs." Eve held up her right arm and pointed to her back.

"He broke my sternum and caused the miscarriage when he was kneeing me while I was bent over." She held up her left hand and pulled down her gown with the right. "They think I broke my hand when I was punching back at him by the type of break it is." Eve sighed. "Boxer's fracture is what they called it." Eve smirked at the irony. "Did Adam show you the video?"

Mrs. Johnston waved her hands. "There is no way I could have sat there and watched something like that." She bent over and covered her face for a couple of moments and then sat back upright. "All the dark coloring and the swelling will soon fade away. After a week or so, you won't see the bruising anymore."

Eve smiled. "I wish the bones healed that fast." Eve pressed her lips flat. "I'm going to miss a ton of class time. It's hard for me to move and breathe, let alone get up and walk around."

"That's why I came to see you." Eve waved her hand to cut her off.

"I already decided that I won't be able to attend next semester. It's not fair to you or the other students, and I don't want anyone to think I've had special treatment." Eve's face saddened.

Mrs. Johnston burst out, "Stop now and listen to what I have to say." Eve was shocked for a moment at her teacher's rant. She pulled two files from her satchel and set them on the table in front of her. She pointed to the smaller one.

"This student has an A and will graduate with honors. She is a decent designer and is good at what she does. She will go on and create wonderful spaces for her clients." She smiled as she opened it up. "This person is on track to finish their work by the end of next semester."

She pulled a couple of pages out, and Eve recognized Stephanie's projects. "She has good drive and uses her time wisely to get everything done." She put the pages back into the folder. "Of all my years of teaching, she's one of my best students and will get offers for employment right away, and she can't hold a candle next to your work."

She pressed her fingers on top of the larger folder. "This student blows all the others out of the water." She opened the larger folder and thumbed through page after page of Eve's work.

"If she turns in her current project and then slowly works on her next client call, she will have completed everything required of her through next semester. So, I don't care if it takes her six months to turn in her next two projects. She has earned her spot at the top of the class and will graduate after this winter semester." Mrs. Johnston's face shifted to a full smile.

"I was hoping she would finish sooner and come back and be a student teacher for the remainder of the course. Help give pointers to some of her struggling peers." Mrs. Johnston smirked as she put both files back into her satchel.

"You really want me to continue?" Mrs. Johnston nodded her head, yes.

"Continue and advance. I can see a teaching career in your future." Eve's smile faded.

"I'm sorry. That won't be my future. Unfortunately, with my requirements back home, I'm bound to my community. Remodeling older buildings has always been my plan for helping. And someday, this responsibility will be handed down to my children, and so on." Mrs. Johnston pressed her lips together.

"I don't know or will pretend to understand your situation, but it seems to me that, as the person in charge, one would be able to take steps to remove themselves from that responsibility, or their children from that tether." Eve could see the concern in her teacher's face.

Eve was going to try and explain the chain of responsibility but decided not to. "It felt like a huge burden at first, but I wasn't guided properly, like my brother was. Now I see it as an opportunity. Each person can decide how to help their community, separately from their required duties." There was a knock on the door, pulling her away from her train of thought.

Thomas entered with her lunch tray, and Eve scanned the tray as he set it down in front of her. "Why do they always put Jello on the tray for every meal? Is it such a treat here?"

"You have swelling in your esophagus from being intubated, which makes it harder for food to go down. You will be able to eat and drink only soft, moist foods for now. This is called a Soft Esophageal Diet," Thomas replied and softly nod his head.

"Thank you, Thomas. No one else explained that to me. Now I understand it better. I just wish I could order ice cream instead." Eve turned to Mrs. Johnston and winked. "Perhaps after dinner if they keep me that long." But Eve didn't want to stay that long. She would rather sleep in her own bed with one of her husbands than on the hard hospital bed.

After her teacher was gone and her lunch was done, Eve was determined to start moving around. She went slow at first and found that using her good hand caused pain to the broken ribs on the same side. She couldn't use her broken left hand, but found that leaning on her left elbow hardly hurt anything.

There was not going to be any sleeping on her favorite right side for a long time, so she needed to utilize her left side better. Before long, she was able to go from lying down to sitting up, and standing. She carefully walked with her pump to the door.

"Hold up there, Speedy." Thomas went to the closet, grabbed another hospital gown and covered up her exposed backside. "We don't need to cause a three-stroller accident as you go by, flashing your assets at everyone." He began to laugh.

Eve wanted to laugh but knew it would hurt, so she just smiled. "It's good to hear you joke. You're hilarious." She started going for a leisurely stroll along the hospital floor and it felt better than she expected. When she got to the nurses' station, Thomas took her picture as she posed with her nurse.

She then sent the picture to both the guys. 'Look whose ugly mug is up and out for a stroll. Going to see if I can get discharged tonight. Really want to sleep in my own comfortable bed.' She included a wink emoji. Hopefully, they got the hidden message that they need to figure out who's coming over tonight.

She turned back to her nurse. "So, what do I have to do to bust out of here?"

Her nurse smiled. "You have already done the hard part. Your medicine pump is good until 7 p.m. You can go home after that if the doctor signs off on everything. And I don't see him not approving your discharge."

She then sent another text to the guys. 'Nurse says after 7 p.m.' Eve included a kiss and a heart emoji this time.

Jessie responded, 'Even all bruised up, you are gorgeous. I will be there at 5 p.m. to eat dinner with you. When they release you, I will take you home.'

'I agree. Even if the outside is blue, we know the beautiful woman inside. I will also be there for dinner, but will leave when visiting is over,' Adam texted.

When Eve and Thomas got back to the room, she had a special request of Thomas that she hoped he didn't mind performing. She was just inside the door, making her way to the foot of the bed when Thomas shut the door. "Thomas?"

She turned to face him, and he was standing at attention. "Yes, Madame?"

"I need photo documentation of my injuries, just in case something crazy happens. Do you mind?" Thomas stiffened up at the request. "I'm not asking you to be sexual. Besides, I don't want those specific body parts in the pictures." Thomas nodded his head and picked up the phone from her hand, but Eve could tell he was still nervous. She took off her gowns, and she could see sadness in his reaction.

"I'll be okay. I'll just stand in the center and let you move around to get the angle you need. Let me know if you need me to lift an arm for the ribs. Don't be afraid to take off a bandage, so long as we put it right back on." He quickly moved from area to area and turned away when they were done for her to put a gown back on.

After their short thirty-minute walk and injury photo shoot were done, she slowly climbed back into bed and was feeling tired again. She spent a few minutes looking over the pictures and did a little editing to remove sensitive body parts, but otherwise, they were great pictures. Thomas had the fishing network on, and Eve started to doze off, so she decided to lean the bed back a bit and take a needed nap while listening to anglers' fish stories.

Entry 3: Valor

On the way to Eve's room, Adam and Jessie ended up in the same elevator as Jamie. Adam recognized her, smiled, and nodded when he saw her. "Jessie. Do you remember Jamie?"

Jessie studied her face for a moment, then tipped his head up. "Yes, we met in the park when Eve invited you to come to girls' night."

She nodded. "We also met on karaoke night. Stephanie is my cousin," Jamie added.

Jessie snapped his fingers together. "That's right. Sorry, my brain has been all over the place today."

Adam leaned on the wall of the elevator and crossed his arms. "She's also Eve's replacement night shift guard."

Jessie turned to fully face her. "You were the one who helped Eve last night?" She nodded again. "Wow. I didn't recognize you out of your uniform and with your hair down." He threw his arms up and pulled her into a hug. "I can't thank you enough for saving her life." He released her, pulled back, and smiled. "I watched the video. You were like a ninja—leaping at him, spinning him around, and taking him down to the ground."

She stood up straight as her eyebrows furrowed, and she looked back and forth between the two guys. "I didn't know there was a video."

Jessie laughed and pointed to Adam. "It's a good thing our straight-as-an-arrow boy here has two cameras at our wife's place to keep an eye on her." Jessie winked. "Now that we know that he came back a couple of times, we can show premeditation."

Jamie's face went pale as the blood drained from it. "When was he there before?"

"He posted bail on Monday. So, he showed up on Monday night, when I stayed over, and then he came back on Tuesday when the girls were sleeping over."

She gasped. "I was there that night. I want to see these videos and make sure he didn't do anything else that maybe you didn't notice." The elevator came to a stop, Jessie exited and walked on to Eve's room. Adam pulled Jamie's arm and held her back after just getting off.

"I have sent a copy of each video to Thomas already. For Monday and Tuesday, he just entered, looked around, and then left. I didn't notice him leaving or taking anything." He took a deep breath and continued. "Wednesday's video is difficult to watch. I was upset that she didn't fight him off from the beginning, and it looked like she was flirting with him, which made my blood boil to think of her with another man."

He shook his head. "But, after what the officer said about her having training, I did some research, and she followed the steps to prevent or reduce rape injury—even if that means willingly having sex at a less aggressive level," Adam cringed for a moment. "Martin just snapped when she told him she was already pregnant."

They started slowly walking to Eve's room. "However, she did delay him enough until you got there. And that got me thinking that the guards being staged outside on the street is just too far away." They walked the rest of the distance to Eve's room, and Thomas was standing at the door. "Hello, Thomas," Adam shook his hand.

"Good evening, Mr. Stratford, Ms. Gagnon," Thomas replied.

"Hello, Mr. Wachhund," Jamie responded.

"I don't know what type of budget you guys are working with, but if there is an available apartment in the building, it could be utilized as an office or staging area. Then your guards would already be in the building and closer if she hits the panic button. A kitchen is available to make and store meals, cool in the summer, heat for the coming winter, and the advantages go on," Adam continued.

Jamie nodded her head in agreement. "Because of Martin's experience with being posted outside, I think he was watching me and waited until I had to leave and use the restroom. It was when I was down the street at the convenience store when her alarm triggered. I ran all the way back and then up the flights of stairs. I busted in not knowing what to expect." Jamie frowned.

"And with a guard stationed inside, I could allow access to view the front door camera so the guard will know what situation they are walking into," Adam added. "With a bedroom there, your off-duty guards could even rotate sleeping there if they prefer not to travel between their shifts."

Thomas nodded his head. "You guys are right on all points. It's something I could research and discuss with my accountant and see if it would be feasible. Plus, it will be something to take into consideration for future contracts. But right now, the three of us are instructed to stay here. The detective working the case is on their way and wanted to talk to both of you."

Jamie nodded and held up her travel bag. "I'm going to go change and will be back shortly." Adam knew what was coming. This is where he goes to jail for murder.

"I'm going to go in and see my wife. Come and get me when they need me." Adam didn't even wait for Thomas to respond and walked into Eve's room. Jessie was sitting on Eve's bed, and they were hugging. He was so glad to see her upright compared to just lying there motionless like last night. His heart started to race faster as he got closer.

He should have tossed the vow aside when he signed the marriage contract. He should have been making love to this wonderful woman, and now they were coming to haul him off to jail and then to prison. If he had just gotten over his issue and talked to her from the very first day, perhaps all of this could have been avoided.

He started to tear up when Eve noticed him standing there. "Bonjour, Héros." She held her arm open, and he joined in for a group hug.

"Hello, Beautiful." He softly kissed her unbruised cheek. "I see the swelling has gone way down. Your eye is not swollen shut anymore."

She smiled. "It's probably the drugs, but I feel better. Movement still hurts, but I know what to expect when I move certain ways." She reached and placed a hand on the back of his head, paused and winced for a moment, then pulled him in for a passionate kiss. Her lips felt so good on his. He didn't realize how much he wanted to kiss her and was holding himself back.

He softly went deeper, and she reciprocated his action.

"Okay, you guys, a ton of eyes are watching." Thomas' voice filled the room. Adam ended the kiss and rested his head to hers.

"I'm sorry. Just thought I would kiss her while I had the chance." He looked back over his shoulder and saw the detective arrive with a sheriff's officer. He let out a deep sigh and picked up Eve's hand and kissed it goodbye. "I have to go deal with this right now. Please remember how much I love you." He felt his chest squeeze.

Eve smiled. "I love you too." He stood up and slowly let go of her hand, not wanting to let go at all. He then turned and went to face the verdict. When Adam came out of the room, Jamie had just arrived. She had changed into her uniform, and her hair was up in a neat bun.

"Ah, Mr. Stratford. Perfect timing. We wanted to come and talk to you all in person instead of over the phone individually. We have ourselves an interesting case. It started with the death of one Martin Jose Julius Evola. The autopsy came back this afternoon, and their findings were that he had an internal decapitation." Adam sucked a deep breath in and held it.

The detective turned to Jamie. "After reviewing the video, it was determined that when Ms. Gagnon took Mr. Evola to the ground in Ms. de Vogue's defense, was when his primary injury happened." The detective looked around at the rest of the group. "A person can still live with this injury, so long as the cord is not damaged, as evident in the video."

He then turned and faced Adam, and he blew out his breath. "When he broke free of his restraints and pulled his gun, you defended yourself and the other two. It was determined at this time was when his cord was damaged and he perished." Adam's heart sank at the realization that he had killed him. He could have survived had he not hit him.

The detective reached out and placed a hand on Adam's shoulder. This is it. This is where they will cuff him, read him his rights, and then take him in for murder. His heart pounded in his chest, his ears were ringing with the added blood pressure, and he could feel perspiration start to form on his forehead.

"The decision by the coroner was accidental. Unfortunately, he harmed another gal in the process." The detective pointed a thumb in Eve's direction.

Thomas stepped closer. "What do you mean, another?" Thomas asked. He had a confused look on his face.

"The DNA pulled from the coroner triggered several unsolved cases across the United States of rape and murder." Adam gasped and stumbled backward and stopped at the wall. He regained his balance and stood back up.

"There is a total of eighteen active cases across the United States. Ms. de Vogue's is number nineteen, and this will finally give closure to the others that he will no longer be out there doing this." the detective added.

It was clear that Thomas was getting very angry. "I do background and criminal checks on everyone before I hire them. Why didn't this come up?" he demanded as his hands twisted into fists.

"We feel that he attacked people who didn't know him, and the ones who did, would end up dead. He did two or three in one area, then he would move and change his name. The name we have, Martin Evola, is only a couple of years old. From what we can tell, he has had ten different names or different combinations of the same name."

Thomas was clearly still frustrated when he shook his fists. "How do I prevent this from happening in the future?"

The sheriff spoke up. "Do as you are, but I would include a DNA test. If they refuse for any reason, it is enough not to hire and a reason to get police involved. You can then hand off the employee info, and we can run with it, even if it leads nowhere."

Jamie opened her mouth and pointed in. "Ahhh. You can swab my cheek whenever you want, boss." She giggled while making light of the situation.

Adam took a deep breath and couldn't handle the weight pressing on him, and he just had to ask. "Are you coming to arrest us and take us to jail?"

The detective and sheriff looked at each other and started laughing. The sheriff reached into his pocket and pulled out two boxes while the detective pulled out two pages from his folder.

"The great state of New York wants to thank the two of you for your valor in the apprehension of a wanted criminal. For your dedication to protect life, even at the risk of your own."

The detective handed out a certificate to each of them that was signed by the governor and then handed each of them a box with the blue valor ribbon lapel medal inside. Adam was shocked into silence as he stared at the medallion.

The officers congratulated both of them, shook their hands, and left before he could fully process the situation. He turned to look at Thomas.

"I thought for sure; they were coming to take me to jail."

Thomas gave him a firm pat on the back. "Let's go share the good news."

Adam stepped in front of Thomas. "Carefully. We don't need to freak her out anymore." Thomas nodded in agreement.

Eve

There was something different in the way Adam kissed her. And he always kissed her hand hello, not goodbye like he did this time, with both his hands on hers, clinging and not wanting to let go. He looked sad when he turned to walk away, like he knew he wasn't coming back.

Eve watched as her group talked with the two police officers. She noticed that they all stood so rigid and needed to relax, except for Adam who looked like he was about to pass out.

Then Adam lost his footing and stumbled backward to crash into the wall. She jerked her arm up in sympathy but froze in pain instead.

"Jessie. Something's going on out there. Do you think they are discussing Martin's attack?"

Jessie leaned over some to look through the windows. "Hard to tell, but Adam looks like he got caught with his hand in the cookie jar."

Eve continued to watch and felt nervousness grow in her stomach. She decided to get up and go find out.

By the time she made it out of bed and halfway to the door, the three of them were coming back into her room. Adam looked so much happier now. He even had a big smile on his face.

"What's going on out there? Were they talking about Martin? They still need to take my statement. I'll defend both of your actions in saving my life." she said in a huff.

Adam closed the distance and leaned in for a kiss. She eagerly drew him in and pressed against him until it stung her chest. She gasped and pulled back while covering her sternum. "I love you so much, it hurts," she smiled.

He softly held her hand. "Let's get you back in bed, Beautiful. We have news to tell you."

He lifted her hand and gave her a soft kiss. "We'll get some dinner in you and then get you home, nice and comfortable."

Eve didn't know what happened, but everything felt right again.

Lilly

Lilly saw the crushed velvet box with the recognizable Tiffany logo on it. She looked inside and saw a beautiful silver bracelet, covered in charms. Way more than just twelve were attached. She smiled as she rolled her fingers over the different charms. They were meant to be a reminder for her mother from her father, but now, each charm is just another part of the story she gets to read about.

She opened the next book that was filled with photographs. Snapshots of their happy times together stared back at her. She studied their faces, how they held each other. She could see they were happy. Page after page of different places, same happy faces. There were drawings her mother had made along with the playbill from the theater.

The next page was the certificate from the State of New York. The page was slightly faded and the edges were lighter, as if it had been in a frame for a long time. She softly ran her fingers over the gold letters that spelled her father's name. She opened a small blue box and inside was the medal of valor, shining as if it was still brand new. Her father probably never wore it. He didn't seam like the kind of man to make a big deal out of it.

She rolled onto her back and held up the images to the light to see the before and after X-rays of her mother's broken bones. Tears pricked her eyes as she thought about how painful that must have been. It scared Lilly to her core, thinking that someone came that close to almost killing her mother. How just a few moments later could have changed the course of history—her family's history.

She needed a brain break from reading for the night. She went down the hall and knocked on her aunt's bedroom door. "Enter," Sophia called. Lilly slowly pushed the door open and then walked in to see her lying in her bed, reading.

"Oh, darling girl. I can tell you have reached a hard point." She patted her hand on the bed. "Come lie down with me and tell me where you are at."

Lilly walked around the bed and climbed on, then slid in closer to wrap an arm around her aunt's stomach. Sophia squeezed her arm around her shoulders and pulled her in closer.

"I know that vile and cruel people are in the world, but I had no idea that she would have been so close to losing her life by one." Lilly's breath hitched and her tears started to fall. "To be that close to pure evil and survive is amazing. Mother was a strong-ass bitch of a woman." Lilly covered her mouth. "Oops. Sorry for my language."

She was quiet for a moment as she calculated how much more reading, she had to cover. "She truly loved both father and her other husband, didn't she?" she asked, but Sophia didn't respond.

"I mean, wow. The description of the sexual energy between the three of them is truly mind-blowing. From what I read, they both love her and she loves them. I'm now curious how long the throuple will continue. I know that Mother and Father got married and lived outside of Manhattan, but did she have a commitment ceremony with Jessie, and did he live with them?"

She breathed heavily for a moment as she tried to remember the people around her when she was younger. "I mean, wow! Holy ménage à trois, on steroids. But I guess, as a polyamorous woman, she must have had one hell of a sex drive to be able to keep up."

Lilly covered her face as she blushed, and she lay there listening to the steady breathing and heartbeat of her aunt. She felt her body relax as questions swirled in her brain that she knew her aunt wasn't going to answer at this time.

Credit where credit is due.

Play list

Music has always been such an inspiration in my life. Sometimes songs would come on the radio at exactly the right moment I needed them to express how I felt. Oftentimes, while writing these dreams out, a song would play, and I'd know exactly where it needed to be in the story. I have a list that didn't make it into the storyline.

"Show Me the Meaning of Being Lonely" is a song by American boy band Backstreet Boys, taken from their third studio album, *Millennium* (1999). It was written by Max Martin and Herbie Crichlow, with production by Martin and Kristian Lundin. Pg 5.

"Patience" is a song by American rock band Guns N' Roses from their second studio album, *G N' R Lies* (1988), released as a single in March 1989. The song was recorded in a single session by producer Mike Clink. Pg 6.

"Every Breath You Take" is a song by the English rock band The Police from their album *Synchronicity* (1983). Written by Sting in 1982. Label: A&M. Producers: The Police and Hugh Padgham. Pg 14.

"Adore You" is a song by English singer-songwriter Harry Styles from his second studio album, *Fine Line* (2019). It was released through Erskine and Columbia Records as the album's second single on December 6, 2019. Pg 21.

"Dreams" is the debut single of Irish rock band The Cranberries. It was originally released in October 1992 by Island Records and later appeared on the band's debut album, *Everybody Else Is Doing It, So Why Can't We?* (1993). Pg 21.

"Put Yer Money Where Yer Mouth Is" was written by Noel Gallagher of Oasis, an English rock band from Manchester. The song was part of the *Standing on the Shoulder of Giants* album, released in 2000. Pg 26.

"Jessie's Girl" is a song written and performed by Australian singer Rick Springfield. It was produced by Keith Olsen. The RCA record *Working Class Dog* was released in February 1981. Pg 29 & 32.

"Only Girl (In the World)" is a song by Barbadian singer Rihanna from her fifth album, *Loud* (2010). Serving as the album's lead single,

it was released on September 10, 2010. Crystal Johnson wrote the song in collaboration with producers Stargate and Sandy Vee. Pg 45.

"Money" is a song by English rock band Pink Floyd from their 1973 album *The Dark Side of the Moon*. Written by Roger Waters, it was recorded at EMI in London under the Harvest label. Pg 49.

"Boyfriend" is a song by American singer Dove Cameron. It was released on February 11, 2022, via Disruptor Records and Columbia Records, as the lead single from her debut studio album *Alchemical: Volume 1* (2023). The song was written by Cameron, Delacey, Evan Blair, and Skyler Stonestreet, and produced by Evan Blair. Pg 50.

"Your Man" is a song recorded by American country music artist Josh Turner. It was released in July 2005 by MCA Nashville as the lead-off single from the album *Your Man*. Written by Chris Stapleton, Chris DuBois, and Jace Everett. Produced by Frank Rogers. Pg 51

"Woman" is a song by American rapper and singer Doja Cat from her album *Planet Her* 2021. Label: Kemosabe RCA. Songwriters: Amala Zandile Dlamini, Jidenna Mobisson, Lydia Asrat, David Sprecher, Linden Jay, Aaron Horn, and Ainsley Jones. Producers: Linden Jay, Aynzli Jones, Yeti Beats, and Crate Classics. Pg 60.

"I Want to Know What Love Is" is a song by the British-American rock band Foreigner. The power ballad was released in November 1984 as the lead single from their fifth album, Agent Provocateur. Pg 114.

"When I Was Your Man" was written by Bruno Mars, Philip Lawrence, Ari Levine, and Andrew Wyatt, released January 15, 2013. The former three produced the track under the name The Smeezingtons. Pg 122.

"Seven Bridges Road" is a song written by American musician Steve Young, recorded in 1969 for his *Rock Salt & Nails* album. It has since been covered by many artists, the best-known versions being a five-part harmony arrangement by English musician Iain Matthews in 1973.

"Shallow" was written by Lady Gaga with Andrew Wyatt, Anthony Rossomando, and Mark Ronson, and produced by Lady Gaga with Benjamin Rice, released September 27, 2018. Pg 128.

"Bidi Bidi Bom Bom" is recorded by American Tejano singer Selena. It was released as the second single from her fourth studio album, *Amor Prohibido* (1994). Pg 132.

"Why Don't We Just Dance" is a song written by Jim Beavers, Jonathan Singleton, and Darrell Brown, and recorded by American country music artist Josh Turner. It was released in August 2009 as the lead-off single from his album *Haywire*, which was released on February 9, 2010. Pg 134.

"The Reason" is a song by American rock band Hoobastank. Released on January 26, 2004, as the second single from their second studio album of the same name. Label: Island Mercury. Composer: Daniel Estrin. Producer: Howard Benson. Pg 136.

"To Make You Feel My Love" is a song written by Bob Dylan for his album *Time Out of Mind*, released in September 1997. It was first released commercially in August 1997 by Billy Joel for his compilation album *Greatest Hits Volume III*. It is one of the few songs to have achieved the status of becoming a "standard" in the 21st century, having been covered by more than 450 different artists. Pg 138.

"Summertime" is a song written by Craig Wiseman and Steve McEwan and recorded by American country music artist Kenny Chesney. It was released in April 2006 as the third single from Chesney's 2005 album. Pg 171.

"Wonderful Tonight" is a song written and performed by English singer Eric Clapton. The ballad was included on Clapton's 1977 album Slowhand. Clapton wrote the song about Pattie Boyd. The female vocal harmonies on the song are provided by Marcella Detroit (then Marcy Levy) and Yvonne Elliman. Pg 178.

"I Don't Want to Miss a Thing" is a song by American hard rock band Aerosmith, as the theme song for the 1998 science fiction disaster film *Armageddon*. In the United States, it was originally supposed to be a radio-only single, but due to popular demand, Columbia Records issued the song commercially in August 1998. Songwriter: Diane Warren. Producer: Matt Serletic. Pg 181.

"I Just Called to Say I Love You" is a ballad written, produced, and performed by American R&B singer and songwriter Stevie Wonder.

The song was the lead single from the 1984 soundtrack album *The Woman in Red*. Pg 286.

"*Thriller*" is a song by American singer Michael Jackson. It was released by Epic Records on November 11, 1983, in the United Kingdom and on January 23, 1984, in the United States, as the seventh and final single from his sixth studio album *Thriller*. Pg 323.

"*I Put a Spell on You*" is a 1956 song recorded by "Screamin' Jay" Hawkins and officially co-written with Herb Slotkin. The selection became a classic cult song, covered by a variety of artists. It was Hawkins' greatest commercial success, reportedly surpassing a million copies in sales, even though it failed to make the Billboard pop or R&B charts. Pg 325.

"*Monster Mash*" is a novelty song by Bobby "Boris" Pickett. The song was released as a single on Gary S. Paxton's Garpax Records label in August 1962 along with a full-length LP called *The Original Monster Mash*, which contained several other monster-themed tunes. Pg 326.

"*At Last!*" is the debut studio album by American blues and soul artist Etta James. Released on Argo Records in November 1960, the album was produced by Phil and Leonard Chess. Pg 326.

"*I Knew I Loved You*" is a song by Australian pop duo Savage Garden, released through Roadshow Music and Columbia Records as the second single from their second and final studio album, *Affirmation* (1999). Pg 327.

"*With Arms Wide Open*" is a song by American rock band Creed. The power ballad was released on April 18, 2000, as the third single from their second studio album, *Human Clay*. Pg 329.

*

Thank you for taking the time to read Royal Journals. I would love to hear what you thought of my story. Please leave a review on either Amazon or Goodreads.

Join us as the journals, letters, and notes continue in book three…

www.ingramcontent.com/pod-product-compliance
Lightning Source LLC
Chambersburg PA
CBHW051134300726

48978CB00011B/266